01/13

Tiptree

2 2 OCT 2013

9/11

D1152514

THE ISIS COVENANT

www.transworldbooks.co.uk

Essex County Council

3013020337051 4

Also by James Douglas

THE DOOMSDAY TESTAMENT

and published by Corgi Books

THE
ISIS
COVENANT

James Douglas

CORGI BOOKS

TRANSWORLD PUBLISHERS
61–63 Uxbridge Road, London W5 5SA
A Random House Group Company
www.transworldbooks.co.uk

THE ISIS COVENANT
A CORGI BOOK: 9780552164825

First publication in Great Britain
Corgi Books published 2012

Copyright © James Douglas 2012

James Douglas has asserted his right under the Copyright, Designs and
Patents Act 1988 to be identified as the author of this work.

This book is a work of fiction and, except in the case of historical fact, any
resemblance to actual persons, living or dead, is purely coincidental.

A CIP catalogue record for this book
is available from the British Library.

This book is sold subject to the condition that it shall not,
by way of trade or otherwise, be lent, resold, hired out,
or otherwise circulated without the publisher's prior
consent in any form of binding or cover other than that
in which it is published and without a similar condition,
including this condition, being imposed on the
subsequent purchaser.

Addresses for Random House Group Ltd companies outside the UK
can be found at: www.randomhouse.co.uk
The Random House Group Ltd Reg. No. 954009

The Random House Group Limited supports The Forest Stewardship
Council (FSC®), the leading international forest-certification organization.
Our books carrying the FSC label are printed on FSC®-certified paper.
FSC is the only forest-certification scheme endorsed by the leading
environmental organizations, including Greenpeace.
Our paper-procurement policy can be found at
www.randomhouse.co.uk/environment

Typeset in 11/14pt Sabon by Falcon Oast Graphic Art Ltd.
Printed and bound by CPI Group (UK) Ltd, Croydon, CR0 4YY.

2 4 6 8 10 9 7 5 3 1

MIX
Paper from
responsible sources
FSC
www.fsc.org
FSC® C016897

For Shona and Derek,
the very best of friends

IAMESDOUGLAS

I

We walked for two days in the darkness of the Otherworld before we reached Queen Dido's treasury. At times I feared we would be lost in the caves for ever.

The words emerged babbled and almost formless, the voice barely a whisper clinging to the outer edge of existence, like its owner, the frail, silver-haired patient lying on the hospital bed. Seated beside the bed, the tall blond man hit the rewind button on a digital recorder and replayed the two sentences for the fourth time.

We walked for two days in the darkness of the Otherworld before we reached Queen Dido's treasury . . .

It had been like this from the start: tiny fragments of stories in half a dozen different languages, each providing a frustrating glimpse of a larger whole. Tantalizing, but ultimately infuriating. Names whose identity had only become clear from the history books. The doctors called it multiple personality disorder and said it wasn't unusual for a sufferer to suddenly start talking in foreign languages, even those they could never have learned. They didn't have an explanation for it, but it happened. Only the blond man knew that something set this case apart. That was why he'd begun recording the mad ramblings of a brain on the point of self-destruct.

The room in the private hospital was large and airy, but for a moment he found it difficult to breathe. He rose from the cushioned plastic seat and opened the window, allowing in a gust of petroleum-scented air from the constant traffic he could hear rushing along Euston Road a few hundred yards away. A combination of words in the excerpt stirred a memory and he searched the machine's database for a previous recording, his subconscious automatically monitoring the shrill, annoying rush of digitized information for the section he was listening for. '. . . *the caves for ever.*'

It was one of the longer passages and he frowned as he concentrated on the words.

I ordered my legionaries to wall up the cave mouth and, using the surviving priests and their scribes for labour, diverted a stream so that it formed a deep pool, which would conceal the entrance of the caves for ever. When the work was complete I had the workers put to the sword, their bodies burned and their bones crushed to dust so that no earthly trace remained of their existence.

Paul Dornberger listened without emotion to the tale of massacre. More important than the content was the fact that the words were spoken in an archaic, colloquial Latin his researches had confirmed was probably used in Rome around the time of Christ's death. He could read Latin and Greek as well as he could read English, but it had taken several weeks to associate the recording with the language he had read and heard.

The thin figure on the bed groaned, as if he could sense the febrile electricity in the air. Dornberger studied him, aware that he felt none of the affection or sympathy that would be normal in a son.

Queen Dido's treasury.

The three words sent a thrill of almost childlike excitement through him. They conjured up a picture-book image of gold and jewels lying in great heaps; a literal king's ransom. Yet, that was the least of it. What truly mattered was that the words appeared to confirm something beyond understanding and that should rightly have been beyond belief. Something that the old man had revealed during one of the more lucid periods of his relentless downward spiral. Dornberger took a deep breath and walked to the large safe bolted to the floor beside the bed. It was an expensive safe, the most secure his employer's money would buy. He studied it for a moment. The combination of keys and punched numbers were etched on his brain, but he ran each stage through his mind before performing it, because he was a careful man and it was his habit. With a faint click, the heavy steel door opened to reveal a substantial, black velvet bag of a kind sometimes used to protect valuable musical instruments.

He hesitated before picking it up. If he was honest, what was inside made him nervous in a way very few things did. He placed the bag on to the bed and untied the silken strings that closed the neck. No need to rush. The door was locked and, in any case, no doctor or nurse would dare barge into the room without knocking. The material was soft between his fingers as he drew the neck apart, allowing him to see the buttery glint of yellow metal inside. His heart fluttered a little as he reached in to draw the contents clear of the velvet cloth.

This was the physical manifestation of the words on the recorder: what made the impossible possible. The object in his hands stood eighteen inches tall and consisted of a diadem of gold topped by twin horns of the same precious metal, which curved upwards and out, so that the tips ended nine inches apart. Between the horns, close to the base and at the narrowest point, were fixed four clasps in a configuration that would hold an object about the size of a goose's egg. The band of the diadem had been worked with symbols that were recognizably Pharaonic, similar to those on artefacts he'd seen in the Egyptian section of the British Museum. In the centre, between the base of the horns, was carved a single staring eye. Some impulse made him raise the crown and place it on his head. At first the metal was cold against his forehead, but it quickly warmed to the temperature of his body. Blood thundered in his ears, his vision became blurred and for a fleeting moment he truly believed. But the sensation quickly passed and he saw himself reflected in the window: the sharp suit and the ridiculous headdress. A heavy-jawed, unsmiling young man with short blond hair and narrow, pale eyes that people found difficult to read. With a snort of disgust he removed the crown and carried it to where Max Dornberger lay in the bed.

'Well, old man, what if I actually believed your madness? Even if it does exist, how will I find it?'

There was no answer, and he had expected none.

He replaced the crown with as much care as he'd removed it and returned the bag to the safe, punching random numbers into the keypad to engage the lock. When he was satisfied, he leaned over the bed and kissed his father's forehead. If he had seen himself he would have been surprised at the affection the gesture displayed. He picked up the recorder from the top of the safe and stared at it for a few moments, as if he expected it to tell him its secrets, but it was as silent as the old man.

Shaking his head at his own foolishness, he reached for the door handle.

The word was like a whisper on the wind.

'What?' he demanded, but he knew what he'd heard. *Hartmann.*

II

Myron Deloite broke open the double-barrel shotgun with a satisfying snap, blew the dust from the mechanism and carefully slipped the two buckshot-filled cartridges snugly into their chambers. The action made him grin because it reminded him of Wednesday night behind the garages with Soraya. Damn, she was good, was that Soraya. But Soraya didn't come cheap. She liked to be romanced with a little love weed and maybe a couple lines of blow to get her in the mood. It was girls like Soraya that had got Myron into trouble, but he just couldn't stay away from their hot little bodies and busy little hands. Satisfied, he snapped the barrels back into place and polished them with a filthy piece of cloth he'd found in a cupboard of the rented flat. It had once been a fine gun, but someone had crudely shortened the stock by cutting away six inches of polished oak and the dark-sheened metal barrels had been sawn off two inches in front of the fore-grip, making it around two feet long. Ideally, Myron would have preferred a pistol, or maybe even one of them dinky little Mach-10 babies that sprayed out thirty rounds in the time it took to spit, but the shotgun was cheap and Myron Deloite PLC was currently having cash flow problems. The main thing about the shotgun was that it was simple and it made a fucking big hole in whatever you pointed it at. He'd seen what it could do, cos he'd insisted on a demonstration. Ol' Myron might be a little slow, but he wasn't dumb. Din't want no shotgun blowin' up in his face.

He tied a piece of string round the butt and formed a loop big enough so it would go over his shoulder. It took two or three attempts before he got the length right, but eventually the gun hung snugly against his right thigh, with enough slack so he could easily bring it up and fire it from the hip. The long black coat he'd stolen from the bar a few nights earlier hung on a hook behind the door. Now he put it on and studied himself in the mirror. No telltale bulges or awkward angles. He'd have to sit with his leg straight on the Tube, but he could suffer that. He unbuttoned the coat again to make sure the gun was easy to access and tried it a couple of times to get the feel of it. Damn, that was good; felt like he was Clint Eastwood. *Do you feel lucky, punk?*

Myron had watched the mark for three days before he'd eventually found what he'd been looking for. Three whole fucking days standing about in the rain or sitting in expensive coffee shops nursing a cup of mocha with the waitress staring at him like he was a piece of dog shit somebody'd walked in on their shoe. The house to the Tube to his office. Office to the Tube to his house. Never went out at night. Never strayed. Didn't the man do *anything* on his own? It was only when he'd arrived early at the house after an all-nighter that he discovered Mr Man was a *jogger*. Mr Man liked to run round the park at first light, all on his lonesome. And Mr Man was dumb. Because Myron had sneaked along to watch on four consecutive mornings and Mr Man never changed his route, not even to run in the opposite direction. And that meant Mr Man was a dead man.

Myron looked at his wrist. The Rolex watch with the Timex action said 4.35 a.m. and Mr Man's runs started at 6.15 sharp. Plenty of time to get the first train out of Brixton and reach Lancaster Gate in time to make the walk through the park to the spot he had identified as the killing zone.

The image of the hit in his head exhilarated him, but he felt a little sluggish. *These early mornings are killing me, man.* He grinned broadly at his own joke. What he needed was a pick-me-up to clear his mind. He fumbled in the drawer until he found one of the sachets of white powder. Even the sight of it made his heart beat a little faster. Pure Colombian coke. Still owed for, but that was what this was all about. When the business acquaintance who supplied Myron with his recreational substances suggested he could wipe out his debts *and* set himself up with a nest-egg, Myron was in no position to turn it down. He'd done these little jobs before. True, some had worked out better than others, but he was still here, wasn't he? Mr Man was a spoiled white rich boy. He wouldn't know what hit him. Myron poured a line of white powder onto the desk top and snorted it straight from the scarred plastic. It was like a jolt of electricity to the brain. Everything looked better already.

He walked up to the mirror and whipped the shotgun out from under the coat. *Do you feel lucky, punk?*

Jamie Saintclair groaned as the alarm on his bedside clock beeped mercilessly. Christ, why did he keep doing this to himself? He rolled over and fumbled for the button. Don't snooze. If you snooze, you'll never get up. He forced himself out of bed. Sarah would have been up by now, bouncing about like a demented rubber ball and getting dressed in her running gear. He liked to move at a more sedate pace. No Sarah. Not for three months. Off back to the Land of the Free to find herself. At least that's what she'd said. He struggled into his Lycra shorts – not cold enough for the long johns yet – grabbed his T-shirt. It was the one with Picasso's *Guernica* on it that he'd picked up at the museum in Madrid for nine euros – five minutes later he'd seen it in a back-street shop for three. Running shoes, Nike, but in need of replacement. Not quite awake, but ready.

He ambled blearily through the flat to the front door and took the stairs down to the street. Kensington High Street. Not deserted at this time of the morning, but not far off it, thank Christ. He didn't start running immediately, just a brisk walk interspersed with vaguely effective stretches that made him look like an idiot. At last, the park. He took his usual route on the long diagonal up past Round Pond. Slowly at first, letting the blood loosen the muscles, easing his way into the run. Breathing a little laboured, but that would soon ease off. The rhythm came to him without conscious effort and his mind switched. That was the thing about running at this time of the morning: you could do it in your sleep. The thought made him smile, and smiling made him think of Sarah, which made him stop smiling. He hadn't done a lot of smiling since she'd gone. Don't. Think. About. Sarah. It must have worked because the next thing he knew he was up at Lancaster Gate, and making his turn down past the ornamental ponds to the path beside the Serpentine. Did he really need to do this every day? He was young – thirtyish was still young, wasn't it? – and fitter than he'd ever been, thanks to Sarah's early-morning runs and the fencing classes. Anyway, an art dealer didn't need to be a marathon runner. He needed to be a networker. Maybe if he did some early-morning networking instead of jogging he'd make more money?

'Crawk!' He swerved sharply as the raucous cry from the lake and the flutter of large wings announced a decidedly pissed-off heron.

'Sorry for disturbing your breakfast, old chum,' he muttered as he ran on into the trees.

* * *

From his concealed position in the killing ground, Myron heard the distant crunch of gravel. He shifted so that he had a better view up the path between the trees. It wouldn't be doing to shoot the wrong jogger, would it? He glanced up to see a dull leaden cast to the sky. Almost dawn. The path was still artificially lit, but the way the cocaine made Myron feel he could probably have seen in the dark. Not that he was nervous. No, just excited. He hated rich people and this spoiled white boy was rich. He'd watched him go every day from his fancy Kensington flat to his fancy Bond Street office. The white boy had everything. Well, Myron was going to take everything away from the white boy.

The rhythmic sound of running feet came closer and he noted the neon flash as tiny panels on the running shoes were reflected in the pathlights. Closer. Closer. Exactly as he expected. A runner in a dark T-shirt. Head down, deep in thought, but the right height and the right build. Mr Man. His breathing quickened. Closer, still. So close that there was no way he could turn and run. Mr Man. Dead man.

Myron stepped out into the pathway, raised the shotgun so it was pointing at the target's heart and squeezed both triggers.

Jamie almost stopped when the man lurched from behind the bronze statue of Peter Pan into his path. His first instinct was to swerve, but when he saw the twin barrels of the shotgun sweep up to aim directly at him he knew he had nowhere to run except straight at his ambusher. He was going to die, that was fairly obvious, but he wasn't going to die without trying. He screamed, the way the Army had taught him to scream, and launched himself at the man in the trench coat.

Myron couldn't believe that the fucking gun hadn't fired. As the wailing banshee with the face from hell bore down on him, he scrabbled at the trigger in desperation. Nothing happened. It was fortunate for Jamie that the seller hadn't told Myron about the safety button behind the trigger and that Myron had been so excited about the potential of his new toy that he hadn't bothered to ask. More fortunate still, because, as he found a second later when he smashed into Myron's chest and forced the barrels skywards, the safety button doesn't always stop the gun firing. The simultaneous twin blasts deafened them both and in his fright Myron dropped the shotgun, leaving him at the mercy of his annoyed, dangerously scared and belligerent target. Myron was only nineteen and five foot six. Jamie was a well-built six foot odd who'd boxed for Cambridge and been trained in unarmed combat by people who killed other people with their bare hands. It was over in thirty seconds.

'Right, you little bastard,' Jamie growled when he'd manoeuvred his ambusher onto his stomach with both arms behind his back. 'What the fuck is this all about?'

For answer he received a string of inventive curses, a few of which he'd never heard before. He switched position so his whole weight was on a knee in the centre of Myron's spine and Myron responded with a satisfactory yelp of agony.

'Look, my trigger-happy friend,' Jamie whispered in the other man's ear, 'whatever happens you're going to the police, the question is whether you go in one piece or not.' He pinned Myron's right arm with his knee and took the left wrist between his hands. 'Now we have a choice here. I can break every one of your fingers one by one, which feels a bit like this.' There was a sharp crack and Myron shrieked in genuine agony. 'That, by the way, is only dislocated. Or I can go the whole hog and force your arm out of your socket and you'll never be able to use it again.' He put a little more weight on the arm and was rewarded by another shriek, followed by a whimper as he released the pressure. 'So let me ask again. What is this about? Why did you try to kill me?'

'Didn't,' Myron gasped. 'Was just going to mug you. Was desperate. Wanted cash for smack.'

'Dear, oh dear, you're going to have to come up with something better than that. You must think I'm as dim as you are.' He sighed and took a tighter grip on the arm. 'One more time.'

'Don't!' The would-be assassin cried. 'Look, I'll tell. I'll tell. Some punter put a ten-grand contract on you. Kill and collect, no questions asked.'

Jamie almost let him go in his astonishment.

'A contract?'

'A contract, I swear it. Please don't hurt me again.'

A hundred questions raced through Jamie's mind, but only one of them really mattered. 'First I need you to tell me who.'

'I can't.' The voice was shrill with desperation and pain. 'He'll kill me.'

'That's a pity.'

'He denies it, naturally.'

Jamie sat with his back against the gnarled bronze roots of the tree stump supporting Peter Pan as he listened to the plain-clothes detective.

'Says he was minding his own business and you jumped out and assaulted him.'

'The gun will have his fingerprints on it,' Jamie pointed out.

'Of course it will. But it would help if he didn't have the injuries he has. That arm of his is a right mess.'

Jamie shrugged. 'Man with a shotgun. Man in his shorts. A fairly obvious case of self-defence, I'd have thought, Inspector.'

'I'd have thought so, too, Mr Saintclair, or you'd be up there in the paddy wagon with him. But you never know these days. Bastard lawyers and a liberal judge, anything can happen. Course, I didn't say that.'

'No, you didn't.'

The detective pulled out his notebook. 'One thing I need to ask? This contract, if it exists, can you think of anyone who might want to kill you?'

It happened that Jamie had been asking himself just that question. Neo-Nazi nutcases. The Chinese government. Mossad. The list was fairly extensive. Not to mention his enemies in the art world, who might have a more lethal dislike for him than he thought. But one suspect stood pony-tailed head and shoulders above the rest. 'There's a man in the United States I came across last year. We had a coming-together that cost him a lot of money. Howard Vanderbilt.'

The policeman raised an eyebrow and noted the name. '*The* Howard Vanderbilt?'

'Is there anything I can do about it, in the meantime?'

'The contract? We'll send someone round to offer you some advice. Ten grand's not really a lot of money.'

Jamie felt vaguely slighted. 'Advice, that's it?'

''Fraid so, sir.'

'Maybe they'll give up on it after this?'

'You don't really believe that, do you, sir?'

'No,' Jamie admitted. 'I don't.'

III

'No scraps for you here, Saintclair.' The words were uttered with that peculiar mix of sneer, condescension and chumminess that takes even the biggest snob a lifetime to perfect. It was a week after the assassination attempt and Jamie Saintclair turned, tempted to mete out the same treatment he had to the currently indisposed Myron Deloite. Instead, he forced himself to greet the speaker with a smile.

'Hello, Peregrine.' He nodded, pondering regretfully how much a broken nose would improve the purple boozer's face. But Sir Peregrine 'Perry' Dacre had recently been appointed an adviser to the Keeper of the Royal Collection and wielded an influence that was astonishingly well disguised by the shiny suit, smelly armpits and permanently vacant expression. Perry was a vicious, acid-dripping gossip with a reputation for groping lowly female interns, but in Jamie's present parlous financial state he had decided, reluctantly, that the man must be humoured. They turned to study the seven-foot painting that dominated the wall of the London gallery where Dacre had peevishly agreed it could be included in an exhibition of Italian Baroque art.

'Charles One had an eye for the ladies,' the older man mused.

By Charles One, Jamie deduced that Dacre meant King Charles I, the monarch reputed to have added the painting to the collection. Clearly, rubbing shoulders with royalty gave you a familiarity denied lowly outsiders. But it was true. She was quite something. Dark of eye and pale of flesh, the young girl's cupid-bow lips pursed as she looked up at the cherubic angel who had appeared miraculously from the ceiling, as if wondering whether to swat it or eat it. Although he'd clothed her in what looked like someone's spare curtains, the artist had still managed to capture the rare beauty that had drawn the eligible men of Rome to her and had eventually led to her death. St Agnes was said to have marched cheerfully to her martyrdom and Jamie hoped that if it ever came to it, he would go with the same grace.

The opportunity came more quickly than he bargained for.

'One of Domenichino's finest, I'd say.' Dacre's nasal bray attracted attention from all around, which was exactly what he'd intended.

As it happened, Jamie agreed with him. It was

certainly one of Domenico Zampieri's best works and a near perfect example of what was called Bolognese classicism; all unaffected clarity, purity of line and subtle harmony of colour. Still, his only reply was a mildly perplexed 'Hmmmhhh'.

'You don't agree?' The piglet eyes narrowed suspiciously.

'Oh, yes, Peregrine. It's just . . .'

'Just what?'

Jamie dropped his voice to a whisper. 'It's just that I was in the Vatican museum the other day. You know Genaro, of course?'

'Of course.'

'Well, I was talking to one of his assistants about the Sybils.' Zampieri had painted two near identical canvases of the Cumaean Sybil, one of which hung in the Pinacoteca building in the Vatican, and the other in the Borghese Gallery. 'It seems there's talk of re-classifying one of them as "school of", which could call into question some of his other works. I'm sure I heard a mention of poor Agnes.' He waited just long enough for the wine-dyed skin of Peregrine Dacre's face to fade to a pleasing pale pink. 'Samantha, hi! I really must go, Perry; lovely to chat with you.'

He attached himself to a tall, blonde gallery assistant passing with a plate of canapés. She glared at him. 'What are you up to, Jamie Saintclair? I'm not sure we're talking yet.' She glanced back to where Dacre was staring pop-eyed at the Domenichino. 'Still, you seem to have taken the wind out of the Pink Baboon's sails, so I suppose I might forgive you.' Samantha stopped abruptly and turned to study him. He knew she was seeing beyond the dark hair that flopped untidily over the intense green eyes and the thin-lipped mouth with the determined set, to the last time they'd met. She was gorgeous and leggy – they all seemed to be gorgeous and leggy – and typical of her breed. A double first in some spired cathedral of learning, spent her winters skiing at Klosters, her summers on somebody's yacht in the Med and popped in to work to say hello to her chums every second Tuesday. He'd thought it would be like making love to a piece of fine china, but she'd treated him to the filthiest four hours of his life and insisted it would only have been better if someone called Charlie had got involved as well. The memory made him groan inwardly and Sarah Grant's face filled his vision. It had been her decision to go back to the States, but that didn't make the guilt any less real.

'You all right, Jamie darling?'

He grimaced and waved at the canapés. 'A touch of indigestion.'

A lined, half-remembered face beamed at him from across the room, but Samantha steered him in the opposite direction. 'You'll thank me later,' she whispered. 'That dreadful little man bored me silly for half an hour about some grubby pieces of torn manuscript some other dreadful little man has found in Paris.' To Jamie's certain knowledge 'that dreadful little man' was one of Britain's most eminent Roman scholars, but he couldn't get Sarah Grant and the Raphael out of his mind. For six all too short months Sarah had enriched his life and the Raphael they had discovered together in a lost Nazi bunker in the middle of the Harz Mountains had looked like making him rich. But eventually the American-born Mossad agent had realized that the Jamie Saintclair who had accompanied her halfway across Europe dodging bombs and bullets wasn't the same man who had settled all too quickly into his old London routine. After a tearful farewell she'd left for Boston to think things over and, in his heart, he knew she wasn't coming back. At the same time, the Raphael teetered on the edge of that permanent limbo the art world reserves for things it doesn't quite understand, and all payments were put on hold.

Which left him more or less where he had been before the Doomsday affair. Not quite penniless. Not quite unemployed. A fledgling art dealer whose career had taken a wrong turn when he'd tracked down a Rembrandt stolen by the Germans from a family of Parisian Jews, destroying the reputation of one of his peers and attracting the permanent scorn of Establishment figures like Peregrine Dacre. It was only thanks to old friends like Genaro di Stefano in Rome, who recognized his innate talent for spotting an unlikely kink in an otherwise pristine provenance, and people like Samantha, who, for reasons unknown, genuinely liked him, that he was able to hover on the fringes of his old world, picking up enough scraps to stay in business.

She eased him effortlessly through the crowded room towards an annexe, her eyes scanning the fringes of the crowd. 'There's a chap I thought you should meet. We were chatting and I mentioned your name. It turns out he might have a commission for you. Where is he? Over there. Oleg, darling!' She waved to someone walking through the door and, before they disappeared, Jamie had an impression of curling dark hair and substantial bulk surrounded by a flurry of attentive minders. 'Bugger,' Samantha sniffed. 'Bloody Russian billionaires. All money and no manners. Look, this is incredibly boring. Why don't you take me for a drink later?'

Before he could answer, something trilled in his jacket pocket, attracting glares from everyone within hearing distance, including Samantha. He remembered belatedly that he'd forgotten to switch off his mobile phone.

'Sorry,' he said, grinning awkwardly and putting the phone to his ear at the same time. He made his way to the door and out into the hall where a few people waited for the attendants to bring their coats. At first he couldn't place the voice, but as the chatter faded behind him he realized it belonged to his lawyer.

'Jamie? How the hell are you?' The tone was suspiciously cheerful.

'I'm fine, Rashid. I thought you'd be in some sleazy wine bar by now?'

'Actually, I was, but I had a call from Berlin I thought you'd want to hear about.' Despite himself, Jamie felt a surge of optimism. Here it was at last. 'The international committee appointed by the *Staatliche Museen* is agreed that the Raphael is authentic. That it is indeed *Portrait of a Young Man*, which was taken from the Czartoryski Museum in Cracow . . .' His voice tailed off into uncertainty and Jamie's inner glow faded to ashes. 'The problem is the two experts they brought in to rubber-stamp their report. We have one who says he can't be a hundred per cent certain and that there's a statistical possibility that it's by one of Raphael's apprentices. The other says outright that it's a fake.' Rashid hesitated, waiting for a response, but Jamie found he didn't have anything to say. He noticed Peregrine Dacre staring at him from the doorway, a sleepy half-smile on his ruddy face. 'Look, Jamie, it's crap. The chap has no evidence, just says he has a gut feeling. But it throws doubt, and they can't afford any shadow of doubt hanging over a Raphael, especially a Raphael with the history this one has. So it's back to square one. A new committee—'

'Did they say who this expert was?'

'That's the surprising thing. He's English, has a fine reputation. You might know him. Sir Peregrine Dacre. Something to do with the Queen's art collection.'

Ten feet away Dacre smiled and raised his glass in a salute. Jamie felt a roaring in his ears and his vision turned red. In his mind he covered the distance to the door in three strides, took Perry Dacre by his scrawny neck and twisted until he felt a satisfying crunch. But when his eyes cleared, the doorway was empty and Rashid's voice sounded as if it came from underwater.

'We'll press the Princess Czartoryski Foundation for an interim payment. It's in their interest to have the Raphael back and I know they have no doubts . . .'

Jamie shook his head to clear it. 'Look, Rashid, this is a lot to take in. Can I call you back in the morning?'

When he rang off, he felt like a boxer who'd just done fifteen rounds. To go back inside and agree to that drink with Samantha, and all that would inevitably follow? No. That would mean having to endure Dacre's smug face, and somehow he didn't feel quite up to Samantha right now.

'Can I have my coat, please?' He handed the ticket to the attendant and waited. A second later the phone went off again. Fuck. What else could go wrong?

'Rashid, I said—'

'Herr Saintclair? I have *Polizeihauptkommissar* Muller for you, sir.'

Jamie felt the hairs rise on the back of his neck. The last time he'd met Lotte Muller had been outside the *Frauenkirche* in Dresden after landing her in the political, diplomatic and legal manure storm that had been the climax of the Doomsday affair. Somehow it didn't seem likely that she was about to offer him her sympathy over his Raphael problems.

'Herr Saintclair?'

'*Kommissar* Muller. What a pleasure to hear your voice again.'

A moment passed while the German police commander tried to work out if she was being mocked, but the hint of a smile in her voice when she resumed said not. 'I truly wish I could say the same, Herr Saintclair. Not, of course, that it is not a pleasure to speak with you, but that I wish the circumstances were different.' A familiar chill settled in Jamie's lower stomach. He should have known that no matter how bad things were, they could always get worse. His suspicions were confirmed when Muller's voice took on a tone more suited to a Bavarian undertaker. 'I was made aware of the attack that took place against you recently in London, and I was asked to make certain inquiries. You may or may not be aware that, as a result of your . . . relationship . . . with Herr Vanderbilt your name was placed on what is known as a "watch list" in the United States. You are familiar with this phrase?'

'Yes, I have an idea what it means.' His voice sounded oddly harsh in the earphone. Jamie was certain in his own mind that Vanderbilt had ordered his grandfather's death, but the tycoon had escaped justice by pinning the blame on a junior executive fortuitously blown up by an Al Qaeda car bomb.

'As a result of those inquiries, I received a courtesy phone call from the Federal Bureau of Investigation.'

'The FBI?'

'Of course, yes, the FBI. In any case, the name Jamie

Saintclair came up in a routine surveillance report filed in New York city two days before Christmas.'

'More than a month ago.'

'Yes, more than a month ago. It appears that even the Fed . . . FBI is not immune to the inertia of what you in England call the festive season . . .'

'And this report said?'

He could imagine the thin lips pursing at the hint that she get to the point, but Lotte Muller would not be hurried. 'On the twenty-third of December a conversation took place between two suspects known to be involved in organized crime within the continental United States. I was not provided with the location or the identity of the suspects, but I do know that the name Jamie Saintclair was mentioned in connection with a one-hundred-thousand-dollar contract taken out by a person or persons unknown.

'Herr Saintclair?'

He took a deep breath. 'Yes, I'm still here.'

'Naturally, you are aware what is meant by a contract?' There was another long silence, which she took as confirmation. 'You must understand that the people under surveillance were third parties – I believe go-between is the term – and there is not enough evidence for their arrest. It is also not unusual in these cases for the task to be sub-contracted, perhaps to someone in the United Kingdom. However, it is the considered opinion of the FBI that as a result of the failure of the first attempt on your life, a suitably qualified individual will be dispatched to England in due course, with the specific instruction to kill the British art dealer Jamie Saintclair.'

IV

'Jesus, will somebody check if Charlie Manson's still in jail?'

After five years in homicide, Detective Danny Fisher could have predicted the essentials of what she was about to see in the house just off the expressway in Brooklyn Heights, but the specifics tested even her legendary composure. She stood in the doorway and took in the scene with eyes long trained to look beyond the human tragedy to the physics and the mechanics of death. Six bodies in the spacious, open-plan room. The father, tall, slim and dark, strung up naked by the arms from a light fitting fixed to the ceiling and, from the blackened scorch marks that disfigured his body, the source of most of the burned-pork smell that almost overwhelmed the rank, sewer stench of bowels emptied by terror. The mother, blonde and tanned, with what had been a good body, was strapped to some sort of makeshift frame, her arms wide and her legs spread.

Fisher studied her face. She would have been beautiful but for the horror that marked her end. The torn shreds of a silky peach nightgown partly covered the body, her features were a mask of blood, one breast had been sliced off and Danny didn't like to guess what else had been done. Young folks, in their mid-thirties maybe, but she could confirm that later. The four children, three girls and a boy, aged between approximately four and thirteen, lay slumped in a row on a large couch, their blond heads matted with gore and their hands secured behind their backs with plastic ties. All of the dead had four-inch strips of brown plastic tape across their mouths.

'You think it's a drugs hit?'

Fisher pursed her thin lips and glared at her partner, who wore the same shapeless blue protective suit. Hank Zeller should have known better than to ask her to speculate in front of the help.

'I doubt if even the Colombians would have tortured the kids. Time of death?'

The coroner's technician looked up from where he was working over the body of one of the children.

'Best estimate? Between one and three this morning. Maybe I can narrow it down more when I get a core temperature. The adult male is no good – there's too much residual heat from his burns affecting the body. My best chance is with the female, but I'll need more time.'

Fisher nodded. It meant the killings had probably

happened between five and seven hours earlier. She had uniformed cops checking with the neighbours for signs of any unusual activity. If they were lucky some insomniac would have seen or heard the killers' vehicle. The gags explained why no one had been alerted by screaming and called 911.

She and Zeller waited another hour while the forensics and fingerprints people checked every inch of the house for possible evidence, sifting through the piles of paper strewn across each room from drawers that had been torn out and upturned, and taking minute samples of dust and fabric.

'We're done.' The crime scene manager wiped a hand across his brow.

Fisher gave him a look that didn't require any translation. He produced a noncommittal shrug. 'The place is smothered in prints; all shapes and sizes, but I think you'll find they're mostly either family or friends. We have smudges on the light switch, the light cable and on the tape used to gag the victims. My guess is that your perp or perps wore gloves. Big help, huh? One thing: from the position of the smudges on the tape, I'd say the material used on the father and mother had been positioned and removed more than once. Okay? I'll send in the medical examiner. Let me know when you need the coroner's guys for the bodies.'

The tall detective nodded and waited until she and Zeller were alone with the dead.

'So what do we think?'

Zeller stared intently at the scene. 'They were after information. But what kind of information? The dead guy is a hardware store manager. No known criminal contacts. We sent a blue-and-white to check out the store. There was no sign of illegal entry. No sign of a search. Whatever they were looking for, they found it here.'

He studied his partner as Fisher took up the story. Tall and rangy, with piercing electric-blue eyes, Danny Fisher was an enigma even to her closest colleagues at the 84th Precinct building on Gold Street. She had a reputation for never socializing with her fellow detectives, which, in their peculiar male-dominated world, had led to the inevitable questions about her sexuality: never proved. Zeller had heard the stories about the guys who had tried to make a move on the thirty-three-year-old and the painful consequences that followed. He had no intention of joining their number.

'Silent entry,' Fisher said confidently. 'They didn't force the front door and the chain was in place, so most likely they got in through the French doors at the back of the house. They were quick and they were efficient. Parents first. Gun to the head while they were sleeping, maybe, and threaten the kids. That would be enough to keep them cooperative. Bring them down. Truss them up and gag them. That's when the real fear would have come. Maybe they brought the kids in to watch, maybe not.' She paused and stared at the four lifeless pyjama-clad bodies. 'I think probably not. That came later.

They would have started with the father. Just a little light grilling with the blow torch to loosen him up. He must have known by then there was no escape, that no matter how long he held out he was going to die. He should have talked.' She turned to the woman, still splayed obscenely against the frame. 'But we know he didn't, because then they used the wife as leverage. He had to watch and he knew she was screaming at him inside to tell them what they wanted. Anything to save her from what they were doing. But he didn't.'

'Or he couldn't.'

She nodded slowly. 'Because he didn't know what it was they thought he knew.'

'Jesus, the poor bastard.'

'That was when they gave him the full works.' She stepped in front of the scorched figure and crouched, inspecting the areas of carbonized flesh. What kind of human being would burn a man's balls off? 'The kids were their last chance to get what they wanted. They brought them in, eldest first, baby of the family – his favourite? – last. They must have known they didn't need to use the blow torch, the threat would have been enough. But they did, and that,' she paused to chew on the thought until it turned into a conclusion, 'that, and the fact that the woman's breast has been cut off, makes one of them a sadist. Because it was gratuitous. First they tortured them, so he could feel their pain, then they questioned him. And when he didn't answer, they killed them. One by one.' She looked down at the matted blond curls of the eldest of the four dead children, a slim girl just beginning the transformation to womanhood. 'By smashing their skulls in with a hammer.'

'Sorry to keep you waiting, Detective.' They turned to find the precinct's medical examiner struggling into his coverall in the doorway. 'A floater at the bridge,' he said in explanation.

Fisher raised an eyebrow. Someone being found dead in the water at Brooklyn Bridge was so common it was hardly worth mentioning, and certainly no excuse for holding up an investigation into six homicides.

The examiner saw the look and shrugged. 'Politics. Son of a city councillor.' He switched on a digital recorder and moved quickly to the bodies, making his first brief inspection and at the same time speaking into the slim plastic rectangle. 'First-degree burns on all four child victims, but initial inspection shows the cause of death to be blunt-force trauma to the skull. Adult female has suffered similar burning to the thighs, breast and stomach, left breast removed by a sharp instrument, probably . . .' he bent to inspect the wound '. . . with a serrated edge. Also some evidence of sexual inter-ference, but I won't be able to confirm that until I carry out the autopsy. Again, her injuries would not have been enough to kill her.' He frowned and inspected the area around the woman's neck, which was hidden by her dark hair, then rose and did the same with the strung-up body in the centre of the room. When he was satisfied he turned to Fisher. 'At first I reckoned they must have had their throats cut, and in a way I suppose they have, but it looks as if the major muscles, arteries and veins of the throat and neck have been severed by some kind of ligature. Whoever did it has come close to decapitating the victims.'

'A garrotte?'

He stared at her. 'Why, yes, I suppose that's right. A garrotte. Probably made of some kind of very narrow gauge wire.' He shook his head. 'I've never come across anything like it. These people had knives, certainly, probably guns. Why would somebody use such a primitive weapon when they had other, more efficient tools at their disposal?'

Fisher bit back the comment that it was her job to speculate on the how and the why, not his, but Zeller answered what had been a rhetorical question.

'To make a point.'

Fisher shook her head.

'Because he enjoyed it.'

The doctor nodded wearily and returned to the woman victim as the two detectives set off to inspect the rest of the house. 'Hey, what's this?' The question was to no one in particular, but Fisher joined him beside the body and crouched at his side as he inspected the dried blood on the woman's forehead. 'There's something here.' He removed a pen and notebook from inside the coverall. 'See, you can just make out the faint outline of the wound. It's not like any natural cut or slash I've seen before.' He drew a rough sketch on a page of the notebook. 'See? A circle within a horizontal oval.'

'Some kind of message? A gang symbol?'

'Maybe,' he conceded. 'I'll have a clearer picture when I get her cleaned up.'

Fisher nodded and got to her feet.

'Such a nice family. What did you say their name was?'

Zeller turned. 'We didn't.'

Fisher looked back at the cosy domestic surroundings that had been turned into a scene of mass slaughter.

'Hartmann.'

V

'Obviously we'll keep an eye on you, sir, but I'm afraid there's no question of full-time protection officers or anything like that. Not with the budgets the way they are.'

'I suppose they're all too busy clubbing with Fergie's brood?'

Jamie's attempt at humour didn't go down too well with Detective Sergeant Shreeves, the personal security adviser who had arrived at his tiny Old Bond Street office a week after Lotte Muller's report landed on some poor, unsuspecting copper's desk at New Scotland Yard.

'Perhaps you should be taking this a little more seriously, Mr Saintclair.'

Jamie picked up the piece of paper he'd just been given. 'If it's so serious why am I not being offered something more substantial than glaringly obvious advice?' He read: *Try not to go out alone. Stay away from places that are potentially dangerous. Be careful when answering the door.* For Christ's sake, this will be a bona fide Mafia hitman. He won't knock on my door and ask for Jamie Saintclair, art dealer of this parish. He'll be waiting outside the office with a bunch of flowers and a smile and before I know it he'll have clipped me with a 9 mm disguised as a bloody daffodil.'

'I think you've been watching too many *Godfather* movies, sir.' The plain-clothes officer from the Met gave the hint of a smile.

'Surely there must be something else. Witness protection?'

'If you want to call yourself Neville and live the rest of your life on a housing estate in Hull and never see your nearest and dearest again, I'm sure that can be arranged. They tell me packing fish can be a very rewarding profession.'

Jamie cringed at the thought. In any case, he didn't have any nearest and dearest. His grandfather, his last living relative, had been murdered a year earlier, less than twelve months after the death of his mother. He had never known his father. Correction. He didn't even know his father's identity. For the first time it hit him that if – for Christ's sake, please make it if – he died in the nearish future, they'd be able to hold his wake in the nearest phone box. He could count his real friends on the fingers of one hand. By the time Sarah heard, it would be too late to come back from Boston for the funeral even if she wanted to. Gail, his part-time secretary, currently sent window shopping to ensure a bit of privacy in this cupboard that posed as a corporate headquarters for Saintclair Fine Arts, took on an entirely new significance. She at least would mourn him properly. Samantha would come along out of curiosity to see who else he'd been shagging – God, he hoped she wouldn't be disappointed – and that was about it. His lawyer, a few people he hadn't seen since Cambridge, and Perry Dacre and his ilk to shed a few crocodile tears . . .

He looked up to see the other man studying him with a look that might have been sympathy. 'Maybe it would be a good idea to take a holiday, sir. They tell me the weather's very nice in Australia this time of year.' Jamie opened his mouth to say something equally witty, but he realized Shreeves was being serious. 'If, on the other hand, you decide to stay, sir, there's a good possibility that this is just smoke and mirrors on the part of persons unknown. To be honest, a hundred grand in dollars isn't that big an incentive to send someone suit-ably qualified across the Atlantic to take you out.' He handed over a card. 'If you do see anything suspicious you know where I am, though,' he gave an embarrassed cough, 'in the event of a real emergency it might be better to telephone 999.'

Shreeves got up to go and Jamie squeezed past the desk to see him out. They shook hands in a manful, comradely fashion that made the younger man think of First World War colonels sending their subalterns over the top. It wasn't the most reassuring image.

'Best of luck, Mr Saintclair.'

Thanks, old chap. Where can I get a gun? The thought came from nowhere and for a split second he thought he'd actually spoken it, but Detective Sergeant Shreeves' stolid expression didn't alter as he was ushered out of the door.

Where can I get a gun? He actually owned a gun, but it was a .22 match rifle and it was chained up in a gun club out at Croydon. Three shots in three-quarters of an inch from a hundred yards wasn't bad shooting, but he doubted he'd get far with a rifle on the Tube. What he really needed was a pistol, preferably an automatic, and that meant going beyond the law, to somewhere in the East End or, if he was feeling particularly brave, Lambeth. And there was the problem. He'd learned to shoot in the Army cadets and at OTC Cambridge. He was good, some people said very good. But his mother and his grandfather had brought him up to be the kind of law-abiding Englishman they thought still populated their rose-tinted island paradise. He might bend the law a little, but he wouldn't lightly break it. The indoctrination of a lifetime couldn't be shrugged off just because some Don Corleone lookalike in Little Italy might, or might not, have given the nod for his execution. Still, it was something to be considered. The door buzzer sounded, and he pressed the button that was Saintclair Fine Arts' answer to a security system, at the same time thinking how silly he'd feel if a man sporting a moustache walked in with a silenced Beretta.

Fortunately it was Gail, and she had an enormous polystyrene cup in her hand.

'I bought you a coffee.' She smiled. 'You looked like you might need it after your meeting.'

'Skinny latté?'

She gave an unladylike snort at the old joke. The shop down the narrow street near the office only sold two kinds of coffee: black or white.

'It might have cooled a little; the lift's not working again.'

'Bugger.' Another reason for patrons of the arts to pass them by. The kind of high-rollers he needed to cultivate didn't take well to climbing four flights of stairs.

Gail settled down at her end of the battleground, the big desk they shared that filled most of the office and which was the scene of constant struggle between the forces of neatness and disorder. Jamie took a sip of his coffee and instantly felt revived enough to start trawling online art gallery and auction sites for the profitable work of genius everybody else had missed. This was what he thought of as the 'muck-shifting' part of the job. The big dealers employed dozens of bright-eyed, annoyingly enthusiastic, underpaid interns to do this kind of donkey work, sifting through the fakes and the gifted amateurs and the students who might or, more likely, might not be the next big thing. It was like a combination of blindfolded bog-snorkelling and hunt the thimble, and it wasn't long before he felt as if he was drowning in dross and frustration.

'Look, Gail, it's possible I might have to go away again for a while.'

She looked up from her computer and he saw the puzzlement in her eyes. The previous year he'd spent more than two months away from the office and although he'd been able to pay her for part of it, he knew it had made life difficult. This time he resolved to keep paying her. He'd rented out his grandfather's house in Welwyn Garden City after the old man died. Maybe it would sell this time? He gave her his reassuring smile, but the emotions swept across her face like rainclouds and when she opened her mouth he knew she was going to say something significant, even potentially life-changing, but the phone rang before she could speak.

'Saintclair Fine Arts, may I help you?' She listened for a few moments, nodding occasionally, before putting her hand over the receiver. 'A Detective Fisher for you. American.'

Jamie eventually located his phone under the mountain of art catalogues at his end of the desk.

'Jamie Saintclair speaking.'

'The name's Danny Fisher, Mr Saintclair, detective NYPD.' The female voice distracted him for a moment. It was low and husky and the accent was as thick as East River silt. Something about it told him she was just out of bed, or possibly still in it. He glanced at his watch: 11 a.m., which must make it about six in New York. 'Mr Saintclair?'

'Yes. Sorry. Still here.'

She got straight to the point. 'We, that is the New York Police Department, would like to ask for your help in a case we are currently investigating.' She must have sensed something over the line: hesitation, or scepticism. 'If you wish, I can give you a number to call at police headquarters that would properly establish my identity and we could continue this conversation at a time that suits you better?'

'No, that's fine. I was just a little surprised. This isn't the kind of phone call I usually get on Monday mornings. Of course I'll help you with your investigation. What do you want to know about the attack?'

Now it was her turn to be puzzled. 'Attack?'

'I'm sorry, I thought . . . Anyway, what kind of investigation is it?'

'That would be a homicide investigation, sir. Nice folks, came to a bad end. As it happens, it has the same signature as a double homicide that occurred not so far from you in London. Maybe you read about it. Elderly couple, name of Hartman?' He dredged up a memory. Yes, he'd heard about the killings at one of the up-market new developments out in Docklands. It would have been difficult not to with all the gory details splashed all over the front of the more lurid tabloids and headlines hinting at some sort of psycho on the loose, possibly even ritual sacrifice.

'That's very interesting, but . . .'

He thought he heard a smile in her voice. 'You're

wondering what all this has to do with a man who buys and sells paintings?'

'That's correct, Detective Fisher, but I have a feeling you're going to enlighten me.'

'Actually, I was hoping you could enlighten us, Mr Saintclair. I understand you have another specialty that could be of some use in this investigation: you hunt down items stolen by the Nazis during the Second World War. Would that be correct?'

'It's something I've done, yes.' He sounded more wary than he intended.

'Well, it's a long shot, but I gotta be honest with you and admit we don't have much in the way of leads. What we'd like is for you to help us track down the whereabouts or fate of one of the Nazis who stole those items.'

He sighed as he recognized another wild-goose chase with no profit at the end of it. 'As it happens, Detective, I'm quite busy at the moment.' Gail raised her eyebrows in disbelief, but he ignored the implied rebuke.

'I can fully understand that, Mr Saintclair, but the city of New York would be happy to pay you an agreed professional stipend for any time spent aiding our investigation, and, of course, you'd have the thanks of the people of this great city.' Jamie couldn't help smiling. Detective Danny Fisher was laying it on with a trowel. 'I might add that you may also help to solve a brutal crime carried out against two of your own countryfolk, for which I'm sure your own Metropolitan Police would be grateful.'

He thought about it for all of ten seconds. It was a distraction, but the money made a difference. At least he'd be earning. 'In that case, how could I refuse?' he said. 'How, specifically, can I help you and the NYPD?'

'Ever heard of a guy called Berndt Hartmann? No? Then how about some loony-tunes Nazi outfit: *Geistjaeger 88?*'

VI

Dream or memory? Max Dornberger was barely lucid enough to be aware of the question's significance. All he knew was that, whichever was the answer, the images his delirious mind conjured up were of startling clarity and intensity. It begins with a crisis. An Empire in peril. Funds must be found even from the most unlikely sources.

'I task you with the recovery of Queen Dido's treasure.' The voice had been shrill, more boy than man, but no sane man would mock its owner, for that owner was the Emperor Nero Claudius Caesar Germanicus and he had power of life and death over forty million people. 'You will bring it to me and I will reward you with wealth unimaginable and an honoured place at my side. Here is my seal, my pledge and your orders, which give Marcus Domitius, faithful centurion of the First Cohort of Praetorians, leave to demand what aid he will from any man under the Empire's dominion. Succeed and you will have your Emperor's everlasting gratitude. Fail, and you need not return.'

The sound of his father's faint voice woke Paul Dornberger and he stirred in the cramped chair where he'd been dozing beside the old man. It was the old-fashioned Latin again, but this time he sensed something different. It was as if there was someone else in the room with them. Quickly, he fumbled for the recorder and set it down in front of his father's cracked lips.

Caecilius Bassus was my guide, and no man ever had a worse. An African mystic of low morals and fewer principles, he dazzled my master with his fugues and his conjuring tricks and the single gold ingot that was the centre-piece of his tale. All men knew of Queen Dido, once ruler of despised Carthage, for her story and her end had been recited by most noble Publius Vergilius Maro in his great history of Aeneas. It is a tale of greed and avarice and murder, as, I suppose, is this.

The secret men have pondered for centuries is that of the great treasure, stolen from her brother, the tyrant Pygmalion, and hidden away so that no man's eyes should ever again be inflamed by its glitter. Yet Bassus, that unlikely hero, claimed to have been led to the treasure in a dream, and did he not have the ingot to prove it? He told of piles of gold taller than a man and wider than a four-wheel cart; coins and bullion and priceless gem stones. But there was more. Precious objects wonderfully wrought and steeped in mystery and magic; the treasure of ages. Bassus claimed to be able to smell gold, and when we had docked in Carthage and requisitioned an escort of legionaries from the Second Cohort of the Third Legion Augusta, he led us south. South and west, to the foothills of the Atlas, where we marched and camped and dug, marched and camped and dug, for the nose of Bassus smelled gold in every gully and on every slope, in every cavern and every runnel. If Caecilius Bassus could truly smell gold, then the Atlas are made of it. Yet gold, we found none. From the mountains to the desert. From heat and jagged stone to heat and stifling dust. March and dig. March and dig. Little water and short rations. On the fifty-seventh day, the baggage slaves mutinied for the first time. My legionaries would have slaughtered them to the last man, for no free man will readily bear a slave's insult. I showed them mercy by burying alive only one in ten and making the rest work in chains, where they died slowly, but productively. Bassus, I would gladly have killed a hundred times, but without Bassus and the Emperor's gold I could never return to Rome. So we marched. And we dug. As the African summer became the African winter, he led us on a fool's errand back to the mountains. To the high peaks where it is so cold that men's fingers and toes turned black and fell off and we huddled together like beasts for warmth around the fires. Snow lay deep in the gullies and the ground was frozen solid, but Bassus had the scent of gold thick in his nostrils now, so we climbed ever deeper into the mountains. Where, to the amazement of all, he found it.

The final words were followed by what seemed an endless pause and for a moment Paul Dornberger wondered if his father was dead. He found that he had barely taken a breath since the old man had started speaking. Now he waited in an agony of confusion for the bony chest to rise again. It seemed an age before the instinct for survival triumphed and Max produced a long groaning sigh and resumed his testament in a desperate voice that quickened with every new revelation.

We had moved enough earth to fill a dozen arenas. Now, in a narrow canyon in the highest pass Caecilius Bassus pointed to the mouth of a cave. No legionary likes the dark, least of all a fearsome shadow that might be the entrance to the underworld of the dead. But it must be done. I chose one hundred of the bravest and placed Bassus at the front, where I could reach him with the point of my sword. To create a lifeline to the true world, we tied together every piece of rope and harness and carried every torch and flint, leaving those left behind to survive the cold as best they could. I gave one end of the rope to Cato, the cohort's senior decurion and a man I could trust. He secured it to a scrubby bush and with the ragged end in my hand I led them into the bowels of the earth. The caves seemed to go on for ever and our lives were defined by the reach of the flickering torches and the treacherous, slippery rock beneath our feet. Above, the cold was a piercing, jagged-edged trial, in the caves it ate you from the inside, leaching into your bones and numbing your brain. The men of the Second Cohort had borne every privation with the good humour and comradeship that is the mark of a legionary, but in the cold and the dark their morale crumbled like a mud dam in a winter spate. I reached the end of my tether sometime around nightfall in the world above, the frayed tip of the taut rope that was our only link to the world of men a testament to my failure. But Bassus was a man possessed. He would go on, even if he must go alone. It was around the next corner, or the next, but it was here. We rested, if you could call it rest, for two hours. Five men refused to continue, but I did not chastise them. Instead, I ordered them to stay by the rope until their rations ran out or we returned.

The caves twisted and turned, rose and fell, and were riddled with inscrutable side passages. Even if we reached our goal, without the security of the rope it would take just one wrong turn to condemn us to wander for ever in the darkness. In place of the rope, I devised a chain of men. Each was positioned within shouting distance of the next and able to maintain contact lest they go mad from loneliness in this hellish place. In this fashion we travelled another mile in the time it would have normally taken a healthy man to march ten. We walked with the dead for two days in the darkness of the Otherworld before we reached Queen

Dido's treasury. At times, I feared we would be lost in the caves for ever.

Paul waited for the next chapter in his father's story, but to his fury there was no more, and the old man lay, silent and exhausted, on the bed. With every sentence, Paul had become more convinced that he was witnessing some kind of genuine link between past and present. He didn't understand how, but that was of little consequence. His was a mind trained to ignore distraction and diversion and focus only on the target ahead. He was like a hunting dog, its every sense attuned to the trail. It wasn't just the story, told in such intimate detail, but the living flesh before him that provided the evidence. To his certain knowledge, Max Dornberger had been born on a farm outside Linz, Austria, in December of the year 1910. Yet the man on the bed, even despite his illness, did not look a day over sixty. And he had looked that way for as long as Paul could remember. What other explanation could there be, but the obsession that had ruled his life – and shaped his son's?

Paul's memories were of an unusual childhood, though that didn't mean he looked back on it with any kind of regret. He had been educated by personal tutors and had no contact with other children. The extra-curricular lessons with his father had been designed to exploit and enhance certain talents and tendencies that the old man believed were in his breeding. And if those talents and tendencies did not exist, they had been beaten into him by constant repetition.

He couldn't remember when he had realized his father was evil. Only that by then it didn't matter. A ten-year-old boy isolated in a rambling, ramshackle house in the country; there had never been any escape from what he was to become. Before he could be allowed to inflict pain, he must understand pain. To understand it, he must suffer it. Strapped to the chair. Whipping. Burning. Electricity. So many levels of pain. So many consequences. He had come – at a certain level – to relish the pain, even to be as one with it. And, after he understood the pain, they began to be brought to him. First the animals, so he should know the feeling of the knife in flesh. The exact position of the vital organs and the most efficient way they could be reached. How the cringing muscles trapped the blade like a clamp if it was pushed too far. The scrape on bone if the point missed that vital gap between the ribs. How you could feel the beat of the heart through the knife until the very last spasm of the dying organ. The way a living, breathing entity kicked and bucked when it realized you were try-ing to kill it, even though its brain didn't understand what was happening. All repeated over and over in that cold, dark cellar until he was drenched in blood.

'No! Use your wrist to twist the knife, so the blade itself breaks the suction. Again. Again.'

And after the animals, the people.

Where did he get them?

Little Pauli never knew, but his older self could guess. The lost and the lonely picked up from bars, or anywhere a sedative could be administered unseen; those were the days before all-seeing CCTV surveillance. An offer of a lift home for a staggering drunk; a cup of coffee handed to a homeless vagrant. Nobodies.

It was the eyes he remembered. The eyes had a vocabulary all of their own. Fear, pleading, hopelessness, defiance, hatred. Agony, suffering, fading. Dying.

Of course, it wasn't enough to kill them. First there must be the mock interrogation. The gift of hope. That was when he discovered a new truth: that a man able to withstand enormous amounts of pain could be broken by terror. Rip out a man's right eye and he would do anything or say anything to save his left. Cut off one hand and the thought of living without the other would drive the subject to the brink of madness. Take away a finger and let him know his manhood will be next and he will tell you anything you want to know.

They all talked in the end.

He learned how to carry a man to within a heartbeat of death and keep him there. How to gauge the effectiveness of the pain he was inflicting to minimize the time it took to break his subject. He became adept. And if he ever betrayed that he was enjoying what he was doing, little Pauli would be placed back in the chair, and the learning would begin again.

Eventually would come the moment when the broken, soiled creature in the chair must be dispatched. At first, he had not been strong enough to kill with his hands, although he had been taught the mechanics of it. Sometimes it would be with a knife. Sometimes with a pistol. Poison, administered in various ways. Even once with gas, though this was never repeated because of the time it took to clear the room. But his father's favoured method was the wire. He remembered the quiet, almost seductive voice in his ear as he took hold of the wooden toggles with the link of steel piano wire between them.

'*Wenn Sie die Schleife platzieren, müssen Sie die Hände kreuzen, rechts über links. Sehen Sie, wie es Ihnen die beste Position ermglicht, um den größten Druck ausüben? Nun, ganz langsam, in die entgegengesetzten Richtungen ziehen.*' When you place the loop, you must cross the hands, right over left. See how it gives you the best position to apply the greatest pressure? Now, slowly, pull in opposite directions. Let him know he is dying.

It was only after he mastered the wire that his father had proudly shown him the pictures of the men in grey with the lightning-flash runes on their collars and the people in the striped uniforms with the hopeless dead eyes. And when he had given him the belt buckle with the eagle and made him recite the oath.

He felt a twinge of guilt at the thought of the oath. He knew he had taken pleasure in mutilating the woman in New York and inflicting the kind of pain on the children he had suffered as a boy. It was not part of his mission to take pleasure from it. It meant he would have to cleanse himself later at the special establishment he was a member of.

Still, the deaths had served their purpose. One more avenue to the man he sought closed off to the opposition.

And the computer he had removed from the apartment of the English Hartmans had provided him with a new trail to follow.

VII

Geistjaeger 88? Jamie studied the sparse file on the computer in his Kensington High Street flat. According to Detective Danny Fisher, the two murdered families had one thing in common, apart from the similarity of their names. If you went back a couple of generations their genes converged with those of a Hamburg resident named Berndt Hartmann, and this Hartmann's name had been linked to *Geistjaeger 88*. Most people thought Herman Göring was the Second World War's greatest art thief, but he'd had a few rivals. Hans Frank for one, the *gauleiter* who had ruled over what had been called the General Government – the Nazis' Polish slave state – and had pinched Raphael's *Portrait of a Young Man* from under Göring's nose. Frank, however, was just a bit player. Göring was a man who didn't know the meaning of the word enough. When he stole, he stole on an industrial scale. In 1939 he had created an organization specifically to create the greatest art collection the world had ever seen. The man appointed to run it was an Austrian art historian called Kajetan Mülhmann, an SS officer and the Nazi Special Delegate for the Securing of Art in the Occupied Territories. Mülhmann and his staff travelled the length and breadth of the ever-expanding Third Reich plundering artworks belonging to Jews, 'enemies of the state' and the Roman Catholic Church, prudently siphoning off the occasional piece to go to Adolf Hitler's planned *Führermuseum* in Linz. But what Göring and Hitler had, Heinrich Himmler must have too. Himmler loathed *'der dicke'*, as he called Göring. He also had his own, rather more specialized, reasons for hunting down artefacts and artworks. In 1942, he ordered the creation of a special SS unit specifically for that purpose. It had started off with a grandiose name to match the grandiose aspirations of its founder, but the men who served in it called themselves Ghosthunters and their unit became Ghosthunter 88; eight being the number that corresponded with the letter H in the alphabet, and not, as some historians had surmised, after the celebrated anti-aircraft, turned anti-tank gun of that calibre.

Geistjaeger 88 operated in total secrecy and under the direct orders of Himmler himself, his instructions passed on by his closest aide, SS *Brigadeführer* Walter Schellenberg. The file revealed that the only reason anyone knew of its existence was the testimony of a man called Bodo Ritter. Jamie checked the name on the internet and his lips pursed in disappointment. It was inconvenient, but in the unlikely event that he could dis-cover anything of value for Detective Danny Fisher, that was where he'd find it.

After making the required phone call, he shrugged on his battered hiking jacket and took the short walk through the rain and down into the bowels of the local Tube station. While he waited for the next service to King's Cross he stood with his back tight to the platform wall. Jamie Saintclair had already seen the underside of one Tube train and he didn't intend to repeat the experience.

With Detective Sergeant Shreeves' warnings still sharp in his mind, he took care to find a spot at the end of the carriage with a good view of his fellow passengers: the usual cosmopolitan London mix of ages and classes, colours and shades, submissiveness and potential threat. His eye was drawn to a pair of young Asian men talking quietly by the doorway. They were the right age, and they had the watchful, restless look of career criminals or undercover policemen. He waited for them to make their move, every sinew tensed for the battle for survival that must come in the tight-packed confines of the carriage, but they got off at the next stop. That left an Italian-looking gentleman wearing an overcoat just long enough to hide a sawn-off shotgun, who had also joined the train at Kensington. Christ, he couldn't live like this, spending every waking hour expecting a bullet or a knife. Better not to see it coming at all. To test the theory he sat back on a seat and closed his eyes, only to find himself watching repeat showings of as many variations of his own death as his subconscious could come up with. Maybe Shreeves was right and he should spend the winter on Bondi Beach?

But he wasn't going to Bondi Beach just yet. Instead, he bought a ticket for the 10.45 to Cambridge. It takes just under an hour to cover the fifty miles that separate London and the university city. As the suburbs gave way to intermittent flashes of open fields, he ran over what he had been able to discover of *Standartenführer* Bodo Ritter. The man had carved out a low-key career as an academic in the art department of an obscure south German university. And there he would almost certainly have stayed, but for the discontent with Germany's economic ills that drew him to the increasingly popular National Socialist Workers' Party and their charismatic leader, Adolf Hitler.

At some point in the early 1930s Bodo Ritter had been introduced to a charming Argentine-German called Richard Darré, a rising star in the Nazi party and the SS, and it was through Darré that he met Heinrich Himmler. One of Ritter's main areas of research had been early Germanic folklore. In Himmler he had a ready audience for his theories, which, in turn, won him an invitation in 1935 to join the *SS-Ahnenerbe*, the organization's Ancestral Heritage, Research and Teaching Society. Bodo's later career would show him as a man with an eye for an opening, and he recognized his opportunity in Himmler's fascination with the origins of the Germanic peoples. In a few years he had made himself indispensable and was appointed to the SD, the Reich security service; just another petty bureaucrat in Hitler's industry of repression.

'I hope you have a strong stomach.' Chris, the young research assistant at the Imperial War Museum's records facility at Duxford, placed a file on the wooden desk.

Jamie gave a grim nod as he studied the tattered beige oblong containing who only knew what horrors. It looked as if it hadn't been opened for years, but that wasn't surprising. These days not many people were interested in the international military tribunals that had tried the top Nazis for war crimes at Nuremberg. Everything that needed to be said had been said. All the arguments chewed over in the sixty odd years since. And Bodo Ritter was small fry compared to the men he followed into the dock.

'You said you were mainly interested in Ritter's career after nineteen forty-two?'

'That's right. But I'd also like to get a handle on the kind of men I'm dealing with.'

Chris leafed through the file. 'Then I suggest we start here.' He laid a sheaf of faded papers on the desk. 'This is a copy of Ritter's sworn statement to a civilian lawyer of the US Advocate General's staff in nineteen forty-seven. You have to understand that in Nuremberg terms this was just a sideshow.'

Jamie nodded. 'I know he was tried by an American

military court and not with any of the big names.'

'Good, so I don't have to go into the background. As you can see, the first few paragraphs cover his life before the war, his university career and his subsequent enrollment in the SS. Then . . .' He passed Jamie the documents.

In early 1941, I was frustrated that, although in uniform, I had not been able to make a contribution to the war effort as a soldier. At that time plans were being finalized for what became Operation Barbarossa and I was made chief of Sonderkommando 4, which would operate under Einsatzgruppe C, within the area of the Sixth Army; that is, the Ukraine. During the period of my service as chief of the Sonderkommando 4, from the time of its organization in June 1941 until January 1942, I was assigned, at various occasions, with the execution of communists, saboteurs, Jews and other undesirable persons. I can no longer remember the exact number of the executed persons. According to a superficial estimate – the correctness of which I cannot guarantee – I presume that the number of executions in which the Sonderkommando 4 took a part lies somewhere between 10,000 and 15,000. I witnessed several mass executions, and in two cases I was ordered to direct the execution. In August or September 1941 an execution took place near Korosten. Seven hundred to a thousand men were shot. I had divided my unit into a number of execution squads of thirty men each. First the subordinated police of the Ukrainian militia, the population and the members of the Sonderkommando seized the people, and mass graves were prepared. Out of the total number of persons designated for the execution, fifteen men were led in each case to the brink of the mass grave, where they had to kneel down, their faces turned towards the grave. At that time clothes and valuables were not collected. Later on this was changed. The execution squads were composed of men of the Sonderkommando 4, the militia and the police. Then the men were ready for the execution. One of my leaders who was in charge of this execution squad gave the order to shoot. Since they were kneeling on the brink of the mass grave, the victims fell, as a rule, at once into the grave. The persons which still had to be shot, were assembled near the place of the execution, and were guarded by members of those squads, which at that moment did not take part in the executions. I supervised personally the executions I have described here, and I saw to it that no encroachments took place. Sonderkommando 4 has killed women and children, too. In September or October 1941, Einsatzgruppe C placed a gas van at my disposal, and executions were carried out by means of this method.

I have read the foregoing deposition consisting of five pages, in the German language, and declare that it is the full truth to the best of my knowledge and belief. I have had the opportunity to make alterations and corrections in the above statement. I made this declaration

*voluntarily without any promise of reward and I was
not subject to any duress or threat whatsoever.*
Nüremberg, 6 June 1947
(Signature) Bodo Ritter

A chill descended that seemed to eat into Jamie's
bones. It wasn't the horrors – the deaths of fifteen
thousand men, women and children and God knew
how many more – but the dispassionate way Ritter
described them. No regret, no guilt or sorrow, just a
cold, hard recital of the facts.

And after the facts came the lists. Lvov, Domobril,
Zhitomir, Mielnica, Novo Selista, Volhynia, Zloczow,
Drohobycz, Kamenka and Stryj. Beside each Ukrainian
town a careful accounting for Himmler's number-
hungry bureaucrats. Jews, Jewesses, Jewish children,
communist, partisan; beginning in tens, then hundreds
and eventually, at the Babi Yar ravine outside Kiev, tens
of thousands.

And after the lists, the reality. Witness statements
from soldiers who had seen the horrors at first hand,
from men who had taken part, from survivors who had
crawled naked and bloody from the death pits and,
somehow, lived to tell the tale. Bodies heaped in layers,
with the living made to lie upon the dead waiting to be
killed in their turn. The desperate cries of the wounded.
A small hand reaching out from a sandy grave in a
silent plea to be finished off. Blood welling in fountains
from the earth as the murderers attempted to

disguise the enormity of their crime. Bodo Ritter's war.

'Christ.' Jamie met the other man's eyes across the table.

'Yes, and this is just the tip of the iceberg. There were at least forty *sonderkommando* operating behind the front lines as the Germans advanced into Russia, from the Baltic coast to the Crimea. The Nazis were extremely proud of what they were doing and kept detailed records. Fortunately, some of them survived the war, which is why men like Ritter were brought to justice. Of course, the Wehrmacht and the SS and local militias often did their dirty work for them, so the figures you see in these papers are a minimum. It's likely that between one and a half and two million men, women and children – and that doesn't include Russian prisoners of war – were murdered over a two-year period.'

'He makes it all sound so ... reasonable.' Jamie shook his head at the thought. 'Just another day at the office.'

Chris nodded. 'Men like Ritter didn't think in terms of humanity. Only in numbers. The *Einsatzgruppen* commanders were lawyers and policemen, Nazi party functionaries. Ask them why they did it and they'd shrug their shoulders and tell you they were only doing their duty. Obeying orders.'

Jamie turned to a second, much shorter deposition made by the same man a few days after the first.

In July 1942, I was taken ill. This was not uncommon in soldiers who carried out our task. It was a job that took its toll on even the hardest. I asked to be transferred to a fighting unit, but as a result of my particular expertise being known to the Reichsführer-SS, I was seconded to a new and experimental command – SS-Hauptampt der Kunst und Kulturschätze – which later became known as Geistjaeger 88.

Ritter gave an account of his unit's specific tasks and areas of operation and at the end was appended a list of personnel, almost all of whom were listed as dead or missing.

SS-Standartenführer Bodo Ritter, SS-Sturmbannführer Max Dornberger, SS-Untersturmführer Gerd Wolff, SS-Unterscharführer Berndt Hartmann . . .

By the time he reached the final page of the file, a facsimile of Ritter's death certificate following his hanging at Landsberg prison in 1950, Jamie felt exhausted, but he spent another hour making his own copy of the Ritter testimony before heading for home. As he left the gates of the Duxford complex, the young man he had been with a few moments earlier picked up the phone in his office.

'You wanted to know if anyone took an interest in the Bodo Ritter file?'

VIII

'I think I've got something for you.'

'Sorry, can you repeat that. This line's not too good. Who am I speaking with?'

'It's Jamie Saintclair. From London. We talked about *Geistjaeger 88*.' He hoped the line was bad enough to hide his disappointment that Danny Fisher hadn't remembered him. But Detective Fisher had just finished a fourteen-hour shift that involved a long day scrambling through Brooklyn's biggest garbage facility in the hunt for missing body parts and her numbed mind needed a few moments to recognize the Englishman with the sexy accent.

'Oh. Hi there.'

'I think I've got something for you,' he said again.

'Go.'

It took a second before he worked out that 'go' meant speak. '*Geistjaeger 88* was set up in nineteen forty-two as a rival to Herman Goring's art-looting organization, but it had a slightly more specialized remit.'

'Uhuh?'

'Its task was to hunt down works of art and historic-al artefacts linked to the occult. Himmler believed that if he could harness the power of the past, the Third Reich would be able to build super-weapons that would allow Hitler to bring the world to its knees. We're talk-ing death rays and flying saucers here.' He explained the former Bavarian chicken farmer's obsession with the origins of the Aryan race, which had spurred him to send expeditions to Tibet and Siberia in the search for the underground cities of the Vril, a mythical people said to have been the inhabitants of sunken Atlantis. 'Among other things, he believed that the Spear of Destiny, the lance that pierced the side of Christ as he hung on the cross, had magical powers that would help the Nazis achieve world domination. Berndt Hartmann was one of the men whose job it was to track it down. Hartmann didn't fit your normal image of an SS man. Most of them were just as you see them in all the pictures: tall, blond and very Germanic, in a square-jawed, bullet-headed kind of way. At the start of the war they had to have flawless criminal records and you could be chucked out for having a single missing tooth. According to the sketchy description Ritter gave his interrogators, Hartmann was short, skinny and he'd just been released from jail in Hamburg after doing time for bank robbery. Ritter was a clever chap. When he was appointed to command *G 88* he very quickly worked out that the job required a team with a special combination of talents. One of those talents was an ability to open a locked safe without blowing up or burning what was inside. That's where Hartmann came in. Ritter took a liking to him and he became *Geistjaeger 88*'s safecracker and unofficial mascot. They would have trawled Europe looking for anything of religious or ritual significance. They'd target museums, private art collections, churches for the bones of the saints, splinters of the true cross; that kind of thing. One of Himmler's top men, a fellow called Walter Schellenberg, wrote after the war that he spent months touring churches in Italy looking for the last known copy of the Roman historian Tacitus's work *Germania*, because it was thought to hold the earliest clues to the origin of the German peoples. There's a theory that Schellenberg actually found the sword of Charlemagne, king of the Franks, but if he did it disappeared with thousands of other treasures at the end of the war. That sword is said to have been involved in magic rituals. Himmler loved that type of thing. The occult was his passion.'

'I thought slaughtering Jews was his passion?'

'Actually, he was quite a reluctant killer, physically that is, but that's not the point. *Geistjaeger 88* operated in southern Russia, Romania, Hungary and France, but in the great battles that followed D-Day they were forced to retreat back to Germany with everyone else.

I've found a specific reference to them in May nineteen forty-five as part of a hotchpotch of SS units defending the Reichschancellery.'

'How does that help us?'

'Their commander, *Standartenführer* Bodo Ritter, survived the war. He seems to have got out before they were trapped. Most of the rest were killed, but two of them just disappeared.'

'Let me guess. Hartmann?'

'Berndt Hartmann and Max Dornberger.'

There was a pause as she considered the names.

'What do we know about Dornberger?'

'Next to nothing, except that he was the unit's political officer, which probably makes him a rabid Nazi.'

Danny tested the new information for possibilities for a few moments before discarding it. Something else occurred to her. 'Hey, I almost forgot. I have a picture I'd like you to take a look at. I'll e-mail you right this second.'

He heard the click as she sent the message and they waited for it to drop into Jamie's inbox.

'So what does an NYPD detective do when she's not catching killers?' he said to fill the silence.

'Are you flirting with me, Mr Saintclair?'

He laughed. 'If I am, you should call me Jamie.'

'She sleeps, Mr Saintclair. She works, she eats and she sleeps. Not quite as glamorous as being an art dealer.'

He was about to disabuse her of the preposterous notion that his life was in the least glamorous when the computer gave a distinct 'beep' as the e-mail arrived. It contained an attachment and he double clicked to download it.

'Just bear with me a second.'

'Sure, take all the time you want.'

The image that appeared on the screen was of a stylized single eye, topped by a curving brow, and it looked oddly familiar, except for one thing.

'At first glance, I'd say it looks Egyptian.'

'That's what our experts over this side of the pond reckoned. Trouble is we can't find anything that links the dead family, or any of their potential killers, to Egypt. The question I have to ask you is: do you know anything that might tie it to this Nazi ghosthunter outfit or Heinrich Himmler and his obsession with the occult?'

'Good question.'

'And the answer is?'

'I have no idea.'

He could feel her disappointment at the other end of the line.

'Maybe it would help if I knew where you found the symbol?'

'It was on one of the victims.'

'When you say on, what specifically do you mean?'

'Specifically?' She hesitated, unsure just how much information to reveal. 'Well, Mr Saintclair, it was carved into her forehead with the point of a hunting knife. Now what do you think of that?'

IX

It had been three long days since the last half-conscious monologue. Three days of frustration and doubt. Paul Dornberger had barely dared move from his father's side in case he missed something vital. He had called his employer and asked for a few days' leave, with the excuse that he feared the old man was dying. At times that had been true. Max slipped between semi-consciousness and coma, and for seventy-two hours had barely uttered a word. Paul had spent the first few hours in a fever of anticipation. What happened next? What had they found when they eventually escaped from the perpetual darkness? But later the niggling worm of doubt had begun boring into his brain. Was he going mad? Surely only a madman could believe that Max Dornberger had lived through this two-millennia-old fairytale. There were a dozen reasons why it could be in his father's head. Perhaps he had read it in a book, or it was a scene from one of those surreal movies of the thirties? The old man's mind was crumbling. There was no reason why he couldn't have made it up. In either case, he was wasting his time here. Yet there was another possibility that made it worth continuing. If he discarded the possibility – the insanity – that Max Dornberger was relating an event he had lived through, what if the old man was dredging up a memory of a tale that had been passed down from father to son through the centuries? Word-of-mouth stories told around campfires and on death beds in the old way. A forgotten family legacy buried deep within the subconscious.

On the bed beside him, Max Dornberger clawed his way up to the place of the dream and Paul reached for the recorder as he resumed his saga.

The fifty remaining men of the Second Cohort stumbled blinking from the darkness into the light.

We emerged into a narrow, steep-sided valley in the centre of the mountains, accessible only by the tunnels we had just negotiated. On the far side, carved from the living rock, lay a wondrous sight. Soaring columns of red sandstone flanked the doorway of a great temple.

The valley stretched for a mile from left to right, a bleak, boulder-strewn fissure that looked as if it might have been cut by a giant axe. No living thing, man nor beast, was in sight, and I ordered my legionaries to draw swords and advance in line to secure the temple.

It was the work of moments to cross the hundred and fifty paces that separated the cave mouth and the building and soon we were standing in its shadow on a flag-stoned court. In scale and magnificence, the temple would count as one of the wonders of the world, and was as out of place in this barren wilderness as a gladiator in the House of the Vestals. Intricate carvings of gods and kings covered the walls, which were cut by niches for statues of the queen who had ordered its construction and of strange, half-human, half-animal creatures; men with the heads of dogs, crocodiles, snakes and hawks. And, in the centre of the lintel, a single staring eye. Clearly the eye was Dido's symbol, or that of the god whose will ruled here, for it also adorned the great altar, cut from a single block of stone, which stood in front of the temple steps. The polished surface was stained with the blood of the last sacrifice, but there was worse to come. 'Mars save us.' I heard the whisper from the soldier to my right and saw him make the sign against evil. I could not help following him as I realized what I was seeing. In a shallow bowl carved into the top of the altar lay the body of a child, its belly slit the way an augur might slit a chicken to read from its entrails. In the same instant we froze as a tall figure in a green robe appeared at the top of the stairs screaming insults in a stumbling, heavily accented Latin.

'None who enter the sacred valley may ever leave it. A curse upon the red scourge that defiles this place.' Spittle shot from his lips as he raised a shaking finger

and pointed it at my face. 'A curse upon the seeker. A curse upon the betrayer.' The finger swung to Bassus, who drew back as if he expected to be struck down by a lightning bolt. 'I call upon the all-seeing eye to destroy the usurpers.' This last in a rising shriek which ended in an unmistakable rumbling from our rear that told me that somehow the tunnel entrance had been blocked. I felt the men at my back shifting uneasily and saw the triumph in the priest's eyes.

'Steady,' I commanded. 'You are soldiers of Rome, not some leaderless rabble. Do not be taken in by a charlatan's tricks. What has been done can be undone. These people must be supplied from somewhere. They cannot trap us without trapping themselves.' As I spoke I marched to where the priest waited with a look of perplexed savagery, which I wiped from his face with the hilt of my sword, splashing blood across the stones and snapping his front teeth at the root. He went down with a howl and I hauled him to his feet with my sword point in his ribs, forcing him in front of me into the shadow of the great pillared entrance.

'Torches!'

Ten men followed me inside, while the rest deployed to protect the temple against any threat from without. The torches flared, and for a wonderful moment we were blinded by the light reflected from a million golden surfaces and awed by the riches confronting us. But we had no time to dwell on this magnificence. Uttering a cry in some foul language, the priest slipped from my grasp, and we were attacked from all sides. In that first second I was tempted to form the testudo, the impenetrable carapace of shields that is the legionary's defence of last resort. But a moment's reflection told me these were not warriors who faced us, only mere priests and slaves, old men, women and children armed with hunting spears, knives and scythes. Instead, we retreated in good order to the door and formed line. Our attackers pressed us hard, hacking desperately at shields and armour, but within seconds I heard the voice I had been waiting for. Bassus had at last reacted to the commotion and led the rest of the men to our aid. With a supreme effort we pivoted like a door opening to allow our reinforcements to join us and the slaughter began.

As I moved forward my sword sank deep in the belly of a wild-eyed elder and I rammed him aside with my shield. Following behind, the armoured wedge of my men stepped over twitching bodies as I sought the High Priest among the panicking throng. A flash of green caught my eye and I turned to see him clambering up between two enormous statues on the far side of the temple. Snarling, I hacked my way towards him determined his soul would be mine to take. Before I reached the base of the figures I was confronted by a teenage boy wielding a long spear. A spear in the right hands can be a dangerous weapon, even against a man in armour, but this spear was held like a farmer's hoe and I was inside the point before he made up his mind where he was going to place it. My sword arm rose and I saw the light of hope die in his eyes. He fell back knowing he would never be a man.

'Hold!'

A man in battle kills and keeps on killing until he is dead or there is nothing left to kill, but something in that desperate shout stayed my hand. I looked up to find the High Priest framed by the statues, holding a glittering relic above his head.

'The crown for his life. The Crown of Isis for the boy's life.'

The words stayed my hand and the anguish in them told me this was his son. 'Enough.' My command rose above the clash of swords and the shrieks of the dying. The clamour receded, leaving only the harsh breathing of the killers and the groans of their victims. I placed the point of my sword at the boy's throat and his dark eyes widened as he felt the cold iron.

'Why, priest? What makes your trinket worth a life compared to all this?'

'Of all Queen Dido's treasures the Crown of Isis is the greatest.' He advanced deliberately down the steps still holding the crown aloft. My breath caught in my throat as I noticed for the first time the enormous gem set between the twin horns, its rays flickering like liquid balefire. 'It was created by Isis herself from the gifts of her father Keb, the gold of the earth and a star plucked from the sky, which she named the Eye of Isis and through which she sees all things. It has been passed

down through the ages bestowing immortality on all who wore it.'

He knelt before me and laid the crown, with its golden horns and great diamond, at my feet. I laughed, but my throat felt as dry as the perpetual deserts we had crossed.

'If it confers immortality, why is Queen Dido herself not here to place it in my hands?'

He looked up and I read the contempt in his eyes at the hunger in my voice.

'Only Dido had the strength to set it aside and place it beyond the reach of men.'

'Yet men have come here, and now you offer it up to me. Why?'

His eyes flicked to the boy so quickly I wasn't certain what I'd seen. I increased the pressure on the point and heard a satisfying gurgle of terror.

'Why?' I repeated.

'If you are here, it is by the will of the goddess.' His eyes locked on mine and I saw something beyond human comprehension in them. At the same time his voice grew in strength. I will remember his words till the day the world ends. 'You may have fifty years in each hundred without paying a single day's price, but stay a moment longer and Isis will keep your soul for an eternity of torment.'

'Out. All of you, out.' Bassus darted a suspicious glance at me as he left the temple, and in that moment signed his own death warrant. 'Leave the priest and his son, but remove the rest.'

An hour later, when the screams had faded, I emerged into the light to find every man staring at me and the burden I carried. I wiped my bloody sword on a cloth cut from the priest's green robe.

X

It was another week before Jamie found the time to visit the Egyptian section of the British Museum. At first it seemed simple, but the more he studied the printout of the file Detective Danny Fisher had sent him the more he realized that something was wrong. The all-seeing eye was a common enough symbol in Egyptology, featuring in amulets, pendants and sculptures, but there was something different about this eye. He spent most of the morning in the museum's great domed reading room studying dusty tracts and scholarly works. Well after lunchtime, with hunger gnawing at him like a starving rat, he eventually found what he was looking for and an intriguing pencilled cross-reference attached to it. The only problem was, what did it mean?

He searched for the volume the note referred to, but it wasn't on the shelf where it should be. The tome was so obscure it didn't seem likely someone else had borrowed it, more likely it had been put back in the wrong place. Still it was worth checking.

'I'm looking for a book called *Myths and Legends of the Ancient World*. The computer says it should be on the shelf, but it seems to be missing?'

The girl behind the counter frowned and checked her own computer before turning to an old-fashioned ledger. She shook her head. 'I thought so. The database hasn't been updated yet. This title was reported missing three weeks ago. Stolen. You'd be amazed how often it happens.'

He thanked her, hiding his frustration, and turned away.

'Oh, hang on,' she called. 'Yes, I thought I was right. We actually have another copy of *Myths and Legends*, only it's in our foreign-language section. Would that be of help?'

When he was certain he had what he was looking for he returned the books and walked across the Great Court and through the pillared entrance onto Great Russell Street. Normally, he would have taken the Tube to Bond Street, but instead he decided to walk back to the office to give himself time to consider what he'd found. His route took him across Tottenham Court Road, and a few minutes later he reached Oxford Street. The quickest way was straight on, but somehow the thought of forcing his way through hordes of damp shoppers didn't appeal, so he turned down towards Soho Square and then west, letting his feet find the way. It wasn't until too late that he realized he was being followed. Two of them, in jeans and what the kids called 'hoodies' – thick sweatshirts, with all-encompassing cowls that hid their faces. The one on the right was in blue and the other dark brown. Jamie cursed himself for not taking the more obvious route and felt a chill that had nothing to do with the weather. Idiot. How could he have lowered his guard like this?

He glanced back a second time and confirmed his first suspicion. Young men, lean and hard, their fitness apparent in the way they carried themselves. If they'd been muggers they would have walked with a certain amount of aggressive swagger and tried to distract him with some sort of diversion. These men were like Cruise missiles locked on to their target. They were less than twenty paces away and keeping in step with quick, purposeful strides. Fight or run? He looked around for an escape route, but they'd caught him in the perfect place, a narrow street of bars and nightclubs whose shuttered fronts wouldn't be opened for hours yet. Run then; he was certain he could stay ahead of them until he reached the relative safety of one of the busier streets. But even as he made the decision he saw it was too late. Two more appeared at the end of the road, hands hanging loose by their sides and making their way directly towards him. He crossed the road, just in case he was wrong, but they mirrored his movement and he knew that behind him the followers would be doing the same. His heart rate increased and he fought to control his breathing. He wasn't frightened, not yet, only prepared. The world slowed and he knew it would stay that way until it was over. He slipped his hand into his pocket and about-turned so that he was walking directly towards the men who'd been following him. Their faces were just visible in the shadow of the hoods, and he could see the consternation on them. The fact that there were four aggressors was oddly reassuring, because you didn't need four people to shoot somebody in the back of the head. A few paces separated them now. The thought occurred to him that he might be wrong, and that they were going to let him pass, but the man on the left went for his pocket and then there was no going back.

The sock full of damp building sand had been sitting uncomfortably in Jamie's pocket all day. He swung it backhanded at full extension so it took brown hoodie on the point of the jaw. For the victim, it was like being on the wrong end of an uppercut from Mike Tyson. His head snapped back with a horrible crunch of breaking teeth, and he went down with his eyes crossed as his legs collapsed under him. Even as his man was falling, Jamie continued his spin, reckoning that the element of surprise would have frozen blue hoodie in place. He didn't have time to worry about the men behind him, but he heard a shout that told him they weren't far away. As it turned out, blue hoodie was quicker than he looked. By the time Jamie faced him he was inside the most effective range of the improvised sap with a knife in his right hand and coming in at a crouch. Jamie blocked the knife thrust with his left wrist in a way that would have made his close combat instructor proud and raised his right foot and brought his boot down on the inside of his attacker's left knee, drawing a satisfying cry of agony as blue hoodie joined his friend on the concrete. But the clock in his head told him his time was almost up. He spun to face the new threat, flailing with the sock even as some kind of spring-loaded blackjack landed on the nerve midway between his shoulder and his neck. Even cushioned by his overcoat's shoulder pad, the numbing shock ran down his right arm and the sock fell from his nerveless fingers. At the same time an explosion of agony swamped his body and filled his brain with red light. He was already going down as his legs were kicked from beneath him and he twisted his head to avoid smashing his face on the rough concrete.

'Look what the bastard's done to Jimmy.'

A boot thumped in his ribs, but the pain barely registered amid the waves of agony still radiating from his injured shoulder.

'Cunt!'

Someone kicked him in the stomach, knocking all the air from him, and he tried to struggle to his feet to escape the flailing boots. How could he have forgotten the cosh? This time it was his left side, and he might as well have been paraplegic for all he could do to defend himself as he fell back face first with the dirt and dog-pee smell of damp pavement in his nostrils.

He could hardly move a muscle. Even as the thought gelled, one of them – he thought it might be blue hoodie – took a half-hearted kick that grazed his cheek, but nonetheless hurt like hell.

A hand twisted in his hair and raised his head from the pavement.

'The man says to back off.' The voice snarled in his right ear, but it seemed to come from very far away. 'You got that, fucker? The man says to back off.'

He tried to respond, but his brain struggled to make sense of what he'd heard. Back off? Back off what? Which man? Without warning his face exploded as his nose was smashed against the ground. Tears filled his eyes and he tasted iron in his mouth.

'I said, you got that fucker? Nod if you understand.'

Somehow he must have managed to nod.

'Cos if you don't, next time we won't be so fuckin' gentle. In the meantime, here's something on account. For Jimmy.'

XI

Paul Dornberger straightened his blue silk tie and walked up to the unassuming wooden door set into a ten-foot-high stone wall topped with electrified razor wire. As he reached it, he pressed the bell and looked upwards with a smile into the unblinking eye of the security camera. Inside the house, he knew Gerard, the monosyllabic Brummie, would be studying his face with those cold eyes of his and using the facial identification software to ensure he hadn't been substituted by someone who'd had plastic surgery. With a soft click the door opened to reveal the tanned features of Vince, the former Delta Force sergeant. There was that moment – no day was complete without it – when Vince looked disappointed he couldn't shoot him, but it quickly passed and the Californian lowered his Heckler & Koch MP5 and ushered him inside. It was unusual to see anyone other than an armed policeman carrying weapons in London, but this house had been designated an outstation of the embassy of the former Russian republic of, and now independent, Moldova and was diplomatic ground. What went in and out in the diplomatic bag was of no interest to anyone but Oleg Samsonov. The neighbours might have been alarmed at the amount of weaponry often on show in the gardens, but there were no neighbours, because the owner had bought both adjoining properties. Up the gravel path, accompanied by Vince all the way, past the cameras and between the sensors to the house, a huge modernistic cube of a place, all brushed steel and blast-proof mirrored glass. The main accommodation lay on the upper floors, with the ground and basement devoted to the kitchens, servants quarters and garaging for the owner's ten-strong fleet of identical limousines and his sports cars, none of which, to Dornberger's certain knowledge, he had ever driven. They approached a glass door set in the corner of the ground floor and Dornberger punched in today's code. Again there was the click as it opened onto an enclosed stairway. Up the stairs, all twenty-four of them, safe in the knowledge that Gerard was watching his every move and at the first sign of suspicion he could isolate the stairway and fill it with incapacitating gas. Finally, he reached the top and another keypad, before the door opened onto the security area.

Gerard looked up from his monitors. 'You're three minutes late.'

'And a good morning to you, Gerard. I was visiting the old man in hospital.'

Gerard nodded and typed the information into his computer, where every deviation in routine had to be recorded.

'Mornin', Paul.' Kenny, the former Australian SAS man, gave him a grin that disguised the fact that he was the deadliest killer in a house full of deadly killers. 'Any improvement in the old fella?'

Dornberger shrugged. 'They're doing their best.'

Kenny nodded sympathetically and opened the steel door to the main apartments.

His glass-fronted office was along a corridor lined with thirteenth-century Russian icons and just off an enormous lounge area. In the centre of the lounge stood a large cube of what looked like stainless steel, which Paul Dornberger knew rose to form the core of the top three floors of the building; a multi-storey panic room whose lock combination was known only to the owner and his wife and which was designed to survive the collapse of the building and anything but a nuclear explosion.

On his desk a secretary had placed a list of the owner's particular interests for the day and he spent an hour on the computer and the phone gathering the information he would need for his briefing to the world's forty-first richest man.

At precisely 10 a.m., he stood up and knocked on the door of Oleg Samsonov's office overlooking the park.

'Come.'

'Good morning, sir.'

They spoke English at the billionaire's insistence, but Paul Dornberger would have been perfectly at home in Russian or any one of several other European languages. Linguistic ability was only one of the reasons he had been considered for the job as Samsonov's personal assistant.

'What's first for today, Paul?'

'The usual overview of the world economy, sir. There's a situation developing in Greece that might interest you.'

He saw the predator's eyes brighten. Oleg Samsonov could smell weakness the way a big cat scented blood and his reaction would be just as deadly. The son of a high-ranking KGB official, before *perestroika* Samsonov had been in charge of importing computers for the Young Communist League. Where others saw the end of the system that had nurtured them for a life-time, Oleg saw opportunity. He had foreign suppliers, a network of outlets, all he needed was import licences and the money to make it work. Using a combination of hard work, utter ruthlessness and his father's contacts, he created a business empire within two years and had his own bank by the end of the third. But banking in post-Soviet Russia could be a dangerous business. Oleg's rivals and business partners turned out to be remarkably accident prone and he could see it was only a matter of time before he joined them. His big chance came in 1995, when he used the bank as collateral to diversify into oil, gas and steel in the great auction of

Russia's state industries. By the time of the economic collapse that inevitably followed, the bank, now forced to default on its loans, was a millstone around someone else's neck. Success didn't make a man popular, especially success bought at the price of so many livelihoods. As the new millennium dawned he moved, with the blessing of his friend Vladimir Putin, to the heart of the world's financial capital, where, for a member of the planet's most exclusive economic club, he kept a relatively low profile. Others could have their football clubs and their super-yachts. Oleg Samsonov was just a man looking for his next billion and his next step up the ladder of the world's rich list. In law-abiding London he could feel safe from disgruntled Kazakhs who resented the profits of their mines and their oilfields ending up in offshore banks, rather than being reinvested in their impoverished cities, and from his former friends in the *bratva*, who still didn't understand that dumping them with a worthless bank was just a good piece of business. Naturally, he knew that the greatest danger came from those closest to him. Other Russian oligarchs valued the loyalty of their countrymen, but Oleg knew people who had been killed by friends they had known from childhood. The only loyalty Oleg Samsonov valued was the kind that could be bought at a price no other man could afford. That was why his safety was in the hands of a former SAS captain turned security adviser who chose his operators mainly from amongst the veterans of his old regiment, apart from a trusted few outsiders, like

Vince, who he'd worked with in Iraq and Afghanistan. There were twenty of them and they worked round the clock in shifts of six.

The two men continued working until Samsonov called a halt and left to have lunch with his family in their private quarters on the floor above. Dornberger would return to his desk for coffee and a pastry. That was another of the things that endeared him to his employer. Like the security guards, he was unmarried and lived a monk-like existence that allowed him to devote all his energies to the man who paid his wages.

The billionaire turned in the doorway. 'Oh, Paul, I almost forgot. How is your father?'

'Still fighting on, sir.'

'The hospital people are doing their jobs?'

'Of course, sir.' Samsonov wasn't interested in the health of an old man, only that he was getting value for money. After all, he was paying for the treatment. 'And thank you, sir.'

The Russian nodded.

A few minutes later a young boy darted into the office a few paces ahead of his harassed English nanny. The child launched himself into Dornberger's lap and Paul smiled and ruffled the dark hair. He was a good boy, with his father's quick intelligence and his mother's fine-boned good looks, but like all boys of his age he had too much energy packed into that slight body.

'Hey, Dmitri, can't you see I'm busy? They'll be waiting for you at lunch.'

He handed the child back to the nanny, who led him away protesting in a high voice.

As they disappeared up the spiral staircase, the smile faded and for a moment the carefully tended mask slipped to reveal another man. The phone rang.

'Dornberger.'

He listened for a few moments before replacing the receiver.

Another step forward.

XII

'Good God, Jamie, what happened to you?'

Jamie Saintclair smiled, as well as he was able with a nose that felt like a burst football. He'd received a few more digs in the ribs for his trouble, but eventually his attackers had tired of their fun and run off, one of them with a satisfying hobble. On reflection he wished he'd broken the yob's leg; then again it would probably have earned him a spell in casualty.

'No real harm done,' he winced. 'I'll look a lot better once I've had a chance to get cleaned up.'

It was only then that he noticed the tall figure silhouetted against the sunlight in the office window.

'This is Detective Fisher, er, Danny. She's here to see you . . . from America.'

Jamie had one of those moments of startling clarity that only occur on a few occasions in a man's life. Like the moment the Emperor realized he was wearing no clothes. He had two options, he could go into babble mode, which was his natural inclination, or he could present her with the man she was expecting, sophisticated and cosmopolitan, only in a torn overcoat, with a battered face and a bloodied nose.

He chose option two and stepped forward to shake her hand. It would have worked better if he hadn't tripped over the waste-paper basket.

'So what did happen to you?' Danny Fisher asked, after Gail had disappeared downstairs to fetch the coffees.

Since he had no idea why he'd been targeted, Jamie decided there wasn't any point in giving her the details. Instead, he settled for brevity. 'Muggers. I was just unlucky they picked on me.'

Shrewd, professional eyes evaluated his injuries, checked them against his explanation and then locked on his own to draw him in, mesmeric and slightly mocking. A warning bell inside told him now was the time to turn and run, but he had nowhere to go and in any case he was in no shape for flight. One step at a time.

'Uhuh? Always better to give them what they want. Not that I tend to have too much trouble with that type of thing back home. These guys can tell a cop from a block away. What did they take?'

'Nothing, actually. Some people came along while I was struggling with them.'

She reached out, her fingers not quite touching the bruise on his face. 'Must have been quite a struggle. You're a lucky guy, Mr Saintclair. I have a soft spot for hero types, but you coulda' got yourself killed.'

He found himself smiling. Detective Danny Fisher gave the impression of being very tall and her body seemed to be composed entirely of sharp, knife-edged angles that made him think any kind of physical contact would probably tear him to ribbons. The face wasn't what you'd call beautiful; actually, not even pretty. Mouth a little too wide, nose a little too long and blue eyes that were a little too hard, like glittering sapphires, but it was the kind of face you knew you'd always remember without seeing it twice. Her presence dominated the tiny space, but that had more to do with personality than physical stature.

She gave the matchbox office another survey, taking in the worn carpet and peeling paintwork, the managing director's desk with the managing director's exhibition catalogues heaped at one end and his secretary's barren desert of pristine efficiency at the other. Between them a narrow no-man's-land where untidy and tidy fought it out for supremacy. 'You're the guy who found the Raphael picture, huh? That Jamie Saintclair?'

He wished she'd tried a little harder to hide her disbelief. 'That's right.'

'Only I expected something a little more . . .'

'Spacious?' He supplied the word she was looking for, but her reaction told him it wasn't the right one.

'Spacious, yeah. They said you got some kind of huge reward. Millions, even.'

'They?'

'These guys, the ones who recommended you.'

He shrugged. 'They always say that.'

'So you didn't get a bean for tracking down a hundred-million-dollar painting? That seems a little harsh.'

A playfulness in her voice made him need to explain. 'There was a suggestion of a finder's fee, but the German government didn't take too kindly to the small matter of withholding evidence in a murder investigation, so there's a delay.' The British government hadn't taken too kindly, either, but that was another story. 'We have ten experts who say the Raphael is what it says on the tin, but two – there's always two – who want to get their name in the papers by proving it isn't. One of them believes, or says he believes, it's a fake, the other says it's by one of Raphael's apprentices, but then you could say the *Mona Lisa* was by one of Leonardo's apprentices and you wouldn't be far wrong. It should all be worked out quickly enough, but quickly in the art world means about thirty years. You're American?'

She gave him a look that said 'Are you kidding?' only in capital letters.

'It's just the last American I met turned out to be an Israeli.'

'Didn't work out, huh?'

He found himself saying more than he'd intended: 'She wasn't certain who she really was, and I was more in love with the person I thought she was than the one she turned out to be.'

'Story of my life.'

He blinked. Danny Fisher had a way of keeping people off balance that was going to take a bit of getting used to. Fortunately, Gail gave him the chance to recover when she barged through the door juggling two coffees and a substantial parcel.

'You had a delivery,' she said breathlessly. 'Feels like another one of your picture books. Do you mind if I head off, Jamie? Remember I said I was meeting my mum?'

'Picture books?' Fisher asked when the other woman had left.

'When I can afford them, I collect books on Rembrandt,' he explained. 'This is probably from the research foundation.' He pushed it to one side. 'I, um, didn't . . .'

'Expect to find me here?'

'Yes, that's right. I didn't . . . It was a surprise.'

'Well, things were a little slow back in Brooklyn and I had vacation time coming.' Now it was her turn to shrug. 'I've never been to London, so . . . it seemed like a good idea to drop in.'

'Drop in?' He didn't bother to hide his disbelief.

She turned to look out of the window. If you craned your neck you could just see the far side of the narrow street four floors below. 'Guy out there's been standing opposite your entryway taking a real keen interest in some expensive jewellery for more than thirty minutes. Only he doesn't look the type to be buying a wedding ring. You seen him before?'

Jamie squeezed past the desk to her side. The man was dressed in what used to be called a donkey jacket, a rough workman's coat that for some inexplicable reason was now back in style. A black ski hat hid most of his head. He might have been in his thirties. Jamie was certain it wasn't one of his attackers and that he hadn't seen him in his life. 'No.' He became acutely aware of her perfume, and a scent below the perfume, a kind of earthy purity mixed with the wool of her sweater.

'When I see a guy like that, my hand starts twitching. Being without a piece.' She saw his look of mystification. 'A gun . . . it takes a little getting used to. That wasn't exactly true, what I said before. Truth is we've kinda run out of places to go with the Hartmann investigation Stateside, so I decided to come to London. Officially I'm liaising with your Scotland Yard, but on my own time, which they don't particularly like. Unofficially, I'm hoping the key to the Hartmann case is here. After all, this is where the second killings took place.'

He leaned back against the desk. 'That seems above and beyond the call of duty and, if I might venture an opinion, quite a long shot.'

She stared at him, the blue eyes simultaneously calculating and evaluating.

'There were four Hartmann children. Just babies really.' Her lips twitched in a melancholy smile. 'Blond hair, pretty, must have been full of life. I have nieces just like the girls. The killer had smashed their heads in one by one with a hammer, but even though her hands were tied, the eldest had tried to fight him right to the end. One way or the other I will find that man, Mr Saintclair, if it takes till hell freezes over. You believe that?'

Their faces were three feet apart.

'Yes, I do. Call me Jamie.'

She nodded slowly.

'All right . . . Jamie. This is your territory. Where do we go from here?'

He took his time.

'I think we have two options. Either we follow the Hartmann trail or we follow the eye.'

'The eye?'

'At first it seemed simple enough. There are two culturally significant symbols depicting the eye in Egyptian iconography. The Eye of Horus and the Eye of Hathor, also known as the Eye of Ra. These are copies I took of the symbols.' He spread out two sheets of paper on Gail's end of the desk and placed the printout of the eye Danny had sent beside them. 'They're common on temple friezes and on amulets; what are known as *wadjets* and which were believed in ancient times to have special healing powers.'

'Soooo . . .' Danny Fisher chewed the end of her right

thumb as she pondered the pictures. She noticed immediately what it had taken Jamie an hour to work out. 'Looks like we can forget about Hathor and concentrate on this Horus guy?'

'Possibly.'

'But Hathor is depicted as the right eye. Horus, is the left, like ours.'

'That's true, but I'll come back to that later. Let's say you're right. Where's the link to the killings? What makes Horus special?'

'You're the expert, Jamie Saintclair. I'm just tagging along on this one.'

The words were accompanied by a grin and he grinned back. 'Hardly, but I do know a few things about him. He was the son of the god Osiris and the goddess Isis.' Danny looked up. Ears trained to pick up a suspect's every nuance had detected *something* there. 'According to legend, his father was given the throne of Egypt rather than his older brother, Set, Horus's uncle. Set, as you'd expect, wasn't too happy about this, so he tricked his brother into climbing into a wooden chest, sealed it and threw it into the Nile.'

'Sounds reasonable.'

Jamie nodded. 'Just your average Egyptian family row.'

'But Set had underestimated the determination of Isis.' There it was again, she thought. 'Somehow she recovered her husband's body and along with another god called Thoth, came up with a ritual that would bring him back to life. Set had other ideas. He stole back the body, chopped it into fourteen pieces and scattered them all over Egypt.'

A memory of two days of hell amongst Brooklyn's landfill made her cough. 'Jesus, Saintclair, I came over here to get away from all that. What does this have to do with Horus?'

'Patience, ma'am, I'm getting there. The long and the short of it is that Isis eventually brought Osiris back to life and he became King of the Otherworld. That's the Land of the Dead, so life is possibly the wrong word. It was Horus's fate to avenge his father and kill Set. While they were fighting, Set tore out Horus's right eye, but since he'd been a good son, the gods gave him it back. Thus, the Eye of Horus, a gift from the gods.'

Danny walked to the window and looked out into the silver-grey mist of the falling gloom and the first faint lights that heralded dusk. 'So, we have a link to a family feud. Brothers falling out and a son's revenge. That could be interesting. It's not a line of investigation we've considered so far. I'll get someone on it tomorrow.'

'But?'

'But I think unless there's a real psychopath in the family – which I admit we can't rule out – the manner of the deaths make it unlikely. Someone took pleasure in those killings, especially the wife and kids. It just doesn't seem like a revenge attack by a relative. Anyway, if you were going to make a point about Set and Osiris wouldn't you cut the husband into fourteen pieces and scatter him from Brooklyn Bridge?'

'There may be another possibility.'

She turned from the window to face him. 'I had a feeling you were teasing me, Saintclair. I'm beginning to like you.'

Something in her voice gave him an inward shiver. 'Which takes us back to Hathor. This lady is a bit of a puzzle. She was a sky goddess and celestial nurse, which makes her a force for good. But as the Eye of Ra she was the goddess of destruction and slaughter.'

'So? We've already agreed that the Eye of Ra isn't our eye.'

'That's true, but Hathor is sometimes depicted as a cow, or wearing a headdress of a cow's horns with a sun disk between them, like this.' He drew a rough sketch, the horns first curving out, with the circle between them. 'The problem is that she's not the only goddess associated with the cow, and there's a suggestion that Hathor might be a mix of, or have been mixed up with, another goddess.'

'Let me guess, Isis?'

'How did you know?'

'Don't ever play poker with a cop, Jamie, you got more twitches than a gopher with an itch.'

'Thanks for the advice.' He grinned. 'So Hathor and Isis have a lot in common and I decided to do a bit of digging. Their filing system was a bit chaotic, but I found this in a back copy of the *Journal of Egyptian*

Studies from the early nineteen hundreds. It's only one academic, but . . . see for yourself.'

He handed her the note he'd taken and she read: '*From a study of fragmentary evidence discovered at a number of significant sites, I believe I can postulate with some degree of certainty, that Isis, in her guise as the Mother Goddess, was at some point portrayed in Pharaonic friezes by a single eye. The Eye of Isis, although in the style of the Eye of Horus, differed from it by the addition of a blood-red tear in the right corner.*'

Danny didn't need to look at the printout.

'That mark in the corner.' Her voice took on an extra urgency. 'The coroner was of the opinion it was caused by the perp being hurried or over-enthusiastic while he was carving it into the victim's forehead, or maybe as she struggled. But it could be a tear, huh?'

'That's what it looked like to me.'

She shook her head. 'This is all great, but I still don't see where it takes us. Unless we can link the dead folks to some sort of weird cult, or this *Geistjaeger* bunch to Cleopatra's grandma and a little Egyptian hocus-pocus, we're no further forward.'

'That's true,' he admitted. 'But what if I told you the Eye of Isis may not be just a pretty picture on a Pharaoh's wall?'

Danny Fisher didn't try to hide her disbelief when they met for breakfast next morning at the British

Museum. 'Come on, Jamie, this is a book of fairytales.'

'Not fairytales, Detective, myths. *Myths and Legends of the Ancient World*, to be precise; except it's in the original German.'

Mythen und Legenden der Alten Welt was something of an anachronism amongst the thousands of scholarly tomes that lined the shelves. Written before the First World War, it must have been unashamedly populist, with half a golden sun at the centre of its red cloth frontispiece above the title, the gold-leaf rays reaching out to the margins. He scanned the pages, taking in a collection of stories that included Britain's Arthur legend and the Holy Grail, the fate of Atlantis and the lost city of Eldorado; but the bulk, and what would have been its greatest attraction, featured stories of lost treasures: wrecked Spanish gold ships, pirate hoards, the accumulated riches of the Knights Templar, buried in the crypt of some twelfth-century baron.

'This is the one we're looking for.'

'I can't read German.' Her tight smile told him she wasn't a morning person.

'I didn't have time to copy it out properly yesterday,' he explained. 'So the quickest way would be for me to translate and you to take notes. Okay?'

She reached into a cavernous handbag and came out with a digital recorder, which she placed on the desk beside them. 'Notes, huh?'

No, definitely not a morning person.

'The odd thing is that the English version of the book

107

was stolen three weeks ago.' He shrugged. 'I suppose it could be just a coincidence.'

'Why didn't you tell me that before? When you're investigating a murder there's no such thing as coincidence. So what does it say?'

'It tells the story of the legendary and supposedly mythical Queen Dido's Treasure. It's a tale that first surfaced in Virgil's *Aeneid*.' He looked at her for confirmation that he didn't have to repeat the story of Rome's original founder and his flight from Troy and was rewarded by a dangerous narrowing of the eyes. 'But it must have had a much earlier provenance. The treasure was amassed by Dido's husband Sychaeus, a Phoenician priest, who had gathered it from all over the Orient. But her brother, Pygmalion, King of Tyre, decided he wanted it, and in short order he slaughtered old Sychaeus. But in Dido, Pygmalion had an adversary as cunning and ruthless as he was. Before he could do anything about it, she'd loaded the treasure onto ships and sailed into the sunset, first to Cyprus and then to Carthage, where, very conveniently, she was made Queen.' He grinned. 'So she's royalty and she's rich, but is she happy? Not our Dido. Because she knows that somewhere out there in the Med, Pygmalion is still on the prowl and beyond the Atlas Mountains a host of gold-hungry Numidians were stirring. So what does she do with it? She buries it for all time away from the eyes of man.' He paused and Danny gave him a 'So far, so what?' look. 'And that would have been that, except that around sixty-five AD a man called Caecilius Bassus appeared at Emperor Nero's court in Rome with tales of a vast cave filled with gold. Bassus even described the way it was stacked and the size of the bars. Nero, whose excesses had all but bankrupted the Roman Empire, badly needed cash and decided to send an expedition to collect it. Now, if he wasn't as mad as Bassus, Nero might have stopped to ask himself why his benefactor hadn't brought a lot more of the evidence with him. As far as we know, the expedition was never seen again.'

'Maybe I'm missing something, but what has this to do with my murder investigation?'

'The visit of Bassus and the dispatching of the expedition are recorded by the Roman historian Tacitus, and repeated by a later author, Suetonius. The reason this is interesting is that, as far as I know, the surviving texts describe Dido's treasure purely in general terms. This is the only version of the story I've ever seen that goes into any real detail.'

'So?'

'*Of all the treasures, the greatest was the Gold Crown of Isis, wondrously wrought by craftsmen of old, and at its centre, the great gemstone known as the Eye of Isis.*'

XIII

The scent of blood filled Paul Dornberger's nostrils as he studied the bank details downloaded from the computer of the English Hartmans. He remembered the old man's desperate dance as he fought the loop of steel that slowly compressed, then carved through, the flesh of his throat. A shame the woman was already dead and not able to appreciate her husband's demise. But that was the pity of it; someone always had to die first. He frowned at the memory of the blood-spattered walls. Had such violence been strictly necessary? Could it be that he was going mad? He realized it was the second time in a week that he'd asked himself the question and fought an unfamiliar feeling of nausea. Gradually he recovered and forced himself to concentrate on the job at hand.

The documents recorded monthly payments of just over a thousand pounds from a company with an address in St Helier, Jersey. Substantial enough to make a small difference to a retired couple living in London, but not large enough to attract the attention of Her Majesty's Revenue and Customs. Perhaps, the kind of payments a man with a substantial fortune might bestow on distant relatives he had never met? Of course, it could be a pension payment from some employment Dornberger wasn't aware of, but the Hartmans had been most meticulous in maintaining their financial records and he could find no other reference to it. Jersey was the key. The Channel Islands didn't just provide a convenient low-tax haven for people with large amounts of liquidity who wanted to keep it that way. They were home to small, discreet law offices, which, for a price, were prepared to provide accommodation addresses for shadow companies formed to disguise their owners' true purpose. He stood up and went to the window overlooking the park. It was dark now, but he knew someone would be out there watching the building. Just as Kenny or one of his colleagues would be in the observatory on the roof of the complex scanning the surrounding area with night-vision goggles to complement the high-tech, infrared and heat-seeking cameras that automatically scrutinized the surrounding area. For a moment he felt the pressure building in his head. Time was running out like sand slipping through his fingers, yet he had never felt closer to Berndt Hartmann. Twenty years of his life had been spent hunting down the minutest traces left by that name. He had sought him in Germany and Spain, in the

United States and South America, but inevitably the trail, never more than a faint, ghostly aura, had gone cold. A hundred times, he had screamed inwardly at his father to give up the quest, but always the old man had driven him on. It was only in the past year, as Max Dornberger's body and mind began to fail him, that his ravings had finally revealed the reason for his obsession.

He picked up the phone and dialled a familiar number.

'I have a job for you.' He read off the address in Jersey. 'I want to know everything about the company. Who's behind it, who's behind them, where the money comes from. Everything. Yes, I know what it could cost. Has cost ever been an issue in the past?'

He replaced the phone and considered what else he could do.

His whole life had been moulded for this. Every lesson in the cellar, every beating, every Latin verb and Greek subjunctive, the languages that sat so comfortably in his head. The sterile, disciplined years at university when so many temptations had taunted and tormented him. Hartmann and the Crown, always Hartmann and the Crown. It must be fourteen years since his father had noticed that some other force was following a similar trail. At first, it had only been the tiniest of hints: an obscure ancient text accessed twice in a single year, a break-in at a museum that was of interest to the Dornbergers. Slowly, it became clear that the target was the Crown of Isis. That was when the hunt began to discover who was taking such an interest and why. The who had eventually become apparent. Even after all these years, the why still had to be answered. Why was a Russian billionaire called Oleg Samsonov spending a small fortune to trace a mythical artefact he couldn't be certain even existed? To discover the answer, his father had devised the plan for the long, patient operation to infiltrate Paul Dornberger into the Samsonov organization. First the menial job in a company two steps distant from the Russian – an office boy, but an office boy with talent and energy who soon became noticed. When a colleague became swamped with work what was more natural than that Paul, the cheerful workaholic, should offer his help? How about if he took over the Maxwell account? That brought new contacts who noticed that good old Paul was always willing to do more than he was asked. Hey, did you know that good old Paul can speak Russian? And just at the time when we're doing more and more work for the Russians. He's young, he's enthusiastic and he's talented. We've got to have this chap. Patience and more patience. Eventually a brush with the outer rings of planet Samsonov. The meeting. The timely intervention. A few hundred thousand saved, his fluent Russian displayed. It was pin money, but it was the kind of thing Samsonov's people noticed. He'd felt their light fingers fumbling about in his life. The odd looks from neighbours of the flat he'd rented. What was it? Your Mr Dornberger's up for an award, Mrs B, can't say what it is, but before Her Maj can hand these things out we have to know if there are any little *peculiarities* in his life. Of course, we'll have to ask you to sign this. Not seen the Official Secrets Act before, have we? And at work, those little signs that Paul Dornberger was on the way up. The nod from the director who'd never acknowledged him before. The unlikely smile from the MD's witch of a secretary. Once inside the Samsonov empire's headquarters, it had been remarkably easy. Oleg Samsonov was a man who took an interest in his staff and he had soon noticed the pleasant young man with the inquiring mind and a talent for discretion, a combination that, in his experience, was unusual. All it had taken then was more patience.

As Samsonov's personal assistant he had an overview of his employer's activities given to few other men. The keystone was the billionaire's investment company, which gave him control of many dozens of businesses across Europe and Russia. But business was only part of it. Like many of his kind, Samsonov knew little of art, but didn't let that stand in the way of acquiring a substantial collection of the world's great works and many others that either took his fancy or were expensive enough to warrant his respect. His acquisitions were made through a network of dealers, mostly respectable, but some not. His taste, if it could be called taste, was towards simplicity and beauty. He distrusted most modern art, because it had yet to find its true value, but, though he disliked Picasso, he also recognized his investment potential and owned several of his works. Many of them were on show in the apartments, but Paul suspected that the most valuable, and quite possibly a number of rarities whose origins didn't stand up to legal scrutiny, hung in the panic room, where Oleg could admire them without being disturbed by lesser mortals.

It had been almost two years before Paul felt secure enough to begin the hunt for evidence that Samsonov retained his interest in the mythical Crown of Isis. The hints had been there. Instructions to dealers to carry out discreet enquiries into private collections of Egyptian artefacts. A payment to a Swiss bank account which, to Paul's certain knowledge, belonged to a Berlin-based specialist in the art of breaching museum security. Researchers employed to carry out searches through the archives of particular museums, many of which Paul recognized from his own efforts. The question was: had they reaped any reward for their labours? The answer to that lay in Oleg Samsonov's personal files and hidden behind an encrypted security wall that Paul Dornberger hadn't dared attempt to breach. Fortunately, there was another way. Calculating that the researchers and dealers were unlikely to have been told of the significance of their target, he simply used his authority to contact each of them in turn to ask for an update on their position. The message? No progress. He couldn't be a hundred per cent certain that the Berlin break-in artist had been unsuccessful, but the fact that the agreed, up-front payment had not been followed by a bonus, led him to believe that was the case.

He had asked his father why they put so much effort into shadowing Samsonov when they already had the Crown. The question had earned him a dangerous stare that had reminded him of the hours in the cellar.

'Fool! In seeking the Crown, the Russian seeks the Eye, because without the Eye the Crown is nothing but a golden trinket. No man, not even a man as rich as Samsonov, would expend hundreds of thousands of pounds to possess such a thing. Somehow, he has learned of the true nature of the Crown of Isis's power. As he gets closer to the Crown he will inevitably come across Hartmann's trail. With his resources he will track down the thief much more quickly than we would ever be able to and where he leads you will follow.'

He had nodded and moved to go, but his father was not finished. 'Paul.' The voice was tired and looking back to that day he could recognize the first weariness of the old man's decline. 'There is another reason. When Samsonov finds Hartmann's trail, it is inevitable he will also find my own. If that happens there may come a time when you have to deal with our Russian friend. Do you understand?'

XIV

'The Eye of Isis is a jewel?'

He could see the excitement building as the calculations ran through her mind. '*And at its centre, the great gemstone known as the Eye of Isis,*' he repeated.

'A diamond, you reckon? A great big diamond.'

'A diamond or a ruby. Remember the red teardrop on the eye symbol. That would make sense.'

'How big is a *great gemstone*? How much would it be worth today?'

'Let's not get carried away, Detective,' he laughed. 'We're talking about a single reference in a single book. And not from a historian or an academic. You said yourself this is a book of fairytales.'

'But it must have come from somewhere. It's too specific. The description is too precise. You don't make stuff like that up.'

'Don't kid yourself, it may be a hundred years ago,

but these guys were in the business of selling books.'

She gave him her shrewd look. 'But you don't believe that.'

He didn't reply. The truth was that he wanted to believe in the existence of an enormous unknown diamond.

'How big would it be? Gimme your best guess.'

He shook his head. 'I don't know enough to make a guess. Wait here.'

She sat for five minutes, taking in the very English unfamiliarity of what was going on around her in the museum until he returned with another book.

'The only big diamond I know anything about is the Koh-i-noor, which is part of the Crown Jewels, that's—'

'Yeah, Jamie,' her voice dripped with sarcasm, 'I've heard of the Crown Jewels.'

'Well, it says here that the Koh-i-noor, also known as the Mountain of Light, is the size and shape of a small hen's egg. About this,' he made an oval with his thumb and fingers, 'and it weighs about 109 carats. That's after it was cut and polished for Queen Victoria in the mid-nineteenth century, on the personal orders of Prince Albert. Before it was cut it weighed in at 186 carats.'

'They cut it in half?'

He nodded. 'It was very controversial at the time. Many people thought Albert, who wasn't particularly popular, had botched things by insisting it be cut. The Eye of Isis referred to in the book, if it ever existed, would have been uncut – we're talking about two-thousand years ago – but I suppose there's a likelihood it was polished in some way.'

'So how much?'

He stared at her. 'Priceless.'

'C'mon, Saintclair, you can do better than that.'

'The Koh-i-noor has never been bought or sold. It may be about three thousand years old, which could make it contemporary with our jewel. Throughout its history it has been gifted, bartered or plundered, mostly plundered. Anything that valuable has been paid for in blood.'

'How much?' she insisted.

'A hundred million pounds, at least. Possibly many hundred millions of pounds. Call it a billion dollars, but it could be as much as ten billion. We'll never know, because it will never be sold.'

'And the Eye of Isis?'

'Potentially the same,' he admitted. 'But only if it exists.'

'Oh, it exists all right,' she said with utter certainty. 'You said anything that valuable has been paid for in blood. Well, the Hartmanns paid for it, and the British Hartmans, and God knows how many other folks. And if it exists, it must have left a trail.'

They studied each other for a few moments, oblivious to the bustle around them. Eventually, Jamie broke the silence. 'Who's the top British expert on Ancient Egypt?'

She frowned at him. 'Now how would I know that?'

'Sorry,' Jamie laughed. 'I was talking to myself. Bad habit. One of many. Anyway, it was a stupid question, because they'll be able to tell us over there.' He pointed across the Great Court to the entrance to the Egyptian section.

'Why do we want to know?'

'I said we had two options, follow the Hartmanns or follow the Eye. Well, you're going to follow the Eye. In the meantime, we've been so focused on the Eye, if you'll pardon the pun, we've forgotten about the Hartmann connection. I'll dig up everything I can about the last days before the Fall of Berlin and we can meet up again tomorrow.'

'Okay,' she said in her slow drawl. 'But I have a better idea. How about we meet up later and you take me out to dinner. Somewhere fancy. I'd like that.'

He grinned. 'I'd like that too.'

The first two experts on Danny's list were, not surprisingly given it was the digging season, working on projects in Egypt, but the third was happy to meet her. Professor Helen Dayton opened the front door of her terraced house in Richmond carrying a feather duster and with two fair-haired toddlers wrapped around her legs. Fisher introduced herself and they shook hands.

'Please excuse them.' The Egyptologist smiled. 'I've only been back from Cairo for a week and they're still a little hyper. To be honest, I'd much rather be up to my neck in dust dealing with lazy Egyptian labourers and argumentative archaeologists, not to mention venal officials from the Department of Culture. Come through into the study while I find them something to occupy themselves with. Coffee?'

'No thank you.' British coffee and the American variety seemed to be only distant relations, although it was better than the warmed-up water they called tea.

She was ushered to a book-lined room with a view over the garden and waited until the other woman returned, still carrying the feather duster, which she absently pushed into an umbrella stand made from an elephant's foot. Two leather chairs sat either side of the window.

'This is lovely.' Fisher gestured to the lawn beyond the window, with its apple trees and flower beds where late roses still bloomed among the greenery.

'All down to my husband and the previous owners, I'm afraid. I don't have too much time for gardening.'

Fisher smiled at the subtle hint and got down to business.

'Firstly, Professor, thank you for agreeing to help. We're very grateful.'

'You said it was some kind of investigation?'

'That's right, a homicide investigation. A young family.'

Helen Dayton's head came up. In Fisher's experience most honest citizens were happy to help the cops, but the mention of murder always shook them a little.

'And you're working with the British police?'

'Correct.' She produced her identification and the accreditation she'd been issued at New Scotland Yard.

'Well, I'm not sure how I can contribute, but what can I help you with?'

Her face paled as Fisher explained the Egyptian symbolism found on Elizabeth Hartmann and the theory that the killings could be linked to the goddess.

'So you see, anything you can tell us about Isis might be of use in explaining why the victims were chosen.'

Helen Dayton rose and went to the window. Fisher waited for her to gather her thoughts. Finally, the other woman nodded to herself. Danny Fisher had deliberately made the question as broad as possible to allow Helen to relax into her role as expert witness. She listened as the Egyptian specialist went over the Isis/Osiris/Horus myth that Jamie had already explained.

'Isis is the divine mother and goddess of fertility. In the Egyptian pantheon she holds her place among the very greatest and is one of the few deities whose worship was exported beyond the borders of Egypt. Temples dedicated to her have been found all over the Roman Empire, even in Rome itself. She was believed to be the most powerful god in the ways of magic, which, I suspect, is what endeared her to the Romans. She had the power to destroy life with mere words, but she is also the only member of the Egyptian pantheon credited with the ability to resurrect the dead and offer them new life.

'I think you are correct in linking the symbol you found to the goddess. Von Bulow, though his work was dismissed by his rivals after the outbreak of the First World War, was a very meticulous archaeologist and scholar. His paper on the Eye of Isis was the product of years of research. I have no doubt the Eye existed in the form he suggested.'

'What about in another form?'

'I'm sorry?'

Danny consulted her notes, although she had no need to. 'I'm talking about *the great gemstone known as the Eye of Isis*. The one that is associated with the Crown of Isis.'

The words were interrupted by a high-pitched shriek from the adjoining room, followed by the sound of infant squabbling. Helen pursed her lips, but Fisher couldn't be certain whether the children had annoyed her, or the question.

'The *Eye of Isis*,' she placed unnecessary emphasis on the words, 'as you suggest it, does not exist, in any context that I'm aware of. I am an academic, Detective, and as such I deal in fact, not fairytale. I'm aware that over the years there have been whispers about some fabled jewel, but these kinds of stories exist in many different cultures. The "Great Mogul" diamond seen by Jean Baptiste Tavernier in 1665 in India was mythologized into three or four different enormous stones, but is now accepted to be the uncut Koh-i-noor. As far as I know, this all stemmed from a few scraps

from a so-called "lost version" of Tacitus' *Annals* . . .
You know who Tacitus was?' Danny nodded, wondering why every Brit seemed to think she was an idiot.
'The "book" was supposedly discovered in a convent
archive in Italy in the nineteenth century and taken to
Berlin in nineteen forty-four, where it conveniently disappeared. It was an elaborate fraud that spawned a
conspiracy theory, nothing more, Detective Fisher.'

Danny Fisher resisted the temptation to dispute the
academic's hypothesis, but she had another question.

'Does that mean the Crown of Isis doesn't exist
either?'

'Oh, the Crown of Isis *existed*. There is plenty of
evidence of that.' Helen went to one of the shelves,
selected a book and flicked through until she found the
page she wanted. 'Look, you can see it here.' She placed
it where Fisher had a view of the page. 'On the right of
the stele is Cleopatra.' She smiled. 'Yes, Detective Fisher,
Cleopatra, wearing the double crown of Egypt and
looking surprisingly manly, is pictured – and named in
the inscription below – making an offering to The Lady,
Isis, seen feeding the baby Horus at her breast and
wearing her own headdress, or crown. The Crown of
Isis was a diadem, topped with the stylized horns of a
cow, and with the sun disk between them. The sun disk
would have been beaten gold, and when the headdress
was worn by the priestess at the two great festivals
dedicated to the goddess, from a distance, it would have
seemed like Ra himself was shining upon them, the

goddess was wearing a star plucked from the sky, or perhaps a great diamond.

'I'm sorry to disappoint you, Detective, is that all?'

'Just one thing, Ma'am. You said the Crown of Isis *existed*, past tense. What happened to it?'

For a moment, Helen Dayton's face went blank and Danny saw the lie that was about to emerge as clearly as if it was written in lights on her forehead. Before she could say anything another burst of screaming froze the words on her tongue and she excused herself to see to the children.

Danny gathered up her things. When Helen appeared in the doorway with a tiny figure in each arm, she was certain she was about to be invited to leave. But the academic sighed and kissed the head of the girl in her right arm.

'You said children were killed? Murdered?'

Danny nodded.

'You won't find this in any books, because no academic would want to be associated with it. It is gossip, no more than that. It may have reached some of the more wild conspiracy sites on the internet, but if it has I have never heard of it.'

'Yes?'

'In the resurrection myth associated with Isis, there's a hint, no more than a hint, that for the dead to become the living, a price must be paid. A blood price.'

'Human sacrifice?'

Helen Dayton's face might have been set in concrete,

but she managed a vigorous, almost spastic nod.

'There's more. I had a colleague who planned a research project on the Crown of Isis. He came up with a wild theory, which he would only talk about with trusted friends. One night when he was drunk he said that he was on the point of proving that the Crown had reappeared at certain times through history. Times of strife. And that each time it appeared, it was associated with magic, witchcraft and murder.' She hugged the babies closer. 'Child murder.'

Danny Fisher caught her breath. 'Where can I get in touch with this man? It could be important.'

Helen shook her head and Danny saw tears streaming down her cheeks.

'I'm afraid that won't be possible.'

XV

'So this Gerald Masterton died in a car crash?'

'I've already checked.' Danny answered the question in his voice. 'No suspicious circumstances. He'd visited a bar after work. Hit a tree on a blind bend.'

'Just bad luck, then?'

'Uhuh, another of those coincidences.'

A waiter brought their first course. Jamie had chosen an upmarket Italian restaurant just off Portman Square, on the basis – he'd seen it in the movies – that all Americans like Italian food. When Danny Fisher arrived every eye in line of sight had checked her out. She wore a black silk suit with a slightly mannish cut, and she didn't walk, so much as prowl. He wasn't sure whether she reminded him of a film star or some sort of big cat.

'Hey, this is great,' she said through a mouthful of salt cod. 'You do classy darn well, Jamie Saintclair.'

'Comes with the job,' he admitted cheerfully. 'My clients are hardly likely to be impressed with the office, so I have to bring them to places like this, feed them fit to burst and get them drunk. Come to think of it, it'd probably be cheaper to rent a bigger office.'

'I hope you're not trying to get me drunk.' She held up her glass for a refill of the Piedmontese red he'd selected to go with the grouse they'd both chosen.

He filled it within a quarter inch of the rim. 'Never crossed my mind.'

The food was so good they waited until they'd finished eating before resuming their discussion.

'So what do you think?'

'You're the detective.' He shrugged. 'But for me it begins to make more sense. The Eye of Isis may or may not exist, but if certain people believed they could lay their hands on a billion dollars' worth of diamond that would give them more than enough motive to torture and kill. It provides a reason for the deaths of the Hartmanns and the Hartmans, even if it takes us no closer to finding out who did it.'

She nodded slowly. 'I'll go along with that. We have the symbol carved into the woman's skull, which links us to the Eye of Isis, and that gives us our motive: greed. But where do Masterton and his theory fit in?'

'Maybe, it *was* a coincidence?'

'I refer you to my earlier answer, counsellor.'

'It sounds like something out of a Dracula movie. Historical artefact keeps turning up through the ages and suddenly the local population starts being thinned out.'

'She said kids, remember. And kids have died.'

'True. But from what you've told me, the Hartmann children died for a reason, albeit a shitty, monstrous reason. They weren't sacrificed, not in a sense that I'd understand it, because there was no evidence of ritual.'

She went silent and he could see her running the alternative scenarios through her mind. He waited until she was satisfied. 'Okay,' she said. 'It's progress, of a sort. Now tell me about your day.'

'Firstly,' he took a sip of water, 'I think your initial instinct about Hartmann was correct. We have two sets of victims with a link to a man last seen in Berlin in nineteen forty-five. The Crown of Isis is exactly the kind of artefact that *Geistjaeger 88* was set up to find. If it was hidden somewhere in Europe the most likely time for it to surface was in the chaos of war.'

'Plunder, like the Koh-i-noor.'

'That's right. Plunder. Secondly, Hartmann was a thief. Let's just say, for instance, Ritter, and Dornberger and Hartmann smash down the door to some mansion or chateau. Chances are they are there for a reason. A tip-off, or information collected from someone in a concentration camp by means we don't want to think about? They search the place for whatever it is that they've been told they'll find there. Probably take it apart. But Hartmann, the thief, stumbles on the Crown of Isis, with its whacking great diamond. Does he hand it over? Not on your life. This is his chance to make sure that, whoever wins, he has a very comfortable start to the post-war era.'

'The Crown of Isis is a sizable object, remember.' Danny giggled and it was odd to hear a little girl's laugh from a full-grown woman. 'He could hardly just put it down his pants.'

'Don't underestimate Hartmann. I have this mental picture of someone young, resourceful and cocky; a kind of Nazi Artful Dodger. He would have found a way. Maybe he broke it up. Anyway, the point is that whoever killed those people in Brooklyn and out in Docklands believed Hartmann had found the Crown of Isis. The question is, did he find it during the war, or after it?'

'During, I think we're agreed on that.'

'Then Berlin is the key. And Berlin is where I've spent my day.'

The waiter approached their table, but Danny waved him away. 'You said that Hartmann and this guy Dornberger took part in the defence of Berlin. I got the impression that maybe you knew more than you were telling me. Now how could that be?'

'You didn't pick up on the reference to the Reichschancellery, then?'

'I thought it was some kinda Nazi telephone exchange.'

He smiled at that. Danny Fisher liked to play the wide-eyed Yank innocent on her first venture beyond Hoboken, but the reality was that she had a brain as sharp as a switchblade. He suspected she knew as much about the Reichschancellery as he did, but she wanted him to spell it out.

'The Reichschancellery in Berlin was the official residence of Germany's head of state. When the Russians closed in on the city in the spring of nineteen forty-five, the chancellery and the Reichstag, the parliament building that was nearby, were their primary targets.'

'All right.' She nodded. 'I get that.'

'The people who defended the Reichschancellery were billeted in a bunker nearby.'

'So?'

'Hitler's bunker.'

'Holy shit!'

'Precisely.'

'So Hartmann was there at the end?'

'He was certainly there until the last week in April. Quite a few German units, particularly SS units, actually fought their way into Berlin as the Third Reich was collapsing around them and everybody else was trying to get out. Either they still had faith that Hitler would save Germany or they were prepared to defend him to the end, even if it meant their own deaths.'

'The real fanatics, huh?'

Jamie shrugged. 'Fanatics, but brave men. The SS knew exactly what their fate would be if they were captured by the Russians. If they surrendered to the Americans they might be roughed up a little and there was a chance they'd be shot, but the best they could hope for from the Red Army was a bullet in the back of the head.'

'If you don't mind me saying so, this doesn't sound like our guys. Hartmann and Dornberger were Himmler's licensed plunderers, not real soldiers. And from what you tell me about Ritter, he may have killed thousands of innocent people, but he was a bureaucrat at heart, a pen-pusher.'

'You're right,' he admitted. 'But in those final days of the war, the Nazis needed every able-bodied man they could lay their hands on. There's a photograph of Hitler during the defence of Berlin, handing out the Iron Cross to soldiers who single-handedly destroyed Russian tanks. In the picture he's patting the cheek of a boy who can't be more than fourteen years old. The German equivalent of Dad's Army.' He saw her puzzled frown and smiled. 'A sort of home defence force – it was called the *Volkssturm* and consisted of men between the ages of sixteen and sixty. By nineteen forty-five sailors and Luftwaffe ground crew were fighting as infantry. The chances are that the men of *Geistjaeger 88* were reluctantly swept up into some SS battle group. The soldiers they ended up fighting beside in Berlin were a unit of French SS volunteers under the command of *Brigadeführer* Gustav Krukenberg. A month earlier, the Charlemagne Division had marched out of a station in Poland straight into the German defence line on the Eastern Front with more than seven thousand men, by the time they were forced back to Berlin there were fewer than a hundred of them.'

Danny Fisher held up her hand. 'Hang on just a

minute. I don't know much about World War Two, but I do know that the French were on our side.'

'Well, yes and no.' Jamie smiled. 'The Free French under General de Gaulle fought on the allied side, and so did the Resistance, though not as many of them as they'd like you to think. But until August nineteen forty-four, France was divided into the Occupied north and Vichy in the south, which was run as a German client state and actively collaborated in Nazi policies like rounding up the Jews. Marshall Petain, the Vichy leader, was a First World War hero and rabid anti-communist. He encouraged his young men and members of the *milice*, a kind of local militia, to fight for the Germans in Russia. For an organization that began life as the epitome of the Aryan ideal, the SS turned into a surprisingly cosmopolitan institution. It already had the Wiking Division, which was composed of Norwegians, Danes, Dutchmen and Belgians, Balts and even a few Britons. They would have welcomed the French with open arms, especially after they'd seen how they could fight. It seems that Ritter had already slipped away, probably on some concocted mission for Himmler, who was by now playing both ends against the middle and negotiating with the Allies, but Hartmann and Dornberger were trapped in some of the hardest, dirtiest and most dangerous battles of the war. They would have been battered by artillery, fighting day and night from burning ruins and cellars to counter Soviet probes, hungry, scared and entirely without hope. The men of the Charlemagne Division, or what little remained of it, made their name as tank killers. They'd stalk the Russian T-34s through the streets with magnetic mines and *panzerfaust* rocket launchers, kill the accompanying infantry and blow up the tanks. The Red Army lost at least a hundred tanks in the battle for central Berlin and those few Frenchmen are credited with destroying at least fifty. But gradually the noose tightened and the last remnants of the French SS and the men who fought with them withdrew to make a final stand at Hitler's bunker in the garden behind the Reichschancellery.'

Danny chewed her lip as something occurred to her. 'If Hartmann and Dornberger were caught up in that kind of horrendous battle, why are we so certain that they survived?'

'Because we know exactly where they were on the morning of the twenty-ninth of April nineteen forty-five – the day before Hitler and Eva Braun committed suicide and three days before the final surrender.' She took a deep breath and he realized he was stretching her patience. 'The reason we know they were there is because our two heroes carved themselves their own little place in history. According to at least one source, Max Dornberger and Berndt Hartmann were the SS men who executed Hitler's brother-in-law, Hermann Fegelein.'

XVI

Max Dornberger felt his blood rise as the images flashed through his mind like a home-movie reel. The cave and the Crown and hot blood on his hands. Tearing down the walls of some nameless eastern city where the sand now gathered in the skulls and sang through the exposed ribcages of the slaughtered population. Riding into Rome at Alaric's side with the women screaming and men choking on their own balls. Charging knee to knee with Murat at Marengo and Borodino. As so often, he found himself questioning his own certainty. How could it be real?

But the Crown was real. The Eye was real.

And that meant Hartmann was real. Berlin was real.

Dust and death. Living – no, it could not be called living, let us instead say existing – in cramped cellars where the air was so foul that you chewed on other men's shit and drank their sweat, while you waited for the katyusha mortar strike that would bury you alive.

Red, swollen eyes staring blindly from below steel helmets and Hitler Jugend caps in the flash of an exploding artillery round. Rats' eyes, only they weren't rats, they were the worn-out husks of human beings. Men and boys who hadn't slept for a week clinging by a thread to what remained of their sanity. A shout. 'Ivan kommt!' Jackbooted feet charging for the doorway. Hanging back as long as you could as Hauptsturmführer Fenet led those crazy Frenchmen past with their 'fausts and their magnetic anti-tank mines, but not for too long because, SS or not, the kettenhunde military police liked nothing better than to string up a shirker from the nearest lamp post. The breathless, heart-pounding dash through streets choked with the remains of bomb-shattered buildings and piles of rubble that stank of festering corpses. Halt. Disperse for ambush. Crouching behind a burned-out Mercedes staff car, ears straining for the telltale tortured shriek of tank tracks on concrete. Hands shaking as they clutch the warm steel of the new banana-magazined Sturmgewehr 44 assault rifle that marks you as SS as clearly as the lightning-flash runes on your collar or the blood group tattoo on your arm. There it was! A nerve-fragmenting clatter of diesel engine. Savage shouts in the demonic language of the barbarian. Wait. Wait. Be invisible. Let them pass. They are careless. As exhausted as you are. They think they are already the victors, their minds on the fat fräuleins and the unlimited vodka and schnapps that will be their reward for all the years of struggle and sacrifice. Vermin. The first sight of a creeping figure in a soot-stained brown uniform, then the gun barrel that heralds the silhouette of the tank. A T-34, thank Christ, and not the Stalin with its thicker armour. Wait. Don't let them see you. This is not your time. This is not the way it should be. A flash, instantly followed by the distinctive thump of a panzerfaust and the takatakatak rattle of fully automatic fire. Nerveless fingers find the composure to throw a stick grenade. A scream you realize is from your own throat mingling with the shrieks of the wounded and the dying; the big rifle bucking in your hands as you seek targets by sense among the shadows in the thick smoke from the burning tank. Enemy or friend, in the madness of battle it is impossible to tell. All that matters is it's not you. Two figures rolling on the ground in a welter of grey and brown. Bright blood spurts in short jets from a punctured throat, like a scarlet rose flowering in a monochrome landscape. A child's face is frozen for ever in a final moment of terror. The Ivan rises snarling from his victim to be dispatched by a short burst from the MG-44. In the odd oasis of calm that follows, Vaulot, the tank killer, sprints past with a funnel-shaped H3 magnetic mine in his hands, hunting a second T-34 that no one else has noticed. Another explosion. More firing. More screams. A whistle: the signal to withdraw. Back to the cellar, only there is a lot more space now. Berlin, April 1945. And always at your heels, like a faithful hunting dog: Hartmann.

Hartmann with his rat's face and his rat's cunning. Slim and agile and quick as a circus acrobat. The hands, too delicate for a soldier, with long fingers made for playing the piano. Hartmann the thief. Once a thief, always a thief. I should have remembered that.

Hartmann came to the unit in late '43, with the smell of the jail still on him. Nineteen, but looking years younger, he'd been in an SS uniform for less than a month and at first he was in awe of the veterans around him. But he was good, and being good made him popular. When he crouched before a safe, he found an inner stillness that was almost beyond human. When his fingers worked the dials he was like a great conductor directing an orchestra.

But Hartmann would always be an outsider. The veterans of Geistjaeger 88 had served in the east. We had seen things that had changed us. The unit was always under pressure from Himmler to deliver and often that meant taking extreme actions to extract information. Sometimes, I suspected Hartmann was too squeamish for the job, but, as we lost more men to the Ostfront, he became part of the G88 inner circle.

We all saw the end approaching and had made our own arrangements, but the final collapse came so quickly that the men of Geistjaeger 88 were taken by surprise. We had been carrying out research and interrogations at Auschwitz in late January when the Russians broke through. Events pushed us north and west, towards Berlin, where we were forced to present ourselves for assignment at SS headquarters in Prinz-Albrecht-Strasse. At first, our written orders from Himmler kept us safe. Geistjaeger 88 made its home in a fine requisitioned apartment on Wilhelmstrasse and spent Germany's dying weeks cataloguing the Reichsführer's personal art collection and counting on its leader to get them out of the shit. But one day in early April, Ritter disappeared and Geistjaeger 88 went to war. A mere fifteen strong, we joined Battle Group Charlemagne of SS Division Nordland, tasked with the defence of Sector C as the Red Army attacked across the Oder. We were reluctant soldiers, Hartmann and I, unlike most of our comrades. For us it was fight or die, because those unwilling to fight were strung up on every corner with placards round their stretched necks. In those last days, I thought of nothing but escape, but there was no escape as we were forced street by street towards the city centre. All I knew was that, somehow, I had to get to the Crown and use it for the purpose the gods had intended.

Early on the morning of the 29th we were ordered back to the bunker. The shattered remnant of Battle Group Charlemagne staggered through flurries of artillery, ignoring the deadly hail as if it was a summer shower. Black smoke billowed from the upper storeys of the Reichschancellery as we carried our wounded past the guards. The main entrance to the complex lay behind a reception hall and the first thing that struck you was the silence. For the first time in ten days there was no sound of Russian shells, no snap of tank fire, no buzz-saw rasp of machine guns. No sudden death waiting to take you before the next heartbeat. Just the groans of the wounded and the snarls of harassed staff officers trying to create some semblance of order among the chaos of the Third Reich's Armageddon.

'SS-Sturmbannführer Dornberger and Battle Group Charlemagne reporting on the orders of General Krukenberg.' The adjutant at the desk smiled disbelievingly at the snap of heels and stared at the thirty grimy, bloodstained scarecrows crammed into the stairway, barely eight or nine of them unwounded, before checking a sheet on the metal desktop.

'I have no orders for you yet, Sturmbannführer,' he said dismissively. 'You will have to wait.' He turned back to his papers.

I drew my pistol and placed it on top of the file he was reading. 'My men need food. They haven't eaten for three days.'

He looked from me to the four stone-faced guards who stood with machine pistols pointed directly at my chest. A moment of doubt, before he decided he had better things to do than kill insubordinate SS officers.

'Take these men to the dining room,' he told an orderly. 'See that they're fed.'

'And somewhere to sleep.'

He shrugged wearily. 'Shoot me if you must, but I'm afraid you'll have to take your chances. You'll see.'

The orderly led us through the gas-proof door.

Imagine the Seventh Pit of hell and the Last Judgement combined, but in a dank, concrete tomb where only the stifling, over-used air gave a semblance of warmth. The upper bunker had been partitioned into thirteen or fourteen rooms, with accommodation for Goebbels and his brood in two rooms to the left and the guest and guard quarters to the right. It had a wide central corridor that doubled as a dining room and a conference area. Somewhere in the labyrinth must have been a kitchen and storerooms. An unkempt horde of uniformed men and women crammed the rooms, some of the men drunk and the women less than half-dressed. Others slumped by the walls as the younger Goebbels children played around their outstretched feet, untroubled by the all-pervading stink of sweat and fear. And defeat. We looked in astonishment at the food and drink piled all around: champagne being drunk direct from the bottle; meats, cheeses and bread filling the tables that weren't being used for more carnal purposes. The men of Charlemagne exchanged glances before frenziedly diving on the food. I liberated a bottle of pilsner, a loaf and some ham and found a place by the wall; Hartmann joined me, laying his machine pistol at his side. The last thing I heard before I plunged into a dreamless sleep was his whisper.

'How the fuck are we going to get out of here?'

For all I knew it might have been an eternity, but what seemed like only minutes later I was prodded awake by someone kicking my foot. I opened my eyes to find a man standing over me in the uniform of an SS general and automatically leapt to my feet. Hartmann stayed where he was, but I could tell he was awake.

'So Heini's removal men are here for the grand finale,' Gruppenführer Johann Rattenhuber sneered. 'Which is more than you can say for der treue Heinrich. I wouldn't be trumpeting your loyalties around here. Your boss has sold out to the Americans and is trying to save his skin. The Führer would have him hanging from a meat hook if we could lay our hands on him.'

I kept my eyes on the far wall and my mouth shut. If the head of Hitler's personal bodyguard wanted me to speak, he'd tell me.

He studied my uniform. 'Sturmbannführer, eh? You must be Dornberger. Come with me, I have work for you. You too, trooper. You can stop pretending to be asleep. And bring your weapons.'

Hartmann got to his feet like a scalded cat and together we followed Rattenhuber to the far end of the bunker, while the drunken throng parted in front of him as if he had the Angel of Death on his shoulder.

'Swine,' he spat contemptuously. 'Have fun while you can. The Ivans are welcome to you.'

A blond child of about four stepped in front of him as we reached the end of the conference room and he bent to pat her head. 'Ach, Heidrun, liebling, where is your mama? You must find her and tell her Papa wishes to talk with her.' A second older girl appeared and took her sister's hand.

'*I will, Uncle Johann.*'

'*Thank you, Helga.*' *They stepped aside and Rattenhuber shook his head and sighed.*

Beyond the conference room lay a second gas door. He stopped in front of it and turned to us.

'*Through this door, you hear nothing, see nothing and say nothing. Understand?*'

Without waiting for a reply, he pushed past four SS guards and down two sets of stairs that led to a long hallway. In the centre of the far wall was another door, with yet more guards. We waited while it was opened and I could sense Hartmann's growing fear. We had heard rumours about Hitler's final refuge; the last thing we had expected was to be invited to share it. Beyond the first door was a second, which led in turn to a broad corridor with rooms to right and left. Compared to the fevered atmosphere above, this was like entering into a monastery. Officers walked between offices without giving us a glance, speaking in muted whispers that were drowned by the low hum of the generator.

Rattenhuber knocked on the second door to the right.

'*Enter.*'

The man behind the desk wore a pristine brown uniform and had a moon-shaped scar on his forehead. He looked like a provincial butcher with too much liking for his own pork. At a smaller desk in the corner of the room a slim, dark-haired secretary sat with a pencil and notebook in her hands. She sniffed as she caught the scent of unwashed bodies and her eyes widened at the

143

filthy uniforms and unshaven faces of the intruders.

'What's this?' the man demanded.

Rattenhuber nodded towards a steel door at the rear of the room and Reichsleiter Martin Bormann glared. 'Get on with it then.'

The general drew his pistol and pulled a key from his pocket.

He turned to us. 'Ready.'

I unshouldered my assault rifle and heard a rattle as Hartmann did the same.

The door swung open to reveal a tiny cell and a dishevelled, defeated-looking man sitting on the floor with his back to the wall and his head down. The prisoner's hands were manacled in front of him and he wore the remnants of an SS uniform, from which every insignia of rank had been torn, leaving a few threads hanging. When he looked up, his eyes were glazed and red-rimmed. I could see that he recognized me and my heart stopped as he opened his mouth to say something.

'The prisoner will remain silent,' Rattenhuber barked. 'Get up.'

Hermann Fegelein used the wall to help himself unsteadily to his feet.

'Bring him.'

Bormann did not look up as we pushed Fegelein out of the office and turned right into the corridor. Fegelein had always been Himmler's favourite, tall and handsome and reputed to be one of the finest horsemen in the Third Reich. Now he looked like a football with all the air kicked out of it. He staggered like a drunk and his clothing stank of stale urine. As we walked, he muttered to himself, but the only word I could identify was 'betrayed', repeated over and over again. I recognized all the signs, but I could feel Hartmann's confusion. He looked at Fegelein and saw an SS Obergruppenführer: a general of cavalry and holder of the Knight's Cross. Nazi aristocracy; the husband of Eva Braun's sister Gretl. All I saw was a dead man walking.

We continued into a long conference room, again with doors giving access to both sides, and from one of them emerged a stooped figure in dark trousers and an olive-green jacket.

'Where is Greim?' the familiar harsh voice demanded.

General Rattenhuber froze and his arm shot out. 'Heil Hitler.'

Adolf Hitler turned to look directly at us. Dark eyes glared from a pale face, the flesh puffy with fatigue. He took in our filthy clothing at a glance and he began to shake with fury. 'What ...?' He stumbled to a halt as he recognized Fegelein, turned on his heel and disappeared back into the room he'd come from.

'Get him out of here,' Rattenhuber hissed. 'The stairs at the end of the corridor. Quickly.'

I prodded the prisoner with the barrel of my MP-44 until we reached the stairway. 'You go ahead,' I ordered Hartmann. 'We don't want him making a run for it when we get to the top, do we?'

145

The stairs rose in steep flights as if we were in some sort of tower. Halfway up the rattle of boots confirmed that General Rattenhuber had returned.

'Move, we don't have all day. Use your rifle butt if you have to.'

When we reached the top, Hartmann was waiting, his rifle covering Fegelein as the condemned man climbed ahead of Rattenhuber and I. He backed out of the doorway and we followed into an open space surrounded by walls and the rear of the Old Reichschancellery. The ground had once been laid out with paths and shrubbery but it was churned up by shell holes. In the centre stood an ornamental turret that doubled as a ventilation shaft for the bunker.

'Right, let's get this over with,' Rattenhuber said.

'No, please ...' Fegelein's voice shook as the general pushed him back against a wall and covered him with the pistol. An artillery round exploded somewhere nearby, but no one even flinched.

'Hermann Fegelein, you have been found guilty by court martial of cowardice in the face of the enemy, leaving your post without orders and high treason. The sentence of the court martial is death by firing squad. Do your duty.'

This last was to Hartmann and I. I raised the Sturmgewehr to my shoulder, but Hartmann froze like a rabbit in a hunter's spotlight.

In his final moments Fegelein straightened to his full height and looked directly at Rattenhuber. 'I swear by

almighty God, this sacred oath: I will render uncondi-
tional obedience to Adolf—'

'Fire!'

The first rounds from the assault rifle took the Nazi
party's former golden boy in the lower stomach and he
jack-knifed forward into a stream of steel-jacketed
bullets that slammed him backwards against the wall.
The torn body slumped sideways, leaving a bright
smear of scarlet on the concrete. Fegelein's leg was still
twitching spasmodically as Rattenhuber marched up to
him.

'Pig. *A pity you didn't remember your oath to the*
Führer when you were trying to run away with your
mistress.' He aimed his pistol and put a bullet into the
already shattered head. 'You,' *he pointed at Hartmann.*
'Since you don't appear to be good for much else, get rid
of this filth.'

Hartmann looked from the body to me. Fegelein had
been a big man, and well set. I shrugged.

'You heard the general. There's a gardener's hut
across by the wall. Find a shovel and bury him in the
corner.'

While Hartmann dug the grave, I sat on a nearby
bench and lit a cigarette. Odd how peaceful it could be
in the spring sunshine even with the Devil's orchestra of
distant battle competing with the sound of birdsong. An
idea formed.

'Will this do?' *Hartmann looked up worriedly from*
the shallow scrape he'd created. Sweat dripped from the

narrow nose and his black hair was plastered across his forehead. He always had been a lazy little bastard.

'Deeper,' I ordered.

It was another ten minutes before I was satisfied. By now the sound of nearby artillery had intensified and the two guards had retreated inside the shelter of the bunker's rear entrance.

'All right, get him.'

He dragged the body across to the grave and it flopped in with the legs up one side and the boots still visible.

'You'll need to get in and sort him out properly,' I pointed out.

Hartmann gave me a schoolboy's look of petulant rebellion, but reluctantly obeyed. I waited until he was in the grave before I picked up the Sturmgewehr and cocked it. He froze when he heard the familiar sound.

'You didn't think you'd live through the war, did you, Hartmann? What a foolish notion, that with all these millions of men dying you of all people would survive. It was always part of the plan to get rid of you, only a matter of when.'

He looked up at me and the dark gypsy eyes were without fear. It struck me that he was actually quite brave. But then a lot of people I'd had in this situation had been quite brave. 'I did everything you told me to. We were a team.'

I shook my head. 'You were never part of the team, Hartmann. The team mascot, perhaps, but times *change. It's your misfortune that, apart from me, you are the only man alive who knows about the Geistjaeger 88 retirement fund. That is about to change.'*

'Fuck!'

'Indeed, Hartmann.' I threw the cigarette aside and lifted the assault rifle. He cringed as his body anticipated the storm of bullets, but I made him wait for a few moments. The artillery had been getting closer. The next barrage would cover the sound of firing.

The first round fell about two hundred yards away, the second a hundred. My finger tightened on the trigger.

When I regained consciousness the sun was in my eyes and the taste of blood on my lips. A gentle hand raised my head and someone poured warm liquid into my mouth. It took a few moments before I realized where I was. A weary-looking medical orderly dabbed at my skull with a bandage that was already soaked with blood.

He saw my panic and grinned. 'You know what they say about head wounds. You're lucky it was a bit of stray concrete and not a shell splinter or I'd be picking up your brains with a shovel.'

I tried to raise my head, and it was like being struck by lightning.

'Take your time. Ivan is having his lunch.'

'Hartmann?'

The orderly shrugged. 'When the barrage stopped

*you were on your own, apart from the poor bastard in
the hole over there.'*

My head felt as if it had a fairground ride inside it,
but my blood turned cold. Hartmann was gone. The
Crown? No, I'd kept it well hidden. Hartmann couldn't
know about the Crown. Still, I couldn't afford to take
the chance. I waited for my head to clear before
struggling to my feet. 'He must have gone back to the
unit. I need to find him.'

'Sturm,' the orderly said, 'you're in no fit state to go
anywhere. Come inside and sit for a while.'

'Just patch me up. You know how it is. You serve
with these men. I can't leave them now, just when they
need me.'

He looked at me as if I was crazy. 'Suit yourself.' He
began wrapping a linen bandage round my head. When
he was satisfied, he turned to go. 'Look after yourself,
Sturm. Nobody remembers a dead hero.'

It took me almost an hour to get back to the apartment on Wilhelmstrasse, moving from house to house
and dodging shells and military police patrols along the
way. Deserters hung like ripe fruit from every lamp
standard and tram pylon. The strangest thing was that
some of the shops were still open for business, selling
whatever stock remained before Ivan came and stole it.
The apartment was on the first floor and the solid oak
door was locked, I shot out the lock and kicked my way
inside. Stacked all around the main room were the
things that would have drawn Hartmann here. Cases of

fine wine and French brandy rubbed shoulders with tins of foie gras and caviar, hams, bread and whole cheeses. Berlin might eat shoe leather, but the men of Geistjaeger 88 would only go hungry when the rest had starved. I checked the room where Hartmann had slept, but it was empty. It was then that I felt the first real stirrings of panic. The Crown. The little shit knew about the Crown. I charged upstairs to the room where I'd hidden it. Hartmann must have heard me and he had barricaded himself inside, but I fired a long burst that shattered the door and hit what was left with my shoulder. I looked frantically to the wood panelling where I'd cached the Crown and fear froze me for an instant when I saw that it had been ripped out. A glint of gold to my left. I whirled, with my finger on the trigger, but the bolt clicked on empty after just three shots. Hartmann was crouching by the window, staring at me with desperate eyes. Roaring in fury, I charged towards him with the rifle raised like a club to crush his skull. But Hartmann had always been a slippery little bastard. He dropped the Crown and threw himself backwards through the window with a crash of splintering glass. Fumbling with the new magazine I ran to where he had disappeared and loosed a burst at him as he staggered away from the mound of sand that had broken his fall. Only then, with a surge of relief, did I turn to the Crown of Isis – to find that although I still possessed the Crown, the Eye was gone. Hartmann had the Eye of Isis.

XVII

'I'll see you back to your hotel.'

Danny Fisher gave him a look of amusement. 'I'm a big girl, Saintclair, I don't need a babysitter.'

'Think about it,' he urged. 'You don't know London. The streets can be dangerous at night and a trained killer might come in handy.'

'Trained killer, huh?'

'Two whole weeks at Sandhurst, retired bored witless. All that effort to get in and then for some reason the Army lost its allure.'

Now the look was appraising. 'I didn't figure you as a quitter.'

'It came as a surprise to me, too. Think about it, while I . . . have to . . . er, go.' He picked up the leather briefcase that had sat at his feet throughout the meal.

'Do you always bring your work to dinner?'

He grinned. 'It seemed a good idea at the time.'

When he returned he was wearing his overcoat and carrying Danny's. He helped her into it.

'What's the decision?'

'Sure, why not? Maybe you can come up for a coffee?'

The expression on his face made her laugh.

'You really don't know us Yanks very well, do you, Jamie?'

When they left the restaurant, they walked southwest, through a soft drizzle and in the general direction of Hyde Park. After a few minutes, Danny Fisher put her arm through his, and he squeezed it. They didn't talk. Somehow there didn't seem the need.

A hundred yards behind, dressed in a black jogging suit and trainers, Paul Dornberger kept pace with them.

It had been pure chance that he had discovered the name Jamie Saintclair in a file on Kenny's desk. A source at the British Library had tipped Samsonov's people off about an unusual and sudden interest in *Myths and Legends of the Ancient World* and someone had decided action was required. Dornberger disapproved of the oligarch's choice of the street gang to try to scare Saintclair off. In Samsonov's position, he would have done quite the opposite and hired the art expert. Saintclair's file didn't make impressive reading until the recovery of the Raphael painting amid some murkier dealings with neo-Nazis and a multi-national corporation that rivalled even Oleg's in scale. Humble start in life. Good degree at Cambridge, followed by his failure to make the grade at Sandhurst and a modest career in the art business. But his pursuit of the Raphael had shown great tenacity and excellent deductive powers. For the moment, this was a man to be watched, not provoked. The question was: exactly how much did Saintclair know about the Eye of Isis?

Dornberger kept to the shadows, occasionally switching to a side street and jogging the next few hundred yards, to reappear with his running jacket inside out and the reflective surface visible. At first glance the pair ahead gave the appearance of being relaxed and unwary, but there was something about the woman that rang an alarm bell and Paul dropped back into the shadows. Saintclair's file hadn't mentioned a recent girlfriend or partner, but the body language was too comfortable for mere acquaintances. He made a mental note to have her checked out and his hand strayed automatically to the toggles at his neck. A car with two men in the front seats drove past close to the kerb and conspicuous by its lack of speed. The passenger took an unusual interest in the two walkers, right up until the moment they drew parallel, when he turned his head away and the car speeded up. It had been skilfully done, and the couple walking arm in arm took no apparent notice, but Paul Dornberger felt the hairs on his neck rise. He took a mental note of the number plate and moved a little closer to his targets. Curiouser and curiouser.

* * *

'So why did a girl like you decide to become a cop?'

'I was brought up with cops. My old man was a cop for twenty years, before he took the bullet that crippled him.'

'That's tough, I'm sorry.'

She shrugged. 'It didn't put him in a chair or anything. He just couldn't walk the beat any more. He'd seen enough of desk cops to know he didn't want to do that or be in charge of the drunk tank at a precinct, so he left and started up his own security company. Did pretty good. What about your pop?'

'I never knew my father. Not even his name.' It was said without emotion, but she knew instinctively what the words cost to say and she hugged his arm closer, so he could feel the curve of her breast against it.

'Ever think about finding out?'

'All the time. I have a letter from my mother that might have his name in it, but I've never opened it.'

She stopped and turned to stare at him. 'Why the hell not? It would drive me crazy.'

He smiled. 'A couple of years ago I would have said the same, but after last year and what happened with the Raphael, it was . . . different. For the first time in my life I knew who the real Jamie Saintclair was, so I didn't need to know, if you can understand that? Anyway, knowing my mother it's probably an instruction to wash behind my ears and change my socks every day.'

Danny caught sight of an ornamental building lit by

spotlights beyond the trees in Hyde Park and went to look at it through the metal fence. Jamie stood in the centre of the wide pavement and waited.

'That's what I love about London. There's always something to see.'

'There is,' he agreed. 'The sad thing is that when you live here, you barely notice it.'

She was still peering through the fence when he saw the man walking purposefully towards him. It was the coat he noticed first – a dark seaman's jacket that screamed out a warning. Then the eyes, like machine-gun slits and focused, in a bull-nosed, angry face. The man's arm was already lifting by the time he saw the gun, a big automatic with a long cylinder attached to the barrel. Silenced then, as if that mattered a damn now. He must have shouted, because Danny turned towards him with a mixture of fear and horror on her face. She was too far away to help, but she was already moving. His briefcase was in his left hand, and instinct told him to use it as a shield. But instinct was too slow. The long cylinder kicked up and to the left, he heard a sharp 'phut' and felt the breath knocked out of him at the same instant. As he was thrown backwards his mind registered a second bullet hitting him somewhere in the chest, but he was already fading. No pain yet, just an all-over numbness, but he knew it would come. Amazingly, he was still falling. Did the world always slow when you were dying? He heard the crack as his head hit the concrete – no shortage of pain now – and for a second his vision went red. His lungs fought for breath, competing against the hurt that had been done to body. As he lay paralysed a dark presence loomed over him, blocking out the street lights. For a moment he thought he was already dead, but his vision cleared to reveal a dark tunnel with a hand and narrow, heavy browed eyes way above it. He turned his head away to avoid seeing the bullet that would finally kill him.

The gunman ignored Danny Fisher's scream and looked down the barrel into Jamie Saintclair's confused eyes. A hundred grand and a vacation. Easy money. His right forefinger took up the pressure on the trigger. Two to the chest and one in the head. Nobody ever survived that. When the flying handbag smashed into his head he literally didn't know what had hit him, only that it was large and heavy and followed up by a screaming banshee that lashed out with a kick that knocked the gun from his hand. Jacko Bonetti had been in plenty of street brawls in his time. He knew when to fight and when to run. The mark was dead or well on the way there. His opponent might be a chick, but she had the moves and she had the jump on him. He had a momentary concern about the handgun, but he was wearing gloves and by the time it was traced to the guy who supplied it, Jacko would be back where he belonged on 47th Street. He sprinted back up the street towards Mario and the waiting car.

Danny's first instinct was to go after the shooter, but she'd seen Jamie go down hard and now she ran to his side. She knelt and scrabbled at the buttons of his over-coat, cursing her fumbling fingers. Two rips in the cashmere showed where the bullets had struck and her heart sank at the lack of blood that pointed to almost instantaneous death. 'Stay with me, Jamie,' she whispered desperately. 'We hardly got to know each other.' At last she got the coat open and tore at his jacket and shirt where she could reach the wounds.

She froze.

'You bastard.'

'That's a bit harsh.' His voice sounded as if he'd swallowed a mouthful of river gravel.

'You complete bastard. So that's what you were doing.'

'Mmmh.'

She pulled back the shirt and studied the two silver splashes where the bullets had mushroomed against the web of Kevlar fibres.

'What kind of guy wears body armour on a first date?'

'It seemed like a good idea at the time,' he managed, before the lights went out again.

'Okay, mister. You have some explaining to do.'

She sat by the assessment bed where Jamie lay bare chested, with various electrical monitors attached to his skin and two enormous bruises merging over his heart. A nurse had drawn the curtains round the bed to allow them some privacy.

'I suppose I do owe you an explanation,' he admitted.

'Damn right you do.'

'I don't think this has anything to do with your case.' He told her about the Raphael and the Sun Stone and the possibility that Howard Vanderbilt had taken out a contract on his life.

'And you didn't think to tell me this before?' The blue eyes flashed dangerously. 'You didn't feel it might be a good idea to let me know I might be standing next to a walking shooting gallery.'

'It was only a remote possibility.'

'So remote that you went out and bought a bullet-proof vest.'

'That was in the way of a present,' he protested. 'A gift from a Detective Sergeant Shreeves.'

'Who took the threat seriously enough to send it to you,' she pointed out.

'He was only covering his backsi . . . hedging his bets.'

For a moment he thought she was going to walk out and he knew he would always regret that. He also knew there was nothing he could say that would stop her. She made him wait, but when she spoke again there was authority in her voice. 'If we're going to work together, this is the way it goes. You let me know anything, and I mean *anything*, that might have an impact on our personal security and I'll do the same. Of course,' she gave him her best bad-cop stare, 'I haven't been holding anything back. Okay?'

He nodded. 'Okay.'

'I'll call some folks and see if I can get something done about Vanderbilt. It could take a little time, but they'll ask a few questions, throw a little weight around and maybe he'll back off. Meanwhile, is there anything you'd like to get off your chest?' She pointed at the electrical spaghetti. When they finally finished laughing he told her about the 'muggers'.

'That's exactly what they said?'

'Exactly. *The man says to back off.*'

'And you've no idea who *the man* is?'

'None. My first thought was that it might be a message from Vanderbilt.' He brushed his fingers lightly over his chest and winced. 'But recent experience suggests that he's into more direct action.'

'Could it be to do with anything else you've been working on?'

He shook his head. 'I've gone back over everything. I've made a few enemies, but not that kind of enemy.'

'Then we have to assume that the man wants us to back off from trying to find out what happened to Berndt Hartmann and, if it exists, the Crown of Isis.' She pinned him with hard blue eyes. 'This is my job, Jamie, but there's no reason for you to get yourself killed. Maybe you should get out now?'

He grinned at her. 'Not until hell freezes over.'

XVIII

'Why Danny? Daniella's a perfectly nice name. Or is that what they call you at the precinct? Tough-cop banter?' All he knew about American police procedure had been learned from a TV programme called *NYPD Blue*, but she didn't object. The doctor had told him to rest for a couple of days and they'd ended up at his Kensington flat, where to his surprise and delight, one thing had led inevitably to another.

'It's been Danny for as long as I can remember. Only person calls me Daniella is my mom. Started out as a joke. I've always been tall and skinny and when I'm a kid there's this short, fat actor; sorta borderline famous, right? So the other kids see me and they shout out, "Here comes Danny de Vito." Funny, huh?'

'Maybe not so funny.'

'I hung out with a crowd of boys, could outjump 'em, outrun 'em and outfight 'em. So it kinda stuck. You thought I was a lesbian, right?'

'Er, course not?'

'Don't worry, happens all the time. A gal tall as me and with no tits has either gotta be a clothes horse – what is a clothes horse, by the way?' He explained: wooden, railing, hanging for the use of. 'Right. I like that. Anyways, gal like me has to be some kind of model or a dyke.'

'I like your tits. They're small, but perfect. Like rosebuds.' He leaned over her and took her left nipple in his mouth, sucking it long and slow. She gave a purr of pleasure. Reluctantly, he detached himself. 'I bet you're popular with all the girls, though?'

'Sure.' She grinned. 'I have to fight 'em off.'

'Er . . . ever not fight hard enough?'

Her nose wrinkled and he thought he'd pushed it too far, but she was only considering what, or what not, to reveal. 'It's happened,' she admitted. 'Wanna hear about it.'

Well, he did, but the abstract fact of it was already having an obvious effect. 'Maybe another time.' He took her hand and drew it to him. 'But you like this, too.'

'Oh, yes, I do like that.' Her fingers closed over him and began to move; a soft fluttering like an angel's wings. 'And you like when I do this, right?'

Something like an electric shock ran through him. 'Mmmmhhh.'

'And when I do this?' She lowered her head so that the dark hair fell over his lower body like a silken veil and he couldn't quite believe what was happening down there.

'Maybe not too much of this,' he choked. 'It might spoil the fun for later.'

But she was having far too much fun right at the present to listen to him.

She came out of the shower room wearing his ragged dressing gown and a towel around her head and still managing to look like the Queen of Sheba.

'So where do we go from here?'

'You mean *we* as in *us*?'

'No, idiot.' She slapped him on the shoulder. 'Just because you've had your wicked way with me doesn't mean we have to get married. *We* are just doing a little fooling around to pass the time. I mean where do we intrepid investigators go next?'

He picked up the book he'd been reading and showed her the image on the cover. It was a black-and-white shot of a soldier in the act of placing a flag on top of a large building. The flag was the only element in colour: a scarlet background with a yellow hammer and sickle.

'*Berlin: The Last Hundred Days*,' she read. 'Any good?'

'It has every last detail, but one in particular caught my eye.' He opened it at the page he'd marked. 'There.'

'*As the Russians closed in on the diplomatic quarter an astonishing, almost Medieval, barter system thrived. People would swap a sack of coal they had hoarded over the winter for a single egg or a bottle of clean water. A car would not buy a loaf of bread. In one instance, a Wilhelmstrasse jeweller reported how he had been approached by a soldier trying to sell an ancient artefact that could only have come from a museum.* So? It could have been anything.'

'I know, but Wilhelmstrasse is the street that runs close by Hitler's bunker. I've tried to call Sir William Melrose to find out if he has any more information, but he's out of the country for a week researching his latest masterpiece. In the meantime, I thought we might go out to Berlin and do a little sleuthing.'

She was rubbing her hair with the towel. She stopped and stared at him. 'You're kidding, right?'

'No, Danny. I'm not.'

'Jesus, Saintclair, that's what I call a long shot.'

'Actually, a long shot is what I'm trying to avoid. I thought if I was in another country I might be a bloody sight harder to hit. Besides, Berlin is where Berndt Hartmann disappeared.'

'Seventy years ago. You said he was around twenty back then? One way or another he's old bones now.'

'You mean you won't come with me?'

'I'm here to do a job, Jamie. I didn't come equipped for a European tour. What would we do for money?'

'While I was in hospital my lawyer called to let me know the Princess Czartoryski Foundation had agreed an interim payment for finding the Raphael. It's not huge, but it means that, for once, I'm in funds. Look, let's go. Think of it as a holiday.'

Her eyes narrowed. 'This isn't just because you want to shack up with li'l ol' me for a few days, is it?'

Jamie grinned. 'Guilty as charged, m'lud. To be honest, because of my past experiences, Germany wouldn't be number one on my holiday destination list, but I've always fancied Berlin.'

'In that case, when do we leave?'

Two days later they were on an early-morning flight out of Gatwick for Berlin. Schonefeld airport caters mainly for budget airlines and is about ten miles from the city centre. It has few facilities that make it an attractive destination, but it does boast an excellent S-bahn link, and less than an hour after walking out of the terminal they reached Friedrichstrasse station. Jamie had chosen a hotel nearby and Danny surveyed the streets as they walked the two hundred yards there.

'So where is the Berlin Wall from here?'

'It's about a quarter of a mile that way. We can go and see it if you like, once we've got rid of our luggage. It's a little too early to check in; maybe we could have lunch?'

'Sure. We're in what was the East now, huh? I'd expected something a little greyer.'

Jamie waited until they'd crossed the street. 'Never underestimate German efficiency. It didn't take them long to turn communist East Berlin into what passes for a capitalist paradise. Hotels, bars, boutiques, shopping malls; they all sprang up within a couple of years. I suspect the place is unrecognizable now to the people who used to live here. This is our hotel.'

It didn't look much from the outside, but the interior was modern and bright. They left their bags with reception and had a coffee while Jamie retrieved a guidebook from his backpack.

'I thought we could go along the river, past the station and then come round until we reach the Unter den Linden, before we get back here and, er, freshen up for dinner.'

She laughed at the hint of an invitation in his voice. 'Freshen up, huh? Is that what we're calling it?'

'Yes,' he said, hefting the bag. 'And the quicker we get going the quicker we get back.'

They left the hotel and turned right towards the River Spree. 'If Dornberger and Hartmann escaped from the bunker,' Jamie explained, 'the likelihood is they did it the day after Hitler's suicide when the last survivors of the Charlemagne Division and the bunker guards broke out under the command of the Führer's deputy, Martin Bormann. This is the road they would have taken.' He pointed towards the river. 'Imagine that bridge with a Tiger tank charging across it and hundreds, maybe more than a thousand people, right behind it. It blasts its way through a Russian barricade at the far end before being knocked out by an anti-tank gun, leaving all those behind it exposed to machine guns, mortars and artillery.'

'It doesn't seem possible.' She struggled to equate the image of carnage – the dead and the dying sprawled across the narrow roadway, the tank burning in the distance – with the quaint cast-iron structure flanked by pretty riverside cafés. 'It all just seems too . . . tranquil.'

'Don't be fooled. On May the first, nineteen forty-five, this was the centre of hell on earth.'

They crossed the bridge and strolled along the riverside walkway westwards past busy bars and restaurants. The golden days of Autumn were just a memory, but it looked as if Berliners refused to be beaten by a little bit of cold and drizzle because the outside tables were all packed. To their left, the far side of the Spree was dominated by the bulk of Friedrichstrasse Bahnhof. The great brick, glass and iron structure looked like a leftover from an earlier industrial age, but Jamie recrossed towards it on a footway beneath the railway bridge.

Danny gave him a look that he'd been getting used to. The one that said: *What the hell are you doing now?*

'General Mohnke, the chap who organized the breakout, was no fool. While Bormann and the rest were trying to fight their way across the Weidendammer Bridge there, Mohnke quietly disappeared with a group of the bunker's secretaries and walked across this *completely unguarded* footbridge.'

'Every man for himself, huh?'

'That's right.'

'And did this guy live to fight another day?'

He nodded. 'I suppose you could say that, but just the one. They were all captured by the Russians the next night.'

They continued round the great curve of the river until a landscape of modern structures in glass, concrete and stainless steel dominated their vision.

'Wow,' Fisher said. 'I'm impressed. Does that building actually cross the river?'

Jamie consulted the tourist guide. 'I think so, but it's maybe just an enclosed bridge. According to this, it's all part of the new government district. The parliament, offices, that sort of thing.

The one I'm really interested in is the big building with the dome. What's up?'

She'd seemed distracted since they'd crossed the river, stopping occasionally to glance in shop windows and loitering in places where there was nothing to see.

'I'm not certain yet. Don't worry. Just keep walking.'

If one thing was guaranteed to make him worry, it was someone telling him not to, but he ignored the urge to look behind him and kept walking, past a broad avenue that opened up to their right, then a huge stone building that overshadowed everything around it.

'Well, wow again, Saintclair. You make quite a tour guide.'

'If you think this is good, just wait until we get to the front,' he promised.

They walked onto a damp lawn as wide as two football fields and stretching far into the distance, before turning back to stare at the enormous structure with its Romanesque frontage and glass dome.

'This is the Reichstag,' Jamie explained. 'The building that's on the cover of our book.'

'Where Hartmann and Dornberger were fighting the tanks?'

'No, that's the Reichschancellery. It was across there.' He pointed to his right. 'Way beyond the Brandenburg Gate. This was what the Russians coveted most, though. Stalin had made it his aiming point and told his generals he wanted it by May the first. It turned into a crazy race between Zhukov and Konev that probably wasted the lives of tens of thousands of soldiers. The Germans fought for every room and every floor. When the fighting was over it was left a shattered ruin, but now they've completely restored it.'

'You know you asked me what was wrong before?' She kept her voice casual and her eyes fixed on the Reichstag dome. 'Well, there are a couple of hot-looking chicks taking an awful lot of interest in us.'

'That happens to me all the time. Do you think they're following us?' He smiled at her and turned to where two young blonde women in tailored jackets and tight jeans stood twenty yards away, openly staring at them.

'Well,' she said slowly, 'they were at the airport. In the next carriage on the train, got off at the same station and followed us here from the hotel. What do you think?'

He ignored her sarcasm. 'I think this is a popular place. Maybe they're staying at the hotel.'

'Sure and they followed us across the bridge and then back over the footbridge and never took their eyes off us the once.'

'What do you want to do about it?'

Very deliberately, she looked the two women over. 'I don't take them for killers and besides, this isn't the place you'd choose for it. Being the political heart of Berlin it has to be crawling with undercover cops. I figure that either they're very dumb or they're very badly trained in surveillance, or they wanted us to see them. Whichever is right, I think the professional thing to do is to go and ask them.'

'Well, let's do it.'

They started to walk towards the two girls, but without changing expression, the pair walked quickly away in the direction of the Reichstag. Jamie and Danny ambled to a halt and watched them go.

'You want to follow them?'

He shook his head.

'If they don't want to speak to us, they don't want to speak to us.'

'And they might be leading us into an ambush.' She smiled.

He smiled back. 'That too.'

'Hey, you said you were going to show me the Berlin Wall.'

He led her towards the Reichstag and as they crossed

an area of tarmac in front of the building he pointed to the ground.

She studied the area he indicated. 'That's it?' she said incredulously. 'That's the Berlin Wall?' She was looking at a twin line of bricks running to left and right.

'That's it. There are still a few small sections standing, but most of it was wiped off the landscape, if not the map.'

Danny Fisher shook her head. 'Well, I guess we should go back to the hotel and do some of that freshening up.'

'I guess we should at that, young lady.'

She punched him on the shoulder. 'And later I want to see a bit of this fabled Berlin nightlife.'

'I'm pretty sure we can arrange that, but we can't be back too late.'

'And why would that be?' she demanded.

'Because tomorrow we're going to do what we came for. We're going to see a man about a crown.'

XIX

I stowed the Crown in my rucksack and attempted in vain to follow Hartmann's trail. Every road or alley I tried was blocked by either a Russian patrol or a Wehrmacht defence line. The artillery fire was almost constant now, with the whip-crack of the high-velocity Soviet tank guns much closer than before and Russian bombers flying low over the city entirely unmolested. Explosions rocked the ground and smoke filled every street. As I ran between the shell bursts I raged at Hartmann's betrayal. The Crown of Isis was my sacred responsibility. Without the Eye would the Crown retain its power? Little by little I was forced back towards the bunker and found myself in Wilhelmstrasse. I took a last chance to search the rooms again, in the unlikely hope that Hartmann had hidden the jewel there before he fled, but found nothing. Close to despair, I stocked up on what supplies I could and prepared to head back towards the Reichschancellery. It was as I was leaving that I came across the boy.

He was hunched in a doorway, terrified, a handsome blond child of not more than eight years old. Tears streamed down his face and he didn't look up when I crouched beside him.

'Where are your parents?'

He shook his head.

'Do you have somewhere to stay?'

Again the shake of the head. I searched in my pack until I found some captured American chocolate and tore the wrapping from it.

'Here, try this.' His eyes widened as the scent of the sweet cocoa reached his nostrils. He snatched the chocolate and crammed it into his mouth as if he never expected to eat again. Gradually, a smile wreathed his face. 'What is your name?'

'Kurt.'

I held out my hand. 'Well, Kurt, come with me. I have somewhere you will be safe from all this.'

His hand felt soft and warm in mine as I led him back to the apartment.

When it was done, I felt nothing. It was confirmed. Without the Eye, the Crown of Isis was just a golden ornament. Hartmann had destroyed me and I vowed that I would hunt him down if it took until the end of time.

There was no question of attempting to get out of the city alone. The only people with the power to escape the cauldron of fire that Berlin had become were the men in the bunker. With a heart like stone I trudged back through the rubble to rejoin Adolf Hitler.

No one questioned my absence; only a madman or one of the true faithful would seek refuge at the gates of hell. Inside, a lethargy hung over the occupants that had not been there a few hours earlier. Then, it seemed, hope still existed, however unlikely, of a rescue by Wenck's Twelfth Army. Now, that hope was gone. Hitler had already sent out messengers with copies of his last will and testament and Rattenhuber, who was almost affable, revealed that the party's Golden Pheasants were planning their escape, even as they were exhorting the men of the Berlin defence to fight to the last man.

'You should join them, Dornberger,' he said. 'Break out and link up with Schorner.'

I talked with Colonel Weiss, aide to General Burgdorf, and he said he would be glad to accept me, but when I heard his plan to find some kind of silent electric boat and sail to freedom down the Spree I knew that I was talking to a lunatic. I decided to stay where I was and wait for a better opportunity.

Sometime in the night I woke under a table as a nervous little man in a brown uniform and a Volkssturm armband was led past and into Hitler's private quarters.

'What's happening?' I asked my companion, an SS doctor called Stumpfegger.

'The boss is getting married.' He grinned and the glaze in his eyes told me he was either drunk or taking his own medicine. 'Do you think he'll take us on honeymoon with him?'

A few minutes later the bride and groom emerged into the conference room to be congratulated by Bormann and Hitler's generals. It was the first time I had seen Eva Braun. Despite the circumstances, she was radiant in a black silk dress, cheerful and animated with a word for everyone. The Führer, his face lined and grey, looked more like a harassed father than her husband. In the hours after the wedding the air in the bunker grew thick with tension. SS and Wehrmacht officers vomited where they lay and the stench from the toilet block was intolerable. Everyone knew that the Russians were only a few blocks away. The next act in the tragedy would soon begin. In the meantime we could only wait.

Stumpfegger was a friend of Bormann's and I never strayed far from his side. If any man could get out of Berlin alive, it was Foxy Martin. But at around noon on the day after the wedding Rattenhuber approached me and gave me another job.

'Take two men and go with Kempka. Just do as he says and don't ask any questions.'

Erich Kempka was Hitler's chauffeur and a coarse brute of a man, he led us back up the stairs and across the garden towards the Reichschancellery garage. The carcass of a German shepherd had been thrown carelessly beneath a bush beside the path. I recognized the dog as Hitler's favourite pet.

'Poor old Blondi,' Kempka muttered. 'Leading the way to the fucking Fourth Reich.'

Inside the garage, gasoline cans were stacked high beside four big Mercedes limousines.

'We need at least twenty,' Kempka ordered. 'Take them across and stack them beside the entrance.'

'What are they for?' demanded one of the SS men.

Kempka looked at the guard as if he was an idiot and shook his head. 'Don't fucking ask.'

For me, these events held no mystery. Petrol in an open space meant only one thing. I remembered the stench of decomposing bodies in a Ukrainian field; the careless unfinished business of a sonderkommando. Men, women and children. Jews. Skin stripping from the arms and legs as the militia carried them to the funeral pyres. Leaping flares of gas from exploding stomachs. Blackened long-dead figures writhing in the flames as if they were still alive. The all-pervading odour of roasting meat.

'Right,' the chauffeur said when we had finished. 'Let's get back inside.'

Downstairs, we were cleared from the lower bunker to leave Hitler and Eva Braun with the men who had been with him right from the start. Bormann, Magda and Joseph Goebells and Artur Axmann, the one-armed Hitler Youth leader, who had appeared at the Führerbunker with his usual immaculate timing. About forty minutes later one of the SS door guards appeared in the upper complex and announced drunkenly to his *disbelieving audience:* 'The chief's on fire. Do you want to come and have a look?'

In the nightmare that was the last hours of the bunker nothing was too surreal. Hitler's death reinvigorated Bormann, who issued orders to non-existent armies and made his plans to break out to join the new Nazi government that had been formed by Admiral Donitz. He cheerfully announced that his first act would be to order the execution of Himmler. At the same time as he was telling his soldiers to fight to the last man, he ordered General Krebs to cross the lines and organize a ceasefire. In contrast, Goebells and his wife wandered the corridors like ghosts, their last link with reality gone. At some point during the late afternoon Stumpfegger came to sit at my side. He lit a cigarette and it shook between his fingers.

'That's it. They're all gone,' he said. 'I didn't want to do it, but they said I had no choice.'

'Who's gone?'

'Goebells and Magda.' I shrugged. I had never liked the crippled little bastard and his harpy of a wife. He continued: 'The children died first. One by one in their beds. Poison. Magda insisted.' He started sobbing, which was odd for a man whose name was notorious for the experiments he had conducted at Ravensbrück concentration camp. What were a few children more or less?

I muttered some insincere consoling words.

'You're a good fellow, Dornberger.' He patted me on

the shoulder and his voice dropped to a whisper. 'Stick with me. We're going out tonight. Bormann, Mohnke and a few others. Mohnke has arranged tank support.'

I was going to survive.

We were due to leave at 9 p.m., but there was so much confusion that it wasn't until two hours later that we gathered in the main entrance, Bormann, Mohnke, their aides and the secretaries. Bormann carried his machine pistol as if it was a feather duster and his fat form looked ridiculous in a combat uniform and a steel helmet. He made a little speech about sticking together and how everyone would be rewarded for their loyalty when we reached safety. No one believed him.

By what route, I never knew, but somehow we made our way through streets raked by an apocalypse of shell and small arms fire until we reached Friedrichstrasse Bahnhof. Somewhere along the way we had lost Mohnke and most of the secretaries, but no one, least of all Bormann, cared about that. The night was carved apart by tracer fire and every now and then terrified faces were lit by the flashes of explosions. It was 1 May and Germany was dying.

Word of the planned break-out had spread and hundreds of soldiers and civilians crouched in the lee of our 'tank support'; a single Tiger and a Sturmgeschütz IV assault gun that were to lead the attack on the Weidendammer Bridge across the Spree. I wished I had gone with Mohnke.

Without warning, the Tiger roared out of hiding and

across the bridge, blasting away as it went with 88 m cannon and machine guns. Astonishingly, it caught the Ivans half asleep and smashed through the first Soviet barrier. Bormann and the rest of the bunker escapees held back and then made a mad rush in the Tiger's wake. An almighty clang rang out and the big tank first stopped, then burst into flames, eviscerated by an armour-piercing round. The uniforms of the surviving crewmen smouldered as they baled out onto the street. Machine guns opened up, mowing them down as they tried to escape, before turning their barrels on the desperate SS men, landsers and the women and children who sought their illusionary protection. Bodies tumbled like skittles and broke apart in a storm of lead and steel. A thousand must have been killed or wounded in those first minutes. I was knocked over by the blast that destroyed the Tiger, along with Bormann and Stumpfegger, but somehow we survived the holocaust of fire. I saw Axmann go down wounded. He recovered quickly, and staggered to his feet.

Three more times we tried to break through, three more times the slaughter was repeated and the assault gun joined the Tiger as a glowing heap of twisted scrap iron. By now the SS men had forced a way across the bridge, but we were caught in a rat trap. I found myself with Bormann; Axmann, who was still bleeding from his wound; Stumpfegger, the doctor, and the Reichsleiter's dark-haired secretary, Else Kruger. At Bormann's insistence, we headed west, until we reached the Lehrtersstrasse Bahnhof. Axmann, who was no fool, decided to go it alone and set off north. I was tempted to accompany him, but I convinced myself there was safety in numbers and we headed north-east along the railway tracks. It seemed that by some miracle we had discovered a safe path through the fighting that raged like a brushfire all around us. But the illusion only lasted seconds. A sudden flicker in the darkness ahead and Stumpfegger went down with a terrible cry, torn apart along with Bormann by the burst of machine-gun fire that scythed through the party. I felt the heat of passing tracer rounds to left and right as I hurled myself to the ground and heard a clatter as something metal hit one of the tracks. Else Kruger lay beside me, still as death, but I could see from her breathing that she was unhurt. Slowly and silently we began to crawl away backwards. She gave a sharp cry and I thought she must have been hit. But when I turned, I saw that the Crown of Isis had fallen from my pack. She was holding it and staring in wonder.

'This belongs to the goddess.' The words spanned the ages and fell like tombstones on my ears. It was impossible. How could she know? I made a panicked grab for the Crown, but she snatched it away, her eyes filled with a kind of ecstasy. 'We must return it to her.' For answer I gave her the sole of a metal-studded jackboot in the face and tore it from her grasp, at the same time hauling my pistol from my belt. Else saw the murder in my eyes and realized she had more to fear from Max

Dornberger than the Russians. As she got to her feet I raised the Walther and aimed it at her head, but a desperate hand clawing at my leg created a momentary distraction. I looked down to see Bormann, mortally wounded and pleading for help. He seemed surprised when I pointed the pistol and blew a hole in his fat face.

By the time I turned back, Else Kruger had vanished.

XX

'Herr Saintclair? Fräulein Fisher? Please take a seat.'

'Thank you, Herr Direktor.'

'You enjoyed your tour of the Neues Museum?'

Danny Fisher gave him her brightest smile. 'It was fascinating,' she assured him, attempting to disguise the fact that after her tours of the Pergamon Museum and the Altes Museum on Berlin's aptly named Museum Island, she was footsore and all but museumed out.

'We are very proud of our facility,' the director continued. 'You will know that we have only just reopened after many years of work and an enormous amount of effort?'

'Of course,' Jamie chimed in with a little flattery of his own. 'The displays are magnificent.'

'Thank you.'

'I was particularly interested in your Egyptian collection.'

'A favourite of mine, also.' Their host nodded

gravely. 'It was not possible to recreate the original Egyptian courtyard, but our bust of Nefertiti is world-renowned. It is probably the finest example of its kind. Now, how can I help you?'

Jamie took a deep breath. 'We are interested in the museum during the period between nineteen thirty-nine and nineteen forty-five.'

'Then I am afraid you may be on a wasted mission.' The other man frowned and his fingers played absently with a gold fountain pen. 'You see, the Neues Museum closed on the outbreak of war and never reopened. Fortunately, in common with the other museums on the island, our greatest treasures were evacuated, first to the basement of the Zoo flak tower, which was the strongest and most secure building in Berlin, and later to the salt mines in Thuringia. Only the least valuable artefacts remained and most of these were lost in the bombing raids that almost completely destroyed the building in November nineteen forty-three and February 'forty-five.'

They'd had a similar answer at their previous meet-ings. Still, Jamie decided to persist. 'I'm trying to discover the whereabouts of an artefact that might have gone missing during that time, perhaps in the latter stages of the war.'

'Missing, Mr Saintclair?' The director gave a bitter laugh. 'You joke with me, surely. For ten years, every-thing was missing. The contents of all three museums were "liberated" to Soviet Russia. Some of the items, such as the Pergamon Altar, were returned in the late fifties and restored to their original positions, or as much as was possible, taking into account the destruction of the buildings that housed them. Other, smaller, but still valuable artefacts were not returned for many years. Some are still *missing*.'

Jamie apologized. 'I meant to be neither foolish nor naive, Herr Direktor, only to place the question in its widest possible context. Perhaps it would help if I was more specific.'

'Perhaps.'

'The artefact in question would be an Egyptian crown, mounted with the cow's horns that typically represent the goddess Isis, but . . .' he hesitated, 'with some form of precious stone replacing the metal sun disk.'

He expected the other man to laugh, as the other two museum chiefs had, but the director surprised him by frowning and picking up the telephone on his desk.

'Could you bring me the contacts file, please, Gerda? Thank you.' He pursed his thin lips. 'The Neues Museum has been open for less than a year, Herr Saintclair, but we have been on site for several, dealing with many questions. Your enquiry has reminded me of one of them.'

A young secretary appeared and placed a green file on his desk. He picked it up and waved it.

'Of course, everything must be on computer, but in many ways I am a very old-fashioned man and some things I prefer to keep on paper.' He began leafing through the sheets in the file. 'Yes, here it is. June, two thousand and seven. A researcher for a very eminent English historian presented himself in person to make the enquiry. The . . . specific question he asked . . . was . . . yes: At any point during the latter stages of the Second World War did the museum lose, mislay or have stolen an Egyptian artefact, specifically,' he smiled from Jamie to Danny, 'a crown, probably of the later period, and adorned with cow's horns and inscribed with the Eye of Horus. Of course, our answer was negative,' he said apologetically, 'as it must be now. As far as I am aware, the museum has never had contact with any such artefact, unless it was in the form of a frieze. There, does that satisfy you?'

'May I ask who the English historian was?' Fisher said.

The director pondered for only a second. 'Of course, it is no secret and, in any case, I know that the book he was researching has recently been published. His name is Sir William Melrose.'

'We need to speak with this Melrose guy to find out what he knows that we don't.' Danny's voice betrayed her excitement. 'For the first time I feel as if we're actually making some progress.'

'You're right, Jamie agreed. 'But there's no point in rushing back to London now. His office said he'd be in Japan until the end of the week. We might as well enjoy

Berlin while we have the chance. I thought we could visit the site of the Reichschancellery this afternoon and then maybe try the Reichstag?'

'Sure, but can we find a bar first? My feet feel as if I've walked to Egypt and back. Did you notice the researcher's question referred to the Eye of Horus?'

'Yes,' Jamie admitted. 'But I don't think it means anything. You have to remember that neither Melrose nor his researcher had seen the actual crown, all they had was a loose description from a jeweller whose world was disintegrating around him. If the jeweller said it was inscribed with an eye, Melrose, who isn't an Egyptian expert, would automatically conclude it was the most common version. The Eye of Horus.'

They walked to Schlossplatz and turned into the Unter den Linden, where they found a suitable bar to rest their legs. Jamie ordered two beers and a plate of bratwurst, which they ate with fresh bread and mustard that was so hot it must have come out of a volcano.

'Okay, Saintclair,' Danny laughed as she wafted her mouth with the back of her hand, 'I feel like I've been tanked up with rocket fuel. This gal is ready for anything.'

They walked together up the famous street towards Pariser Platz and the Brandenburg Gate, stopping now and again to look in shop windows. Occasionally, Jamie swept the streets for the two girls who had followed them the previous day, but either they had improved their surveillance techniques or he and Danny were on their own.

'Do you ever feel as if this is just a game compared to what you usually do back home?' he asked. The electric-blue eyes studied him for a long moment and he had a feeling she was trying to read his mind for the real question behind the question.

'No.' She shook her head. 'For one thing, I needed a break. I've been working non-stop for about nine months now and I could feel myself burning out. A change of scenery is just what the doc ordered. And it's not a game. I said today that I felt we were making progress and that wasn't just garden manure. Look, I've probably worked on a hundred murder cases. A lot of them are simple. You have a suspect, you have a motive and you have evidence to make it stick. But there are plenty like this, where you start with nothing and it takes time to build a case. Okay, it's not the kind of case the department likes, but if you stand your ground, don't allow yourself to be sidetracked and keep right on going, whatever happens, then the chances are you'll get there in the end. I'm not a quitter, Jamie. Tell me you aren't, either?'

'I'm not a quitter, Danny.'

She kissed him on the lips, slow at first, but then hard and deep, so it took his breath away.

'I knew that, idiot. Now where is this place?'

'This is the Wilhelmstrasse, where Melrose said the jeweller was offered the Crown. It should be round here.' He led the way along a narrow alleyway off the main street. 'Don't expect too much,' he warned.

They reached their destination. For once Danny Fisher was lost for words. It took her a full minute to find the ones she needed.

'Hitler's bunker – the place where he died – is a *parking lot*?'

They gazed around the flat open space surrounded by grubby apartment blocks built decades before. Rows of parking bays filled with Mercedes and VWs and Fiats and Renaults were separated by low wooden rails and surrounded by shrubs and spindly trees. It seemed a terribly banal use for a piece of ground that had seen the end of a generation of evil that had consumed tens of millions of innocents.

'The Russians would have wanted to obliterate it, but the bunker was constructed with two-metre-thick reinforced concrete. It looks as if the German Democratic Republic decided the best way to wipe it from history was to bury it.' Jamie stepped off the road as a dark van advertising an electrical business swept into the car park and found a bay close by. The driver opened his window, lit a cigarette and started reading a newspaper at the sports pages. 'In some ways it makes sense. Why leave something that could become a shrine to a monster?'

'So this is where it happened.' Danny Fisher looked around at the blank windows of the tower blocks, her expression somewhere between awe and sadness. 'Berndt Hartmann was here all those years ago. But did he have the Crown of Isis?' She swivelled to face Jamie and he took her in his arms. 'Do you ever wish you could turn back time?'

Before he could answer, a silver car drew in behind them and he heard the click of the door opening. 'Jamie Saintclair!'

The voice was so full of genuine pleasure that he turned to meet it with a smile. At the same time his mind was trying to work out who he knew in Berlin and wondering at the coincidence that they'd met. Then he remembered that when you're investigating a murder there are no coincidences. It took a millisecond for the features to register.

Danny Fisher saw him freeze. 'Jamie?'

'Run, Danny!'

But he knew it was already too late. You couldn't escape the ghosts of your past.

He faced up to the man from the car, tensed and in a fighting crouch, ready for what was certain to come. At his back the sound of the sliding door in the van's side was followed by a rush of feet and a sharp cry that told him Danny Fisher was taking on whoever had emerged. The temptation was to turn and help, but he knew that the real danger was here in the man in the dark suit with the thin smile.

'What do you want, Frederick?'

'Why you, Mr Saintclair. You.'

In the same second his arms were pinned to his side and his world went black as some kind of evil-smelling hood was pulled over his head. At least two men dragged him off his feet and threw him bodily into the van where more hands were waiting to pinion his wrists with plastic ties. He felt a bolt of pain as his back was rammed against the metal side of the van. He sensed that Danny must be somewhere opposite him and he opened his mouth to give her some pointless reassurance.

'Dan—'

Bright colours exploded in his head as something very hard hit him on the side of the skull.

'No move. No speak. Or you get hurt proper, huh?'

The words were in heavily accented English and in a tone that convinced him the owner meant what he said. Better, in any case, to wait and preserve his strength. That was the advice from the escape and evasion instructors. Then again, they also said the best time to escape was in the minutes after you were captured. Conclusion? The E and A course had been a complete waste of nine hours in the freezing cold, plus four tied to a boiling radiator with a bright light in his eyes and four hulking paras taking turns to kick him in the balls.

As the van sped away, Jamie's racing mind fought for calm. Two minutes ago they'd been standing in the drizzle chatting about an East German car park. Now they were trussed up like Christmas turkeys in the back of a van going who knew where and at the mercy of . . .? Somewhere beyond the shock, his subconscious was working on that question. Frederick. How could it be Frederick? Frederick should be in jail or in hell, where he belonged. Frederick shouldn't be walking the streets of Berlin. Frederick was, or had been, the leader of the paramilitary wing of the Vril Society, a shady neo-Nazi organization whose origins went back beyond the Second World War. Taking its lead from Heinrich Himmler, the Vril Society was dedicated to discovering the source of the Aryan race and tapping the mythical powers of its founders. At least that's what they claimed. For Jamie Saintclair, Frederick and his kind were the devil spawn of men like Bodo Ritter and Hitler. When they were bored they'd go out and take over someone else's country and the more blood spilled, the more glorious the victory. Not that knowing his enemy gave him much comfort. Frederick was not only ruthless, but cruel, with ice water in his veins and not a shred of pity in his make-up. The last time Jamie had seen him had been outside the *Frauenkirche* in Dresden, bathed in the blue flashing lights of a dozen police cars, trying to explain away a crate of machine pistols and at least two dead bodies. The questions queued up in his head. How had the Vril tracked him down? Was this kidnap to do with the attack in London? Or the Crown of Isis? The Crown was exactly the kind of artefact that would interest a society who got their kicks from secret rituals in the basement of Himmler's planned SS Disneyland at Wewelsburg Castle. It was even possible that Ritter himself had been a member of the society. His mind reeled with a dozen unlikely possibilities. In all of them the outcome was better than the most likely, and the one he feared most. That this was about simple revenge.

A few feet away, Danny Fisher cursed herself for a fool. She should have reacted more quickly. She'd been lulled by the smile on Jamie's face as he'd turned to meet the man from the car. When the four guys had jumped from the van, she'd got in just one good hit before they'd swamped her. Now she was helpless to fight the suffocating hood or the plastic ties that were biting into her wrists. The ties stirred a memory and her mind was momentarily filled with that scene of horror back in the Brooklyn house. The Hartmanns had been pinioned with plastic ties just like these before . . . Well, whatever happened she would not submit to that. Better off dead. She didn't know how, but, if it came to it, she'd find a way. She attempted to use the van's motion and the pressure on her back to figure out how far and in what direction they were travelling, but the map in her head was soon a scrambled mess. Hell, she could barely have found her way back to the hotel. Fear gnawed at her insides, but that was only natural. Anybody who wasn't scared in a situation like this was either lying or lobotomized. It was a question of ruling your fear and not allowing it to rule you. She hung on to the certainty that as long as you continued to function, there was a chance. And all she needed was one chance. But Christ, she was lonely. She hadn't even been certain Jamie was in the van until she'd heard the German scumball tell him to shut up. For the moment, she didn't let the whys or wherefores occupy her. Whether it was about the Crown of Isis or the contract out on him didn't matter. This was about Jamie. Thinking about his reassuring presence brought her a moment of strength. She had a suspicion their kidnappers might be underestimating Mr Jamie Saintclair. Beneath that slightly bumbling academic exterior she'd sensed a hardness, a kind of titanium core, that wasn't like other men she'd known. If it came to it, she decided, she could rely on Jamie Saintclair to go the extra mile. All they needed was one chance.

XXI

The door of the van slammed back with a booming echo that told Jamie they were in some sort of barn or warehouse. It wasn't much information, but enough to give him a glimmer of hope. Better to be wherever they were than in a field where the likelihood was that the inside of the hessian sack was the last thing he would ever see. He braced himself as two men manhandled him out and held him until he found his balance.

A shrill protest reached him through the material of the hood. 'Get your fucking hands off me, you fucking pervert.'

Danny Fisher's voice contained no hint of fear and despite their plight he felt a surge of pride. Whatever happened next, they were still together and that dramatically increased their chances if it came to a fight. It was a tactical error. Maybe Frederick wasn't the mastermind he thought he was. Jamie held that thought as his captors guided him across what felt like a concrete floor and up two flights of wooden stairs. He heard a door open and rough hands propelled him through.

Inside, someone pushed him and he felt a moment of fear as he fell backwards, only to be brought up with a bump by some sort of chair. He heard a yelp that said Danny was still with him. It was followed by the sound of shuffling feet, until he calculated that at least six or seven men must be in the room.

'Close the door. All right, remove the hoods.'

The light hit him like a train from a tunnel and it took a few seconds to become aware of his surroundings. He'd counted right. Seven of them, including Frederick. He instantly recognized the type. Regulation dark clothing that was a kind of uniform if you knew what to look for. Either leather jacket and jeans or an expensive suit, though one ugly customer was in a tight black T-shirt, showing off shoulders like a mastodon. Close-cropped hair apart from one with his long hair tied back in a pony-tail. From what he could see, every man had a weapon of some sort; pistols mainly, either to hand or, in the case of T-shirt Hulk, in a shoulder holster that looked suspiciously like a Special Forces' pattern. And if that seemed like security overkill for two bound captives, pony-tail was toting a sub-machine gun, for Christ's sake. Clearly, Frederick was keen to ensure there'd be no repeat of Jamie's previous miracle escape.

Danny was to his left, closer to the door, and, like him, forced back into a cheap office chair. She had her head up and a dangerous look in her eyes. He met the look with one he hoped would be similarly reassuring. He'd never been in much doubt where this was going, but if he had, the plastic sheeting that covered the floor and the rubber padding that lined the walls would have clinched it. It was the kind of room you held noisy, messy sports like mud-wrestling in. Or alternatively, the kind where you killed people who had become a nuisance. On the one hand, the room gave him a shred of comfort, because if Frederick had been going to kill them immediately they'd already have been in a shallow grave. On the other, it meant that either Frederick wanted to know something and was going to have a little fun finding it out, or he was going to have a little fun anyway. The up side was it gave them more time, the down side that it was likely to be time bought at a painful price.

Oddly, he felt no fear at all, only the inner calm and a fine, growing, but contained rage, that was the familiar precursor to terrible violence.

'You have no idea what joy it gave me to see you parading around Berlin's sights with your whore, Mr Saintclair. It was, as I believe the English saying goes, like Christmas coming early.' Frederick spoke in a distinctive Berlin accent Jamie remembered well – why was it he only remembered it now? – and the little joke raised a few grins among his men. The German words mostly meant nothing to Danny, but she understood *whore* well enough. She spat at her captors like a cornered wildcat, but Frederick only smiled. He was enjoying himself. 'You are losing your touch. I preferred your previous girlfriend, the Jew, to this stick insect.'

Jamie felt like tearing the smile off the other man's face, but he met the words with a shrug. 'In that case why don't you let her go. She's nothing to you. She's nothing to me. Whatever it is you want, I'm the one you need, not her.'

'If you're going to talk about me, Saintclair, talk in English. I assume this vulture can speak it.'

'Oh yes, I speak it quite well, Miss . . . Please, the lady's bag.' One of the men handed him the voluminous handbag Danny had carried. He searched until he found her purse and rifled through it before giving a low whistle. '*Detective* Fisher.' He shook his head. 'I am afraid that New York's finest must remain with us, Mr Saintclair. I am sure she will find it instructive, even entertaining. Perhaps she will see a new side to you?'

'This is just wasting time. What do you want?'

'Want? I want what I am owed. You owe me a life, Mr Saintclair. You remember Erik, from Paderborn, whose skull you smashed in? I never forget debts, or the people who owe them.' The name wasn't familiar, but Jamie remembered a tall man who didn't look in great shape after thirteen and a half stones of Clan Sinclair landed on top of him. The good news, if there was any, was that Frederick didn't appear to know that he was also responsible for the timely and well-deserved end of Gustav, the Vril Society's pet torturer.

'Erik was just one of your foot soldiers, Frederick. Cannon-fodder. How much can he be worth?'

'A life for a life, Mr Saintclair.' The German oozed reason like a bank manager turning down a loan for a kidney transplant. 'Your life for his.'

'That would be a pity, because I have something to trade.' An eyebrow rose and he knew he'd hit the mark. 'How is all your Nazi mumbo-jumbo going? I recall you put a lot of faith in the Sun Stone.'

'The Sun Stone no longer exists, Mr Saintclair, I seem to remember you proving that most conclusively.'

Jamie nodded at what amounted to a compliment. 'But you Nazis had also mislaid something just as important. What if I could find you the gold centrepiece to the Wewelsburg Sun. The centrepiece that would allow you to translate all the rune symbols carved into the marble. Whatever that leads you to has got to be worth a couple of lives.'

Frederick's eyes glittered. The Black Sun at Himmler's Wewelsburg Castle had been one of the clues that led Jamie to the hiding place of the Sun Stone, but the golden centrepiece, which was the key to all the information on the Sun, hadn't been seen since the final days of the war. For a moment it seemed the German would take the bait, then he laughed.

'How can you find something that no longer exists?'

'That's what I do, old chap,' Jamie said patiently. 'I found the Sun Stone, didn't I?'

Frederick shook his head slowly. 'Not possible.'

'Walter Schellenberg.' He could almost see the Nazi's ears prick up. The charismatic Schellenberg had been

Himmler's counter-intelligence chief, a will-o'-the-wisp character perfectly at home in a world of shadows. 'Walter Schellenberg holds the key. I'm willing to bet that Schellenberg was the last man out of Wewelsburg Castle before the demolition charges were set.'

Frederick was tempted. Jamie could see it in the storm-grey eyes, but eventually he shook his head again, emphatically this time. 'Ah, Mr Saintclair, if it was only me . . .' He stepped aside to reveal the big man with the muscles pulling his T-shirt over his head. 'You remember Gustav, of course. How we all miss Gustav. Let me introduce Jurgen, Gustav's brother. Jurgen was most upset at his brother's death. If I remember rightly he promised to rain all manner of biblical punishments on the perpetrator. And now,' Jurgen's smile resembled the grinning skull on an SS death's head ring, 'thanks to your timely arrival in this fair city, he has his opportunity.'

Jurgen pushed himself forward into the centre of the room and drew what looked like a butcher's skinning knife from his belt. Danny Fisher gave a little cry and for the first time Jamie's body told him it was time to be scared. Very scared. He could see the rippling blue sheen where the blade had been sharpened to a razor edge. He tried to push himself back, away from the advancing German, but the men behind him laughed and held him in place. Jurgen bent low over him, eyes bright and the flat, moon face inches from Jamie's, so he could smell the other man's sewer breath. Very slowly, the knife came up to his waist and his body cringed away from the awful curved blade. With a sharp snick Jamie felt the plastic ties falling away from his wrists and Jurgen backed away, grinning.

The Englishman let out a long, slow breath and felt something ready to explode inside him.

Frederick laughed. 'Jurgen has always planned to take you apart, one piece at a time and with infinite patience, but he is a warrior, as well as an artist. He wants to see how well you can fight.' Casually, he threw a knife, the twin of the one in Jurgen's hand, at Jamie's feet, as the others made a ring with the two men at the centre.

Jamie's brain screamed that there had to be a way out, but the warrior inside told him that was just the fear talking and he buried it deep. He studied his opponent. If Frederick was giving him a knife, it was because he *knew* Jurgen was better with it. And that was only the half of it. Stripped to the waist, the German was massively muscled and his height gave him a longer reach. Something told Jamie that, despite his size, Jurgen would be quick, too. His brother had fought in Afghanistan and enjoyed inflicting pain. It looked as if it ran in the family. He ignored the thrown knife and the ring of bright expectant eyes and slowly removed his jacket, unbuttoned his shirt and shrugged it off so he was Jurgen's smaller, leaner twin. He also removed his shoes and socks, which brought a sneer from the other man.

When he was ready, he stood for a few moments allowing his mind to clear. It wasn't anger or hate he needed now, but ice-cold calculation. The man who tried to match Jurgen blow for blow was a dead man, but if he couldn't outfight him, at least he could try to outthink him. In many ways it made it simpler that this was a fight to the death. Black and white. He had no illusions what would happen if he won, but he was certain of one thing. Before he died, Jurgen was going to be saying hello to his brother. He bent to pick up the knife, his eyes never leaving the other man's.

The trick in knife fighting is not to be mesmerized by your opponent's hands. He'll posture with his left to draw you, while lunging with the blade. He'll hypnotize you with his knife hand until you see every move but the one that kills you. Don't watch his hands; watch his eyes – that was what the unarmed combat instructors at the OTC had always said. The problem was that Jurgen was too good for that. Jamie knew it the moment they faced up to one another, each man circling to get the measure of his opponent's reach, and his balance. Searching out any weakness. Jurgen's knife hand swayed, jinked and darted, but his eyes never left Jamie's face, nor betrayed any of those swift, graceful movements. The grin had gone, replaced by the sardonic smile of a professional at work. He had patience, too. After the initial ritual dance, like two cobras swaying in a deadly courtship, Jamie expected a first rush to test his defences. It never came. Gradually, he realized what was happening. To test his theory, he offered Jurgen a potential opening, but the German's smile broadened and he continued to circle. Now Jamie was certain. His opponent had a plan. He had made his promise to Gustav. In Jurgen's tiny mind, Jamie had already been turned into a bloody obscenity, taken apart piece by piece; all that was required was to execute that plan. And that gave Jamie confidence. Jurgen was good. But was he that good?

A flash of exquisite agony gave him his answer.

'Shit!' The jeers of Jurgen's Nazi comrades filled the room. First blood. Where had that come from? Jamie glanced at his shoulder. An inch of skin was missing and blood trickled wine red down his right arm. Jurgen raised his arms in a victory salute. The gesture was arrogant and contemptuous and it almost killed him. Jamie feinted right and lunged, the point of the skinning knife aimed at the German's protruding belly-button, the strike so fast and so precise he could almost feel it enter the flesh. Jurgen had been expecting it, but even so he was almost too slow. He abandoned the counter-stroke he had planned and danced clear, but the wind of the blade whispered on his flesh like a child's kiss and he realized he had been a millimetre from being disembowelled. The eyes hardened and Jamie knew there would be no more salutes. Still, he reasoned, Jurgen wouldn't abandon his plan so lightly. That was Jamie's edge. Jurgen was like a gladiator performing a piece of theatre for the Emperor, and the longer it took, the more exquisite the end would be. Jamie only wanted to kill. Jurgen wanted him to attack, because that would make it easier. But that was all right, because now Jamie understood that Jurgen's vanity was his weakness, he was happy to give him what he wanted. Jurgen needed many openings to make his plan work. Jamie only needed one.

He built up the speed of his movements, circling and dancing, first in, then out, the knife weaving glistening patterns in the artificial light. Inside the circle, Jurgen turned, always facing his opponent, but Jamie saw a faint hint of concern in the close-set eyes, because he was only barely moving fast enough, and he knew it. Jamie's bare feet allowed him to dance over the plastic sheeting, where Jurgen's trainers, with their notched soles, moved it with them. Jurgen glanced at his feet and Jamie struck. He darted inside, at the same time bringing the blade round in a slashing arc designed to sever the German's carotid artery. Jurgen, and every man in the room, thought he had reacted too late. He swayed away from the blade, but it pursued him like a hawk diving on a sparrow. A splash of bright scarlet signalled the hit and Jurgen screamed in fright. Jamie heard Danny's cry of triumph and felt the volcanic surge of victory deep in his loins. But it was only momentary. A man with his throat cut doesn't keep moving. A man with his throat cut sways and bleeds and falls and dies. Jurgen raised a hand to his left ear, which had been sliced diagonally, with the lower piece flapping against his neck held by a thin strip of skin. A line of blood appeared where the knife point had traced the flesh of his cheek.

Jurgen was hurt, but like a wounded big cat it made him more cautious, but no less dangerous. Jamie was unaware of the savage delight that etched his face and sent a shudder of concern through his enemy. He had tasted blood and he wanted more. He darted in a second time, hoping to take advantage of Jurgen's shock, but the big man knew how close he had come and retreated into a defensive crouch. They fell into a rhythm of move and counter-move, thrust and counter-thrust. The minutes passed and Jamie felt his arm beginning to tire. Once more, he created what he thought was the killer opening, but this time Jurgen was ready and as Jamie swerved away his hand flicked out like a striking viper. The knife point scored Jamie's left cheek-bone and his vision disintegrated into a fiery cauldron. He knew Jurgen would be coming for him and he slashed blindly with his blade. But when his sight cleared Jurgen was standing back with the grin restored to his face. He reached up to touch the scar on his own cheek.

'*Schlager*,' he laughed.

Jamie knew a *schlager* was the heavy sword used in years past by German students to inflict scars of honour during fencing contests. But those were tests of skill, not fights to the death. That was when he understood this was a battle he could never win.

Frederick barked an order to continue, and Jurgen

moved in for the kill. They resumed their circling, Jamie reduced to trying to stay alive and seeking an opening that seemed increasingly less likely to come, and Jurgen, his confidence restored, now doing the probing and dancing. Another near miss opened Jamie's left breast just above the nipple and that galvanized him into a new attack, but he could feel the fatigue eating at him. He had to finish it now. Or die.

Feigning a slip, he allowed his feet to go out from under him at the same time praying that Jurgen would see his opening and go for the kill. It was a risk, but a calculated one, because if he was quick, the way he had fallen would carry him under the knife and into the killing zone. The downside was that if Jurgen was quicker, Jamie would be at his mercy for the vital split second it would take to plunge the blade into his body. As he hit the plastic he heard a crash as the door slammed back and a shrill voice that shouted, '*Hande hoch.*' Inexplicably, Jurgen froze and his knife arm dropped. Jamie was already rolling beneath his opponent's guard and he came up in a fluid movement that brought the skinning knife in below Jurgen's breastbone. He sensed the moment it broke the skin and entered the sucking embrace of the flesh, and the instant it pierced the frantically beating heart. Jurgen screamed and screamed again, but Jamie kept forcing the blade up and up, deeper and deeper. He felt an elemental, visceral joy that men in battle must have shared through the ages. Death-bringer. Survivor. Victor. More alive than

he'd ever felt before. Until the next war, the next battle
or the next fight. The German's mouth opened and
closed and his eyes bulged. Blood sprayed from his
nostrils into Jamie's face and a flood of warmth covered
his knife arm. As he twisted the knife and pulled it free
he heard the sharp chatter of a machine gun and the
thud of a body falling. Jurgen's shuddering body
crumpled into the widening pool of blood at his feet.
When Jamie looked up, the men who had made up the
circle behind Jurgen stood with their mouths open and
their hands above their shoulders. He turned with the
knife still in a death grip ready to kill and kill again. It
was puzzling that the audience had been increased by
four figures dressed in ski masks and black overalls who
now stood inside the doorway covering the room with
cocked Heckler & Koch machine pistols. Against one
wall, eyes wide open and a string of ragged holes stitch-
ing his chest, lay the pony-tailed stormtrooper with the
sub-machine gun. Frederick stood beside him, his face a
mask of fury.

Jamie advanced on the Vril's paramilitary leader until
a soft hand touched his shoulder.

'It's all right, Jamie, we're safe now.'

XXII

Danny Fisher had never witnessed anything more magnificent and she had a sense of the feral, animalistic delight experienced by a spectator in a Roman amphitheatre.

She knew the memory of the knife fight and the knowledge that its end meant her certain death would return to haunt her, but it was the look of savage certainty on Jamie Saintclair's face she would remember for ever. He couldn't win. He had known that. Even if he had somehow managed to disable the giant German, Frederick would have had him killed. Yet he had fought, and the spirit that had sustained him had helped to sustain her. She knew that if Jamie had died and they had come for her, she would have fought them with her feet and her teeth until they killed her. When Jamie fell she had believed it was the end for him, and for her.

Then the miracle had happened.

The door had burst back and two slim figures in

black jump suits and ski masks had appeared with the barrels of their machine pistols threatening every man in the room and shouting at them to raise their hands up. After the initial shock most of the Germans had dropped their guns and raised their hands, but the fool with the machine gun had made one move too many. The figure on the left had switched aim a fraction and fired a short burst that threw him back against the wall.

Within seconds, the two gun-toting figures at the door were joined by two more and one of them cut Danny free with nimble, delicate fingers that surprised her when she felt them against her skin.

'We're safe now,' she repeated, leading Jamie back to the chair.

The words penetrated, but they didn't have any meaning. He seemed to be caught somewhere between two worlds. A moment earlier he had been at the centre of a blaze of light and anything had seemed possible. Now the light was fading and he suddenly felt very tired. Slowly, he began to dress, his hands automatically doing the right things, even though his mind was still in another place. He was aware of putting on his shirt over skin tacky with Jurgen's still-damp blood. Danny helped him with his socks and shoes, then draped his jacket over his shoulders.

'*Hände auf den Kopf. Legen Sie Ihre Waffen auf den Boden und Rücken gegen die Wand. Irgendwelche Tricks und du bist tot wie dein Freund.*'

A woman's voice, but a woman who had proved she

was prepared to back up her words with bullets. The surviving Nazis, including Frederick, did as they were ordered and retreated until their backs were against the wall where a gesture from the machine pistol forced them to their knees. Another of the masked saviours kicked the abandoned weapons into a heap near the door. She started to put them in a rucksack, but, before she'd completed the job, Danny Fisher selected one and cocked it.

'We must go now,' the leader said.

Jamie stared at her. He had no idea what was going on, only that he and Danny had been about to die and these people had saved them. He heard Frederick's voice as he moved towards the door. Despite his defeat it was thick with menace.

'This is not the end, Saintclair. We do not forget. You will be looking over your shoulder for the rest of your short life.'

Danny didn't move. 'Just one more thing. You, up!'

She pointed the pistol at Frederick, who rose to his feet with a sneer of contempt on his face.

'Whore,' he spat.

Jamie winced as he saw Danny smile. She had positioned herself perfectly. Her foot swung in an arc to land directly between Frederick's legs. The Vril's leader doubled over with a choked groan and before he could recover she smashed her knee into his face and brought the butt of the pistol down on the back of his neck so he collapsed to the floor as if he'd been shot.

'For the record,' she held the gun carelessly against her thigh as she surveyed the rest of the men, 'I am a detective with the New York Police Department. If anyone else wants to call me a whore, now's your chance.'

They drove from the warehouse in a Mercedes van with blacked-out windows. Two more of the Vril lay by the doorway, left unconscious when the assault team – that's how Jamie now thought of it, he'd only seen a more professional infiltration in an SAS demonstration – had broken in with Taser shock devices and gas grenades.

They were well away from the warehouse when the front passenger, the woman who had led the assault, removed her ski mask and shook her dark hair free. She was older than the speed of her actions had led Jamie to expect. Startling green eyes shone from a face that had known suffering and disappointment, but still retained a fine-boned beauty that reminded him of a Modigliani portrait and hinted at an origin in southern Germany or the Alps. Jamie expected the others, there were five of them altogether, to follow suit, but they made no effort to imitate their leader.

She saw his puzzlement. 'It would be preferable if you remained unaware of the identity of my sisters. Also that you keep any questions you may have until we reach our destination.'

He looked at Danny and she nodded. 'Of course.'

Suddenly Jamie felt very sleepy and his eyelids began to droop. Danny dabbed at his brow with something damp. He reflected muzzily that it seemed to be the role of the women in his life to wash other people's blood from his face. Maybe there was a message there?

By the time he woke they were parked in front of some kind of remote country house; three substantial floors of white stucco with a red tile roof and a garden screened off from the surrounding farmland by bushes and trees. They got out and the van drove off without a backward glance from the other passengers. Inside the house, their hostess showed them upstairs to a large bedroom, with a window that looked out over trees and fields.

'You will find your personal effects from the hotel here. I thought it sensible that you did not return there, Germany is not safe for you now. It will also give you a chance to change your clothes, Herr Saintclair.' She said it politely, but the words contained steel. He realized for the first time that he stank of sweat and fear and was still stained with another man's blood. 'The washroom is through the second door on the left.' He opened his mouth to thank her, but she wasn't finished. 'Of course, you will have many questions. When you are rested, perhaps you will join me downstairs in, shall we say, one hour?'

Jamie nodded, reflecting that this was one formidable lady, but Danny hadn't been brought up to be quite that polite.

'We'd just like to express our gratitude for rescuing us. I believe you saved our lives back there.' The other woman nodded graciously. 'May we be allowed to know your name?'

She smiled, and, in that instant, looked ageless. 'I have many names, Detective Fisher,' she said enigmatically, 'but you may call me Athena.'

Exactly an hour later a maid ushered them into the main room where Athena waited for them by a drinks cabinet.

'May I offer you wine, or perhaps you would prefer something a little stronger after your . . . adventures?'

Danny accepted a glass of wine, but Jamie opted for whisky, which came large, over ice and, unless his nose mistook him, was some sort of well-aged single malt. Athena took a seat by the window. She had switched her black jumpsuit for jeans and a designer sweater that set off her trim figure to good advantage. She waited until they were comfortable.

'Where do I begin?'

Jamie took a sip of his whisky and exchanged glances with Danny Fisher. She nodded.

'All right,' he said. 'Perhaps you'd care to tell us how you managed to be at the warehouse at just the right time to save our necks. I'm assuming that the two young ladies who followed us on our arrival in Berlin were your people, but the fact that you were able to do what you did, when you did, speaks of not just good intelligence, but first-class resources and exceptional organization.'

Athena nodded thoughtfully. 'You speak like a soldier, Mr Saintclair, but I suppose that is not surprising given your background.' Jamie raised his eyebrows at that. 'Oh yes, we know a great deal about you, but not about you, Detective.' Fisher acknowledged the smile. 'Our influence in the New World is not yet so extensive. We had information about your investigation, which was of interest to us, and we were able to gain access to your travel plans. You were followed, and we were happy that you knew you were followed, because we wished you to be aware that we were no threat. But when a genuine threat appeared in the guise of our Neanderthal Nazi friends, the decision was taken to make the surveillance more covert. That was how we were able to follow you after your abduction and how we had the time to draw together the necessary resources and to make our timely intervention.'

Jamie saw the hook being dangled, but for the moment he decided to ignore it. Danny was about to ask a question. She picked up his warning glance and relaxed back into her chair.

'And for that we have to again thank you. You saved our lives.'

'I am not so certain that we did, Mr Saintclair.' Athena said solemnly. 'Anyone who saw you overcome the large gentleman with the knife would have been very foolish to take your defeat for granted. You reminded me of one of the warriors of old; wrathful, certain, dangerous and without fear. A Zealot of Josephus's time, perhaps, or a gladiator who stood with Spartacus. A man who does not fear death is a man to be feared.'

Jamie accepted the compliment with a shrug. 'But a man just the same, and all it takes to kill a man, however wrathful, is a single bullet.'

'A man to be feared just the same,' she admonished. 'I, for one, am glad that we were on time, but I would warn you not to overestimate our capabilities. It was very fortunate for you that we were in Berlin, where we could count on the aid of suitably qualified friends. We will help you when we can, but it will not always be like that.'

'Maybe I'm speaking out of turn here, ma'am, but who is "we"?' Athena turned to face Danny, and for the first time, Jamie saw uncertainty on her face.

'How much to tell? Tell all and you would think me mad. Not enough and you will think me a mere fantasist . . .'

'We have seen enough of the reality of who you are to believe whatever you tell us,' Danny insisted.

'All, then.' Athena nodded. '*We* are The Sisterhood, or more correctly The Sisters of Isis.' She paused to allow the impact of her words to register. For a moment it seemed to Jamie that all the air had been sucked out of the room. 'The history of our Order goes back much further than the cult of the Othergod, whose face was the Nazarene, Christ, and whose disciples first courted then betrayed us. They seduced the god-emperors of Rome and poisoned their minds, so that we, who were foremost and eldest, were reduced to worshipping in the darkness. We worship in the darkness still, but still we worship.' She waited to allow some reaction to this heresy, but Jamie Saintclair and Danny Fisher had seen enough of God's handiwork to be suspicious of His motive, if not his existence. 'Isis is the Mothergod,' Athena continued, 'who gave birth to heaven and earth and will nurture them till darkness falls or she is driven from the minds of man. She is the divine womb of all mankind. She is The Lady, greatest and most illustrious Queen of Egypt. Without Isis,' her eyes flicked to Danny, 'woman would forever have been the chattel of man, a mere vessel, and of no more import than the cows in the field. Once, our temples were the glory of the world, now they lie in ruins or are crumbled to dust. All but one. Her influence and her grace spread across the civilized world, but her grace was too gentle, and she was supplanted. She can never return, but she survives, and her influence can once again be felt upon the fabric of our world.'

Danny kept her face expressionless as she registered the significance of Athena's reference to The Lady. Jamie had his own questions, but it was Danny who had the stage. She said: 'Then this is about the Crown, or the Eye.'

'That is correct, Detective.' Athena acknowledged the

truth with an aristocratic inclination of the head. 'But the Crown and the Eye are one. Without the Eye there is no Crown of Isis. Two hundred generations ago, when Rome was still a swamp beside the Tiber, a great civilization thrived on the black earth flood plains of the Nile. Even then, Isis was very ancient. She was revered among men and women alike, and they believed it was the tears of The Lady that provoked the great inundations that each year were the source of Egypt's prosperity and power. Thousands, led by the Pharaoh and his court, flocked to worship her at the great temple of Abu-Sir, and the focal points of the year were the two great festivals: the one for the annual rebirth of the world, and the other to celebrate the resurrection of Osiris.'

She paused, staring into the far distance and Jamie had the odd feeling that their surroundings had disappeared. It was as if he was listening to some priestess of ancients talking matter-of-factly of her own time, and that time was now. Then Athena's eyes focused and her habitual serenity was replaced by a grimace of pain.

'The centrepiece of every ritual was the Crown of Isis, forged in Memphis in ages past by Osiris's greatest craftsmen from Nubian gold, and at its heart the Eye, the gift of the stars, placed in The Lady's hand by Ra himself. The Crown was invested with the power of the goddess and under her benign influence Egypt never suffered the traditional blights of plague or famine. While Isis was strong, no widow went without, there

216

was justice for the poor and shelter for the weak. Egypt prospered and her Pharaohs amassed great wealth. But prosperity and wealth provoke envy. Such was their faith in The Lady that the Pharaohs became convinced of their own invulnerability. They neglected the strength of arms that had protected them for generations, and became fixated on art and culture. They became weak and indolent. And beyond their shores another power was growing: a sea people, hardy and cruel, too lazy to amass their own wealth, but greedy for the wealth of others. They attacked without warning and swept through the Delta, leaving all in flames. The temple burned. The Crown of Isis was taken.'

Jamie broke the silence that followed: 'The Phoenicians, or their forerunners.'

'I see that you are familiar with the legend of Queen Dido's treasure, Mr Saintclair. Good, that will save us time. So, Egypt began the long decline. The age of the pyramid and the sphinx was past. Over the centuries, Isis continued to be worshipped and her Crown was copied and replicated, but its power could never be reproduced, because the true power was in the Eye, Ra's gift to the goddess.'

Danny couldn't contain her impatience any longer. 'But where does the Sisterhood come in?'

'My apologies for the history lesson, Detective.' Athena smiled. 'It is so long since I have told the story that I am too tempted to prolong it. The story of the Sisterhood begins with the destruction of the temple.

Women had always been at the heart of the Cult of Isis, and when the temple burned, her priestesses were slaughtered or taken as slaves. All but a group of novices finishing their training at Philae, the other great Isiean centre in the south. They returned, shocked at the sacrilege and the loss of the cult's greatest treasure, and so distraught that they would have taken their own lives and joined those they had loved and lost. But one of them was a true daughter of Isis. She it was who brought them together and told them that they were now the keepers of The Lady's memory. They pledged to tend the flame, enact the rituals and nurture her faith. They would restore the temple, and when that was done they would spread the word of Isis far and wide. But the most solemn promise was that they would find the Crown and return it to the goddess.

'They and their successors made the Cult of Isis great again, and as Egypt waned, they carried the faith to Athens and to Rome, and once more The Lady was a power across the lands. And always, they sought news of the Crown. There were whispers that it had been found among the lost treasure of the Carthaginian queen, Dido, then, for centuries nothing. A new civilization thrived in the east, where a cruel and bloodthirsty despot was said to have enlisted the power of the goddess to give him dominion over the world. More whispers, stories and rumour.'

It was a powerful story and it explained the ability of the Crown to seduce and enslave, but Jamie wasn't prepared to let Athena off so easily. 'We appreciate the *history lesson*, but can anything that is coveted by so many be quite the force of good you claim? For instance, we've heard that the Crown may have re-appeared at different times over the centuries,' he met Athena's stare, 'and that far from being a benign influence, it was associated with witchcraft, magic and death?'

The German woman's eyes flashed. 'There have been many attempts to tarnish The Lady's name, and not only by the followers of the Othergod. Octavian, who became Augustus, claimed our rituals were porno-graphic.' She shrugged. 'Of course, a fertility rite would have a sexual element, but what could be more pornographic than forcing men to fight to the death against other men for entertainment?'

'That still doesn't answer my question,' Jamie persisted.

Athena rose to her feet and walked to the window. 'It is true that through the ages the Crown has been associated with evil and abomination. The Crown of Isis is a potent talisman. Legends attach themselves to such things. Because she was able to restore Osiris's soul, Isis was said to have power over life and death. At the end of her mortal life that power became in-extricably linked with the Crown. It was believed that under certain conditions a person who wore the Crown would be given the gift of eternal life. But if such were the case, would Isis herself not have chosen that path?'

'I suppose that would depend on the conditions?'

She took a deep breath and her voice became harsh, almost manly. '*You must spill the blood of a first born of good family beneath the first light of the sickle moon. Only then will the gateway to the next life open.*'

It was a few moments before the full import of the words sank in. When it did, Jamie flinched at the horrors that lay behind them. 'Are you saying that one person has owned the Crown of Isis for twenty centuries, killing a child whenever they felt the power of the Crown begin to subside?'

'No, Mr Saintclair; that would be beyond madness. But the Crown certainly has the power to mesmerize, bewitch and bemuse. What if it was passed down from hand to hand and the legend passed with it? A kind of contagion, which convinced men that, whatever the evidence, possession of the Crown gave them the capability of resurrecting themselves, as long as they had the ruthlessness to meet the conditions.'

'Jesus,' Danny breathed. 'A hundred generations of child killers.'

'Not quite how I would have put it, Detective, but yes, that is what we fear.'

'Then they have to be stopped.'

'But how?' Jamie demanded.

'I believe the answer lies with you and Detective Fisher, Mr Saintclair. The ways of Isis have always been mysterious. Can it be a coincidence that you came to our notice in England and a few days later you are in

Berlin, where we have been focusing our search for the Crown without success for the last sixty years?' She saw his look of puzzlement. 'One of our number infiltrated the higher reaches of the Nazi party and recognized the Crown among their plunder when she was trying to escape Berlin in the chaos of nineteen forty-five. It was the first physical evidence of its existence in two millennia.' She explained how Else Kruger had had the Crown within her grasp on the night of the break-out from Hitler's bunker and how it had been torn away from her.

'Hartmann.'

Now it was Athena's turn to look puzzled.

'We believe a man called Berndt Hartmann was in possession of the Crown of Isis in May nineteen forty-five,' Jamie explained.

'Oh, no, Mr Saintclair, our informant was most precise. The man who carried the Crown was an SS Sturmbannführer called Max Dornberger. But the point is, you found your way to Berlin. That is why we helped you, because we believe you are being guided by the goddess. Because we believe that you and Detective Fisher have been chosen to find the Crown of Isis. If we can do anything to aid you, we will, but there is one condition. The Crown must be returned to the Temple of the Lady, where it can be used to atone for the sins committed in its name for the past two thousand years.'

XXIII

'Hey.' Danny Fisher nudged Jamie's arm. 'A girl likes to be shown a little attention.'

'Actually, I was just wondering exactly who the Berlin Ladies Sewing and Sub-machine Gun Circle were.'

'Cops,' she said emphatically. 'Berlin's answer to a SWAT team, or maybe one of those elite anti-terrorist units that have grown like mushrooms since 9/11. It would make sense for the Sisterhood to infiltrate their people into something like that.'

He nodded. 'Athena referred to them as her Order, which makes them sound fairly military, a female Knights Templar . . . They were—'

'I read *The Da Vinci Code* on the way over, Jamie.'

'In any case, you're right. If the Sisterhood has survived two thousand years of persecution and living and worshipping underground, they'd need to know how to look after themselves. Even Athena's name is significant. In Greek mythology she was the goddess of wisdom, courage and just warfare. The companion of heroes.' He looked over his shoulder. 'I suspect they may still be around.' They were sitting in a small cafeteria tucked away off the main concourse at Tegel. Athena had advised against taking their scheduled flight back from Schonefeld in case Frederick's men were aware of it. Instead, they were flying out of Berlin's biggest airport in seats booked at the last minute.

'So, Hartmann or Dornberger? Which trail do we follow? They can't both have had the Crown of Isis.'

'I don't know,' Jamie admitted. 'But the first thing we need to do is talk to Sir William Melrose. From what his researcher told the Neues Museum, it's pretty clear that his source had a good description of the Crown. If that's the case, what other information does he have? And why didn't he use it in the book?'

'All right,' she agreed. 'I'll go along with that, but aren't you forgetting something?'

'That a hired killer might be waiting for me when I open the door to my flat? Yes, I had considered it.'

'So what are you going to do about it?'

He grinned. 'I thought I might move in with you for a few days.'

Paul Dornberger couldn't believe he'd lost Saintclair. Over the years with Oleg Samsonov he had painstakingly worked to create an organization within an organization: a small group of investigators and highly skilled individuals who believed they were acting for the oligarch, but were actually doing Dornberger's bidding. Thus far, Saintclair had come into contact only with the very fringes of the Hartmann investigation which had taken up so much of Dornberger's life. That made him of interest, but of fairly low-level interest. The murder attempt had made him more significant. For a time Dornberger worried that some new and unknown force might have appeared from below the radar, but his subsequent investigations seemed to discount that possibility. The private inquiry agent tasked with keeping a discreet watch on the art dealer had reported little or no activity in the days following his release from hospital, apart from a visit from the as yet unidentified woman he had taken to dinner. Then he had disappeared.

Disappointingly, Saintclair's secretary had stalled every attempt to glean any further information, either by telephone or by visits from potential 'customers', and they'd had to abandon the attempt when it became obvious that she was becoming suspicious. A search of Saintclair's flat and office had been equally unrevealing, but had allowed them to plant bugs in his phones.

It seemed their only option was to wait until the quarry turned up.

But there *was* still one loose end and Paul Dornberger didn't like loose ends. He couldn't allow a rogue element to blunder around London getting in the way of the operation and potentially threatening everything he'd achieved. The hotel his people had pinpointed was only a dozen blocks away in the West End and he'd reconnoitred it the previous evening, confirming what they'd already learned by hacking into the computer system. The two men were lying low, existing on room service, booze from the mini-bar and cable-channel porn movies. Harmless enough for the moment, but the very fact they were still in London pointed to a second attempt to kill Saintclair.

It was nine thirty in the evening when he used a cloned card to gain entry to the hotel's service area. Not late enough to alarm them, but late enough that they'd be sluggish from food and drink and just about to settle down in front of *Prom Girls in the Shower*, or whatever constituted tonight's entertainment. Once inside he changed into the green overall with the hotel group's logo and retrieved a workman's toolbag from his rucksack.

In room 508, Jacko Bonetti lay with his eyes closed listening to Mario's commentary of what was happening on the screen. Christ, couldn't he shut up even for one goddam minute? After five days cooped up together the glamour of their situation had long since worn off. How was he to know the mark would be wearing a vest? There was no other explanation for Saintclair's survival. He had hit him clean. Two right over the heart. No man could survive that. Well, the next time it would be two in the head and brains on the sidewalk. *Get up after that, you prick.*

He was going through the hit in his mind when he

heard the gentle knock on the door. It was a knock they'd experienced a dozen times during their stay. Routine and unthreatening. Unusual only for the timing.

'Who is it?' Jacko's hand instinctively crept below the pillow where the replacement automatic was stashed.

'Room maintenance.'

Jacko exchanged glances with Mario, who shrugged. 'We didn't call for none.'

'I know, sir, but the previous occupants of this room reported a faulty window catch. It will only take me a minute to fix it.'

'Switch that off.'

'Aw, Jacko—'

'Switch the fucking thing off.'

Jacko went to the door and opened it to reveal a cheerful, bulky man in the familiar green overall worn by the hotel's cleaners and maintenance staff. 'Okay, but make it quick.' He went back to the bed, his right hand hovering by the pillow.

'Thanks for this.' The engineer marched directly to the window. 'It'd be more than my job's worth if it was put off for another day.' He fiddled around with a screwdriver. 'That'll do it.'

'That's it?'

The bulky man nodded and was heading for the door when something caught his eye. He frowned and pointed at the phone by Jacko's bed. 'Can't trust anyone

226

these days.' Before Jacko could react he was kneeling beside the bed. 'See, bare wires.'

Automatically, Jacko followed the pointing finger, but all he saw was the nozzle of a small spray can. He opened his mouth to shout a warning, but the nozzle emitted a single concentrated puff and his whole world froze. He couldn't move. He couldn't speak. He willed his fingers to reach for the gun that was mere inches from them, but they wouldn't obey his ice-bound mind.

Dornberger held his breath until he knew he was safe from the gas, which had been developed by the KGB to help in the forced return of defectors.

Mario heard the soft 'phut' of the spray being released, but his brain was already anticipating the return to the 42-inch plasma screen of a dozen naked, soap-covered female bodies. He turned and looked up into the engineer's smiling face.

'I have an appointment to see Sir William at three.' Jamie smiled at the woman who answered the big oak door. 'The name is Saintclair.'

'Of course, sir.' She ushered him inside with old-fashioned courtesy. 'Please come in. Sir William will be with you in just a moment.'

She took his coat and led him into a wide room with a wine-coloured carpet and matching walls hung with paintings of ships and seascapes. He was admiring a vibrant oil on canvas of a sea battle when a tall, balding man entered, dressed in worn jeans and a ragged blue cardigan.

'*HMS Agamemnon*'s somewhere in the smoke in the background. My great, great whatever grandfather served as a mid in her at Trafalgar. The 'seventy-four taking on the big Frenchman in the centre is *Superb*.'

'A beautiful picture. One of Pocock's?'

The man's manner, which had been offhand, became appraising. 'Of course, you're that Saintclair, the one who found the Raphael. Reason I agreed to meet you, actually. Intrigued. Have to 'scuse the skivvies, but I've been working on my transcriptions.' Sir William Melrose spoke in clipped, machine-gun-burst sentences that for Jamie would always be the speech pattern of the military man, which in turn reminded him that his host had sidestepped the family's naval tradition and gone on to command tanks instead of destroyers.

'Your secretary said you've been in the Far East.'

'Mmmmh. Burma and Japan.' He waved Jamie to one of a pair of antique Chesterfield settees. 'Publishers weren't too happy about it. Not commercial enough. Forgotten Army's still forgotten, poor buggers. Still, if you're going to do it, do it right, what? Both sides. Very old, of course, the Japanese survivors. Penitent, which was a surprise. Still, the name will sell it hopefully.'

Jamie nodded in bemused agreement. 'I was reading your book about Berlin recently . . . In fact, I'm just back from there.'

Sir William smiled. 'Wonderful city, spent many

happy months there. Not quite the atmosphere it had in the Cold War, but the Jerries don't hang around. If Stalin had had his way he'd have bulldozed it and salted the ground. Didn't dare after he'd given half of it to the Yanks. Something in the book you wanted to chat about?'

Jamie explained how he had stumbled across the passage about the ancient artefact, and the meeting with the Herr Direktor that had confirmed the description of an Egyptian crown. 'I wondered if you had any more information about the circumstances?'

The author nodded slowly. 'A murder case, you say? Odd a chap in your line being involved in a murder investigation. Odder still that you're looking at evidence from more than half a century ago . . .'

'All I can say, sir, is that I'm helping the New York Police with the background.'

'Mmmmmh.'

'I also wondered why you hadn't mentioned the crown when you had its description?'

'Simple enough, really.' Sir William got to his feet and motioned Jamie after him. 'No corroboration. Nothing to say where it might have come from. Could have been a child's toy. Too outlandish, you see. It would have been sensationalist. Tempted, but one must maintain one's standards. Mary?' he shouted. 'Tea for two in the writing room, there's a dear. Biscuits, too. The chocolate digestives. Now, tell me all about this bunker where you found the painting . . .'

They descended a stone staircase with a cherrywood banister into the basement of the building.

'Can't write without my files,' Sir William explained. 'Only place in the house big enough to hold them all. Had to find somewhere else for the wine.' He led the way into a room lined with wooden shelves packed with files of every shade and colour. In the centre stood an ancient desk as big as a battleship, equipped with an equally antiquated manual typewriter. 'Can't be doing with all that modern rubbish. Leave the inter-whatever to my researchers. Too much distraction, you know. Sensory deprivation. Only way to write. Now, where are we? Yes, here it is.' He waved a languid hand at one wall. '*Berlin: the Last Hundred Days*. A hundred sections, one for each day, naturally. Black files for the SS and the Nazi hierarchy. Grey for the Wehrmacht. Red for the Soviets and Comrade Stalin. Green for the Allies, and brown for the civil administration, including our chums the Gestapo. Now, what day did we say it was?'

'April twenty-ninth. The day before Hitler shot himself.'

'Of course.' The author smiled dreamily. He ran his hand along the wall of files caressing the spine of each one, until he reached a slim brown volume. 'Not a lot of civil administration left by then, of course. Surprising they held it together at all. Fear. And discipline. But mostly fear. You can read German?'

Jamie assured him he did and Sir William handed him

the file. 'Take as long as you like with it. If you need any copies, just let me know. We've all sorts of technical wizardry upstairs.'

'Ah, Mary, thank you, my dear.' He accepted a tray from the secretary. 'Milk and sugar?'

Jamie nodded distractedly, leafing his way through the file until he found what he was looking for. It was a single photocopied sheet of *Geheime Staatspolizei* headed notepaper recording a contact report between *Kriminalassistent* Krebs and informant Zeigler, a jeweller on Wilhelmstrasse. The time was given as 15:47 hours on Sunday 29 April 1945 and the place as the jeweller's premises at Wilhelmstrasse 94.

Regular weekly contact meeting: Note – Informant displayed uncharacteristic nervousness, but this may have been a result of nearby artillery fire.

Informant Zeigler begged to report a suspicious customer on the morning of 29 April. Suspect knocked loudly on door of Informant Z's shop premises and refused to leave until door was answered: suspect described as male, thin and of small stature, and dressed in the uniform of an SS-Unterscharführer. Suspect carried a brown hessian bag of reasonable proportions, which he opened on entry to reveal a curious object, which suspect claimed was a crown of Egyptian origin. Informant Z described a coronet of gold, or gold-like substance, decorated with a single stylized eye and mounted with the horns of some animal. In Informant Z's professional opinion a central feature of the piece appeared to be missing. Suspect was visibly agitated and in a hurry. He wished to exchange the crown for its approximate physical value in gold coins or small diamonds. Believing that the item could not have been obtained legally, Informant Z terminated the meeting and suggested the suspect return later, at which point Informant Z contacted Kriminalassistent Krebs. Investigator's conclusion: suspect is almost certainly a criminal element attempting to sell looted material. Action: further investigation required. Signed: Walter Krebs, Prinz-Albrecht-Strasse, 29 April 1945.

'Astonishing, when you think of it, that our friend Krebs may have been typing that note at the very moment the Russians were knocking on the front door of Gestapo headquarters . . .' The author's voice faded into the background as Jamie flipped idly to the next page in the file, another report by the same agent. Suddenly he found it difficult to breathe.

'Are you all right, young man?'

XXIV

'Hey, you're looking a little shaky?'

Jamie laid the envelope on the bed in Danny Fisher's hotel room and retrieved the copies of the two Gestapo reports. He handed the first to Fisher.

She nodded as she read. 'I don't know why you're so down. This is great. The guy in the *Unterscharführer*'s uniform has got to be Hartmann, so it confirms we're right to follow the Hartmann trail. The thing that was missing was the Eye of Isis. It would make sense for a thief like Hartmann to try to offload the Crown, but hold on to the Eye, which had the benefit of being more portable and infinitely more valuable. Maybe this Dornberger guy eventually got the Crown, but Hartmann kept the Eye. And for us, it's the Eye that's important.'

'I'm not down. I think I'm in shock. All this stuff about the Crown of Isis being stained with blood was just a story until I read this.' He handed her the second sheet.

Suspicious death, Wilhelmstrasse, 29 April 1945. 16:50 hours.

On returning from contact meeting with Informant Z (see separate sheet LZ1-005) my attention was drawn to the body of a young male that had been recently discovered in a garden off the main street. Under the circumstances, this was not an unusual occurrence, but on investigation the unidentified child, of Aryan appearance and aged around seven years old, appeared not to have died on site from shrapnel or blast injuries, but had suffered a wound to his throat using a sharp instrument that had almost severed the neck. Investigator's conclusion: subject may have been the victim of Soviet infiltration patrol or communist fifth columnists. Action: no further action possible due to deteriorating local situation. Signed: Walter Krebs, Prinz-Albrecht-Strasse, 29 April 1945.

Danny read the words, then reread them with even greater concentration. She tried to picture the scene among the devastation of Berlin. A small, blond figure lying across a pile of rubble, his blank eyes staring at a smoke-filled sky. Lost, orphaned or abandoned, it didn't make any difference now. Two people standing over him. The finder, by now wishing he'd walked away, and the Gestapo agent, Krebs, probably thinking the same. The boy's head would be thrown back, the wound . . .? Yes, that was the key. The wound.

'Hartmann had the Crown in Wilhelmstrasse a few hours before the boy was killed,' Jamie said. 'And from what we know now, if he had the Crown, he had the motive. I've always thought of Hartmann as a bit player, the innocent link between the past and the present, but it looks as if Hartmann was as possessed by the Crown as everyone else who held it.'

Danny shook her head. 'Let's not jump to conclusions, Sherlock. We know that a day later it was Dornberger who had the Crown. Who's to say that Dornberger didn't kill Hartmann and the kid and steal the Crown for himself?'

They stared at each other, knowing they were going down the same road and entertaining the same doubts.

'We need to know what happened afterwards,' Danny said slowly. 'Somehow we have to find out if Hartmann or Dornberger escaped, and what happened to them if they did? Is that possible?'

Jamie shook his head. 'I don't know. These people didn't exactly advertise what they did after the war.'

'Yeah, how do you go about tracking down an old SS man? I thought they all changed their names and skee-daddled off to Argentina, like that Doc What's-his-name.'

'Mengele,' Jamie said absently. 'A lot of them just vanished into Soviet prisoner of war camps and never came back. The lucky ones like Mengele were smuggled out by ODESSA, the SS escape organization that had been set up when they saw what was coming, or with the help of the Roman Catholic Church.' He saw the look on her face. 'Oh yes, it's a murky area, but well documented. The worst of them changed their names and their faces, although, oddly enough, now that I think of it, some of them are quite proud of their past. They even have an Old Soldiers' organization.'

'Like the American Legion?'

'That's right, a sort of Legion for the Damned.'

'Well I'll be . . .'

'What we need is an introduction.'

'And where are we going to get that?' Her face creased in a frown. 'Maybe London is crawling with ex SS men, but they aren't likely to introduce themselves and, even if they did, I doubt they'd send us an invitation to their next square dance.'

Jamie went to the window and looked out over the London roofscape towards the distinctive outline of the Gherkin. 'There is one possibility.' His voice made it clear it wasn't a particularly welcome possibility. 'It might be pointless. On the other hand, it might be dangerous. Even if it works, I'll end up owing a man I'd rather not be in debt too.'

'Except the other option is to walk away.'

'That's right. The other option is to walk away. And for the sake of the Crown of Isis's next victim we can't do that.'

'May I speak to David, please?'

'There is no David here. I believe you have the wrong number.'

I wish. Jamie smiled bitterly. 'Perhaps he no longer calls himself David.'

'You have a nerve calling this number again, Mr Saintclair. You exposed me to a great deal of needless trouble, not so say risk, and you cost me the services of a very good operative.'

'How is Miss Grant?'

'What makes you think I would know?' the other man demanded. Something in the way he said it confirmed Jamie's growing suspicion that Sarah Grant had returned to the fold.

'Please pass on my regards, if she gets in touch.'

A half-grunt of disbelief.

'At great risk to myself, I lured the Vril Society out into the open for you. I'm sure you made good use of that.'

'The Vril Society is an irrelevance, Mr Saintclair. Our only interest was in the Sun Stone. It took a large amount of money and effort to discover what you already knew. That it no longer existed. I have very painful memories of the meeting with my supervisor at which I had to explain that. So tell me, why should I talk to you?'

'Because I also removed Walter Brohm, Gunther Klosse and Paul Strasser from your most-wanted list. I'm sure that was a cause for celebration in certain quarters.' He took the silence that followed as confirmation. 'I'm interested in getting in touch with some former *Kameraden*. You will have heard of *Geistjaeger 88*?'

A snort of disgust made David's feelings clear enough. 'Not just an irrelevance, but a joke. Perhaps if you discover the Spear of Destiny or the Ark of the Covenant you will get back in touch?'

'I can assure you this is no joke, David,' Jamie hurried on before the other man could hang up, 'but a matter of life and death. People have already died and others may be at risk. I can't believe a man with your background would leave them to their fate.'

There was another long pause while David made his decision. 'I think if we had any sense we would discontinue this call and terminate our relationship now, Mr Saintclair, but there is a possibility that at some point in the future you may be of some practical use to us. Do you understand what I am saying? This might not be in your best interests.'

Jamie knew exactly what he was saying and he was certain that David was right. Who would have thought selling your soul would cause such a physical pain? Still, he was too far in to turn back now.

'I need a way to reach the Old Comrades' Association. I thought you might have a suggestion.'

'Call me on this number in two days.'

David was still as he remembered him. Short, tanned and powerful: a pocket battleship of a man in a smart suit and open-necked shirt, who could break your neck with a flick of his wrists and his smile wouldn't even falter.

'How was our old friend Frederick when you last met? Berlin, wasn't it?'

Jamie laughed. So he'd been right. Mossad did have a source inside the Vril Society. So much for being irrelevant. 'If you'd ever tried poking a cobra with a stick you'd know. Isn't this a strange place for you to be meeting someone?' He looked up into the nave of the church, where time had blackened and cracked the seven-hundred-year-old beams.

David didn't take his eyes of the altarpiece. 'Not so strange as you might think.' He reached into his pocket and withdrew an envelope, which he handed over. Jamie hesitated, not certain what to do next. 'Open it, please.'

He worked the flap free and pulled out two sheets of paper. David saw his look of surprise.

'Yes, quite interesting that you should already be acquainted. Page one is a biography of his life that you will already be familiar with. The second page is an alternative and entirely accurate account of his activities between nineteen forty-one and nineteen forty-six.'

Jamie shook his head, even after so many surprises this was difficult to believe.

'What if he denies it?'

'Oh, he certainly will. First he will feign shock that you, his friend, have accused him. Then he will laugh it off; a joke perpetrated by his friends. If you press him, he will deny it outright. Enemies attempting to smear him. A hangover from the time when he risked his life for good old Blighty in the fight against Communism.

That's when you show him a copy of this.' He handed over a picture of a man in uniform, smiling broadly as he fixed a noose over the head of a boy in a flat cap. Beside the boy a pretty girl with wild blonde hair looks on so disinterestedly that it takes you a moment to realize she is already dead, choked by the thin rope around her neck. 'Clearly he enjoyed his work.'

Jamie read the second page of the document again. 'Why . . . ?'

'Because, despite what you read there, he was small fry. Not worth the effort of unmasking. There are thousands like that. Latvians, Estonians, Ukrainians. All former SS with blood on their hands and welcomed into your country. They even set up their own social clubs. At one time, there was a feeling that he might be useful and the material could be used to persuade him to help us. Now, because of his age, he is a dwindling asset. Thus . . .'

'Thank you.'

'You understand that it is up to you to make this work, Mr Saintclair? And that our agreement is still binding whether it does or not.'

Jamie nodded.

'Good. Here is a card with a new number to use. I have decided to discontinue the old one.'

Jamie took it and studied the name. 'Benjamin?'

The other man produced a tight smile. 'David was becoming a little stale.' He got to his feet. 'Good luck, Mr Saintclair. I do not envy you your task. Even for the most righteous, it is difficult to dabble in these waters without becoming a little contaminated. And should this lead you back to Germany, please be careful. The Vril Society may be an irrelevance, but that does not make Frederick any less dangerous.'

XXV

'I should really call in at the office to let Gail know I might be gone for a while longer.'

Danny gave him one of her looks. 'So you stay away from the apartment, but you're happy to walk into the office in broad daylight? Why don't you pin a notice on your back saying shoot me? Give her a call, but not on the office phone, on her cell. Okay?'

'All right,' he said, 'but I can't hide for ever.'

He rang the number and Gail answered on the third ring.

After the usual pleasantries and a briefing on the latest business she came out with the information he'd been expecting, but hoped not to hear. 'I'm so glad you called, Jamie,' she said. 'I've been frightened for you. We've had some very odd phone calls and a couple of unlikely "customers" asking questions about your new female assistant.'

Jamie looked to where Danny lay on the bed studying

the newspaper and making a call of her own. 'We need all the customers we can get, Gail.' He forced himself to be cheerfully reassuring. 'If we turned away the weird ones we'd be out of business in a fortnight. Look, that's what I was phoning you about. Why don't you take a week off and spend some time with your mum? I'm trying to set up some meetings in Germany and I won't be in the office for a while.'

'I could do that.' He sensed the reluctance in her voice. 'But if there was anything I could do to help. Anything at all . . .'

He closed his eyes. Was she saying what he thought she was saying? Life couldn't be that complicated.

'No, that's fine, but look, we'll have a chat when I get back. Increased responsibilities, maybe a pay rise . . .'

When he rang off, Danny was doing the same.

'Thanks for your help, sir.' She laid down the phone, picked up the newspaper and handed it to him. 'Page four. One of the stories down the side. Just a few paragraphs because Scotland Yard is trying to keep a lid on it for now.'

He found what he was looking for. 'Two American tourists found dead in a hotel room. Police are treating the deaths as suspicious and have asked for any witnesses to come forward?'

'That's right, two American tourists with a rap sheet you could use as a parachute and a cocked .45 pistol under their pillow.'

'Our guy? That would be quite a coincidence.'

She nodded slowly. 'And we don't do coincidences. But that's not the juicy part.'

'I'm not sure if I'm going to like the juicy part.'

'The way they died. The very specific way they were killed. According to your cops, their throats were cut by some kind of metallic ligature. That's precisely the same MO as the Hartmanns in Brooklyn and the London Hartmans.' She picked up the Gestapo report on the boy's death in Berlin from where it was lying on the bed. 'Which, in case you hadn't noticed, is also uncannily similar to our unknown child victim in nineteen forty-five.'

'Hartmann must be in his eighties. Dornberger nearer a hundred. They're not running around London killing people with a piece of piano wire, for Christ's sake.'

'Maybe not, but someone is.'

'Why would our man – assuming it is a man – kill someone who was sent from the States to kill me? It doesn't make sense.'

'None of this makes sense, Jamie. We just have to try to make sense of it. What does he achieve by killing them?'

The seconds lengthened into minutes as he turned it over in his mind. 'I think there are two possibilities.' She nodded for him to carry on. 'Either he wanted them out of the way to have a clear run at me at a time and place of his choosing – he wants me dead, but for some reason not now – or he wants me to keep looking for the Crown of Isis . . .'

'Which means . . .'

Their eyes met. 'We're closer than we think.'

'Why not a combination of both? He killed them because he thinks you can lead him to the diamond and once you have . . .'

Jamie told her about Gail's strange calls and visitors and got up to close the curtains. He looked out from the window and saw a hundred others staring back at him from a dozen tower blocks. The killer could be behind any one, which triggered a worrying possibility.

'How did he know where to find them?'

'As your Sherlock Holmes would say: *Elementary, my dear Saintclair, elementary*. He knew where to find them because he was watching us when they hit you. But I don't think he is now.'

'I'm not sure I go along with that, Danny. I prefer to stay nervous.'

She shrugged. 'Suit yourself. If he knew *where* I was the chances are he'd know *who* I was. If that's the case, why would he be asking your secretary about your new female assistant only a few days ago, while we were still in Germany? I think he lost us.'

Cork Street, in Mayfair, had been the centre for London's most successful commercial art galleries for as long as anyone could remember. It was close to Jamie's office in Old Bond Street and he regularly made the rounds in the search for business and the hope of being offered a decent cup of coffee. Cork Street wasn't the kind of place you were likely to pick up a bargain, but sometimes, if a gallery owner was keen to move a picture on, Jamie might be offered a commission. Micky Janelis ran his business from a discreet townhouse in the small mews that cut off at a dogleg from the main street. The only clue to his line of work was the Renoir self-portrait in the front window that may, or may not, have been genuine but that to Jamie's certain knowledge had never been offered for sale. Micky was an old-school collector who specialized in the Impressionists and revelled in his self-appointed role as the street's elder statesman and relentless *bête noire* of all things modernist. He was a diminutive, untidy man in a rumpled suit and spotted bow tie, with spikes of grey hair that shot like fireworks from either side of his bald head. From what Jamie had heard, Micky could have comfortably retired a couple of decades earlier, but claimed it was only his passion for art that kept him alive.

When Jamie pressed the entry buzzer and Micky discovered who it was, he greeted the younger man like an old friend.

'Jamie Saintclair, as I live and breathe, I thought you was dead, or off to Tahiti, chasing the ladies like Gauguin with the profits of that Raphael I heard about. You come to spend some money with Micky, huh? You spreading it about? Come, I got something to show you. Just in this week. Look.' By now he'd blown through to the gallery like a mini whirlwind with Jamie in his wake. He pulled back a black velvet curtain in the centre of the wall. 'Just for you.' There was a twinkle in his eye as he unveiled the picture. 'What you think, eh?'

It was a very simple painting. Just a tree- and gorse-covered hillside overlooking the sea. The hill all green and gold, dappled with pale flowers, trees twisted and spindly-trunked with shadowed, drooping canopies, and the sea a light sapphire shot with splashes of aquamarine. But it was the sky that told him what it was. Clouds that were solid, but also ethereal, seeming to move across the immense blue vastness with the graceful ease of swans over the surface of a lake. At first, you thought they were white, but when you looked more closely you saw the purples and the golds, the azure and the peacock, and in the distance, the ghostly threat of a storm. It was one of his early pictures, Jamie decided, when he was learning his craft, but you could already see in that sky the first stirrings of the Impressionism that brought him his fame.

'I thought all Monet's stuff was in the big galleries or private collections?'

Micky Janelis huffed. 'Rich men, they get bored, they come to Micky.' He said it as if that was what fate had always intended for him. 'You like it?'

Jamie forced a smile, though inside his guts were churning. 'Like it, Micky, yes, but want it? No. How about old Pierre-Auguste in the window? Always fancied that. How much?'

'Jamie, Jamie, Jamie.' The old man shook his grey

head. 'You know he gave that painting to my grand-mother in Paris when the Prussians were on the doorstep and everybody thought they were going to die. It's a family heirloom. It would be like selling one of the kids.'

They wandered through the gallery, Micky talking about the market with a relish that belied his years. 'Genius has never been a better investment, you mark my words. You got yourself an Old Master, one of the greats, you stick it in the vault for a year and you make twenty million, no problem. You want a coffee?'

'Actually, Micky old chum,' Jamie chewed his lip, 'I was hoping for a word in private.'

'You want a loan?' Micky asked when they were in his oak-lined office. 'Maybe I hear that the finder's fee for your Raphael is stuck in traffic. Micky don't give loans, but for you, I break a rule, just this once, okay?'

'It's not money, Micky.' Jamie's heart and his feet were telling him to get up and walk out, but he remembered the contents of the second sheet of paper and stayed where he was. 'I'm looking for an introduction to some old friends of yours. Some old army friends.'

Micky sat back in his chair. The smile was still there, but it was as if a veil had closed over his eyes. 'You know Micky wasn't in no army, Jamie. You heard the story. Micky was a refugee . . .'

'Sure, Micky,' Jamie reassured him, 'I've heard the story. Everybody has. You were a slave labourer for the Nazis. East Prussia, wasn't it? Then the forced march ahead of the advancing Russians. Frostbite and eating your shoe leather and drinking bloodstained snow. What was it you said one time? Oh, yes. Our yardsticks were the corpses of the fallen. Anyone who lay down never got up again. But Micky was tough. Micky never lay down and Micky made it?'

'Sure, Jamie, or Micky wouldn't be here. Why you joking with me? Why you teasing an old man?'

Jamie took the envelope out of his pocket. 'Like I say, Micky, I'm looking for an introduction to some old friends.' He placed the second sheet of paper face up on the desk between them. 'You say you were never in the army? Well, I have a different version of the Micky Janelis story, and maybe Micky isn't such a hero. Are you telling me you never heard of the Rumbula Forest?'

The old man's face didn't so much go pale, as a sickly mustard yellow, but he hadn't lived with a lie for sixty years without learning how to act.

'Sure, I heard of the Rumbula Forest. Every Latvian heard of the Rumbula Forest. That doesn't mean every Latvian had anything to do with what happened there.' He picked up the paper and threw it back across the desk. 'What is this shit, Saintclair? You abuse my hospitality and my friendship over this Soviet bullshit propaganda. Get out of here.'

Jamie picked up the paper and read: '*In November nineteen forty-one, I was one of some twenty-four thousand Jews taken from the Jewish Ghetto in Riga to the Rumbula Forest. The able-bodied men were* separated from the women and children and the old, but for ten kilometres I was able to march beside my father and my twelve-year-old brother, Jacob. A number of people were killed on the way because they could not keep up, either by Germans of the Aktion Squad or, more cruelly, by men of the local militia, the Arajs Kommando. I was frightened, but my father reassured me. When we entered the forest, my father and brother were singled out by a local man who was known to me. He forced them out of the column at pistol point and pushed them into the trees. I did not know what to do, but it seemed better to follow them. My father and brother were ordered to dig a deep pit, while the other man watched, calmly smoking a cigarette. When the pit was completed to his satisfaction, he ordered them to return the spade they had used. He picked up the spade and I saw him smile before he brought it down with all his strength, edge first, on my father's head, splitting his skull in two and exposing his brains. Then he did the same with my brother. I was standing ten metres away among the trees while he used the bloody spade to fill in the pit. I escaped into the forest, where I fought with partisan units until October nineteen forty-four. The local man's name was Mikhailis Janelis, a boy I had known from school. This is my testimony. Anna Gurenstein.'

'Tas ir jāšanās muļķības! Get out! Get out! Get out! And take your manure with you.' Micky's hands shook as he gripped the desk and a vein in his neck pulsed ominously. Jamie wondered if he was about to have a heart attack, but he stood his ground.

'And Mikhailis Janelis' military record? Is that bull-shit, too, Micky?' He slapped the execution photograph on the desk and the gallery owner recoiled as if it was a hissing snake. 'You've changed a lot, Micky, but not your smile. I recognized that fucking smile as soon as I walked in your door. I wanted to punch it off your face, and if you don't cooperate I might just do that yet.' He carried on relentlessly. 'Volunteered for the Latvian SS Legion in early nineteen forty-two; fought at Leningrad until forced to retreat in spring of 'forty-four. Accused of war crimes during the retreat. I'm assuming this is one of them, Micky, but with your record I'm pretty sure there was worse. Trapped in the Courland Peninsula until late nineteen forty-four, wounded and evacuated to East Prussia. Evacuated from Konigsberg to Germany. Surrendered to troops of the US Ninth Army on the fourth of May nineteen forty-five.'

'War crimes?' Micky spat. 'What the fuck do you know of war crimes? Terrorists. Back-shooters and mutilators. At least the Americans treated us as what we were. Patriots. *The Waffen SS units of the Baltic states are to be seen as units that stood apart from the German SS. We do not consider them a movement that is hostile to the United States,*' he quoted from memory. 'Does it also say that I stood guard with my comrades at the Nuremberg war trials as an ally? Does it state that I advised the CIA on Latvia during the Cold War.'

'No it doesn't, Micky.' Jamie felt the anger draining from him as he exchanged stares with a defeated old man. 'So it looks as if your former allies have all abandoned you. Maybe they didn't know about Anna Gurenstein and the Rumbula Forest, but they do now.' He picked up two sheets of headed notepaper from the desk and placed them in front of the other man. 'I need a name and an address, Micky, of a contact in the Waffen SS – the man who gave me this reckoned you still keep in touch with your old mates – and a nice polite letter of introduction asking him to cooperate with me. Do that for me and we'll forget this ever happened.'

Micky's shoulders slumped. His hand shook as it reached out to pick up a pen and began writing. 'You're a fool, Jamie, out of your depth. They will eat you alive.'

'I'll take a chance on that, Micky.' The Latvian pushed the papers across the desk. Jamie picked them up along with the photograph. 'Perfect. If it helps, which I doubt it will, this could save someone's life. I'll leave you with the other stuff, but I'll take the picture, if you don't mind, just in case . . . I'll say cheerio now. I doubt we'll be seeing each other again.' He turned to leave. 'And by the way, I'd have that Monet checked out again, there's something not quite—'

The familiar click of a gun being cocked froze the words on his tongue and when he looked round Micky Janelis was pointing a small, shiny, but still very dangerous pistol at him. The hands that held it were shaking a lot, but not enough to miss from four feet and the dead eyes said he had nothing left to lose.

'Don't be an idiot, Micky. Think of your kids. If you kill me all that's going to happen is that the people who gave me this stuff are going to send it to the *Daily* fucking *Mail* and you're not only going to be in jail, but all over the front page labelled as Britain's last Nazi war criminal. Just put the fucking gun down, please. This is getting to be a bit of a habit and it's not good for my digestion.'

Micky shook his head. 'You don't understand. You could never understand. My father was a police sergeant in Riga. A big man. We had a good life until the day in nineteen forty the Soviets took over and the NKVD came and took him away. He had been denounced as a Nationalist by one of our Jewish neighbours. When the Germans threw the Russians out we found his body in a mass grave along with two hundred others. He'd had his head smashed in and we could only identify him because of his police uniform. When the Nazis started killing the Jews, I was glad.' He nodded slowly, as if he was speaking about someone else. 'Yes, I was glad. I volunteered to help guard them, but that was not enough. You must help with the dirty work. I discovered the Jew who denounced my father quite by accident. As soon as I saw him I knew what I must do. I didn't even notice the girl.'

There was a long silence, and Jamie noticed the gun

had stopped wavering and was aimed right over his heart. In the unlikely event he survived this, bullet-proof underwear was going to become part of his permanent wardrobe. He considered pleading for his life, but from the look in Micky's eyes that wasn't going to help.

'I go to Mass every day and say a prayer for those people, and all the rest, the ones whose faces will never leave me. I pray for their forgiveness and my salvation, but if God hears, He never responds. For sixty years I have had to live with what I have done. And now, this?' He shook his head and tears fell on the scattered papers. 'Now this.'

'Well, Micky, old boy, I'm afraid that's between you and your conscience. Now,' Jamie said carefully, 'if you are going to shoot me, it might as well be in the back as the front. So I'm just going to turn and walk out of that door. As I say, this is between you and your conscience, so if you let me walk out of here, you'll never hear from me again.'

Very slowly, he turned until his back was to the gun. He opened the office door as gently as if he was defusing an unexploded bomb and his spine cringed in anticipation of the bullet that was undoubtedly coming his way. It was almost with disbelief that he found himself in the gallery on the way to the front door. With a last glance at the Monet and a silent prayer of thanks, he reached for the door handle.

The sharp crack of the small-calibre pistol snapped the silence in two. For a moment he wondered if he'd been shot after all, but it was followed a second later by the clatter of the gun falling to the floor. His first instinct was to get out before he had to explain to the cops what he was doing here with a dead man. His hand actually touched the door handle before he changed his mind and walked back through to the office.

Micky Janelis was in his chair, his head thrown back and the pulse of blood from the little hole in his forehead weakening with every passing second. The hooded, unseeing eyes told their own story. Behind the dead man the wall was splashed red on white with a random modernist pattern that might have pleased Jackson Pollock, but would have mortally offended Micky. Fortunately, none of the splashes appeared to have reached the surface of the desk. With one hand Jamie scooped up the incriminating documents and crushed them into his pocket.

'Goodbye, Micky,' he said. 'No hard feelings, old son.'

XXVI

'I don't know how I let you talk me into this.'

'Think of it as the Venice of the north. Just as wet, but not quite so warm.'

'It doesn't say anything about that in this guidebook.'

'Well, it wouldn't, I've just made it up, but Hamburg has many other attractions for the discerning American on her first tour of the European continent.'

'Surprise me,' she said with a yawn.

'It contains some beautiful architecture, though quite a bit of it is modern, because between them the Eighth Air Force and the RAF more or less wiped it off the map in nineteen forty-three.'

'Reminds me of London.'

'That was the Luftwaffe.'

'Touché. Carry on with the tour,' she ordered. 'We'll be landing soon.'

'It's where the Beatles were discovered in nineteen sixty-um-something.'

'I prefer classical.'

'Excellent.' Jamie brightened. 'Best place in Europe for theatres, opera and museums.'

'You're making that up, too.'

'Not the bit about the opera.'

'It's also the birthplace of Berndt Hartmann,' she pointed out. 'Formerly of the Waffen SS and bearer of the cursed Crown of Isis, and despite our close encounter with the heirs to Adolf Hitler in Berlin you are once again about to drag me kicking and screaming into the lion's den, dragon's lair or whatever metaphor best suits a social club filled with elderly former mass murderers. Can you be a former mass murderer? I guess not.'

'Why did you say cursed?'

She shrugged. 'Figure of speech, I guess. A lot of people who come into contact with it seem to end up dead. Why?'

'I took another look on the internet before we left and ended up on one of those conspiracy sites, the kind that say Hitler and Elvis are still alive and taking turns on Shergar. One of the things it said about Isis was that there was a passage in a tomb associated with her that said, and I quote, *May you be cursed by the gift of long life.*'

Danny felt a little shiver before she remembered something she'd meant to ask in the hurricane of activity that followed Jamie's decision to pursue the Hamburg link. 'Hey, you didn't say much when you came home from that meeting with the old guy?'

'No, I didn't.'

'How did he take it, the past coming back to haunt him after all those years?'

'Oh, as well as could be expected is probably the best way to put it.'

'Yeah?'

'Yeah.'

He closed his eyes as the plane began its descent.

When he'd left Micky's gallery the first thing he'd done was call David and explain what had happened. Unsurprisingly, the Mossad agent was more concerned about covering his tracks than the fate of the former SS man.

'You left nothing behind. None of the document-ation.'

'No, I thought it best for everyone that there was no link to his past.'

'Good, it could have been awkward with the original owners of the information.'

'He was an old man, better his family never knew.'

'He was a mass murderer, Mr Saintclair, who took part in the killings of at least twenty-five thousand Jewish men, women and children. Don't feel any sympathy for Micky Janelis. If there was any justice he would have been dangling at the end of a rope fifty years ago. Every breath he took since was an affront to God and humanity. Now, what I would like you to do is to place the papers and the photograph in an envelope and send them to an address I will give you. Please do not be tempted to copy them. That would be very unwise.'

'I don't want anything to do with them ever again,' Jamie assured him. 'There is one thing I'd like in return, however.'

'Your persistence is becoming a little irritating, Mr Saintclair. Don't, as you say, push your luck.'

'The telephone number Micky gave me is for someone in Hamburg. It would be helpful to have some background on the city and the . . . political situation there.'

'By political situation I assume you mean how great is the current influence of the SS?'

'That's correct.'

'I will call you back in fifteen minutes. In the meantime, get as far away from the gallery as possible.'

Jamie was sitting in a coffee shop when the call came.

'You are alone?'

'Of course.' *But why would you ask that?* he thought. 'Do you have anything for me?'

'After the war and the Nuremberg trials it was opportune for the SS leadership to lay low, but by the early nineteen fifties, and with Germany in political turmoil, the leadership began to flex their muscles again. In nineteen fifty-three, senior members of HIAG – *Hilfsgemeinschaft auf Gegenseitigkeit* – a self-help organization set up by SS veterans, met in a Hamburg restaurant called the Ferry House. They were there to be courted by a local politician called Rolf Schmidt. Does the name mean anything to you?'

'There was a Rolf Schmidt who became Chancellor of Germany.'

'Precisely. Herr Schmidt was looking for votes and the SS were still a powerful enough force that he felt that they could guarantee them. Not long after that, Konrad Adenauer, who was then Chancellor, met with former SS-Brigadeführer Kurt Meyer – you may know him better as Panzer Meyer – a man found guilty at Nuremberg of being responsible for the shooting of twenty-three Canadian prisoners of war. Meyer was a senior official of HIAG and had huge influence over its membership and was one of those responsible for having SS pensions restored to parity with those of the Wehrmacht.'

'So the SS is still a power in Hamburg?'

He heard the shrug in David's voice. 'Times change. Men get old and they forget. HIAG was still a power in the sixties and seventies, the veterans formed social clubs and held parades, but in the eighties the tide turned against them. A new generation of Germans looked back and saw the SS for what they were: not heroes, but murderers who had prolonged a murderous regime. Officially, the organization disbanded in nineteen ninety-two.'

'Officially?'

'In reality, they went underground. The social clubs

changed their names. The rallies were held in secret locations by those who remained. Despise them if you will, but do not underestimate them. They are old. They are not the men they were. But they are still dangerous.'

'What about the number?'

'A gentlemen's drinking club in the heart of one of the city's less salubrious areas. I leave it to you to guess what kind of gentlemen. I truly wish you luck, Mr Saintclair.'

'Venice, huh?'

Jamie pulled his coat tighter round him and brushed off another ageless hooker offering the delights of a threesome at a local hotel for 100 euros, all in, as it were. Balls of sleet slanted through the street lights and turned the roadway between the nightclubs offering nude table dancing and the gaudily lit sex shops into a neon rainbow. Shivering prostitutes lined the route and men with greedy eyes and sharp-suited minders looked out from alleyways like conger eels waiting for their prey to come close enough. The Reeperbahn is Hamburg's best known red-light area, but the city has plenty of other streets where you can get anything for any price. Steindamm was one of them.

'Maybe you should have stayed in the hotel.'

'What, and missed all this fun?'

She was grinning at him and he grinned back.

'Hey you, pretty lady looks like Sigourney Weaver. You wanna get high? Teddy got just what you want.'

The speaker was a slim young man in a Guns N' Roses T-shirt with a knowing smile and a handful of powder-filled sachets on open display. Danny Fisher didn't even break stride. 'Fuck off, or I'll break your fucking arm.' His boy spread his arms and shrugged. His smile didn't falter and he walked on, looking for his next potential customer.

'Where are we supposed to meet this guy?'

'There's a bar called the Pussy Katt. We stand outside and someone will be there to give us directions.'

'Are you kidding? I thought we had directions?'

Jamie shrugged. 'This is the way he wants to play it.'

They walked on up the street, scanning the garish signs for the Pussy Katt. Without warning, Jamie found himself confronted by a heavily made-up girl with straight dark hair who flashed her long fur coat open to show she had very little on beneath it. 'You like what you see? You and the lady. Two hours, three hundred dollars. Or I can bring a friend, boy, girl, your choice.'

Danny Fisher snarled a warning and Jamie raised his hands in what he considered a non-threatening gesture of dismissal, but the girl stepped between them and rubbed herself up against him, her teeth nibbling his ear. 'Athena sent me.' He froze as he heard the name. 'They are following you, be careful. I will try to stall them.' She stepped back and he realized the make-up disguised the shadow of a face he had last seen by the side of the River Spree. And something else, too, that he hadn't been aware of. A resemblance to the woman who could be her mother.

Before he could respond, she laughed in his face. 'Fuck off, man,' she said incredulously. 'For that price you wouldn't get to screw one of the dogs down by the docks.'

Danny Fisher had been about to step between them, but she hesitated and the girl walked quickly away. Jamie took her by the arm and pulled her into the nearest doorway for what, to all appearances, was a passionate clinch.

'What the fuck is going on, Saintclair? That girl—'

'She's one of the Sisterhood,' Jamie whispered. 'I think it was one of the girls from the Reichstag. There was something familiar about her. I think she may even be Athena's daughter. Don't look round, but Frederick's here somewhere.'

He felt her freeze.

'What do we do now?'

'We have to lose them and find the Pussy Katt fast. She said she'd try to stall them.' They heard a commotion twenty yards further back. Loud male and female voices arguing in German, before the female's rose to an outraged shriek. 'And it looks like she's succeeding. Come on.'

The sign above the Pussy Katt was a life-size cartoon of Catwoman complete with whip, breasts of enormous proportions and long legs in thigh-length boots.

Jamie looked around desperately for their contact.

'Classy joint,' Fisher muttered. 'If we stand here long enough I could make a few bucks. Aw, shit.'

The source of her irritation was the boy with the broad smile and the drugs. He walked up to them, but when he spoke he wasn't selling and his voice didn't match the smile. 'You were told to come alone, just the two of you. What's with the company?'

Jamie closed his eyes. For Christ's sake, how many people were following them? It was like the Lord Mayor's parade. 'If we have any company, it's not because they were invited.'

The dark eyes searched the street around them. 'You people ... Okay, this is how it happens, yes?'

'We're listening.'

'You go up to the bar and there's two doors to the left. You take the first. You walk straight through and down the corridor until you get to another door that leads onto an alley. Go down the alley, turn left at the bottom, then first right. Left at the bottom and then first right. Don't stop for anything. You got that, English?'

'I've got that.'

'What then?' Danny Fisher demanded.

'Someone will pick you up.'

'This is bullshit.'

Teddy sneered. 'You wanna walk away, be my guest.'

'Come on.' Jamie made the decision for them. They walked into the bar where a few single, middle-aged men watched a bored-looking naked girl dancing round a pole on a dais. No one moved as they entered and only the girl's eyes flicked in their direction, meeting Danny Fisher's with a look of sisterly resignation. Jamie took the first door, which led to a urine-scented corridor and then out onto a poorly lit alley. The occasional over-bright window opened up contrasting scenes of family life or drug-induced squalor and the smell of cooking food fought with the nauseous odour of a long-blocked drain. Above them, the overhanging trees cast eerie shadows, and every shadow contained a threat. They hurried over the rough cobbles, avoiding the anonymous patches of darkness.

When they reached an intersection in the labyrinth, Danny stopped. 'Left here,' she said. 'Have I asked you this before, Saintclair: how the fuck did I get into this?'

He tried to think of something reassuring to say and failed. 'It could be worse.'

A bitter little laugh gave him his answer. After another fifty yards a narrow passage, barely wide enough to take two people, opened up to their right.

'This can't be it,' Fisher groaned.

'The man said first right.'

'I'm not—' As Jamie made for the entrance a long scream of pure agony echoed through the narrow streets.

'Where did it come from?'

'Somewhere up ahead.'

'Let's go, Danny. We haven't time for this. He said not to stop for anything.'

But she took his arm and when he saw the look in her eyes, he knew there was no walking away.

'I'm a cop, Jamie. This is what cops do.'

They broke into a run until, in the distance, they could see two figures struggling against a wall. Jamie cursed, certain that they were interrupting two people having sex. Then he saw the arm draw back and punch again and again into the other body. 'Hey!' At the shout, the attacker made one last savage lunge and ran off up the alley, disappearing round the nearest corner.

By the time they reached the scene, the victim of the assault lay writhing in the shadow, each breath a desperate razor-edged sob. Danny knelt over the twisted figure and instantly recoiled with her hand over her mouth. 'Oh, Jesus.'

Slowly, Jamie's eyes adjusted to the deeper gloom. She had dark hair and might once have been beautiful, but it was difficult to tell, because her face had been horribly carved open by a dozen knife strokes. The thick fur coat still covered her body, but the spreading pool of darkness on the cobbles told a story of other unseen wounds. It was the girl from the street. Athena's daughter. Wide, liquid eyes mirrored the horror of what had been done to her. She tried to speak but even as they watched she gave a shudder and a fountain of blood spilled from her torn mouth. Desperately, Danny knelt beside her and spoke into her ear. 'Your sisters and The Lady will meet you on the other side.' Did she imagine it, or did the dark eyes lose their fear before they faded into sightlessness?

Jamie bowed his head over the dead girl, but he became instantly alert at the sound of running feet from the direction the attacker had disappeared. He stood in front of Danny, but she moved to his side.

'You go high, I'll go low,' she muttered.

A silhouetted figure careered into sight and when it registered the two shadows ahead, a hand swooped to its waist and Jamie saw the bright flash of a blade.

'High,' Fisher reminded him. But Jamie had already recognized the distinctive T-shirt.

'Did you do this?' he demanded as the young drug dealer walked into sight.

Teddy looked wild-eyed at the murdered Sister of Isis and shook his head wordlessly. 'Quick,' he said, 'this way.'

Danny hesitated, but Jamie pulled her away from the body. 'There's nothing we can do for her now.'

Teddy led them back to the narrow passage and into a maze of alleyways that twisted and turned so much that within minutes Jamie had no idea what direction they were moving in. As they ran, Danny's hand groped for his and he squeezed it, trying to give her the reassurance she was seeking.

'Why did you say that to her?' Even as he asked it, he knew the question should have been more nuanced. What he really wanted to know was how she had *known* what to say.

'A hunch.' She shrugged, but her voice said it was something much more powerful. 'It just seemed right.'

As they ran, he kept darting glances over his shoulder. It seemed unlikely anyone would be able to follow them in this warren, but he was out of his depth and he knew it. Even Danny Fisher had more idea what they were doing than he did. Somehow, the Sisterhood had found a way to follow them, ready to give what help they could in the search for the Crown. But even they had no answer to the sinister force that had stalked them in their turn, a force so ruthless it had cut down their representative without a second thought and with a savagery that was clearly intended to send a message. The girl had said 'They' were following, and he had automatically assumed it must be Frederick and the Vril. But how had Frederick found them? It could just as easily have been whoever had hunted down and butchered the men who had been sent from America to kill him. The ruthlessness was all too evident, but there was a pattern to his killings that just didn't fit here. And there was a third possibility: what if the Sisters of Isis had enemies of their own? A secret society would always inspire fear of the secrets they kept, and a society that had survived for two thousand years would have no shortage of secrets. He had so many questions and no answers and he had a feeling things weren't going to improve any time soon.

It seemed the alleys could get no narrower when Teddy turned into a gap between two buildings that would only allow them through in single file. At the rear of the larger of the buildings, a metal stair climbed to an anonymous doorway on the first floor.

Their guide's eyes shone in the darkness.

'We are here.'

XXVII

Beneath the first light of the sickle moon.

Paul Dornberger frowned and checked his calculations, though he knew the answer well enough. The old man's time was running out.

He tried to remember the first occasion his father had mentioned the children, but his mind was blank. Had it been in the cellar? He could never truly know that, because the visions of what had happened there were never complete. They arrived like star-shells over a battlefield; a burst of light, a moment of stark illumination, a fleeting shadow, then back into the darkness. But they always left that lingering doubt. Had he truly seen what he thought he had seen? Done what he feared he had done? It struck him that there was some memory that even a mind saturated with so much blood had to repress for fear of the consequences it would bring. He felt a surge of an unfamiliar emotion that brought with it a shudder. The realization came as a shock. It was *there*, somewhere inside this kaleidoscope that was his head, but Paul Dornberger didn't dare to access it. Beyond a hidden door in his tortured mind was the secret that made him who he was. But he was too *frightened* to look for it.

Oleg Samsonov appeared in the doorway.

'Are you all right, Paul?'

Dornberger forced a smile. 'Of course, sir. By the way, I have these papers for you to sign.'

'Fine, but come upstairs.' Samsonov gave an embarrassed grin. 'I've left my reading glasses in the big lounge.' Dornberger smiled back. His employer was notoriously shy of admitting any deficiency. It was a measure of his growing trust that he revealed even this minor physical fault. Paul followed the other man up the spiral staircase to a room that took up two-thirds of the second floor of the building. Above this were the family bedrooms and dressing rooms and the state-of-the-art gym, and above that a helicopter pad hidden behind blast-proof walls. The space, it was more than a room, was enormous, a vast floor of the finest Finnish ash hardwood, scattered with oriental carpets from Isfahan and Tabriz, each of which would have paid Paul Dornberger's annual salary twice over. In one corner hung the largest and most expensive flat-screen television that money could buy. In another, a Swedish sound system that had cost as much as one of Oleg's Ferraris. The space had been designed somehow to produce separate acoustic zones, so that Oleg could be listening to music at the same time as Dmitri watched cartoons and his film-star wife Irina was entertaining her friends by the enormous picture window that looked over the park. Marble busts from Rome and Greece jostled with modern sculptures on strategically placed pedestals. And in the centre, its exterior hung with fine art worth millions, the panic room.

'You're putting in a lot of extra hours lately on these merger deals.'

'Maybe you should give him some time off?' Irina Samsonov kissed Paul on both cheeks, while Dmitri pawed at his hand with a shy smile. Oleg picked up his son and hugged him.

'I don't think Paul has any of those treats he doesn't believe I know about. Maybe later, Dimi. Ah,' he sighed, 'here they are. If there is one thing I detest it is getting older, but even money cannot buy you youth.'

Irina kissed her husband on the lips in a show of genuine affection. There was nothing artificial about Oleg Samsonov's wife, neither the love she showed her family nor the beauty that seemed to light up any room she entered. 'No, but it could buy you laser surgery, if you weren't so frightened.'

Oleg shook his head ruefully. 'No man, certainly no Russian, goes into hospital unless he needs to.'

He signed the documents, reading each one with care before putting his pen to it.

'You should let Paul see your new acquisition,' Irina suggested. 'After all, he's almost one of the family. He bought it while you were in New York. How did that go, Paul?'

Dornberger smiled. He had a momentary vision of terrified faces and the particular salt-sweet scent of burning flesh. 'I think we'll see the fruits of it before too long.'

Oleg glanced at the panic-room door and frowned. 'No, we have things to talk about. Perhaps another time.' Paul nodded and bit back his disappointment. If Irina was excited about whatever was in the panic room, it must be something special.

They walked back downstairs and Oleg went to his office, leaving Paul to deal with the papers. Dornberger's mind drifted back to his earlier inner conflict. The Crown and the knife. The ever-presents in his life. It was still difficult to believe that what he had learned in the past few months was true. Yet how else could his father be explained? How else could he be explained. His father's creation. Always the outsider. Never loved. Never treated as a child should be. His life had revolved around the Crown and the knife and Hartmann. A small bleep from his computer alerted him to a message in his super-encrypted e-mail basket. He opened it and read. It was a complex message with a number of attached documents and it took time before he understood its true meaning. The contents took his breath away. One step. Just one more step and he had him.

XXVIII

A shaven-headed teenager dressed in a dark bomber jacket and black jeans met them at the top of the stairs.

'Friends,' Teddy assured him.

'Sure,' the boy grunted. 'But friends still gotta be given the once-over. Orders.'

Teddy shrugged and ushered Jamie forward. The hands that ran over his body were surprisingly gentle, but thorough – whoever taught the boy knew what they were doing.

'Tell him if he tries that with me I'll tear his freekin' head off.' Danny stood with her arms folded.

Jamie translated. The boy shrugged and produced his best high-school English.

'You don't get searched, you don't come in. Suit yourself.'

'You can wait outside,' Jamie suggested.

'Sure, when hell freezes over. You put one hand in the wrong place, mister, and your girlfriend will be the one who's crying.' She submitted to the search with a glare that would have lowered the temperature considerably in Satan's realm, and they were ushered through the metal-studded wooden door.

Inside, a short bar dominated one corner; worn leather benches lined the walls, providing seating for a few scattered tables, at one of which three old men in shirtsleeves sat playing cards and muttering while a fourth watched. The cards were slapped down in quick succession followed by a triumphant cackle from the victor as he picked up the winning hand.

Teddy nodded to a door at the rear of the club. Jamie and Danny exchanged glances. They'd already decided that Jamie would do the talking and that they had no option but to trust their hosts. Jamie followed Teddy while Danny went to sit in the corner near the card players.

Behind the door, an office. Bare, nicotine-stained walls with flaking paint, three olive-green filing cabinets, a large ornate safe that might have been looted from a Hungarian bank, and a wide desk with a scarred red-leather top and a desk lamp that gave the room its only illumination. In an ashtray beside the lamp a cigar smouldered, the smoke spiralling in uninhibited tendrils through the rays of the lightbulb. At the desk, a silver-haired patrician – in another setting, Jamie thought, he would have been a count or a prince – sat mountainous and solid, despite his obvious great age. Even now it was possible to see the ghost of the laughing eyes and matinee-idol looks that must have had the girls chasing after him in the grey uniform with the silver lightning flashes on the collar. The man looked up and sent a message with his eyes. Teddy turned to go.

'Wait,' Jamie said. 'A girl was killed on the way here. She was stabbed. He had a knife.'

Again the slightest flicker and Teddy was at the old man's side, whispering into his ear, then sliding past Jamie to stand behind him. Not a threat, exactly, but . . .

'He says he knows nothing about the girl. You were being followed. Two men. Maybe they were there to protect you – from us?'

Jamie shook his head. 'No. You said to come alone. We came alone.' At the same time an image of David's face appeared. Who knew how the Israelis worked? It was possible, but if it had been Mossad, Jamie doubted even streetwise Teddy would have spotted them.

'You lost them when you came through the bar, but he went back to check. Found only one. That's when he came to you. The first time he saw the girl she was already dead. Then he brought you here. Does that satisfy you?'

It didn't seem to matter whether it did or not. He knew it was all he was going to get. He nodded and there was a slight click as Teddy closed the door behind him. Once they were alone, the other man allowed the silence to lengthen and Jamie felt the ice-blue eyes searching his soul.

'Where do you think you are?' It seemed an unlikely question, but appeared to demand an answer.

'I'm in a gentlemen's drinking club in Hamburg.'

The leonine head shook slowly.

'No, you misunderstand your situation.' He picked up the cigar and pointed it at the door. 'You and your lady friend are one step from the tomb. You think you can just walk into our world and walk out again? That's not how it works. If I believe what you say, maybe you do. I don't believe what you say: two bodies are floating in the docks. A blow to Hamburg's tourist trade, but what the hell, there are plenty more tourists.' He smiled at his joke, but it was an undertaker's smile. 'Who killed Micky Janelis?'

The room seemed to grow twenty degrees colder and Jamie was surprised he was able to keep his voice steady. 'Micky killed himself.'

'And how would you know that?'

'Because I was there when he did it.'

The head came up. 'Why would Micky do a thing like that? Micky was a happy-go-lucky kind of guy. Everybody liked Micky.'

Jamie hesitated. With some people you could get away with a lie or a diversion, but not with this man. 'Maybe he thought someone was going to tell the world the truth about his past.'

'You?'

He nodded.

'You'd have done that to Micky?'

'No.' He shook his head. 'Micky was my friend.'

'Maybe Micky should have chosen his friends more carefully?'

'Maybe.' It took all Jamie's nerve to hold the blue eyes. 'But sometimes there comes a point when you even have to sacrifice your friends. I thought a man who's done what you've done would understand that?'

For the first time he noticed there was a clock somewhere in the room. He could hear a laboured ticking somewhere in the background. Eventually, the other man reached below the desk and opened a drawer. Jamie held his breath for what came next. And what came next was a bottle filled with a clear liquid and two glasses which he filled to the rim. He pushed one towards Jamie and raised the other in salute.

'To Micky.'

'To Micky,' Jamie poured the rough liquor down his throat, blinking as it exploded in his stomach and set his body on fire.

From somewhere a picture magically appeared on the desk as the glasses were refilled. 'Me and Micky, Kharhov, 'forty-three, when his *kompany* was seconded from the Leningrad front. I was eighteen when that was taken, and with the *Leibstandarte*.' He grinned. 'Hitler's bodyguard. The best. Let me tell you about Micky. Micky hated the Reds more than any man on this earth. Sure, we sometimes killed prisoners. They sometimes killed prisoners. So what? It was war. They'll tell you that the Eastern Front was a nightmare. Hell on earth.

No. The Eastern Front was a soldier's paradise. Every man knew that if he was captured, he was dead. So you fought until your last bullet; and when that was gone, you fought with your entrenching tool, then your knife and finally with your teeth and your bare hands.' He lifted his hands so Jamie could see them. Strong workman's hands that looked as if they should still bear the bloodstains of half a century earlier. 'We were the walking dead, and that made us the gods of the battlefield. Micky wasn't real SS, not Waffen SS anyway, but I liked Micky. Problem was, he *enjoyed* killing prisoners. One day after we recaptured Kharkov I saw him pop twenty in a row and he never stopped smiling. Maybe they were commissars, maybe they weren't. Twenty men and women kneeling in front of him. Pop. Pop. Pop.' He pointed a finger and pulled the imaginary trigger in imitation of a hand gun. Jamie tried to square the image of Micky's perpetual grin with the penitent Micky had claimed to be, praying for the souls of his victims, and failed. 'I heard the Latvian Legion was wiped out in Courland, so I never expected to see Micky again. Then one day in the fifties he turns up in Hamburg. I'd got lucky; shrapnel in the leg fighting with the Hitler Jugend at Caen. Fortunately, the Canucks didn't shoot the wounded, although they shot just about everybody else. By the time Micky knocks on my door, I'm in business for myself and working with HIAG helping out the old *kameraden* who weren't so lucky. He needs help, he says, he's back fighting the Reds, but this time with the

CIA. I laughed, because the CIA was a big joke back then, but he was serious. They wanted to run agents into Latvia from Hamburg; Micky had convinced them he could put together the organization to make it happen. We have the people, we have the expertise – everybody in Hamburg knows someone who has a boat. So for about three years the SS is working with the Americans against the Soviets, and getting well paid for it. In maybe 'fifty-four, Micky's star is fading and the Yanks work out that everybody they're sending into Latvia is being snapped up soon as their feet hit the beach. The work dries up, but Micky is still smiling. He's always been interested in art, he says one night when we're having a drink at the Ferry House to wind up the operation. "I'm going to start an art gallery; would you know anyone who has any art to sell?" Now, Micky, he knows what happened in the war, in France and Italy and the Netherlands, when everybody was putting away their nest egg for the future. You were a trooper, you stuck a gold candlestick down your boot. You were a general, you filled a convoy of trucks with everything you could lay your hands on: paintings, sculptures, gold and silver bullion. Some of it was destroyed, some recovered by the Allies, but a lot of it was still around in attics and bank vaults and nobody had any idea what to do with it. "Give me a little at a time," Micky says, "just the small stuff, no Old Masters, I'll sell it for you at best price and take a commission." So that's how Micky started in business, and we've been in business ever since. I miss Micky.'

He dipped into the drawer again and came out with a pistol that Jamie recognized as a Walther P-38, oiled and gleaming and dangerous. He laid it on the desk in front of him and spun it until it came to rest with the barrel pointing directly at Jamie.

'Why did you come here?'

Jamie pulled a sheet of paper from his pocket and laid it on the desk beside the gun.

'I'm trying to find out what happened to this man. It could save his life.'

The other man read it, sucking his teeth, and shaking his head. Eventually, he shrugged.

'Maybe I can do something, maybe I can't. It was a long time ago. Plenty of people disappeared because they wanted to and for good reason.' He laid the paper back beside the gun. 'Come back in two days and I'll have an answer for you.'

He poured himself another drink and Jamie left him staring at the picture; an old man forever imprisoned by his youth.

Back in the club, Danny was dealing cards to the old soldiers. One of them looked up with a grin.

'For God's sake take her away. She's raping us.'

XXIX

Dancing flurries of snow drifted through the smoke and sparks to melt in the flames from the burning building.

'Are you sure this is it?'

Jamie couldn't drag his eyes away from what had been the SS drinking den.

'Yes, I'm sure.'

They stood on the edge of a big crowd that had crammed into the alley to watch the fun from behind a police barrier about fifty metres away. Firemen appeared with a hose and began to spray the roof and windows, but it was already much too late. The flames had eaten away at the roof joints and super-heated slates exploded in batches, cascading in shards onto the street. A few minutes later the roof collapsed into the building below with an audible 'whump', sending a new eruption of flame and spark high into the Hamburg sky.

'What are we going to do now?'

It was a question Jamie had been asking himself, but, fortunately or otherwise, it had answered itself. Or that was the message he was getting from the gun barrel being screwed painfully into his armpit.

'Come with me.' He half turned, but the boy who had frisked them jammed the pistol all the harder. 'I said come with me, that doesn't mean anything else.'

Danny was close enough to understand what was happening. Jamie saw her tense, but he shook his head. Whatever went down, the only way they were going to find out was to play this hand as it fell. Downstairs this time, to a basement bar where the SS patriarch sat behind a table with four other men. The white mane lifted and his pale eyes fixed the newcomers.

'This is your doing?'

The boy was still somewhere behind them and there had been another man in the shadows through a beaded curtain that led only who knew where. This time Jamie understood for certain that if he said the wrong thing they would never leave the bar alive.

He shook his head. 'I think it might be the people who are also looking for Hartmann. Men who want to see him dead. They must have tracked us to you somehow.'

The mouth set like a steel trap and he watched the calculations working through the old soldier's mind. This wasn't the first time this man had pondered the life and death of a fellow human being. Jamie just hoped he'd made it a bit more difficult. The expression didn't change, but at some point a decision was made.

'You find out who these people are, you tell us and we deal with it.' It was an order, not a suggestion. A moment's hesitation and an envelope passed across the table.

'Maybe he will, maybe he won't and maybe he'll kill you.'

'Zurich?'

'It looks like the address of some kind of lawyer's office. Forchstrasse.'

He recognized the look.

'It's just another step. A link in the chain. But if we don't go we'll never know.'

'Okay, but my time is running out, Jamie. I can't afford to go running around Europe on a wild-goose chase.'

Jamie stared at her. It wasn't what he wanted, but he had to make the offer. 'Maybe it would be more sensible if I went alone?'

She thought about it and shook her head. 'No. Not yet. One more step, and then maybe . . . but not yet. I'll book the flights.'

'Better if we get the hotel to organize a hire car,' he suggested.

'Are you nuts? It must be what . . . five hundred miles from here to Switzerland. Maybe six. Two hours on the plane, a full day by car. Two if we get lost up the wrong Alp.'

He went to the window and studied the streets and canals below. 'The people who killed that girl and burned down the club are still out there. If we take the plane they can put someone on it, or have someone waiting at the other end. Driving will take longer, but if it's six hundred miles, that's six hundred miles of road we can use to lose them. We don't have to put a destination on the form, all we need to say is that we're touring Germany.'

Two hours later they headed south, with Jamie at the wheel of the hired Audi. He deliberately kept his speed erratic, driving so leisurely that it brought intimidating blasts of the horn from the lorry drivers who were their fellow users of the slow lane, then pushing the accelerator to the floor so the German countryside flashed past in a blur. Danny searched the road for cars trying to match their speed.

'Anything?'

She shook her head. 'But that doesn't mean they're not there. If they're pros there could be as many as four or five chase cars, switching positions to make sure we don't get a make on 'em.'

Just to be certain, they left the autobahn after Frankfurt and they spent twenty minutes on country roads until they found a *gasthaüs* where they stopped for a beer and sausage.

'So what happens when we get to Zurich?' she asked while they were eating.

'We make contact. We tell . . .' he picked up the sheet

of paper the former SS man had given them. '. . . Herr Kohler a story – not the true story, of course, much too outlandish, but something suitably urgent – a relative who must know if Hartmann is still alive. A legacy, maybe.'

'You think a lawyer is going to buy that? A Swiss lawyer?'

He ignored the snort of incredulity that accompanied the words. 'Maybe the simple mention of Hartmann's name is all it will take? There's no point in making assumptions.'

They'd been on the road for nine hours when they entered Switzerland north of Basel and crossed the Rhine, turning east to follow the line of the Swiss-German border, then south through the gently sloping wooded hills of Aargau. They passed small, immaculately maintained towns that made Jamie wonder if there was a law against allowing your paint to peel or your grass to grow in Switzerland, but the closer they got to Zurich the more urbanized the landscape became. The road crossed and re-crossed the same river several times before entering the city proper. Jamie was tired, but he was relaxed and confident that no single follower could have stayed with them without being spotted. What neither he nor Danny knew was that the surveillance team that had been tracking the hired Audi since Hamburg consisted of a fleet of four anonymous German saloons with a Mercedes SUV as command car. In the mid-town traffic they had the Audi bracketed. The man in the Mercedes calculated he could have made the hit at any one of five places – kill or capture – but he had his orders.

'I think we should be on the other side,' Danny pointed out helpfully.

Jamie grunted and tried to navigate his way round another fiendishly complicated system of one-way streets, avoiding trams and buses that seemed to have priority over everything else. 'You don't say.'

Eventually, they found a way to cross, and, after a twenty-minute detour, worked their way back into the city centre and a hotel close to the eastern shore of Lake Zurich in a district of broad streets, parks and beautiful old houses. Jamie had an impression of a city that was predominantly old, pretty and sprawling, where people minded their own business and would rather other people didn't have cars. Unfortunately, it was too late to find out whether he was right, so they settled for a beer in the hotel bar before they retired to their room. They showered, made the slow, slightly distracted love of people with other things on their minds and slept, Danny dreaming of chase cars she might have missed and Jamie with the feeling that his life had gone wrong somewhere and he wasn't certain how to get it back to where it belonged.

In the morning he telephoned to make an appointment with the lawyer.

* * *

'First you must know that we have no record of a client named Hartmann.'

Danny and Jamie exchanged glances of disappointment. 'Then it seems we have wasted our time and yours, Herr Kohler. I apologize for the inconvenience.'

They made to get up from their seats, but the lawyer, who spoke perfect, if rigidly formal, English, raised a hand.

'Please, I am not quite finished. Although we have no Hartmann on our files I did receive a telephone call yesterday afternoon, warning me that a Herr Saintclair was likely to pay this office a visit.'

'May one ask the source of this call?'

'One may not. But the purpose of the call was to issue certain instructions in the event of such a visit. These instructions brought into action a long-established procedure, which to my knowledge has never been required before.' He handed over a white envelope. 'You should know that I am not aware of the contents of this envelope. Neither do I wish to be.'

'Isn't that a little odd?' Danny asked.

The Swiss gave a thin smile. 'I am merely a conduit, Fräulein Fisher, a transmitter of information, untouched and unaffected by what passes through my hands. I can assure you, in Switzerland this is a most normal situation.' He pointed to a painting of a disapproving, stiff-necked man in a wing collar. 'My grandfather, who founded this firm, would have insisted it was so.'

A secretary ushered them out of the office on to

Forchstrasse, a long, wide street that split Zurich's Eighth District. Jamie tapped the envelope against his palm.

'Well,' Danny said, her voice mirroring the frustration on her face. 'You were right. Another link in the chain, but a goddam daisy chain that just goes round in circles. *I am merely a conduit, Fräulein Fisher,*' she perfectly mimicked the lawyer's stiff, grammatical English, '*a transmitter of information.* Jesus, I wanted to take him by his scrawny neck and shake him.'

'Don't knock it until we've seen what's inside here,' Jamie insisted. 'He talked about a long-established procedure that's never been used before. How long? Kohler's law firm has been around for fifty or sixty years at least. Who's to say that old granddaddy Kohler didn't take the instructions from Hartmann himself?'

'The only way to find out is to open the letter, so get on with it.'

Jamie studied the street around them. If someone knew they were going to be here, that someone was likely to be watching. He took her by the arm and led her protesting into a side street, taking random rights and lefts. He made her wait until they were in a tree-lined park just off the street and she was simmering just below boiling point when he finally tore at the seal and removed a single sheet of paper.

'This doesn't make sense.'

'What doesn't make sense?'

He handed her the letter. 'Proceed to Facet Safes and Strongboxes, Forchstrasse 12, Zurich. Enter by the rear door and await further instructions.'

'Somebody's yanking our chain.' Danny studied the park around them, but the only people in view were a young couple playing with a small girl at the base of a tree, while an older boy climbed to a bench that had somehow been fixed to the branches. 'They're playing with us. Maybe we should just walk away.'

'I'd agree, apart from two things. The first is that this business is less than four hundred yards from here. The second is the name of the company.'

'What about it?'

'Facet has a couple of meanings. It can be a particular feature of something, but it's usually only used for one object in particular.'

'And what's that?'

'A diamond.'

As they left the park neither of them noticed the man who walked up to the front door of one of the houses overlooking the park. Or the fact that he took so long to find his key.

Facet Safes and Strongboxes occupied a large unit in a modern block of shops and flats where Forchstrasse met Kreuzplatz, a wide intersection crossed by tram lines. Four windows displayed an array of ultra-modern safes, alarms and other security equipment. The only lights were illuminating the merchandise and it looked closed for business.

Danny shook her head. 'I'll tell you one thing, Saintclair, if this has been around since the Second World War I'm Abe Lincoln. A little bell is ringing inside my head telling me to get the hell out of here. If you've brought that body armour of yours along, now would be the time to hand it over.'

Jamie ignored her complaints and they found an alleyway that led to a car park serving the residents of the triangular block of flats. Each ground-floor business had a small yard area for storage and deliveries, identified by a panel with the firm's name.

'Here it is.' Danny walked through the double doors that had been left open to reveal the inner courtyard. On the far side, set into the wall, was a wide goods entrance, with a fire door to one side. Slowly, she walked towards it and pushed. 'For a security company they sure have a strange way of keeping the bad guys out,' she muttered as it swung back noiselessly.

They looked at each other. Danny took a deep breath, but when she was about to step across the threshold, Jamie put a hand on her arm. 'I think in this case we'll make it gents first.'

'Be my guest, but don't go trying to be a hero. The first sign of trouble and we are outa here.'

'Couldn't agree more, Detective Fisher. You wouldn't happen to have a Glock 9 mm in that handbag, would you?'

'Just about everything else.' There was a smile in her voice. 'But no, I left my Glock in Brooklyn. Even a cop can't get away with carrying on a 747 jet these days.'

'In that case, "Once more into the breach".'

XXX

The interior of the shop consisted of a gloomy maze of enormous safes and stacks of smaller items like strongboxes, security TV systems and alarms. The only true light came from the spotlights in the front windows, which were mostly blocked by merchandise, and some source at the far end of the shop. A flashing red beam in a globe suspended from the ceiling indicated that someone was monitoring their progress, which was comforting, because it should mean that nobody was going to ambush them. Then again, that could be wishful thinking.

Gradually, they were drawn to the light, which came from what looked like a small and very basic office with a desk at its centre and an unfeasibly heavy door thrown back in welcome.

'Please come in,' invited a disjointed voice that was unmistakably American.

Jamie hesitated in the doorway and he almost had a

seizure when a hand dropped on his shoulder. He turned and looked into Danny Fisher's wild eyes. '*Trap!*' she whispered. His mouth felt as if it was filled with gravel, but he shook his head.

'You wanted to talk, so come in and talk,' the voice persisted.

He took Danny's hand in his and they walked side by side into the room.

'At last.' The tone was good-humoured, even playful. 'Now we can proceed. Please take a seat.'

Two chairs sat behind the desk and they took their places warily. Facing them, above the open doorway, was the lens of a security camera, and Jamie knew that whoever was doing the talking was also watching them on a monitor from somewhere nearby. The voice originated from a microphone set in the corner behind them, which gave him the odd feeling of being surrounded. That feeling was compounded when the metal door of the room silently swung closed with a gentle, but very final 'thud'. They frantically searched the room for an alternative exit, but it didn't take a genius to work out that Danny's prediction had been right and they were trapped.

'Now we have a little privacy,' the voice said.

'Shouldn't you be telling us not to be alarmed?' Jamie indicated the closed door.

'At the moment you will be admiring the interior of the XK-60 vault, our best-selling walk-in safe, complete with eight-inch Titanium-steel alloy walls, fully encrypted locking and guaranteed air tight. Is it a little stuffy in there?'

Jamie swallowed and felt a tightness in his chest. Just for a moment the walls seemed to be closing in. Claustrophobia had never been a problem in the past. He'd done the water-filled pipe thing on army assault courses and felt nothing more than mild discomfort. But then he'd always known that if anything happened the good guys were on hand to get him out. He'd never been stuck in an eight-foot steel box with every breath using up the available air.

Danny sat with her head back and her eyes closed and he wondered if it was despair, exasperation or the fact that she wanted to kill him for getting her into this mess. She opened one eye and confirmed the third theory. 'Did I ever tell you that I really don't like enclosed spaces?'

'You should have enough oxygen for about thirty minutes, give or take,' the voice assured her. 'I am going to allow you ten of those minutes to consider your situation, then we'll have our talk.'

'We came here to talk about Hartmann.' Jamie's voice echoed round the chamber's metal walls, but the only answer was a low hiss of static. Fisher pushed the desk away with a wooden screech and gave the door an ineffectual kick.

'Okay, Sherlock, what the fuck do we do now?'

'We wait. Maybe he's bluffing?'

'That's it?' She didn't bother to hide her incredulity.

'We're not dead yet.' He stared up at the camera, trying to figure out who was watching them and hoping he lived long enough to beat the living shit out of him.

The atmosphere inside the safe was already stuffy. Soon the sweat made their clothing stick to their bodies and the air seemed to be thicker and more difficult to breathe. Jamie knew that was only an illusion caused by his own fear, but knowing didn't seem to help a lot. Danny had taken up a position with her back against one wall and her long legs folded in front of her.

'We're here because they want something, huh?'

He nodded. 'If they wanted to kill us they could have done it in Hamburg. I don't think this is about the SS and the past any more. It's about now. By contacting the jovial Herr Kohler we knocked on a door and gave someone palpitations. Now they have to make up their mind whether to open it and let us step through or . . .' He shrugged.

Danny uncoiled herself and got to her feet. She took his hand and drew him to a point as far from the microphone and the camera as possible. 'So what can we tell them that will keep us alive?' she whispered.

'Hartmann is the key. If this is about Hartmann,' he replied in the same vein, 'whoever is out there is going to want to know why the past has suddenly come back to haunt them. They'll want to know how we got here and who else knows we're here.'

'So we tell him about the Crown of Isis?'

'Unless we think the Crown is the reason he's been

hiding all these years. If it is, the very fact we know about it could give him a reason for letting us rot in here. Ouch!' He touched his ear where she'd bitten it.

'I was looking for something a little more positive.'

'The only way we can play this is one card at a time. If he doesn't have a reason for keeping us alive, we have to give him one. Maybe that's the Crown of Isis, maybe it's not. The Crown is the joker in the pack, but only he knows whether it's the high card or the low. The one thing I'm certain of is that we can't play it too early. Am I making sense?'

'As much as you ever do.'

Another few minutes passed and the air around them became noticeably staler.

'I see you made good use of your time.' Jamie searched for some emotion or evidence of compassion in the voice, but found none. 'Twenty minutes left. Time enough for a game of twenty questions. Well, perhaps not twenty, but enough questions to give you an opportunity to convince me that you have a value. First the obvious: why did you come here?'

Jamie exchanged glances with Danny and she nodded.

'We're looking for information about a man called Berndt Hartmann.'

'A good start, which confirms what I already know. May I ask what makes Hartmann so interesting?'

This time it was Danny who answered. She related

the story of the murders in New York and London and the link back to the SS man.

'Yes, I can see why you'd wish to confirm the connection, but not why you would want to pursue this man Hartmann, who, after all, is much more likely to be dead than alive?'

Danny's head came up. 'Why would you say that?' She hadn't mentioned the details of Hartmann's career in *Geistjaeger 88* or the circumstances of his disappearance in Berlin. 'Berndt Hartmann would be in his eighties now, along with many people who survived the war.'

'Under the circumstances you'll forgive me for insisting that it's I who ask the questions, Detective. I repeat, why would you wish to pursue Berndt Hartmann?' The question was followed by a long, dangerous pause, filled only with the sound of strained breathing. 'Don't take too long. Time – and air – is in short supply.'

'Because . . . if he's alive he should be warned.' Danny felt as if she was walking on quicksand. 'The name Hartmann was not the only thing that linked the murder victims to this man.'

Again, the long pause, as if the man behind the microphone wasn't certain he wanted to know the answer. Eventually, he decided he did: 'And this other thing is?'

'An Egyptian symbol.'

'Go on.'

'One of the murder victims had the Eye of Isis carved into her forehead.'

There was a thump from the microphone: the sound it would make if it had been knocked over. When it spoke again the voice was almost accusing. 'And what makes you think this Eye of Isis is in any way connected with the man Hartmann?'

'I think you already know the answer to that question, sir,' Danny said softly.

She waited for the angry rebuttal. What she didn't expect was the drawn-out sigh they heard.

'You should not have come here. I am truly sorry.'

The utter finality of the words froze whatever Danny was going to say on her lips. Jamie knew he only had seconds before the camera and the microphone were switched off and they were left to suffocate.

'Tell him Max Dornberger says hello.'

XXXI

Jamie and Danny were lying on the safe floor gasping at the last of the oxygen when the door swung open to allow in a rush of cool air that was as reviving as champagne. They looked up to see three young men dressed in casual clothes and carrying automatic pistols. Two of the men were dark haired and pale skinned and appeared to be twins, but it was the third man, tall, spare and with a sandy complexion and pale blue eyes, who threw a pair of what looked like leather hoods in beside the prisoners.

'Put these on.'

Jamie picked one up, but Danny stood her ground. 'The last time somebody got me to wear one of these I ended up in a lot of trouble. You guarantee that won't happen again?'

The man shrugged. 'It's up to you. You put on the hood and come with us or you don't and we close the door again.'

'When you put it that way . . .'

Another van and another blacked-out mystery tour. They drove for forty minutes before the vehicle eventually parked. But the journey held none of the menace of their trip with Frederick, and willing hands helped them out of their seats and across what felt like a gravel drive and into a building. When the masks were removed they were in a bright room with a view of a vegetable garden, but nothing else that would provide them with any clue to their location. Their passports and wallets had been removed during the trip. Now they were returned, which seemed reassuring. Blinking, they studied their surroundings. Set into the rear wall, which backed directly onto the hillside, was the steel door of a massive walk-in safe, which gave Jamie a shiver. Without a word the twins walked from the room and the third man took up position beside the door. A few moments later they were joined by a shrunken gnome of a man with a badly twisted neck, but cheerful, twinkling eyes and an expression of perpetual puzzlement, as if, despite his great age, each day confused him more than the last.

'Thank you, Rolf. Send up the twins with some coffee, will ya?' He waved Jamie and Danny to a pair of white leather chairs and took his place opposite them on a matching sofa. They stared at each other for what seemed like minutes before Danny broke the silence.

'Berndt Hartmann, I presume.'

The old man laughed. 'I like that. Stanley and Dr Livingstone, right? I haven't heard that name in a long,

long time, but sure, call me Hartmann, only make it Bernie. This is a day for memories. Bernie Hartmann. The Eye of Isis. And Max Dornberger.'

'We've been looking for you for some time, Mr . . . Bernie. The last thing I expected to find was a fellow New Yorker.'

'New York, Boston.' He shrugged. 'Fifteen years in the States makes an impression on a man—'

He was interrupted by the arrival of the twins. One of them carried a tray with a silver pot while the other served. There was something about the pale, unsmiling faces and dark hair that was unnervingly familiar. Bernie Hartmann saw Jamie's look.

'You ever see *The Boys from Brazil*, Mr Saintclair? Helluva film.'

Jamie had an image of Gregory Peck as Dr Josef Mengele and darted another startled look at the nearest twin. The old man laughed.

'Just a joke, Mr Saintclair. But you English never did have much of a sense of humour. Too much stiff upper lip, huh?'

'That depends on what we have to laugh about, Bernie. I could swear that about an hour ago you and the Children of the Damned here were hell bent on killing us. Or maybe I mistook that steel tomb for a sauna?'

Bernie Hartmann shrugged and sipped his coffee. 'That was then. Right now I'm interested in how you came up with the name Max Dornberger. Max

Dornberger was a good friend to Bernie Hartmann, but he's been dead a long time.'

Jamie took his time, disguising the confusion left by the second half of that statement. 'Simple enough, Bernie, old boy. According to a book I read, Bernie Hartmann and Max Dornberger were in Hitler's bunker just about right to the end. It also said that you were the two men who executed Hermann Fegelein, Hitler's brother-in-law.'

The smile never left Bernie Hartmann's face, but his eyes hardened and humour was replaced with a look of calculation. 'Wrong on both counts,' he crowed, enjoying the confusion of his "guests". 'It's true I was there and I helped bury Fegelein, but I didn't fire a shot. And the man who did shoot him wasn't Max Dornberger.' He shook his head. 'Bodo Ritter executed Hermann Fegelein.'

'I don't understand.' Jamie's puzzlement was clear. 'Bodo Ritter had already left Berlin when Fegelein was killed.'

Hartmann sat back and closed his eyes. For a few moments they wondered if he'd fallen asleep.

'Ach, maybe it's time to tell it all.' The gnome's eyes opened and the twinkle had returned. 'Somebody should know and who's going to arrest old Bernie now, eh? But I tell it my way, and I tell it from the start.'

He began with his childhood in Hamburg before the war, the youngest of a family of seven children, runt of the litter and always in the shadows because his father blamed him for his mother's death. The more he talked, the more his voice changed. The accent was still pure New York American, all drawn out syllables and Rs gone AWOL, but the cadence was taken over by the kid from Altona: sharp and rhythmic with the occasional crack of a bullwhip.

'The old man worked ten hours a day as a blaster at the quarry, so it was Aunt Gerda who brought us up. Not that she got much thanks for it. We spent more time down the docks thieving than we ever did at school and both my sisters were on the game by the time they were sixteen.' He shrugged. That was just the way life was back then. 'Then one time, it must have been in 'thirty-seven around my thirteenth birthday, Aunt Gerda got ill and the old man had to take me with him to work. He taught me about stone and how it split, and about blasting caps and dynamite and how to make them work together. How much to use to get what effect. I was a natural, he said, I had good hands, steady and nimble, and I didn't make mistakes. 'Course,' he chortled, 'you only got to make one mistake in the blasting game. Well, he was a Red, the old man, they were all Reds in the quarries and round the docks. They'd been fighting the Brown-shirts along the *Breitestrasse* on and off since 'thirty-one and he could see what was coming. So he started bringing his work home, in a manner of speaking; half a stick at a time and a couple of blasting caps under his hat. He thought I didn't know where he kept it, but little Berndt wasn't as dumb as he looked. Well, they came for him in 'forty. It's the KZ at Neuengamme for you, Herr Hartmann; five years without the option, unless you'd prefer to use your skills in an infantry pioneer battalion? In the end, it didn't make no difference. It wouldn't, would it? A fifty-year-old man in the combat engineers. Last we heard was a postcard saying he'd made the ultimate sacrifice for Führer and Reich in a great German victory somewhere near Bryansk.'

He sighed and closed his eyes again, as if he was trying to remember a face. 'He wasn't what you'd call likeable, the old man, but I always regret never having a beer with him.

'So here's little Bernie, underfed and scrawny, couldn't get into the Hitler Youth if he wanted to because of the old man's history, and that means no job. All he knows is explosives and how to steal and he has twelve sticks of dynamite and fifteen blasting caps buried down by the shithouse. He wants to help feed the family, but he doesn't know how. Fortunately, his old pals down the docks have an idea. Why don't we rob a store? So we do, the Alsterhaus on *Jungfernstieg*, and it's a peach. They get me in, I do the safe. Everybody gets their share and nobody gets hurt. But this is at the height of Barbarossa, with the Wehrmacht outside Moscow and Stalin beginning to think maybe Siberia's nice this time of year. One night there's a knock at the door. Could have been the Gestapo, but instead, it's Erich, the old man's pal, come to ask a favour; only the

Reds don't ask favours. They're short of funds, he says, and I don't ask what for. Next thing, I'm knocking off banks all over the Third Reich and taking more risks than is good for me. Let me tell you about little Bernie, he's no Red and he's no hero. So little Bernie decides to do one last job – for little Bernie. Only this one goes wrong.

'The crazy thing is that it saved my life. It was the Hamburg bulls picked me up, not the Gestapo, and when they put the screws on me I admitted to the Alsterhaus job as well. If they'd looked hard enough, they could have tagged me for what I'd done for the Reds, and that would have meant a guillotine haircut, but I was a seventeen-year-old kid and not worth the effort. So nobody looked, just then.

'Two years later, I'm out in Neuengamme with the gypsies and the Jews and the Reds and with just about as much chance of staying alive. I thought it was Bernie Hartmann's last hour when Max Dornberger walked into the barracks in his SS uniform and called out my name.'

'You said Max Dornberger was a good friend to you?'

He nodded. 'That's when it started; right there in a stinking barrack room in a concentration camp. Max, he looks me over – I was maybe seven stone back then – and says, "So you're the kid who blows safes. You don't look much." Sure, I say, I blew a couple; no point in denying it. He grins, this kinda knowing way, and I get a cold feeling on the back of my neck. "Yeah, a couple, but I'm not here to take you to Heini's barber for a haircut. I've got a job for a smart kid, if you're interested?"

'Now, don't get me wrong. I wasn't conned by Max, the smiling *Schutzstaffel*; these guys had a way of joshing with you just before they smashed your teeth out with a hammer. But after two years in the KZ and another five to go I knew that the only way Bernie Hartmann was getting out of Neuengamme was in a box. So I played along. Six weeks later I'm being measured up for an SS uniform and I'm cock of the dungheap.'

He saw Danny's look. 'You're asking yourself how Bernie Hartmann could sell his soul to the SS. Well, I'll tell you, lady. Bernie Hartmann was nineteen years old and he was alive. Five feet fuck all and a record as long as my arm and it's all forgiven and forgotten; as long as I do my job. So that's what I did. *Geistjaeger 88* was paradise after the camp. French champagne; and all the girls liked a uniform, even with an ugly little bastard like me in it. I'd looked into an open grave. I knew that life could be short and shitty, so I enjoyed every last minute of it. For three months we swanned around France, living it up and taking what we liked for Uncle Heini. Then everything changed. Bodo Ritter turned up. The Devil incarnate. A man made for a uniform with the Death's Head on it.'

Danny was itching to ask Bernie Hartmann about

Berlin and the Crown and the odd references to Max Dornberger that didn't quite fit, but she had a good cop's sense to stay quiet. Hartmann would get there in his own time.

When he talks of Bodo Ritter there is fear in his voice even now and his eyes flick towards the window as if his nemesis is out there among the trees. Ritter had a nose for the things Heini wanted and that made him important. Ritter garrotting one of his own men. Ritter and the Italian countess who wouldn't cooperate. Ritter's see-saw game with the Italian partisans and a pair of nooses. But always there is the shadow in the darkness. The Ritter story so awful he can't tell it.

'The families who were killed in New York and London were killed with a garrotte,' Danny said quietly.

'Oh, Christ,' Bernie whispered. He looked up at her, the twinkling eyes now dull and confused. 'How could it be? Bodo Ritter is at least ten years older than I am. If he's still alive he must be close to a hundred.'

Then it hits him.

'The diamond. This is all about the Crown and the Eye.'

XXXII

'Bodo Ritter had the coldest eyes of any man I'd ever seen and we were all scared shitless of him. Any man who stepped out of line was sent straight to the Eastern Front and knew he could count himself lucky. From the first day I met him I knew that good job or not, one day Bodo Ritter would be my executioner. Sure, I was the unit mascot, but that wasn't going to save Bernie. It was the way he watched me, like a snake watching a mouse and all the time its little brain is full of the details of the kill. But all the time he was watching me, I was watching him. I noticed that everywhere he went, Ritter carried a leather case with him, like an old-fashioned surgeon's bag. He treated that case like it was his old man's ashes and I knew that whatever was in it must be worth a fortune. But no matter how hard I tried, I couldn't get a look inside. Not until Berlin.' He shook his head and his mood changed again. 'The bastard tried to kill me, but I fucked him. I pinched the love of his fucking life.'

'I still don't understand.' Jamie frowned. 'Bodo Ritter's testimony to the war crimes tribunal said he left Berlin on April the twentieth on a secret mission for Heinrich Himmler. Why would he say that if he was still in the city fighting one of the last battles of the war? Let's face it, a battle which, enemy or not, won the admiration of most of the world apart from Joe Stalin and the Red Army.'

To understand, you have to understand Bodo, Bernie Hartmann told them. Bodo with his animal cunning, always sniffing the wind, always looking for a new opportunity or a new threat.

'He could see what was coming better than any of us and, looking back, he knew things, terrible things, that only a few dozen people in the Third Reich knew. Things that, when they came out, would be the death of him. The big shots, they all made their plans to get out. Bodo wasn't a big shot, so he did the next best thing. He decided not to be Bodo any more. You have to understand that *G88* wasn't a real military unit and we weren't real soldiers. We were a *pinkelwurst* of thieves and conmen, hucksters and pencil-pushers with machine guns. Sometimes we had to blend into the background, like chameleons. When Bodo and Max decided to swap identities while the world was burning down around us, it was almost normal.'

'That's impossible.' Jamie didn't try to hide his disbelief. 'A man in Ritter's position must have been known to dozens of people at the top of SS.'

Bernie Hartmann snorted his disdain. '*You* don't know how it worked and you don't understand how it was back then. Chaos. Sure he might have been spotted wearing a different rank, but so what? All the top guys had different ranks in the Waffen SS and the Allgemeine SS. Fegelein was an *Obergruppenführer* in the Waffen SS, but when Bodo shot him he was wearing the uniform of an Allgemeine SS *Gruppenführer*. Bodo Ritter and *G88* worked to Himmler and Himmler alone. Maybe a couple of secretaries at the hell house on *Prinz-Albrecht-Strasse* might have recognized him, but apart from that nobody in Berlin knew Max Dornberger from Adolf Hitler. I think maybe Rattenhuber, the bunker security boss, suspected something, but he had problems of his own right then.'

'But he went on trial at Nuremberg,' Danny pointed out. 'He stood in the dock with the other commanders of the *Einsatzgruppen*. Surely they would have recognized him?'

'Before the trial,' Bernie explained patiently, 'Max Dornberger spent eighteen months as a prisoner of the Russians, sometimes in solitary confinement, but mostly working down a salt mine. I saw the pictures. By the time he stood in the dock his own mother wouldn't have recognized him.'

Jamie took up the attack. 'That still doesn't explain why Max Dornberger would put his neck in a noose for Bodo Ritter?'

The little German didn't bat an eyelid. 'Max hadn't been looking too good for a couple of months. We thought it was the rations. but before he left Berlin Max told me it was stomach cancer. Bodo convinced Max that he would make sure his wife and kids would want for nothing if he did the swap. He was going to die anyway, what did he have to lose?

'Max also told me to watch my back with Bodo, but maybe I wasn't listening too hard, because the bastard had me cold, sharing a new-dug grave with Hermann Fegelein, and it was only luck or God saved me. When the shell hit the bunker and Bodo went down, I didn't hang about. We had this house up in Wilhelmstrasse, nice big place with lots of rooms. Lots of hiding places, too. I'd been watching him with his bag since we'd got back to Berlin. Hell, it got so he talked to the fucking thing. Most of the time, it never left his side, even when we were playing tag with Soviet tanks. But he couldn't take it to the bunker because everybody was searched on the way in. That meant he had to hide it. But you can't hide anything from a thief.'

He described how he'd run back to the building and searched the room where he knew Ritter had stashed the leather surgeon's bag. It had taken him longer than he liked, but he'd eventually found it. Opened it.

'At first, I couldn't believe what I was seeing. Some kind of crazy gold hat—'

'Describe it.' The words choked in Jamie's throat.

'I can see it as if it was yesterday.' Bernie Hartmann

grinned. 'A circlet of gold, with two horns spiralling up from it, and at its centre, where your forehead would be, an eye that stared at you the way Bodo Ritter's eyes did, but . . .' He hesitated and Jamie wondered if the secret was too great to share. If the old mistrustful Bernie Hartmann had won the fight and they would never know the whole truth. But Bernie was only gathering his thoughts. 'But the most wonderful thing about it was the stone. It wasn't like any diamond you'd see today, not in a jeweller's window. It was rough cut, opaque in places, and dazzlingly polished in others. But it was a diamond,' his voice mirrored the wonder he'd felt on that day sixty-three years earlier, 'a diamond as big as a goose egg. A great big hundred-million-dollar hand grenade and it was all Bernie Hartmann's.

'Thieves are greedy, but we're not stupid.' The old man looked to Danny for confirmation. 'I wanted it all, the gold and everything, but I knew it would be tough to get something as big as the Crown out of Berlin. The first thing I did was take my trench knife and prise open the clasps to remove the stone. When I held it in my hand I'd never felt anything like it. As if I was floating. I'd expected it to be heavy and cold, like a lump of frozen snow, but it was light and warm, so warm that I could feel its energy creeping into my body. I don't know how long I sat there with it in my hands, but it was too long, as if the rock had hypnotized me. Next thing I heard was a burst of machine-gun fire and the front door crashing open and I knew Bodo was coming for me. I stuffed the diamond in the pocket of my camo smock and buttoned it up real tight. I was on my way to the window when the glint of that golden crown drew me back, like a fish to a spinning lure.' He shook his head at his own foolishness. 'I had to have it. I couldn't leave it for Bodo. That moment of greed almost killed me. Another burst of fire, the door splintered and Bodo charges in like the Angel of Death he was. He raises the gun and fires, but a second later he's out of bullets. Bernie Hartmann, he doesn't need no second invitation, he's through the window, sash, splinters and all—'

'Hang on,' Danny interrupted. 'You left the Crown behind? So when did you try to sell it?'

'So you know about that, huh?' Bernie gave her a sly sideways glance. 'You're a pretty clever detective lady.'

'That's right, Mr Har . . . Bernie. A clever detective lady who still wants an answer.'

He shrugged. 'So my memory's a little off. It happens when you get as old as I am. Maybe it didn't happen quite so quick. Maybe I went across Wilhelmstrasse to a jeweller's shop. It was gold, worth thousands of marks; I couldn't just leave it behind? Only the bastard stalled me. He told me to come back later, but I knew he was setting me up for a fall.'

'Okay, you went back into the house and Ritter burst inside. What then?'

'Just like I told you. Straight out the window. Death or fucking glory. I got lucky. Landed in a pile of builders' sand. I got up, checked the diamond was still in my pocket and ran for the nearest alley. That's when he shot me. Bodo Ritter shot me in the arse.'

It was dusk by now, and one of the twins came into the room and pressed a button that automatically closed the curtains and turned up the ceiling lights.

'We'll have dinner in the window room, Matthias,' Bernie Hartmann instructed. 'Do you have any preferences? Vegetarian?' His face twisted into a mock grimace and Jamie and Danny shook their heads. 'The veal then,' he said gratefully. 'And a bottle of the 'ninety-six Montrachet, and put another on ice.'

The window room turned out to be exactly that and confirmed what Jamie had suspected. Bernie Hartmann's home was an enormous mansion house set into a low hill overlooking the eastern edge of the lake.

'Better if I turn off the lights,' their host said. For the next five minutes they stood in silent wonder looking out over the darkening expanse of water as the flat hazy glow on the other side turned into a million twinkling sparks that covered the faraway hillside and coated the surface of the lake with shimmering bands of reds and pinks, oranges and yellows, purples and blues. Dinner came, and with it the finest white wine either of them had ever tasted. Jamie complimented Bernie and the wizened old man grinned.

'You can thank Bodo Ritter and Heinrich Himmler.'

Their puzzlement gave him obvious pleasure, and he continued with his story, except that they both noticed there was an important piece missing, a piece that sparkled like a star fallen from the sky.

'Eventually, the Yanks got me, but they didn't keep me for long and after I got out of hospital I headed for what had been a *G88* safe house south of Munich. I wasn't sure what to expect, but I'd been a regular visitor and the old couple who looked after the place seemed happy enough to see me. It wasn't long before they put me in touch with some old comrades who got me out on a ratline to Italy, then Argentina. Maybe I could have stayed in Germany, but they were trawling the camps for SS then and the *Heimat* didn't look too healthy for the likes of Bernie Hartmann. Argentina might have been great for the Golden Pheasants, but for the small fry like me it was a dump. Just heat and dust and flies so big they coulda had you for breakfast. I laid low for three years working on a farm outside Buenos Aires before I got the papers I needed to allow me to visit Europe legitimately.'

Matthias, or perhaps his brother, appeared to remove the remnants of their meal. Bernie frowned, and poured himself another glass of wine. For a moment, he seemed to shrink into himself, but from somewhere he found the strength to straighten in his chair.

'I'm not proud of what I'm going to tell you now, but I can't change any of it, though please believe me, I've done what I can in the past few years to try to make up for it. *Geistjaeger 88* wasn't just a freeloading operation to hunt down trinkets that might interest Crazy

316

Heinrich; it was part of the plan to turn the SS into the richest and most powerful organization in Germany. Even more powerful than the Nazi party itself. Between nineteen forty-two and 'forty-five, Bodo Ritter and Max Dornberger organized the transfer of hundreds of millions of marks' worth of gold bullion, works of art, currency, government bonds and jewellery to numbered accounts in Swiss banks in Zurich. I became part of this operation in nineteen forty-four when Himmler agreed to transfer most of *Geistjaeger 88*'s personnel to SS units fighting on the Eastern Front and Ritter didn't have no option. We'd dress as civilians and use diplomatic passports to cross into Switzerland at Gaillingen, north-west of the Bodensee. Once we hit Zurich either Bodo or Max would present their credentials at the bank and we'd make the deposit. But this was *Geistjaeger 88* and nothing was that simple. Right from the start Bodo operated a policy he called System H: one for Heinrich and the rest for the boys. Himmler only wanted the good stuff and the relics that fulfilled his fantasies, so what were we going to do with the rest? Donate it to the party? Not a chance. We took what we wanted from a chateau or a villa and torched the place so that we could claim the stuff went up with the house. In the early days that was fine, but the problem was there was just too much loot. Soon we began to look like a caravan from the Arabian nights. So the Zurich trips would have a double purpose: to fill the SS accounts and to top up the *G88* pension fund.

Naturally, only Bodo or Max had access, but Bernie Hartmann isn't a thief for nothing. On one trip I followed Max to find out which bank they were using. Now, the only thing I needed was a way to get at the account. Security in Swiss banks wasn't as tight as it is now, but tight enough. Still, it turned out to be easier than I thought. Every time Max and I came back from a Zurich trip, I noticed him palm something to Bodo. A key maybe? Eventually I worked out that it was a piece of paper that Bodo kept in his billfold, because he thought it was so innocuous no one would suspect what it was used for. That's why, when Bodo was knocked unconscious outside the bunker, I took this from him.' He reached into his pocket and pulled out half of a playing card, torn from top to bottom up the centre. 'The ace of spades.' He grinned. 'My passport to paradise. All I had to do was walk into the bank, say I was Bodo Ritter and present my half of the card and they'd show me to the vault, no questions asked. Then, I'd fill a case with what I fancied and carry it across the street to a second Swiss bank where I'd opened an account in a new name. Bodo Ritter paid for this,' he waved at the picture window, 'my place in Boston and the villa in the South of France. He also paid to set up my security consultancy and the safe manufacturing business, from which I've now retired. You look sceptical, young man? Maybe you think Old Bernie's off his rocker?'

'It just seems so easy . . .'

'Oh, it was easy all right. Our Swiss friends were remarkably cooperative. It's just business, after all, and they're so very good at business. I wouldn't be surprised if the SS account still exists. You think I'm kidding, just look in the papers. Not two years ago a prosecutor from Geneva working on some money-laundering case opened a vault in the *Zürcher Kantonalbank* and found fourteen paintings by Monet, Renoir and Pissarro. The account was in the name of Bruno Lohse, an art dealer who was part of the Göring operation all those years ago. Lohse had been cleared of any crime after the war and continued to work as a dealer. Who knows how many paintings were put in that vault when he opened it?'

'So you made your fortune from money and paintings from the Jews?'

'Don't waste your anger or your disgust on me, Detective Fisher. In the past few years I've heaped enough self-disgust on myself for a hundred lifetimes. In any case,' he smiled, 'this old, wrinkled skin is like rhinoceros leather, it would take much more than that to hurt me.'

'Then let me be equally frank, Mr Hartmann. We didn't come here to listen to your life story, interesting as it is. We came here to find out what happened to the Eye of Isis. Maybe it's time you quit stalling and told us.'

Bernie Hartmann nodded as he made his decision. 'Of course, but I'm an old man and it's getting late. Please be my guests and stay the night. We have plenty of room and you'll be perfectly safe under this roof. Tomorrow, after breakfast, I'll tell you everything. I promise. There's only one thing I ask in return.'

'What's that?' Jamie said warily.

'If Bodo Ritter is alive, kill him. If he's dead, find his grave and put a stake through his black heart.'

XXXIII

Paul Dornberger jumped from the steps of the private jet onto the tarmac at Zurich airport and walked swiftly across the apron to his waiting car. Once inside the gleaming black Mercedes SUV he wasted no time.

'Is everything in place, Sergei?'

'Not yet, sir.' The man beside him flinched at the blind rage in Dornberger's eyes. 'There are complications. The house is on a narrow strip of land between the lakeside road and the Zurichsee. It's walled on all landward sides and covered by security cameras, which we have to assume are monitored twenty-four hours. Given the target's area of expertise, we also have to plan for additional security precautions within the grounds themselves. None of that would matter if there was a suitable position nearby to use as a base for a surprise attack, but the lakeshore is heavily populated and short of taking over a neighbouring property there's nowhere satisfactory. We would be compromised before we could get anywhere near the walls, never mind the house.'

Dornberger listened with growing anger. Like Oleg Samsonov's security team, these men were all former Special Forces soldiers, but there the comparison ended. They were freelancers, Russian and east European mercenaries hired on a mission-by-mission basis and paid for by a special fund Paul had created over the years, and which he alone could access. These people were professionals, they were supposed to supply solutions, not whine about their problems. 'I want to see for myself.'

It took thirty minutes to drive through the town and another twenty to reach the property, halfway along the lake's twenty-mile east bank. One pass was enough to confirm what the Russian said. The attack would have to be at night and the first hint of a vehicle stopping would set the alarm bells ringing. There was no screened parking within a mile. Despite the grandeur of the house and those around it, the area was heavily built up, with homes, shops and factories bordering the road-side, each of them no doubt with their own security arrangements and CCTV cameras.

'If you could give us another forty-eight hours to do a proper reconnaissance . . .'

'No.'

Sergei nodded and his voice regained its confidence. 'In that case, our only option is to come in from the lake. Two assault boats, four men each – we estimate a security team of not more than four men – we come in silent and make our landing among the trees beside the lake. I would suggest dawn, when experience tells us there will be a heavy mist on the water at this time of year. We approach the house in stealth, taking care of any opposition as we go, but when we reach it, we go in hard, stopping for nothing.'

'You understand I want the old man alive?'

'Yes, sir, that's understood by everyone. What about the rest?'

'Kill them all. I don't want to leave any witnesses.' Saintclair and the woman had done their part, they had led Sergei to the house. They were no longer required. In any case, it would have been only a matter of time. He already had Hartmann's identity from the document trail the old fool had left as a result of the donations he had made to the Jews and to his family. 'And for the withdrawal?'

'We've identified a place for insertion two miles to the north, but we plan to withdraw to the opposite side of the lake in the exit phase of the operation. There's a suitable landing ground that isn't overlooked at a place called Vorder Au, directly opposite the target house. We'll sink the boats and return separately to the rented accommodation.'

Paul Dornberger smiled for the first time since landing in Zurich. So close, after twenty years. He had feared the old man might already be dead and the trail gone cold, but he could almost smell the scent of Berndt Hartmann's fear. The payments to the families in New

York and London had been the start of a long paper trail. Electronic penetration of the company named as the proxy of the Jersey lawyer's office had revealed first dozens, then hundreds of regular payments to Jewish support organizations and individual survivors of the so-called Holocaust. Not a Holocaust, his father would have said, but a reckoning. One of those payments had led them from a corporation that manufactured safes in the United States to a small holding company based in Zurich, Switzerland. After that, all it had taken was money.

Hartmann is soft, his father had said, he does not have our strength of will. He will reveal himself.

And now he had.

Twenty years. He could wait another twelve hours.

'We go in at dawn.'

XXXIV

In bed later, they tried to make sense of the day. It had felt like being on one of those fairground rides Jamie remembered from his schooldays: a perpetual spinning and bumping on a sea of choppy, mismatched waves, and all accompanied by a blur of faces and the sickly sweet scent of candyfloss and toffee apples.

'What did you think of him?'

Danny turned to face him, her small breasts peeping over the covers. 'I think Bernie Hartmann would give Pinocchio a run for his money in the veracity stakes. For a while there I wondered why his nose wasn't growing. All that sob-story stuff about his old man and working with the communists. My guess is he was a career criminal who ratted on his friends when he got caught and volunteered to do anything that would get him out of the concentration camp.'

'You can't really blame him for that.'

'No, but it makes me wonder how much we can believe.'

Jamie turned Hartmann's confession over in his mind.

'You're right; there were more holes in his story than a Swiss cheese. I have the feeling our friend Bernie was protecting the picture of himself he'd created since the war. A lot of very bad stuff must have happened during those three years with *Geistjaeger 88*, but Bernie wants us to believe he was just a bystander when the blood was spilled. The reality is that unless he'd been prepared to tie the noose or pull the trigger, Bernie Hartmann wouldn't have lasted five minutes in the SS. Oddly, though, when it comes to the important things, I do believe him.'

Danny nodded and the small breasts quivered invitingly. Jamie reached out absently to stroke one, but she slapped his hand away.

'Not while I'm thinking, Sherlock. The whole thing begins to make more sense. The Crown of Isis existed. Ritter or Dornberger—'

'He was telling the truth about Ritter, I'm convinced of that.'

'Okay, Ritter, then. Ritter has the Crown and Bernie Hartmann has or had the Eye. The dead child in Wilhelmstrasse on the twenty-ninth of April 1945, is evidence, circumstantial maybe, but still evidence, that one of them, probably Ritter, believed in that mumbo-jumbo about the Crown's powers. Sixty years later, someone starts knocking people off who may or may not know the location of friend Bernie, but only after turning the heat on them in the worst possible way.

That tells me that Bodo Ritter . . .' She saw his shake of the head. 'Okay, I grant you it's unlikely, but can we really discount the possibility until we know otherwise? Bodo Ritter, or someone connected with Ritter, is trying to reunite the Crown of Isis with the Eye. All of which makes my trip here worthwhile and makes me just a little more optimistic that I am going to put this guy away for a long, long time.'

'Why now?'

'Why now?'

'Yes, why has it taken sixty years for whoever has the Crown of Isis to decide that he needs to reunite it with the Eye?'

It didn't come in a flash of inspiration, more with the thud of a body falling to the floor. 'Simple, Sherlock.' She snuggled a little closer and placed his hand over her breast where it had been earlier. 'Because Bodo Ritter is dying and he thinks that only the Crown of Isis can save him.'

It was still dark when they heard the soft knock on the door. Jamie switched on the bedside light and threw on the towelling dressing gown he'd found in a wardrobe. When he opened the door, Bernie Hartmann was standing there, fully dressed and grinning like a malignant sprite.

'It's an old man's privilege or an old man's curse, Mr Saintclair, that he doesn't need much more than four hours' sleep. I like to get up about now and watch the sun rise over the lake while I breakfast; I thought you young folks might like to join me and I can finish my little story. Shall we say twenty minutes?'

'I hope you like eggs Benedict? The Swiss, they think tea, bread and butter is fine in the morning. When I was in the States I learned to enjoy starting the day with something more substantial.'

It was still dark outside, and at first all they could see in the picture window were their own reflections, but gradually Jamie became aware of a dull leaden grey beyond it, that grew imperceptibly lighter with each passing minute.

Bernie Hartmann finished his eggs and ham and wiped his lips with a napkin. Matthias, or his brother, removed the plates and brought another pot of coffee. 'The Swiss may know nothing about breakfast, but they make a fine cup of coffee. Last night, I was telling you . . . what?'

Danny stifled a yawn, drawing a glare from the little man. Jamie grinned. 'I do believe that Bodo Ritter had just shot you in the arse.'

'That's right, I landed in that heap of sand and I was heading for the hills when I felt this sting in my left butt cheek. Still got the scar, if you're interested.'

Danny had a vision of something pale, scrawny and wrinkled and was glad she'd finished her breakfast. 'No thank you,' she said politely.

'Your loss.' Bernie's eyes twinkled. Again, the narrative emerged in that curious mix of American vowels and German cadence, and it was punctuated by unlikely cackles of laughter.

'Fortunately, it was just a nick, but maybe it saved my life. The Ivans thought it was fucking hilarious. So there I am, richer than I've ever been in my life and with a hole in my arse, running through the streets of Berlin in an SS uniform trying to avoid a hundred thousand Red Army *Frontoviks* who would like nothing better than to put another hole in me, only this time in the head. I had a pistol, but not a rifle, and what good was a rifle going to do me anyway? There's tank fire ripping through the air, mortars dropping in the streets, long-range artillery with shells the size of a *kübelwagen* bringing down whole buildings. The Ivans are fighting their way to the centre street by street, house by house and room by room, and our boys are defending every cellar and every attic with machine guns, rifles, *'fausts*: a Devil's symphony of sudden death, and Bernie Hartmann's right in the middle of it. Where was I going? The only thought in my head was: *West*. If there was a way out of Berlin, it was west. The first thing I did was get rid of my SS grey. I came to this corner and here was this kid standing like a signpost and staring at me. It was only when I looked again that I saw the hole below his right eye. The kid should have been at school, what was he doing looking round corners in the middle of a battle? By then the idiots in charge were calling up twelve- and thirteen-year-olds for the *Volkssturm*. Well, he'd looked round his last corner and he didn't need his *feldgrau* any more. These kids, they gave them full-size uniforms and they just turned up the sleeves and trousers: one size fits all. So Bernie Hartmann's one step from being a civilian again, eh? By now I'm somewhere near Potsdamer Station, trying to reach Tiergarten, because I reckon I can hide up there till dark and I'll have a better chance of getting out that way towards Zossen. The last I'd heard they were still holding out in the Zoo flak tower. But the further west I went, the more Ivans I began to run into. Shit-brown uniforms and a 7.62 mm welcome on every corner. Any way you looked at it, Bernie is in trouble. I could have wept. I did fucking weep. When night came I found a shell hole in the garden of an apartment block. I was out of luck and out of options. The only chance I had of getting out alive was to take a chance and give myself up.' He paused and wiped his eyes with a handkerchief. 'Well, Bernie's been in a lot of dark places, but this is the nearest he's come to despair. I've got enough dough in that sparkler to last me ten lifetimes, but if I don't surrender, I won't even have one life. And if I surrender with it, some other bastard is going to take it away. The only thing I can do is hide it somewhere and hope that I get the chance to come back for it. Maybe, because I'm a kid, they'll let me go? But in my heart I know that's not true. We'd heard all about the camps and the salt mines. Siberia here I come. Only I won't be coming back.'

By now, the darkness outside the window has been replaced by the pewter grey of old ashes. Bernie heaved himself out of his chair and dimmed the lights. 'You'll like this,' he promised.

'So you buried the Eye of Isis in Berlin and never went back for it?' The disappointment was manifest in Danny's voice. 'It's still there buried under a DDR office block or somebody's new porch?'

Bernie ignored the implied rebuke and resumed his seat, with his back to the door and facing the window.

'You never knew what would happen when you surrendered. Sometimes they'd just shoot you outright, because they had no idea what to do with you. Sometimes they'd ask you a few questions and pop you when they'd got as much as they could out of you. If you were unlucky, they'd kick you to death or bash your head in with a rifle butt. They were very unpredictable, the Ivans. They could give you vodka and be laughing with you one minute, then shoot you because they were bored the next. You didn't want to surrender to no Russian women soldiers, know what I mean?'

Jamie had a feeling he did, but didn't want to think about it too much. He nodded.

'Anyway, I'm pretty much shitting myself when I walk towards this checkpoint with my hands up. An officer with blue shoulder boards and a few men, ragged and dirty with tired, lifeless eyes; maybe a dozen rifles on me all the way. They stand me against the wall, search through my clothes and slap me around a little, just for the fun of it, making my skull bounce off the brick. Eventually, the officer waves them away and begins to question me in pretty good German, considering. "Where your unit? Any tanks nearby? How far to Big House?" Big House was what they called the Reichstag. I told him everything I could. Said my unit was wiped out. Told him about two broken-down tanks dug in somewhere around Potsdamer. But by now I'd seen the feet, maybe six pairs, lying side by side and just visible by the corner of the truck. All the time the officer has been questioning me, he's been smiling, but now the smile is replaced by a look almost of regret and his hand inches towards this big Tokarev pistol at his belt. Bernie, I says to myself, if you don't do something quick, you're a dead man. Now, while this guy has been interrogating me I notice something, without realizing what it is. Then it dawns on me, like a what-ya-call-it? An epiphany. He may look tough, but Comrade Tokarev is a crook. Comrade Tokarev is just another Bernie, trying to get through the war without too much inconvenience. A crook with a sense of humour. Very carefully I bring my hand down between us and I rub my thumb and forefingers together, like this.' He demonstrated the international sign for money. 'Maybe the Ivans do it, maybe the Ivans don't, but this Ivan knew what I meant. He gives me the look. You know, that long look that says, *If you fuck with me I'll have my boys cut your balls off?* Then he says, "How much?" "Diamonds," I say, "jewels, gemstones. A million." I don't know how much he understood, but his eyes opened when I said million and he gave a look at his men that I recognized. I'd seen Bodo Ritter give our guys the same look when he was about to rip them off. "Not far," I says. "I show you." He takes out the big Tokarev and points it between my eyes. "Bang," he says, just in case I don't get the message. With a nod of the head we're off, back the way I came, and he's shouting at his men that it's okay and probably that he's going to shoot me somewhere quiet, which was prophetic, if you like. He pushed me ahead of him, crouching down, wary, so some sniper couldn't shoot past me to get him. After five minutes we reached the street where I'd hidden and scrambled through a bombed-out house to get to the garden. The whole place was wrecked, with piles of rubble all around, and I had trouble getting my bearings. Was this the right block? The right garden? Eventually I realized we'd come in on the opposite side. I saw the bush and I pointed to it, making a digging action. It was only then I saw that he was as nervous as I was, with big drops of sweat running down his face onto that big nose. Why didn't I try to take him, or at least make a break for it? I never gave it a thought. This was a big man, with a big gun, and he knew what he was doing. I'd have been dead before I could move. He motions with the gun and I go to the bush. Take two steps right and point to the ground. He liked that. Not the bush, but a certain distance from the bush. "You dig," he says. I'd dug the hole with my bayonet, but it was easy to do the same with my hands in the disturbed earth. I pulled up the sod and it took me about ninety seconds to find the old can I'd put the diamond in, wrapped in a rifle-cleaning cloth. When I pulled it out, he waved at me to put it on the ground and back off. When I was far enough away he walked forward, still pointing the gun at me, picked up the can with one hand and emptied the contents on the ground. His eyes were a little wild when he looked at me, but they changed when he shook the cloth and saw what was in there. I heard a muttered curse in Russian and his hand was shaking when he reached to pick up the stone. I started to back away. The gun came up, but he smiled like I was his biggest pal and waved at me to go. I turned and slowly walked away in the opposite direction from where we'd come. I think I got to the top of the rubble before he shot me.'

The coffee was cold by now, but Bernie Hartmann didn't seem to notice as he took a long drink from the cup. There was an orange cast to the grey beyond the window, but he didn't notice that either.

'The Tokarev's a big pistol and when the bullet hit me in the small of the back, it punched me forward about six feet. At the same time, my head seemed to be in a red haze and I felt the strangest feeling, as if my neck had exploded. There was no pain, but my mind told me I was dead, so that didn't matter too much. I think I was out before I hit the ground.'

He saw them staring at him and his face broke into a gentle smile.

'So this is the first time you've met a dead man. I congratulate you. When I regained consciousness, it must have been an hour later, because my face was welded to the rock by dried blood. I can be fairly certain Captain Tokarev came over to make sure of me, he was that kind of man. But when he saw the mess my head was in, he must have decided not to waste a bullet. It was one of these curious ballistic irregularities, you see. We wore leather ammunition pouches on harness that crossed in the centre of the back. I didn't even know there was a buckle, but that's what deflected the bullet, so it penetrated the skin, but not the bone, and shot up my back taking nicks out of ribs along the way, before blowing a fucking great hole at the junction of my neck and shoulder. A hole that left a flap of bloody flesh over the base of my skull. He would have believed he had aimed a little high, but the result had been the same. Bernie was a goner. My arm was useless, blood leaking everywhere, and I wandered in a nightmare through burning Berlin, by some miracle was given succour, and by a greater miracle survived. So there you have it. The life and death of Berndt Hartmann. Ah, just in time.'

He walked to the window, where the rays of the rising sun had just clipped the top of the low mountains on the other side of the lake. As they watched, the land seemed to welcome them, and the slope was bathed in a patchwork of greens and browns of every hue, but it was the lake that drew them.

'Yes,' Bernie Hartmann encouraged. 'Enjoy.'

The temperature of the water and the air had combined in some natural meteorological phenomenon to carpet the entire surface of the water in a milky band of fog two metres thick. As they watched, the sun's rays raced across it, turning the white expanse into a sheet of molten gold, like the very centre of a volcano, or the heart of a raging inferno; a swirling, ever-changing canvas that no artist could ever emulate. Danny gasped and Bernie Hartmann turned to her.

'Yes, a spectacle only God could fashion, and from the simplest of elements. Light and air.' A low hum intruded on the silence. Bernie tutted. 'Fishermen. As if anyone could catch fish in a fog.'

He was quiet then for a long time and Jamie tried to hide his disappointment as they prepared to leave. But the shadow was closing in and Bernie Hartmann's face mirrored the shadow's power.

He turned to Jamie. 'Death brought you here, and it seems the possibility of my death concerns you, Mr Saintclair. But you have no need to fear for me. I have lived a lifetime that should have ended sixty years ago. Every second lived since has been stolen from God, and, as a thief, I find that quite satisfying. However, you must know what you are dealing with. You think of Bodo Ritter, or whoever is carrying out these murders, as a man, but you are wrong. Bodo Ritter was the Devil incarnate, and his creatures will carry his stamp. Let me tell you one last story.

'We went to a concentration camp. Dachau, I think. This happened a dozen times. A hundred.' The tone has become matter-of-fact, as if only by distancing himself from his subject can he bear to put words into it. 'A Jewish family, some sort of collector. A relic, who knew what? Another Spear of Destiny or a Torah that talked. Whatever it was, it was lost, but Bodo Ritter didn't believe that. He jokes with the children. Tells the family, *Let's go for a walk*. To the furnaces.' The words are now bound in iron, so controlled he can barely get them out. '*Where is it?* he asks. *I don't know*, says the father. Ritter's smiling as he picks up the boy and tosses him alive into the furnace mouth. Just a kid, maybe five. You ever heard somebody burn alive? You hate God for not striking you deaf. Ritter picks up the girl . . .' His eyes turned puzzled as a high-pitched alarm sounded. 'What . . .?'

XXXV

It was like moving through a sea of gold. The sun-kissed fog swirled around the two Zodiac assault boats as they slid silently through the water towards the bank, landing with a soft bump against the gravel on the lake shore. Instantly, two of the four men on each inflatable leapt ashore to form a defensive perimeter while the others secured the boats and shifted their gear ashore. They were dressed in black ski masks and overalls and each man carried a silenced Heckler & Koch MP-7 machine pistol with a thirty-round magazine, plus four spares. The MP-7 was superior to the MP-5 in that it fired a round capable of penetrating body armour. Paul Dornberger had witnessed Jamie Saintclair's miraculous resurrection and learned from it. When Berndt Hartmann's bodyguards went down they would stay down.

A shadowy figure emerged from the fog. 'One exterior guard,' Sergei whispered, 'standing two metres to the left of the garden-room door.'

Dornberger nodded and gave the hand signals for one man to follow him while the rest prepared to breach the house once the road was open. The plan of the house was etched on his brain and he moved to his right, keeping low as he scuttled silently along the lake front, before dog-legging left past a boarded-up summer house. His course brought him to the corner angle of the main building, and to the bodyguard's left. A single guard was lax, even careless. It meant Hartmann had been in this cushioned Swiss bolt-hole so long that he wasn't taking his security seriously. One man to distract, one to neutralize. He motioned his partner forward with his left hand. Dornberger moved swiftly along the line of the wall towards the doorway. A slight sound caught the guard's attention. He was just a shadow in the mist, but Dornberger saw the barrel of an automatic weapon move to cover the garden area towards the lake shore. Moving swiftly and silently, he took two paces forward and looped the steel piano wire around the man's head. His hands took the strain on the wooden toggles and the guard dropped his assault rifle and clawed impotently at the awful steel vice that had instantly closed his windpipe and crushed his voice box. Now he could feel the sting of it cutting into his flesh. With a single tug, Dornberger could have ended the man's agony, but that was not his way. He liked to feel them struggle, the way a fish struggles at the end of the line, thrashing and kicking but entirely reliant on his tormentor's mercy. He knew it was a weakness and that the only way to remove the guilt was to punish himself for it when he returned to London, but for the moment all that counted was the life slowly ebbing away under his hands, the soft bubbling choke as the wire severed the windpipe. Careful. Careful. Just the right amount of pressure so the carotid artery stayed intact. That would be too quick. Too messy. It would be soon, anyway, the legs were starting to kick and he could smell the soft stink of voided bowel. With surprising suddenness the head flopped forward, Dornberger maintained the pressure until he was certain before allowing the body to slump to the ground. He unlooped the wire, wiped it with a cloth and coiled it tight before re-stowing it in a custom-made pocket in his overall. He turned to find the other man staring at him, his eyes the only things visible in the dark mask. What did he read there? A mixture of fear and puzzlement, but did he also detect a hint of contempt? He would deal with that later. For the moment he gave a soft whistle that set the assault team in motion. In almost the same instant a high-pitched alarm began to sound. Not so lax, after all. Someone had tripped a security beam. He'd hoped to make his entry by stealth, it would have been neater. But that didn't matter now.

'Blow the door,' he ordered. He ran the plan of the house through his head. Beyond the door was the garden room with a bar and changing rooms for guests who wanted to swim in the lake. To the right were the stairs that led up to the main floors of the house.

Sergei moved forward and fixed the charges to the security door. Three of them, precisely weighted and exactly placed to take it off its hinges. They exploded simultaneously with a sharp crack.

'Go.'

Everyone froze at the sound of the alarm and Jamie looked on bewildered as Matthias and a man he hadn't seen before rushed to the stair carrying sub-machine guns. At the same time the third man who had released them from the vault ran into the room carrying a bullet-proof vest, which he proceeded to strap on to Bernie Hartmann.

'Don't fuss, Rolf. It's probably another deer.'

The thump of an explosion and the sound of the door clattering into the room below put paid to any further optimism. Rolf dragged Hartmann to his feet and hustled him towards a door at the rear of the room. Jamie hesitated, drawn to the stairway to find out what was happening. A short burst of machine-gun fire on the floor below followed by a cry of agony gave him all the information he needed.

'Come on, idiot.' Danny Fisher grabbed his arm and hauled him in the direction Rolf and the old man had disappeared. A shout from the stairs froze them and Jamie turned in time to see Matthias firing his machine gun one handed as he dragged his comrade into the room. At the same time the wall above his head appeared to be mauled by a giant invisible woodpecker, creating a blizzard of brick and plaster. Matthias cursed and dropped the wounded man. He began to fire short controlled bursts at whoever was down below. The shots were answered by more eruptions in the walls and ceiling around him. Jamie shrugged himself free of Danny's grasp and ran towards the injured man just in time to see his skull explode in a welter of blood, bone and brain as he caught the full force of a burst of fire. The bolt on Matthias's gun clicked on an empty chamber and he clawed at his pocket for another magazine. He seemed to see Jamie for the first time. The dead man's weapon lay at his feet and he kicked it towards the Englishman. Almost without thought, Jamie picked it up and cocked it. Some kind of very modern, cut-back version of the Uzi. From the corner of his eye he saw movement on the stair, heard the soft stutter of a silenced weapon and winced as the banister by his side exploded into splinters. The Uzi came up automatically, as if he was on the Barton Road firing range, kicking in his hands and raking the area where the dark figure had been. Matthias appeared beside him, the weapon reloaded. 'Go,' he ordered. Jamie had time to reflect that it was the first time he'd heard the bodyguard say a word before he sprinted for the corridor ready to cover the other man as he retreated. He saw Matthias crane forward to get a better shot before the back of the twin's jacket shredded in a spray of red and he collapsed without a sound.

'Come on, Jamie.' Danny stood at the door of the

room where they had originally met Berndt Hartmann. Feet clattered on the stair and he directed a quick burst on the run to slow the intruders down.

Jamie hurtled into the room between Danny and Rolf as the air around him buzzed with the sound of passing bullets. Danny had acquired a pistol from somewhere and she fired it left-handed round the door jamb, sending blind shots into the corridor.

'Why in the name of Christ did we come here?' Jamie's voice sounded high in his own ears, but he didn't care who knew he was scared. They were trapped. The only way out of the room was through the window into the garden and whoever their enemy was would have thought of that. No, they weren't trapped, they were dead. Bernie Hartmann was fiddling with the keypad of the safe. What was the point? Whatever he kept in there wasn't going to be any use to him now. It struck him that it might even be the Eye of Isis, but the thought didn't give him any pleasure. He doubted that whoever was trying to kill them was going to stop just because Bernie threw them a billion-pound diamond. The only thing that would help at the moment was an RPG rocket launcher. Then again, maybe it would be just like Bernie Hartmann to keep a *Panzerfaust* around as a souvenir of the good old days. Danny reeled away from the door clutching her face and he felt a thrill of fear. He moved to help her, but she waved him away. 'Dust in the eyes.'

The Hartmann house had been solidly built with

brick partition walls and Rolf used the cover to fire aimed bursts that were keeping the attackers at bay for the moment. Jamie knelt by the window, checking for the flanking movement that would inevitably come when the gunmen realized they were stalled.

'This way.'

Bernie Hartmann finally had the safe door open, revealing a small space about six feet square. A space that was entirely empty.

'Are you crazy?'

'If you don't get in here you're all going to die,' the old man insisted, his voice surprisingly calm for a man with a houseful of vengeful assassins.

Danny and Jamie exchanged glances. On the one hand it was only delaying the inevitable, on the other, any delay was preferable to being cut to pieces by flying lead. Whether they'd be thinking that in half an hour or so when they were slowly suffocating was another matter, but they could worry about that when it happened. Danny went to stand beside Bernie Hartmann inside the cramped space, then Jamie left his place by the window to join them. Bernie part closed the massive door so there was just space for a man to get through while Rolf continued calmly firing his weapon from the doorway. The bodyguard looked towards the safe, checking that they were inside and Jamie was surprised to see him grinning.

'Now, Rolf!' Bernie's voice was shrill. Rolf fired one last burst and turned towards them just as the wall protecting him exploded into fragments. A DM11 bullet designed to penetrate twenty layers of Kevlar, plus 1.6 millimetres of Titanium alloy plate at a range of two hundred metres isn't going to be stopped by a single layer of bricks twenty feet away, however Swiss and solid. By the time they tore through Rolf's soft tissue, the three 4.6 millimetre rounds of copper-plated steel were mushroomed and misshapen, but had lost little of their velocity. The impact threw him against the far wall in a spray of blood and torn flesh and he was dead before his body hit the floor.

'*Scheisse*,' Bernie Hartmann muttered as he slammed the safe door shut.

For a few moments the little German seemed paralysed by what had happened. He stared at the inside of the door with a look of bemusement until the hammer blow rattle of armour-piercing bullets against steel brought him back to his senses. 'We're safe enough in here,' he breathed.

'Safe?' Jamie was incredulous. 'What's the point of being safe until you suffocate?'

'Safer than Rolf, or the Berger brothers, Mr Saintclair. Would you really rather be out there leaking all over my carpet?'

'So we just wait?' Danny demanded.

Hartmann gave her the look schoolmasters keep for particularly stupid questions. 'You're a policewoman, Miss Fisher; don't tell me you've never heard of a panic room?'

'Sure I have, Bernie,' she studied their surroundings. 'But most panic rooms I've seen tend to have a few more home comforts. Like a regular supply of oxygen.'

They were standing together in the centre of the safe. Whoever was outside had evidently come to the conclusion that he wasn't likely to shoot his way into the safe, even with armour-piercing rounds, but in some ways the silence was more intimidating than the sound of bullets.

'Excuse me.' Bernie Hartmann put his hands on Danny Fisher's arms and moved her so that he could see the rear wall of the safe. 'Where is it? Ah, yes.' He reached up to what looked like some kind of steel reinforcement and pulled. A second later the entire back wall slid silently to one side, revealing a narrow concrete passage complete with emergency lighting. 'Would that be enough oxygen to satisfy you, Detective?'

For a moment his companions were too stunned to speak.

'What is . . .?'

'How did . . .?'

The old man led the way into the tunnel. 'I have been preparing for this eventuality for something like fifty years, Mr Saintclair. As you may have gathered, I am something of an expert on safe design and security. It began as a necessity, became almost a hobby and it would have provided me with a very good living over the years, even without the help of Messrs Ritter and Himmler. When I bought this villa I carried out a number of modifications of which this is only one. It cost rather a lot of money and entailed the purchase of the neighbouring house but one, but I am a rich man and, although at times I wondered if I was merely indulging my paranoia, the thought of what would happen if Bodo Ritter caught up with me made the expense seem worthwhile. Our friends with the machine guns will now be wondering what to do, and while they are wondering we will make our escape. But I'm afraid Rolf's death has affected my plans somewhat.'

Berndt Hartmann set a surprising pace for an old man, scuttling through the passage in a curious sideways gait that reminded Jamie of a land crab. It took them only two or three minutes to reach a metal door at the far end. Hartmann again fumbled with the keypad, muttering numbers to himself. The door opened inwards and they stepped through into the gloomy interior of what looked like a wooden garage, or an engineering shed. It was lined with tool benches, and the smell of engine oil and worked metal hung thick in the air. Facing them was a wide double door with a gap in the centre that allowed in a slanting shaft of light. The old man leaned against one of the benches breathing hard as Jamie and Danny ran to the door and Jamie put his eye to the gap.

'What do you see?'

XXXVI

Paul Dornberger stared at the impenetrable steel door of the safe and felt a surge of fury. Hartmann and his two house guests were inside, he was certain of that, there was nowhere else they could be. The question was did the thief have the diamond with him, or had he used it years ago as collateral to fund his lavish lifestyle on two continents? No, he had to believe Hartmann still had the stone. It was here. He could feel it. He paced the room, avoiding the pile of six bodies sprawled in the pool of blood by the wall: the four Hartmann body-guards and the two mercenaries who had been cut down during the assault. Dornberger knew he didn't have time to attempt to open the safe, even if he had the expertise. In fact, he'd prepared for this outcome the moment he'd realized what Hartmann had done. That was why the bodies were here and two of his men were outside siphoning gasoline from the thief's cars. If, by some miracle, Hartmann survived, he would go into deep hiding and take the diamond with him. That couldn't be allowed to happen.

'Burn the place, and be thorough. I don't want one stick standing on another.'

The diamond would not be damaged in the safe, although its occupant certainly would. In the days after the fire, perhaps posing as insurance assessors, he would bring in a team of experts with the equipment to open it. This room would be buried by the floor above. Because it was cut into the hillside, sealed off by debris, it was unlikely the corpses would be discovered in the immediate aftermath. The cars would be made to disappear, making it seem the house had been empty.

The only thing that bothered him was why an intelligent, and, yes, cunning man like Hartmann should choose to lock himself into a trap. But he consoled himself with the thought that Berndt Hartmann knew exactly what kind of people he was dealing with, and that made his choice very logical indeed.

He walked away as the first flames began consuming the dead.

Jamie gazed across the broad expanse of gravel separating the garage from a fine white house by the lake shore. Water streaked by the last shreds of golden fog. A shallow bay with a long jetty.

And . . .

'Is that yours?'

Danny Fisher forced her way to the door and looked

through the crack at the white float plane anchored in the bay two boat lengths from the end of the jetty. Bernie had recovered sufficiently to join them. He held a set of keys in his hand. 'It's mine.' He nodded sadly. 'But I'm afraid it's not much use without Rolf to fly it.'

'I can fly it.' The two men turned to Danny, varying degrees of disbelief written on their faces. 'It's been a while, but I can fly her,' she insisted. 'She's a Cessna. Not too much different from the Beaver I piloted for a couple of seasons up in New York State. Plenty of take-off room. All we have to do is haul her in, start her up and we're out of here.'

'Couldn't we just jump in a car?' Jamie said warily.

'I'm afraid this is all I have, Mr Saintclair.' Bernie handed Danny Fisher the keys. 'If you fly north-east for the Bodensee, I have a mooring near Eriskirch south of Friedrichschafen.'

Paul Dornberger heard the roar of the Cessna's engine above the Zodiac's muffled 75 horsepower outboard and some sixth sense told him instantly what had happened. He screamed at Sergei to turn the Zodiac towards the sound and cocked his machine pistol. By now the mansion house was well alight and thick smoke billowed across the lake, covering the approach of the plane.

Sergei gunned the engine and followed by the second boat they curved southwards.

* * *

Danny Fisher ignored the impatience of her two passengers and methodically went through her pre-flight checks. It had been ten years since she'd flown a plane like this and though everything seemed familiar enough she didn't want to take any chances. When she was ready, she opened the throttle and nudged the Cessna into motion. The propeller transformed into a spinning wheel of black bars and she worked the flaps to get a feel for them as the twin floats cut through the placid surface of the lake. Gradually, their speed increased and the plane began to buck, because although the waves were small, they existed and they were solid things. Gently, she twitched the wheel to compensate. She sensed Jamie glance at her.

'If you want to fly this thing, Saintclair, why don't you just take over?'

Second by second the engine sound built up to a roaring crescendo, the black bars of the props turned into silver discs and the trees began to rush past in a blur.

'What's that?' Bernie Hartmann squeaked from the rear seat as he struggled out of the bulky bullet proof vest.

A band of white rolled across the lake to their front.

'A fog bank?'

'You don't get fog banks on the lake, just a covering in the morning.'

'Christ!' Jamie followed Bernie's pointing finger. The Hartmann house was bathed in a red glow, with fire swirling from every window.

The plane rushed towards the wall of smoke at a hundred knots, but they were only halfway into their run and Danny knew she still didn't have enough take-off speed.

'What should I do?'

Two low shapes burst from the smoke away to their right to answer her question. Men lay in the bows of each and she could see the twinkle of muzzle flashes as the assault boats turned towards the Cessna. Calmly, she opened the throttle as wide as it would go and the plane thrust forward. If the water had been any choppier the Cessna would have been in danger of yaw-ing off line and flipping over, but it was a chance she had to take. Her course took her at an angle away from the boats and for the moment they hadn't got her range. Now, it depended on just how fast and how good they were. A line of water spouts appeared in front of the nose and a bullet spanked off some part of the plane. Belatedly, Jamie remembered he still had the Uzi and grabbed for the side window.

'You won't . . .' Danny shouted.

But someone, probably the late Rolf, had foreseen just this situation and removed the screw that locked the window in flight. It lowered easily. Jamie knew he had little chance of hitting anything, but no one liked being shot at and it might put them off their aim. He let off a burst with the distinctive buzz-saw rip of an auto-matic weapon. The boats were at the outer limits of the Uzi's effective range, and at an angle of about seventy degrees, but he was pleased to see his bullets strike twenty metres in front of the first boat, which swerved and lost ground.

Paul Dornberger cursed at Sergei to resume the chase and tried to line up the plane in his sights. The target was ten times the Zodiac's size, but, if anything, his chances of hitting it were lower than Jamie's in a bucking assault boat with the angles changing with every passing millisecond. All he could do was fire bursts in the general direction and hope for a hit that would disable the plane. The gunfire confirmed that Berndt Hartmann was aboard. Dornberger still couldn't understand how he'd escaped the house. However he'd done it, the crafty old bastard must have moored the plane within a few hundred metres, probably with the crew in residence. Spray half-blinded him, but when it cleared he had a good view of the plane in profile. If they were going to bring it to a stop it was now or never. He lined up as best he could on the window where the firing was coming from and in an instant of freeze-frame clarity the features behind the gun came into focus.

'Cease firing.' He signalled to the second boat to cut its engine.

Jamie whooped as he saw the assault boats slow in the water, but Danny only had eyes for the smoke. From where she was sitting it looked like a solid wall and she knew that at this speed if anything was hidden in its depths they were all dead. As they hit the cloud, the cabin filled with the stink of burning. For a moment she feared the plane was on fire before she remembered the hammer of Jamie's Uzi.

'Shut that goddam window.'

As she spoke, the smoke cleared and they were through and unscathed, with the lake stretching ahead of them cobalt blue in the winter sun. She pulled back on the control column and the bumping gradually faded as they took to the air.

'Bernie?'

Danny heard the fear in Jamie's voice and her heart came close to stopping. She half-turned to see the old man slumped forward with his eyes closed. Jamie unbuckled himself and forced his way through the narrow gap between the seats. At first, he could see no obvious wound and the only indication of Bernie Hartmann's plight was the grey shadow across his face and the shallowness of his breathing. It was only when he pulled back the dark jacket that he saw the red stain spreading across the old man's shirt. It took him a second more to find the tear in the silk and the wound six inches below Hartmann's right arm. At first he was encouraged that it was too small to have been caused by a bullet. Then he saw the splash of light where the round had entered the fuselage sending splinters of metal through the plane at lethal velocity. The bullet had missed Bernie and exited out of the far side, but one of the splinters had carved its way through flesh and bone. Only God knew how deep.

'We have to get him to a hospital,' he told Danny. 'He needs help and quickly.'

She nodded. By now they were passing over Zurich and she brought the plane round back towards the lake.

With a gasp of pain, Bernie Hartmann raised himself. 'No hospitals,' he hissed. 'Bernie Hartmann's been shot before. He'll be okay. You head Constance. Maybe see a doctor there.' They looked at each other, but before they could make a decision, the old man barked: 'Whose fucking airplane is this, anyway, huh?'

Reluctantly, Danny set a course for the Swiss-German border, putting the plane into a climb. Jamie wrapped his jacket around the old man and settled in beside him for the flight. 'Hold on, you tough old bastard,' he whispered.

They flew on in silence for a while until they hit turbulence and the plane bucked like a rodeo pony, making Hartmann cry out.

'I don't like this, Jamie,' Danny said softly. 'What do we do when we get to the lake?'

'I suppose we do what he says. Find a doctor and get him fixed up. Then try to get back to London.'

'I tell you what to do.' Bernie Hartmann had been listening to every word. 'You go back to England and you settle with Bodo Ritter, once and for all.' Despite his weakness, he managed to give the final four words special emphasis and it confirmed something that had been burrowing away at Jamie's brain since their discussion the previous evening.

'You knew, didn't you? About the Crown of Isis and what it can do? You talked of the Eye and you couldn't have known about the Eye unless Ritter told you about it.'

Bernie shook his head, but his eyes didn't open. 'Not knew. Guessed. Even Bodo couldn't always live with the things he did. He was like two different men. The Devil who was capable of any torture or cruelty reigned within him, but occasionally another man would appear, brooding over what he'd done. The second Bodo would drink to forget. Usually it didn't affect him and he would sit there with eyes that haunt me to this day. Eyes filled with the accumulated terror and pain of his victims. If there is one thing that sustains me, it is that for men like Bodo Ritter there is always a reckoning. But sometimes the brandy would anaesthetize him against his horrors and he would become voluble and almost friendly. A rattlesnake with a smile. And on those occasions he would choose Bernie as his friend. One night, after some butchery or other, he began to play the What If? game. What if you could live for ever, Bernie? What if you possessed something that would make death an irrelevance? Then he said something even more odd. *How can I, who has stood beside popes and kings and matched minds with Machiavelli, be reduced to a mere butcher and a leader of thieves?* I dismissed it as a crazy man's fantasy. *A Crown and an Eye.*

He was clearly mad. But gradually I realized that his madness and whatever was in the surgeon's bag were linked. He never let it out of his sight until those final days and when he thought he was alone, he spoke to it as if it were listening to him. It sends a shiver through me even now. But I never believed it had power, until I saw it for myself.'

'Not something you would give up lightly.'

'No. He would have killed me there and then, Captain Tokarev, if I hadn't told him the rest. I don't think he believed me, but he was intrigued enough to take me to the place where I'd hidden the stone.'

'And then he tried to kill you?'

'It was the chance you took.'

'So apart from you and Bodo Ritter, one other man knows the potential of the Crown of Isis, and that man has the Eye.'

Bernie Hartmann nodded weakly and coughed. Small bubbles of blood appeared between his lips.

'Can we go any faster? I think he's been hit in the lung.' He didn't need to say what effect the wound would have on a man Hartmann's age.

'I'm doing what I can,' Danny insisted testily. She had another, more pressing, problem. They had started out with a full load of gas, but now it was less than a quarter full and draining fast. The only explanation was a bullet through one of the tanks, or more likely a lucky shot hitting a fuel line. If that was the case, they were fortunate to be still in the air, and not a ball of fire hurtling towards the ground, but time was running out with every drop of aviation fuel they lost. She studied the map on her knee. Lake Constance was still twenty miles away. No hope of reaching there. She altered course northwards. If she couldn't get to the main lake, maybe she could reach the leg of the upper lake which eventually became the Rhine.

Jamie noticed the change of direction and leaned forward between the seats. 'Change of plan?' She pointed to the fuel gauge. 'Shit.'

'Right on the money again, Sherlock. We need to find somewhere to put down. Fast.'

He studied the ground from the plane's windows. 'That might constitute a problem . . .'

'Seeing how this is a float plane . . .'

'And I can't see any water. How long?'

The answer was she had no idea. Minutes, but possibly less. The low fuel light came on but she had no idea how much range it gave her. All she knew was she had to land the first chance she got. She dared a glance at the map again. Her eyes locked onto two barely visible blue spots a few miles south of the point where the Rhine flowed from the upper lake.

'Get him strapped in. We're going down.'

'Where?' he demanded.

'There.' She pointed to what looked like a silver coin in the landscape about two miles ahead.

'It looks like a puddle.'

'Well, it will have to do. How's Bernie?'

Jamie felt pressure from the fingers holding his hand. 'He's still with us, but I'm not sure how long he has.'

He bent over the old man to fasten his seat belt. With an enormous effort Bernie Hartmann lifted his head and his eyes opened. Jamie saw his lips move, but the words were less than a whisper and he had to put his face next to the old man's to hear what he was saying.

'You remember what I said,' he wheezed. 'You find Bodo Ritter and you kill him. Tell him Bernie Hartmann will be waiting for him in hell.'

With the final word, the fingers on Jamie's hand tightened convulsively. Bernie Hartmann gave the weary sigh of a man who has suffered enough and was gone.

'He's dead.'

Danny nodded distractedly, already concentrating on her descent. The lake looked like a postage stamp from up here. Ideally, she would have banked and come in from the east, where there were fewer trees, but the fuel gauge read empty and she couldn't take the risk. She guessed it would be just wide enough to squeeze the Cessna in, but guesswork wasn't the best criteria to fly by. 'You'd better get over here and belt up. This could be a bumpy ride.'

Jamie clambered into the front to take his place beside her. He hadn't realized just how small the lake was until now.

She read his mind. 'If I tried to put this thing down on one of those ploughed fields down there we'd be joining Bernie before he even reached the Pearly Gates, and they wouldn't need to dig our graves, because we'd already be six feet under.' The water was flat calm and wind conditions good, but they were the only things in her favour. She came in as low as she dared, using a red farmhouse as her aiming point. As soon as she was over the trees she knew she was too high and coming in too fast. Jamie gripped the door handle with one hand and the seat with the other and braced himself for the impact. The plane was already at maximum flaps and she instinctively throttled back to get the lowest possible landing speed. The effect was to make the Cessna land tail down and instead of cruising forward and being slowed by the water she bounced and gained speed. Somehow she managed to regain control, but when they landed a second time she knew it was already too late. The trees on the far side of the lake hurtled towards them.

'Brace for crash.'

Jamie had the impression of the world turning a somersault at the same time as gravity tried to tear him apart. The safety harness cut into his stomach and chest as the floats smashed into the bank and the Cessna went up on its nose. Suddenly the engine was screaming and shards of propeller flashed past inches from his face, accompanied by the sound of tearing metal as a tree branch penetrated the tail and came within six inches of taking off his head. All his weight was being carried by the strap and everything movable in the cockpit fell past him.

A momentary silence, as if the whole world had decided to stand still, was replaced by the creaking groan of crumpling aluminium alloy, and the ticking of red-hot engine parts. 'Get out!' Danny's shout startled him into motion. The Cessna had settled upside down and slightly on its side, and he noticed his door had burst open. He hit the quick release on the belt to drop nose first onto the roof of the plane and scrambled clear through the opening. He hesitated a few feet from the wreck, waiting to help if she became trapped.

'Don't be an idiot. She could blow any minute. Get the hell out of here.' The Cessna's tanks were close to empty, but the vapour from aviation fuel is more combustible than the fuel itself and ruptured gasoline lines and red-hot engine parts do not make a good combination.

'Bernie . . .' Jamie turned back towards the plane, but Danny knocked the feet from under him just as there was a soft 'whump' followed by a fireball that engulfed the Cessna, igniting the tree branches above and generating enough heat to singe the hair from his forearms.

'Jesus . . .'

'Let's hope so,' Danny said, staring at the burning aircraft. 'But with Bernie it's kinda difficult to know for sure.'

They scrambled away from the wreckage and sat against the base of a tree, hypnotized by the flames that consumed the Cessna and the earthly remains of Berndt

Hartmann; thief, safecracker, SS veteran and millionaire philanthropist. Smoke billowed through the trees and up into the heavens. Jamie found himself hoping it was carrying the diminutive German's soul to be with his God, but part of him couldn't escape the image of smoke from a crematorium chimney. He shivered as the sound of a child's scream split the air, but when he looked up all he could see was a passing gull.

When he turned to Danny, tears were rolling down her cheeks. They reached for each other and he tasted the salt on her lips. 'If we hang around here, we're going to have to explain this,' he said as gently as he was able. 'They'll keep us for days, maybe weeks, and when we finally get out those guys back in Zurich are going to be waiting for us.'

'Maybe that would be a good thing?' She stifled a sob. 'It's odds-on that the men who killed Bernie are the same ones who murdered those people in New York and London. If we can persuade the Swiss authorities . . .'

He shook his head. 'You saw the kind of firepower they had. If they wanted us they'd get us and they wouldn't worry about who they shot along the way. The only chance we have is to fight them on our own ground and at a time of our own choosing. We'll get another chance, but enough people have died already. I think we should walk away. Act like a couple who've lost their way. We'll eventually find a bus or a cab.'

She wiped her eyes with her sleeve. It wasn't much of

a plan, but for the moment she couldn't come up with anything better. 'All right, there's nothing to connect Jamie Saintclair or Danny Fisher to the plane. It's going to be days before they figure out why there's only one piece of charcoal in there. We can go back to London. Regroup.'

'Not London.'

'But you said—'

'I know, but I think I've had one of those epiphanies Bernie mentioned. What's this all about?'

'The Crown of Isis,' she said without hesitation.

He shook his head. 'It's not about the Crown. The Crown is nothing without the Eye. This is about the Eye of Isis. And what's the Eye?'

He read the anger in her eyes, but he persisted.

'The Eye is a diamond.'

'Exactly and if you want to know about a diamond, you go to the experts.'

'Won't the opposition have done that already?'

'Yes,' he admitted. 'But maybe they don't have access to the experts I have.'

'So where do we go?'

'Where else but the diamond capital of the world? Antwerp.'

XXXVII

The man who called himself Max Dornberger experienced one of his familiar fits of panic. Fear rose from his stomach and filled his chest like ice water, crushing his lungs and making it difficult to breathe. It forced its way into his throat and up through the nerves of his face until it entered his brain, exerting a terrible chill pressure that made his skull feel as if it was about to explode. He wanted to scream, but he knew that nobody would hear him in the white desert that was now his existence. He was bleeding to death. Bleeding time.

Somewhere in his head a clock ticked remorselessly. The pages of a calendar turned. He could tell the position of each phase of the moon, as if Isis was whispering its position in his ear. *Ten days*, she said. *You have ten days before I exact payment.*

The price of what she had given him was truly terrible. What did they know about pain, all those he'd sent to the other side? He could feel them gathering in the outer edges of his world, waiting to exact retribution, and he remembered the words of the priest as he died. *May you be cursed by the gift of a long life.* Now he understood. Unless the Eye was returned to the Crown of Isis by the first phase of the new moon he would have failed her and the gift he had received would have to be repaid a thousand times in torture and mental torment. A thousand deaths, each more painful than the one before. A child's voice deep in his fractured mind told him to run, but he knew he had nowhere to go. The Eye was his only hope. He must trust in the son he had created in his image.

And yet, that very thought brought a moment of doubt. For within the depths of the dream loomed another presence that created a different type of fear. A darkened room. The slap of a leather belt on flesh. Sharp, searing bursts of pain. And words, repeated over and over. Why could he not remember the words? Why was it only emotion and sensation that stirred the memories, along with part-visions he struggled to understand? A medal, polished and bright on a uniform of Prussian blue, gilt eagles glinting between the spread arms of a Maltese Cross. Wrinkled, liver-spotted hands clawing for something in his grasp. He saw what it was and the confusion intensified. Was it the Crown that was keeping him alive, or was it his belief in the powers of the Crown? If this was reality, then what of the dreams that had been his life – lives? If the Crown was a lie, why did he see what he was seeing; feel what he felt? Yet if *this* dream was real, what did it make *him*? Squandered. All of it. Every breath wasted. Every moment of his existence an illusion. And at what cost? Suddenly he was a child again, squirming in the grip of strong, merciless hands, but they weren't the hands that had beaten him, or the hands that had tried to wrest the Crown away. He felt pain beyond imagination as the furnace blast of heat charred his clothing and shrivelled his flesh. Flames all around. Jerking and squirming to escape the agony even as he was consumed, still alive as his eyeballs exploded and his body fats made him one with the fire. He screamed as he had never screamed before.

Antwerp. It took them four days to reach the Belgian port. On the first, they'd walked along country roads until they reached the nearest town, holding hands like lovers and hearing the sound of sirens in the middle distance. In time the cops would start asking questions and begin the hunt for the dishevelled young man with the shock of dark hair over his eyes, and his tall, angular companion. They might discover that the mystery couple had taken the bus to Constance and boarded the Allmannsdorf ferry to Meersburg; and possibly even the next few convoluted, energy-sapping steps by taxi and train. But Jamie reckoned by the time they reached Munich they were safe enough. Then it was just a question of replenishing the clothing they'd left in Zurich – he'd called the hotel manager pleading a family bereavement and asked for their luggage to be sent on to his flat in London – buying bags to keep it in and paying the extortionate ticket price for the flight from Munich to Antwerp.

Jamie had called in advance to arrange a meeting with the man whose advice he sought. Fortunately, it wasn't far from their hotel to Samuel Meyer's office in the city's *Diamantkwartier*. As they walked, Jamie tried again to explain the logic that had brought them here.

'The man who took the diamond from Bernie Hartmann in nineteen forty-five was a Soviet political officer who'd fought his way into Berlin, probably with Zhukov's Third Shock Army.'

Danny's face clouded with doubt. 'How can you know that?'

'I checked it out. When the Russians invaded the Third Reich, Berlin and Hitler were the great prizes. They converged on the city from east, north and south, but when they fought their way to the centre they were in danger of hitting each other with their own artillery. Stalin's solution was to create a dividing line through the centre of the city, with General Konev's First Ukrainian Front to the south and Zhukov's First Belorussian Front to the north. The line more or less took the course of the River Spree. Bernie Hartmann said he was captured near Potsdamer Station, which was in the area of the Third Shock Army's attack towards the Reichstag. Anyway, Bernie's captor was wearing blue shoulder boards, which makes him an NKVD officer. You with me so far?'

She shrugged as if she had other things on her mind, but he took it for acceptance.

'So if he survived the war, our man is a member of Stalin's secret police who returns to Russia a hero and with a diamond worth God knows how many millions in his knapsack. What does he do with it?'

'Sell it?'

Jamie shook his head. 'A death sentence, unless he has serious contacts. No, he's clever and he's patient. He knows he can't touch it. Instead, he puts it somewhere safe and keeps his nose clean. He's a party member who's had a good war. If he's lucky and obeys orders, he knows there's automatic promotion. Khrushchev and Brezhnev were both war heroes and they made it all the way to the top. Okay, our man may not have risen that high, but in time, maybe he made it to a position where he had freedom of movement.'

'Then he sells it?'

'Maybe, maybe not. But he definitely wants to know how much it's worth.'

'And this is where he'd come.'

'If the streets of London are paved with gold, the streets of Antwerp are paved with diamonds. Every year, about half the world's polished diamonds are sold within half a block of here. There are four thousand diamond cutters and fifteen hundred traders—'

'All right, enough of the history lesson. Just tell me

how we're going to find this guy when the opposition, who it's now very clear to me possess considerable resources, don't seem to have been able to?' Jamie came to the doorway he was looking for and pointed to the small gold plaque. She read it aloud. 'Meyer and Sons?'

'When Belgium surrendered to the Nazis on the twenty-eighth of May nineteen forty, the Jewish leaders of Antwerp's diamond industry were less concerned than many of their compatriots. After all, the diamond companies made huge amounts of money; they were run by Jews and run efficiently. And did not the Germans prize efficiency above all else? A loss in status was a possibility, but they could survive that. Unfortunately, they underestimated the depth of Adolf Hitler's pathological hatred for their race, the ruthlessness of his henchmen in the SS and Gestapo and that peculiarly German need to tidy up every last messy little irritant and tick it off on their 'to do' list. They also overestimated the loyalty of the non-Jewish Belgian employees who would soon be sitting in their shiny leather boardroom chairs. Of the thirteen thousand Jews who decided, or were forced, to ride out the storm in nineteen forty, only eight hundred remained in nineteen forty-five. With the help of a family of devout Catholics and a sock full of his merchandise, Sam Meyer's father had been one of the lucky ones: he survived to revive an industry that now had a turnover of almost forty million US dollars and employed thirty thousand people.'

Jamie recognized one of the reasons for Herschel Meyer's unlikely survival the moment he set eyes on Sam. The Belgian was tall and broad shouldered, with slicked-back blond hair and intelligent blue eyes; a picture of the successful Aryan businessman in his two-thousand-euro Armani suit and the spectacular stone that twinkled on his ring finger. His greeting was polite, but wary. Sam Meyer's cousin had been the client Jamie had recovered the Rembrandt for and Sam had oiled the wheels with the help of his contacts in South America, but that didn't make them friends.

'Your phone call was intriguing, but not particularly informative, Mr Saintclair. How can I help you?'

He listened politely and without comment as Jamie explained about the possibility of a large, hitherto unknown diamond being offered for sale or valuation by a Soviet official during the Cold War.

When Jamie was finished, Meyer smiled, showing teeth almost as sparkling as the diamond on his finger. 'It sounds like something out of a James Bond movie. You're serious?'

'I know it's unlikely, but . . .'

The big man shook his head slowly. 'So we'd be talking about the seventies or early eighties? A long time ago, but if something like that happened, even back then, I would have had some hint of it.' He waved towards the office window that overlooked Antwerp's Diamond Club. 'We inhabit a small and incestuous world, Mr Saintclair. There are only about ten men I'd trust with this kind of business and seven of them work in that building. The diamond you described – three hundred carats, white, possibly flawless, and yet to be properly cut – would be the stuff of legend. Stones are our lifeblood. We talk about nothing else. If any *diamantaire* had seen a diamond like that, a stone to rival the Mountain of Light or the Great Mogul, word would have been round the bourse in a matter of days.'

Danny Fisher spoke for the first time. 'The man who owned this diamond would have bought his chosen expert's silence either with cash or by the threat of violence, probably both. If he's the type of man we believe he is he would be very persuasive indeed.'

'Perhaps that is true,' the dealer said. 'But we are talking about decades ago. By now the money is spent and any threat would have lost its potency.' He smiled. 'The Soviet Union is no longer the bogey man it once was. New York is still our biggest market, but Russians are some of our best customers.'

'So you can't help us.'

'Of course, I will do what I can. I will be at the club this afternoon and I will ask a few discreet questions. There are also some phone calls I can make. Give me your cellphone number and I will call you tonight if I have any information.'

'Disappointed?' Danny asked, as they left the office onto *Pelikaanstraat*.

'It was always a long shot,' Jamie admitted. 'But I wouldn't write off Sam Meyer just yet. He strikes me as a man who can get things done.' He studied her and realized how weary she suddenly looked. 'You seemed a little distracted in there.'

She hesitated, seeking the right words. 'I have a feeling time is running out for the case . . . and for us. The only reason we're still alive is pure dumb luck. Every face I see, I wonder if it's one of those goons who killed Bernie Hartmann, or Frederick and his merry band of Nazis, or somebody else getting ready to cash in on the contract that's out on you. You're different, Jamie. Harder.' She reached out to touch his face. 'I don't mean that in a bad way. You just seem to coast through it all. Nothing bothers you. After all those years in homicide I thought I was immune to death, but the stories that are associated with the Crown freak me out. How many children have died in an attempt to make the fantasy come true? And how many more if we fail? That's the problem, Jamie. For their sake, we can't afford to fail, but all we seem to be doing is fumbling around in the dark.'

By now they were in a wide park with walkways and ponds. He led her to a bench between two gnarled beech trees.

'You're the cop, Danny. Tell me what else we could have done. Every clue we've followed has brought us another step closer to the Crown or the Eye. Hell, when we started we didn't even know the Crown of Isis existed. And every step closer to the Crown or the Eye is bringing us closer to the men who killed the people in

New York and London. That's the reason you're here. Don't give up on me now.'

She turned to him, but he didn't give her a chance to reply.

'And then there's your career.'

She glared at him, but they both knew he was right. From the moment they'd left London they'd been operating beyond the boundaries of normal policing and in a murky grey area of near criminality.

'Failure to report several deaths, failure to report an abduction – actually, make that two – assault, though I doubt Frederick will be pressing charges, flying a plane without registering a flight plan, crashing said plane, failure to report crash of said plane . . . Ouch!' He rubbed his shoulder where she'd punched him. 'Anyway, the point I'm making is that we can't go back now, either of us. All we can do is keep going until we find the Crown and the Eye.'

'And what then?'

'We'll worry about that when it happens. But the general idea is that you get the bad guy and head back home to take all the glory.'

'All right.' Her lips twitched into a bleak smile. 'I'll buy that – for now. But you have one week to make it happen, mister. In seven days I have to be on a flight to New York.'

Seven days? The figure came as a hammer blow. Their time together had passed so quickly and so naturally that it hadn't occurred to him that it was drawing to an end. Just for a second he thought of suggesting that she give up everything and stay with him, but the absurdity of the idea almost made him laugh. She grinned when she saw the look on his face.

'C'mon, Saintclair, don't be such a sap. Let's make the most of the time we have. Take me back to the hotel and show me some of your crazy moves.'

As suggestions went, it didn't seem like such a bad idea.

The chirrup of Jamie's mobile phone broke the reverential post-coital silence. It was Sam Meyer and the regret in his voice told Jamie everything he needed to know.

'I asked around at the club – people I trust – but nobody's heard anything about a big stone out of Soviet Russia. The considered opinion is that there's no way a diamond like that could exist without it becoming known in the community.' There was a moment's silence as Jamie digested the bad news. He was about to thank Meyer for his help when the Belgian continued. 'I also made a few calls to people who were around at the time, but have since retired. The answer was the same. I . . . These are old-fashioned men, Mr Saintclair, some of them from my father's time. A few of them refused to answer until they knew who was asking. I hope you don't mind that?'

'If you trust them, I'm sure it won't do any harm.'

'Well, one of these gentlemen, Leon Rosenthal,

became quite animated when he heard your name. He asked whether you were the same Saintclair who found the bunker in the Harz Mountains. When I told him you were, he said he'd like to meet you.'

Jamie was still coming to terms with the crushing weight of failure. The idea of hanging around to meet a geriatric Belgian when all he wanted to do was get back to London held no appeal. 'I don't think—'

'Before you say no, perhaps you'd hear me out. For one thing, I'd esteem it a personal favour. Leon Rosenthal is something of a legend in Antwerp and in the diamond trade. He was eighteen when the Germans marched in, but unlike many others, my father included, instead of just trying to stay alive, he decided to fight. Leon formed a resistance unit that helped downed Allied airmen, carried out attacks on the Germans and hid fellow Jews from the Gestapo round-ups. After the war he built the family firm into one of the world's biggest dealers in precious stones, with branches in New York and Tokyo. And that's the other reason you should see him. Leon Rosenthal knows more about diamonds than any other man on the planet. If anyone can give you information about this mythical stone, it's Leon.'

XXXVIII

Leon Rosenthal's red-brick house was set within its own grounds in the upmarket suburb of Aartselaar, about five miles south of the city centre. A housekeeper showed them into the main room where a nurse was just packing up her equipment, and it was a few moments before a heavy-set man with thick white hair and a neat moustache appeared in a wheelchair. At the age of eighty-six, Leon Rosenthal still radiated the fearsome energy that Sam Meyer's history had hinted at. He used the chair like a battering ram, impatiently pushing aside chairs and bulldozing through doors. Narrow-rimmed spectacles with thick lenses framed his milky blue eyes and magnified them until it seemed they were dissecting you.

Like Meyer, the old man spoke impeccable English, and despite the chill he waved them towards a paved area beyond a set of wide patio doors. On the way, he picked up a stone jar and carried it to where Jamie and Danny had taken their seats at a wooden table.

'My only vice in sixty years,' he growled, snipping the end from a large cigar and lighting it. 'They say it will kill me, but what difference is that going to make now? Even when the Americans were blockading Cuba, Fidel Castro would send me a box every month as a gift.'

For a few moments the Belgian sat, oblivious of his guests, savouring the taste of the cigar and contemplating the fading light beyond the edge of the sparse parkland that surrounded the house. Eventually he emerged from his reverie and turned to Danny Fisher. 'Forgive an old man his moment of pleasure, Miss Fisher, and welcome to my home. It is not often these days that this house is graced by the presence of a beautiful woman, although please don't tell my housekeeper that. Claudette still believes she's the same as she was thirty years ago. One of the benefits of poor eyesight and a refusal to wear spectacles.' Danny smiled acknowledgement. 'Mr Saintclair, you will be wondering why I asked young Samuel to invite you here?'

'We're visiting Antwerp because we are interested in diamonds, monsieur. Naturally, it was a great honour to hear that you wanted to meet us.'

Leon Rosenthal gave a grunt of laughter. 'You should have been a diplomat, Jamie – may I call you Jamie? It's my guess that you would have much preferred to be on the flight to London right at this moment. But I have my reasons for wishing to see you, and perhaps you will find some profit in your visit.' He pressed a button on the arm of the chair and a few moments later the house-keeper appeared with a tray on which sat a decanter and three stubby crystal glasses. Rosenthal waved her away and poured three generous measures of glowing amber. 'Please,' he said, indicating the glasses. 'Seventeen-year-old single malt whisky is not a vice, but a simple pleasure, and you would always regret not at least tasting this particular whisky. It is distilled on the banks of a river where I once fished for salmon and every sip brings back memories.' All three drank and automatically sat back as the rich golden glow of the liquor suffused their nerve ends. Leon Rosenthal issued a long sigh. 'Now, Jamie, if you would be kind enough to tell me about the bunker and what you found there?'

Jamie had told the story so often in the past year that it was a request he had no trouble fulfilling. He left out the machine-gun toting neo-Nazis who had hunted them through the Harz Mountains, concentrating on how he and Sarah Grant had unravelled the clues in his grandfather's diary to discover the waterfall behind which lay the secret entrance to the bunker. Leon Rosenthal sat back and closed his eyes as he was led upwards into the darkness, and into the concrete tunnel that held the offices and laboratories of Walter Brohm's research facility. Jamie assumed that, like everyone who asked him to recount the story, the Belgian was only interested in the Raphael painting that had made the bunker famous, and that was where he stopped. But

Rosenthal opened his eyes and pinned him with his round-eyed stare.

'Please, continue. Do not miss out a detail.'

The metal stair, and long echoing corridors, until at last they came to the great steel doors, twisted and buckled by the massive explosion that had been meant to obliterate the entire complex. Beyond them, a vast room the size of a football field, and Brohm's engineering equipment, turned into the world's largest indoor junkyard. Now he had no choice, but to tell of the pursuit that had driven them there, and into the room. Rosenthal's breathing became a rasping tear and Jamie's voice faltered for fear of the old man's health, but the Belgian waved him on.

The room. 'Behind the door we discovered the remains of three hundred scientists and slave workers who had been killed at their workplaces.' He moved on, to the escape, but without opening his eyes, Leon Rosenthal raised a hand.

'Do not cheat me, Mr Saintclair, I beg you. I wish to hear every detail of it as you remember it, please.'

Jamie exchanged a puzzled glance with Danny Fisher. Where was this going? Remember it? He had spent the last year trying to forget what they had found in the room. A sea of bones. Men and women contorted in every form of agony or mere heaps of disarticulated white. And, closest to the door, the girl. The silent scream in the tormented, eyeless face that had reflected the terror of her end, the jagged hole in her skull that was clear proof of the method they had used to snuff out her life. He had reached forward to touch her shoulder.

'Describe her.' Leon Rosenthal's voice had turned savage.

How to describe a skeleton with a hole where the face had been? 'She had long fingers. A piano player's fingers.' An image came to him of a girl. 'She was tall and slim, graceful. She wore a striped grey shift.'

Rosenthal sniffed. 'Yes, they would make her do that.' He turned the chair away from the table and wheeled it back into the room to a large desk, opening a drawer to withdraw a small slip of paper. For a moment he held it in his hands, staring at it, with his shoulders slumped, looking somehow even older than his years.

When he returned to the balcony he handed Jamie a sepia-tinted picture.

'My Hannah.'

At first the name didn't register, then the face swam into focus. A young girl with an almost spiritual beauty, serious, in the photograph, but with a hint of amusement in her eyes that made you wonder how lovely she must have looked when she smiled. Suddenly he was in the back of Lotte Muller's car on the way to the bunker and the German policewoman's voice echoed in his ears. *Another of the victims is his niece, Hannah Schulmann, a laboratory technician who worked closely with him. She was nineteen years old.* In that picture she had been smiling.

'She was working with her uncle, Abraham, on their nuclear programme. I wanted her to come away, to be with me in Belgium, but she wouldn't leave him. He could never survive without her, she said. When she stopped answering my letters I went to Germany to look for her. You can imagine how that was. Brownshirts and SS men on every corner, strutting and crowing. Jewish businesses closed, their windows smashed and their owners branded with yellow stars. Fear, everywhere. Of course, I couldn't find her. They would have taken them all away to some guarded laboratory, then ... Well, we know what happened then. It was what I learned in Germany that made me resolve to fight them when they came. It was because of what happened to Hannah that I survived the war. I never forgot her. I married and had children, but I always wondered what happened to my Hannah. And then you found her for me. I will never forget that, Jamie, and as long as I live I will always be in your debt.'

Jamie felt Danny Fisher's hand on his. He remembered again the eyeless skull with teeth that sixty years later were still like flawless pearls. Gently, she slipped the photograph from his fingers and studied it. Eventually, he found his voice.

'There's no question of debt, monsieur. When we found Hannah and her friends murdered in the bunker, it was a scene I will remember for the rest of my life. It changed me. It is one thing to read of these things, another to see them. To know that some good has come of it helps take away some of the awfulness.'

Leon Rosenthal nodded gravely. 'Yet, perhaps there is some way that I can repay you, at least in part, for finding Hannah. You came to Antwerp for a reason, I understand, not unconnected with those times? Samuel mentioned a Soviet official. I am afraid I know nothing of that. Yet, I have taken an interest since our Russian friends abandoned Communism for the KGB.' He smiled at Jamie's puzzlement. The Englishman opened his mouth to say something, but Danny Fisher kicked his foot under the table. 'We have to call it the flowering of capitalism and it is true that many things have changed. Russians, as I am sure Samuel mentioned, are some of Antwerp's biggest customers. After so many years of austerity they covet things that sparkle. And, of course, should the situation change, diamonds are an ideal, easily transportable currency in times of crisis.' He stopped to take another sip of whisky, leaving the table to return a moment later with a newspaper, which he left folded in front of him. 'From time to time,' he continued absently, 'certain favoured former clients still ask me for their advice. A few years ago, for instance, I spent some time in St Petersburg – a beautiful city; if you have not visited it, you surely must – as a guest of one such client. I was given what you would call the movie-star treatment.' He smiled at the memory. 'Of course, I cannot betray a business confidence by naming the gentleman in question, I have a reputation to protect even now.' He closed his eyes and his voice faded, then recovered slightly. 'I had the oddest dream a few nights ago, about a diamond, a diamond to take your breath away. Imagine it, a man like me, who has seen everything the diamond world has to offer, from the Koh-i-noor to the Cullinan, being so impressed. A white diamond, flawless, yet, in the way it was presented, flawed, because it had never been cut or polished by an expert. My hands itched to cut it, how they itched. I can feel them now, reaching out for it. But, in the dream, the owner would not have it cut. I could polish it, all seventy-five facets, to make the most of what it was, but the integrity must remain unchanged. Of course, I protested. To make the most of what it was, it must be cut. It was a slightly offset oval, but to reach the very heart of it, to bring out the pure diamond that was its soul, it must be cut pear. I cajoled, I even pleaded, but he would not be moved. If the dream was true, Leon Rosenthal would go to his grave regretting that moment.' He opened his eyes with a tired smile. 'Fortunately, it was only a dream.'

'How much would a stone like that be worth?' Danny asked, winning a look of scorn from their host.

'It is not a question of worth, Miss Fisher, but of glory. Even in its cut state, it would have remained at least 275 carats, and would have outsized and outshone the greatest clear pear the world has yet seen by at least one hundred carats. When it was exhibited in London that diamond was insured for one hundred million pounds, which was a fraction of its *worth*. In monetary terms, my diamond would be *worth* ten times as much.'

'Then the man who owned it would have been worth a great deal?'

Leon Rosenthal turned to Jamie with a shrug. 'He treasured the stone purely for its sentimental value. A gift from his father, I understand. Perhaps a leftover from the time of the Tsars, which if it came to light, might be the subject of some dispute with the remaining remnants of the Romanovs. Who knows? Of course,' he opened the newspaper in front of him and flicked through the pages, 'there are many rich men in Russia today. Look at this one, for instance.' He pointed to a picture of a man disembarking from an enormous yacht. 'He gives rich men a bad name . . .' Jamie craned forward to see the name. Leon removed the newspaper with a knowing smile. '. . . unlike the gentleman who invited me to St Petersburg.'

'Did he just do what I think he just did?' Danny demanded as they sat in the back of the taxi taking them to their hotel.

'I think so. To mix a couple of metaphors, he led us up the garden path, then pulled the rug out from under us.'

'After all that bullshit about *my Hannah* and how grateful he was, he had the name and he wouldn't give it to us.'

Jamie smiled and shook his head. 'That wasn't

bullshit. Leon Rosenthal meant every word he said, but Leon's personal integrity wouldn't allow him to give us the name. He's lived all his life by a code of honour as strict as any Samurai. If you look at it from his point of view, everything he'd gained from finally discovering what happened to Hannah Schulmann would have been lost.'

'I'd still like to go back there and hang the old bastard up by the heels till he spilled.'

'I doubt that would work. He may be old, but he was one tough old bastard. I think he liked the idea of challenging us.'

'Yeah. The old bastard.'

Suddenly they were laughing and he took her in his arms and kissed her, feeling the odd mix of hardness and softness that was like an aphrodisiac to his senses.

'Anyway, how many billionaire Russian oligarchs can there be?'

'More than you'd think.'

'Probably,' he mused, 'but I'm betting that only one of them has a father who was an NKVD lieutenant serving in Berlin under Marshal Zhukov on the twenty-ninth of April nineteen forty-five.'

XXXIX

Paul Dornberger stared out of the hospital window and pondered his next move. The Zurich raid might have been a disaster, but the face he had seen behind the machine gun at the Cessna's window created a last opportunity to make up the lost ground.

He had underestimated Jamie Saintclair. Like a will-o'-the-wisp, the art dealer somehow flitted in and out of the action with irritating ease and damaging consequences. How had he tracked down Berndt Hartmann so quickly? Dornberger shook his head. That didn't matter now. All that mattered was that with Hartmann gone and the diamond still missing, only Saintclair could provide him with his next step on the road to reuniting the Eye with the Crown.

News of the air crash had filtered through while he was still in Zurich. A burned-out Cessna float plane. No known survivors. At first he was certain he had lost everything. Only slowly did it emerge that the crashed

386

plane contained a single body. Discreet enquiries revealed the victim as one Berndt Hartmann, retired security consultant. That meant Saintclair had somehow escaped. The question was, where would he turn up next? It had been five days and there was no sign of him either at the Bond Street office or the Kensington flat, both of which were being watched by Dornberger's men.

He looked down at the old man on the bed. Max Dornberger's skin was the colour and texture of old parchment and the flickering eyes sunk deep in circles of bruising. The shrunken figure breathed in short, gasping bursts like an engine about to cut out. Even the best doctors Oleg Samsonov's money could buy had given up on him. Three days. Could he hang on until then? Dornberger's eyes automatically moved to the safe. Was it possible? If a suitable candidate could be found and the ceremony properly reenacted, would it buy him time? No. It was a measure of his desperation that he should even think of it. His father had been emphatic. Without the Eye, the Crown was nothing but a golden trinket. The ritual would only be effective if it was carried out under the right conditions on the first day of the sickle moon. Only then would Max Dornberger be restored. Did he truly believe that? He had to believe it, because if he did not, his whole life had been for nothing. All that pain and death. He had suffered every agony and every humiliation for this. The old man groaned and Dornberger's entire being seemed to collapse in on itself as he was consumed by a terrible emptiness. Once life fled the frail, decaying vessel on the bed, what was left for him? Three days. He must find Saintclair. Every instinct told him that the art dealer was close to the solution. And once he had Saintclair in his power that solution would be his.

Back in the office at the Samsonov complex all he could do was harness his frustration and go through the motions of carrying out his day-to-day work. The billionaire had left to meet a group of Japanese industrialists and Paul, who only had a smattering of the language, had been replaced for the day by an interpreter. He had done everything he could. If Saintclair used one of his credit cards or made a call on his mobile phone he would be alerted. If he appeared either at the house or at the office Paul Dornberger would know within minutes. He even had people checking out London's countless hotels on the off chance that the art dealer had booked a room under his own name. All he could do now was wait. But waiting didn't come easy.

He walked along the corridor to the security room. Gerard was sitting back in his chair, almost horizontal, his eyes half closed but never leaving the monitors in front of him. Kenny sat beside him and they chatted quietly, probably about the hitting power and other merits of automatic weapons, which seemed to be their sole topic of conversation. They looked completely relaxed, but Dornberger knew that was an illusion. A shadow warrior knew instinctively when to conserve his energy. It came just as naturally as the instinct that would turn these men into whirlwinds of death at the first sign of a threat to their client. The Australian looked up and grinned. 'Hey, Paul. The old man given you a half day?'

Paul smiled back, donning the mask that had protected him all his life. 'Even my world has to take a rest some time. Everything set for the German trip?'

It was only conversation, but Paul saw the instant change as Kenny's mind turned to business. 'Sure, Paul. Scout car, decoy, client's car and chase car on the way to the airport. Straight through to the plane. Four men waiting on the tarmac at the other side and the same system on the way to the meet. Wha'dyathink? No problems?'

'No problems. They tell me the nightlife's great in Berlin.'

They both laughed. The chances of any of them getting beyond fifty yards of Oleg Samsonov's side during the visit were non-existent, almost as non-existent as the chances of Oleg going to a nightclub.

'Can I get you guys a coffee?' Kenny shook his head and Gerard didn't even acknowledge the suggestion. 'I'll ask the others.' As he walked past Gerard's monitor, he could see an armed figure standing by the outer gate. It wasn't Vince, who lay on his bunk in the security quarters reading some kind of Japanese manga comic, while the two other men played cards at a small table. All three looked up with the bored watchfulness that was endemic to their kind when they were out of the firing line.

'Coffee?' he asked.

'Thanks for the offer, but no.' Vince smiled. The others shook their heads silently and concentrated on their cards. Paul went through to the small kitchen and prepared himself a cup of the instant he preferred. On the left of the door was a board with rows of hooks that held the keys for Samsonov's fleet of cars, but Dornberger's mind went over what he had just witnessed. The angles and the distances.

He stayed with the guards for a few minutes, drinking his coffee and engaging Vince in desultory conversation about the fortunes of the Forty Niners, which he knew the Californian took an interest in. It was something he did most days and they were as relaxed in his presence as tight-wound men like these ever would be.

When he returned to his desk, he picked up an invoice he'd been keeping for over a week. He had little to do with the day–to–day running of the household. Irina, who in her heart of hearts was a traditional borscht-stirring, gossiping Russian housewife, insisted that it was her way of staying in contact with reality in her gold-plated world. The timing was important. He was careful never to be alone with her and he knew she would be just completing her daily two-hour session with the secretary who helped with the various charities she involved herself in. The household staff worked strictly defined hours and kept to their quarters in the grounds when they weren't on duty to ensure privacy for the Samsonov family. He trotted upstairs to the huge open-plan living area.

Irina was sitting at a desk beside a tall bearded man studying a document. The man explained something and tried desperately to avoid any semblance of physical contact. It was always this way with occasional visitors. Oleg Samsonov's power didn't just make out-siders wary, it induced fear, and Dornberger's knowledge of the darker elements of the Russian's busi-ness interests convinced him that fear was well justified. Eventually the bearded man stood up, and Irina Samsonov rose with a formal smile. 'Thank you, Mr Rudge. Next week at the same time?'

Rudge bowed as if she was a duchess and backed away. Paul Dornberger gave a quiet cough. Irina looked round and smiled when she recognized him. Belatedly she realized she was wearing her spectacles and removed them with a single smooth movement and without a change of expression. In many ways she was as vain as her husband and just as formidable.

'Paul, this is a surprise; what can I do for you?'

He handed her the invoice. 'The bill for the party we gave for the African delegation?'

'Yes, it's dated last week, but it must have got stuck in the post. I need your signature to pay this one because of the amount, which you'll see is above the authorized figure.'

She pursed her lips, gave a rueful smile and signed the back of the paper. 'They do like their gifts. Crystal eggs in the style of Fabergé and every one with a Cartier watch and a set of Ferrari keys. Sometimes, when I'm hosting, I feel like Marie Antoinette.'

He thanked her and turned to leave, but she called him back.

'I promised I would show you Oleg's latest acquisition.' She waved him across towards the panic room. 'Now, we must follow security instructions.' She smiled to show there was no offence intended. 'So I must ask you to turn away while I open the gallery.'

The gallery? It was an odd reference and one that showed the conflicting attitudes of Oleg Samsonov and his wife to the house they shared. For Oleg it was a fortress; an ultra-secure headquarters from which he could rule his vast worldwide empire with the added attraction that it was in the centre of a cosmopolitan, cultured city. A city where the inhabitants tended not to work out their differences with rocket launchers or car bombs, and where a man with money and influence was guaranteed access at the highest levels. Irina, on the other hand, had never shared her husband's insecurity as he gathered his wealth and attempted to consolidate it with hungry jackals barking at him from every side. She understood and sympathized with the dreams that sometimes made him call out in the night, but she could never think of her home as a bomb-proof citadel. She knew that their wealth made them targets, and welcomed the protection it afforded, particularly to little Dimi, but there were no images in her sub-conscious of machine-gun-carrying hordes of Kazakhs or Chechens swarming across the security wall to avenge a hundred intended and unintended slights. So the barriers were an irritant and the guards a necessary, but unwanted, intrusion into her life, and the panic room became the gallery. And within the house she could trust who she chose. Even Oleg had agreed that Paul was safe.

'You can turn now.' She said it with a complacent smile that sought, no, demanded, his appreciation. And he gave it.

'Incredible.' He stepped forward, but she touched his arm and shook her head.

'It's protected so that an alarm sounds and the whole building goes into lockdown if someone other than a family member enters. You must only look.'

'Of course.' He smiled. For a moment he forgot everything as he basked in the golden aura of true genius, an aura that had at its centre a triple sunburst of yellow flowers. The application was almost crude, the brushstrokes confident in their own certainty. A rough vase in glazed green, against a jade background and set upon a mottled wooden surface. Yet the eye barely registered the surroundings, it was the sunflowers that drew it like the flash of an oriole's wing. From deep within their hiding place they seemed to fill the entire room with their glow.

'This is the only one of the series not in a museum,' Irina explained. 'Oleg intends to display it on special occasions, but for the moment it is his personal prize.'

'Then I am doubly honoured.' He found he could barely breathe. 'He must have wanted it very much.'

'Yes, and my Oleg is not deterred by refusal.' She laughed lightly and he knew she was remembering when Samsonov had pursued her around the globe showering her with gifts until she had agreed to abandon her American football star boyfriend. 'Even for him this was an expensive purchase.'

He stepped back to allow her to close the door. The painting stood on an easel in the centre of the room, but his eye was caught by an unusual shape against the far wall close to the door that must lead to the stairs connecting the three floors of the safe haven. She saw his look, and shook her head at her husband's mania for security. Who would put a safe inside a safe room? 'Even I must not look there.' She smiled. 'A family heirloom. Perhaps it is the crown of the Tsars?'

He laughed obediently, but he'd seen everything he needed to see.

Suddenly her face lit the room in the same way the sunflowers had earlier.

'Mummy.' A dark flash flew past Dornberger as Dmitri launched himself into his mother's arms.

'Dimi.' His mother picked him up and whirled him

around. 'Foof!' she said. 'You are getting too big for this. Time you had a little brother or sister, huh?'

'Me. Me. Me,' Dmitri laughed. 'Me. Me. Me.'

Paul Dornberger kept the mask in place as he stepped back to watch the perfectly natural interaction between mother and son. Inside, he felt as if he was being sucked into a whirlpool. Something she had said . . . What was it that had scored the inside of his brain like a red-hot blade? His mind spun as he tried to find something of his own childhood. A mother. A moment of pleasure. He could remember neither. The cold shock of the truth froze the smile on his face. He had been robbed of all this. And what else? It was there, buried deep; a moment of warmth that he had to find if he was to maintain his sanity. He made a grab for it, but it was like a freshly caught fish slipping through his hands. A fleeting moment of contact and then gone. Panic gripped him and he saw concern on Irina Samsonov's face.

'Paul, are you unwell?'

Somehow he pulled himself together and shook his head, but his shirt was soaked with sweat and his whole body felt as if it was a bundle of flickering nerve ends.

'You are very pale. You look like death, poor man. Come, have a seat here.' She abandoned Dmitri and drew him across to a kudu leather couch. 'Stay with Paul, Dimi. Look after him.'

Dornberger went rigid as the boy sat at his side and put his slim arms around him, so he could feel their warmth. The panic grew. It was not supposed to be like this. Dmitri looked up at him with wide, worried eyes and Dornberger could only stare back dumbly until Irina returned to the room with a damp cloth. She placed it across his forehead and put her hand to his cheek, tutting as she felt the heat of it. The cloth moved to his face, dabbing gently and cooling the fire that burned his skin. An unexpected liquid feeling flooded through him and he could have cried out with the desperate need for human contact. This was what a family must feel like. Without thinking, he reached for her hand and took it.

Irina went rigid. 'Paul, please!' The outrage in her voice shocked him and his fingers reflexively tightened. 'Paul!' She pulled herself free and stood up, taking the boy with her and leaving Dornberger alone on the couch, blinking in bemusement. What had he done? He was appalled at his own weakness. He had allowed the mask to slip and now twenty years of effort and invest-ment was threatening to disintegrate. If he lost his job it would take years to rebuild the network he had created within the Samsonov organization. His first instinct, the instinct he had been bred for, was to wipe away any trace of his failure. He stood up and saw the alarm in Irina's eyes as the height and muscularity that had made her feel safe now appeared so threatening and full of menace. But Irina Samsonov was the daughter of Cossacks; her high cheeks flared with colour and her eyes flashed with suppressed fury. When she opened her mouth he knew she was going to fire him on the spot. He moved before she could speak.

'I apologize for my lapse,' he said humbly, bowing his head. 'You are right; I have been unwell for some time. My father . . . when he is gone there will be no one.'

He waited and knew she was searching him for the lie like some steppe shaman; a queen deciding on the fate of her subject. He recognized the moment of decision in the relaxation of her body.

'We will say no more of this for now, Paul. You must take the rest of the day off and we will speak of it again when my husband returns.'

Paul turned away, but not before he had seen the flash of concern in the eyes of the little boy hiding behind his mother's denim-clad legs.

His whole world spun as he returned to the office suite. It could only be minutes since he had climbed these stairs, but it might as well have been a lifetime. It didn't seem possible. All these years he had played this game and now, in a single moment of stupidity, he had jeopardized everything.

He realized he'd left his mobile phone on his desk, and when he walked into the office it was buzzing urgently. When he picked it up his hands were shaking.

'Yes,' he said.

'He's back.'

XL

They made their headquarters in Danny's hotel room and Jamie laid it out as if for a military operation, pulling tables together so they could work side by side with their laptops. He borrowed a flip chart from the conference suite and set it up by the window. On it, he wrote the names of the one hundred billionaires on Russia's Rich List in *Forbes* magazine.

'I think we can discount all those who aren't old enough to have had fathers who fought in the Great Patriotic War,' he suggested, 'which should narrow it down a bit. Also, Leon Rosenthal showed us that particular newspaper for a purpose. The picture was of Roman Abramovich, who owns Chelsea Football Club, getting onto his yacht in Antibes. Abramovich is among the richest of the rich. That means our man is likely to be too. So we start at the top.'

'From what I read here,' Danny looked up from her laptop, 'he's also one of the most flamboyant. His yacht cost something like a billion pounds and is just one of three. He uses them to ferry his family – he has six kids – around the Mediterranean, and when he's not on it, he lends it to his rich friends. Jesus,' she blinked, 'did you know this guy started off selling plastic ducks? Now he's worth ten billion dollars.'

'There's hope for me yet,' Jamie laughed. 'But forget Abramovich. For two reasons: firstly, according to his profile, his father was a construction worker who died in an accident in the Sixties, and second, Leon Rosenthal specifically said he gave rich men a bad name, while the man he met in Russia was the opposite. We're looking for a billionaire with a low profile.'

Danny looked up at the flip chart, which contained many names she didn't recognize, and rubbed her eyes. 'There must be dozens of them here.'

'Well,' he said cheerfully, 'we have to start somewhere. Odds or evens.'

'I'll take odds. So,' she took a deep breath, 'first on the list is Vladimir Lisin, chairman of Novolipetsk Steel. Net worth: twenty-four billion dollars. Born nineteen fifty-six, which puts him in the right age range, but it says here he followed his pop into the Tulachermet steel works, which I guess rules him out?'

'Let's not be too hasty. Put him down as a possible.'

They worked their way from the top of the list, discounting on the grounds of age, background or father's job history, and retaining a few possibles, which Jamie admitted to himself were long shots at best. 'Let's stop for a coffee,' he suggested after an hour. 'What do you think so far?'

'I think that if some of these guys weren't on the rich list, they'd be on the most wanted list. You?'

'To be honest, I'm surprised there are so few dodgy characters, given the kind of murky stuff that was going on after the communists were kicked out. Mind you, there was a kind of natural selection. The weak were either disposed of or forced to go bust, and the real bad guys either are in jail or are Mafia bosses who'd rather not have their name in the paper and keep their wealth secret. There may be a few skeletons in the cupboard among the people on the list, but you could say that about any rich and powerful man anywhere.'

'What I also think is that we aren't getting anywhere.'

'Not yet,' he admitted. 'But maybe that's not a bad thing. He's here somewhere, I'm certain of it. The fact that so few people fit the profile means that when we do find him it will be obvious.'

So obvious that by the time they reached the end of the list they had fifteen possibles and zero probables.

'He has to be here,' Jamie repeated.

'Sure,' Danny said soothingly. 'The essence of all detective work. If at first you don't succeed . . .'

'Go through the possibles again. We said Lisin was unlikely, why?'

'Because his father was a foreman in a steelworks and I can't see an NKVD war hero ending up in a steelworks in Kazakhstan. From what you've told me, that's not the way the system worked, especially while Stalin was still alive. You kept your nose clean and were lucky, you rose through the ranks. If you didn't, it was Siberia, or more likely the Lubyanka and a bullet in the back of the neck.'

'Okay, who's next?'

'Vekselberg, Viktor, head of the Renova Group and worth a cool thirteen billion. Around the right age, but we have no information about his parents.'

Jamie read the *Forbes* biography and clicked through the pages on his laptop screen. He shook his head. 'My gut says no. This bloke had to work to make his money and it was his contacts with the Yeltsin administration that made him rich.'

By the time they had gone through the list for a second time, they were left with just five possible candidates. Jamie ripped the sheet from the flip chart and tore the surviving names off in strips before placing them face up on the bed. He frowned over them for so long that Danny eventually said: 'Do you think he's going to jump up and introduce himself, Saintclair?'

He grinned self-consciously. 'They're all the right age, but their past lives seem to have been wiped clean, which is suspicious in itself. We can't find any record of their parentage on any website, Russian or otherwise. They all made the kind of dramatic rises that could only have been made with the right contacts and backing, which means high-ranking party membership or the KGB.'

'That's true,' Danny said thoughtfully. 'But maybe we've been so caught up in this hunt-the-thimble exercise that we've been forgetting something.' She moved three of the names off the bed onto the floor and pointed at the two survivors. 'Only these could be called the richest of the rich.'

Jamie studied the two names and felt his heart beat faster. 'You, my dearest Yank, are a genius. Get that laptop cranked up and find everything there is to find about these two gentlemen.'

The first thing they discovered was that both men were resident in London, one voluntarily, the other because if he returned to Russia he would immediately be arrested on multi-billion-pound fraud charges.

'Would you say this guy gives being rich a bad name?'

'Maybe not in Russia.' Jamie grinned and stepped behind her, so he could see what was on her screen. 'Anyway, let's not count our chickens. Keep scrolling.'

'Nothing about their backgrounds. They're both relatively low profile for billionaire businessmen. No yachts or football teams or nightclubs. In fact, judging from the picture file they don't seem to get out much, which seems a waste with all that—'

'Wait.'

Her finger froze on the mousepad.

'Where was that picture taken?'

The photograph focused on one man among a group of about a dozen, all wearing dark overcoats. It was only when you studied it carefully you noticed the sub-group; stone-faced young men with alert, searching eyes fixed on different points of the compass, with the picture's subject at their geographical centre.

'At the Cenotaph in Whitehall, November two thousand and six, it says here, I guess that would account for the buttonholes, huh?'

'Poppies,' Jamie corrected. He'd noticed that all the men were wearing the Remembrance Day symbols, but that wasn't what had drawn his attention to the picture. 'Can you home in on that other red spot on his chest just below the poppy.'

She double clicked on the picture and it formed a separate image no larger than the original. 'Not in this program.' She clicked her teeth. 'Maybe if I open it in Photoshop. Depends how sharp the original is. Looks like it was one frame, taken in a hurry before his security detail reacted. They appear to be some tough hombres.'

While Danny fiddled with the computer, Jamie went to the window. It was still early afternoon, but the kind of dull, mist-wrapped London day that turned the city into a patchwork of individual, gloomy Victorian town-scapes filled with rushing figures wrapped in warm overcoats. A sort of between-seasons limbo: the golden days of autumn were nothing but a memory, but winter was somewhere in the future, if the self-generated micro-climate of a city of seven million souls ever con-descended to give it house room. Somewhere out there, the enemy was waiting, and perhaps not waiting, but hunting. The textbook Special Forces-style raid on Berndt Hartmann's lakeside mansion had shown him what they were up against and he had no illusions about his chances of defeating these men. But he had promised Danny Fisher his support and Jamie Saintclair kept his promises. And afterward, when she went back to Brooklyn? Well, he'd have to think about that. She'd hinted, in her clod-hopping cowboy way, that he could go back with her – his business was international, he was as likely to succeed in New York, or not, as he was in London – but somehow that didn't appeal at the breakfast table the same way it did in bed. She was wonderful; exhilarating, exhausting, challenging and infuriating at one and the same time, but, apart from Danny Fisher, his life was here, in his maddeningly English, stuck-up, sometimes horribly vulgar, little corner of this vast cosmopolitan metropolis. She knew as well as he did that when she got on that plane, he'd be there to wave her off. And, then, unless some miracle happened, he would have to face the enemy alone. There was no question of a truce, he was certain of that. These men had left their traces like the scent mark of a leopard, with utter cruelty and ruthless efficiency, on both sides of the Atlantic. Unless they had what they wanted they would never leave him alone. This was a fight to the death.

'It looks like some kind of medal.' Danny's voice cut through his gloom. 'Hard to tell, but it could be a gold star on a red ribbon. There's another one beside it, but it's a little harder to make out.'

'Bring up a website with images of Soviet military decorations!' he ordered.

'Anything you want to tell me, Sherlock?' She looked up sharply at the excitement in his voice. 'Because if you aren't wetting your panties about something all those psychology classes I went to were a waste of time.'

'Why would someone who's never been anywhere near a battle march in a Remembrance Day parade wearing a medal he wasn't entitled to?'

Danny saw where he was going with the argument, but she had to play Devil's advocate. 'He would have been a conscript. Every Russian of his age had to do their national service. Maybe he won it in Afghanistan. Plenty of glory to go round in that one.'

He stared impatiently at the screen. 'Maybe.'

'Or it could be some kind of industrial award. Why shouldn't he wear his Order of the Filled Pig Iron Quota when he's got the chance?'

A page came up on the screen. It had dozens of awards arrayed in rows across the screen. 'Can you refine it?'

'Sure, I'll just add star, see what comes up.'

This time there were many fewer.

'Order of the Red Star,' she quoted. 'Looks like they gave that one out just for getting up in the morning.'

'Our star isn't red, it's gold, maybe you hadn't noticed.' She heard the edge in his voice and grinned.

'Keep your hair on, Sherlock, we'll get there. How's about that? Gold star on a red ribbon.' She divided the screen so that the image of Oleg Samsonov and his retinue was on the left and the medal on the right. 'Could be?' She turned to him.

'Jackpot,' he whispered. After she managed to unwrap him from their spontaneous embrace, she threatened to use the fruit knife in all sorts of interesting ways unless he spilled the beans. 'It looks like a medal. A simple gold star on a red ribbon. But it's actually a title: Hero of the Soviet Union. It was awarded to the bravest of the brave, or generals who were ruthless enough to win their battles at any cost. I doubt Oleg Samsonov won it, but I'm betting that his father did.'

'We can't approach him on a hunch. We have to know for sure.'

'I know. I'm thinking.'

'Well, think fast, pardner, because time is running short.'

He reached to the bedside for his mobile phone, but before he could dial she laid a hand on his.

'I've been thinking, since Zurich and Hamburg, that it's possible that our phones have been compromised in some way.'

'Bugged, you mean? I never let it out of my sight. It's like an electronic tag.' She gave him the look. 'Oh, I see. You mean there are ways they could find out where we are.'

'It's possible. Not to the nearest foot or anything close, and certainly not on the seventh floor of a concrete hotel, but anything that brings them closer to us is off limits.'

He looked at the little oblong of plastic with new understanding and switched off the power button. Instead, he picked up the hotel phone.

'That's not a good idea either, unless you're phoning someone who's not on their radar. It's possible we led them to Bernie Hartmann, but if we didn't the chances are they found him electronically. Bernie was a careful man. If they could do that to him, they can bug your office and your home, and anyone who happens to be in your address book.'

'Aren't you being a little paranoid?'

'Why don't you ask Bernie?'

'The person I'm phoning is not on their radar.'

'You certain?'

'It's Sir William Melrose.'

She thought about it. 'Okaaay.'

He dialled the number and when the secretary answered he asked to be put through to the great man. When Sir William came on the line he apologized for disturbing him. 'Not at all, young man.' The writer's jovial tones echoed in the earpiece. 'A long shift on the Burma Railway can be rather wearing on the senses. Glad to be out of it for a few minutes. How goes the grand quest?'

'It seems to be one step forward, two steps back, sir, but we're making progress.'

'Well, how can I help you make a little more?'

'Would I be correct in thinking that the title of Hero of the Soviet Union has not been awarded too often?'

'Good God, no, what makes you think that? They handed out thousands of the damn things.'

Jamie tried to disguise his disappointment. 'I'm thinking in particular of the battle for Berlin or just prior to it. This would be an award to a relatively junior NKVD officer named, possibly, Samsonov, who was somewhere near Potsdamer Platz on the twenty-ninth of April.'

There was a low moan from the other end of the line and Jamie wondered if Sir William was in pain, but the author was mentally dredging the voluminous mountains of research in his brain. 'Yeeees, that would make him part of Zhukov's Third Shock Army, almost certainly with the 150th Rifle Division under Pereveretkin. You're not after the chaps who raised the Red Banner over the Reichstag, are you? Entirely different names I'm afraid. Yegorov and Kantaria, and neither of them was NKVD.'

'No, sir, I'm afraid this chap wasn't quite so famous.'

'On the other hand, not many of the NKVD people became Heroes of the Soviet Union, unless it was their generals. They tended to command blocking detachments, you see, the people who shot down their own chaps when the attack faltered. Not a particularly heroic job. Seems even Stalin thought that. Samsonov, you say?'

'We believe so.'

'See what I can do. Might take a few hours. Can you give me a call tomorrow morning?'

'Of course. Around ten?'

'Excellent. Hey, ho. Back to the rice and mealies.'

He told Danny the outcome of the conversation.

'Damn. We can't afford to wait another day. We have to do something now.'

'What do you suggest? Pop around and say, "Dear Oleg, we think your old dad might have been an NKVD man who looted a fabulous diamond during the Second World War. Hand said sparkler over and we'll say nothing more about it. Oh, and by the way, someone's probably coming to kill you." I'm not sure that would work. Apart from the fact he'd think we were mad, at this very moment we have no idea where he lives.'

She rewarded him with a look that would have withered a cactus. 'So what do we do?'

'Well, we have time on our hands and,' he bounced suggestively on the mattress, 'a perfectly good bed. I'll leave it to your licentious mind to work out the rest. Afterwards, you dress for dinner and I'll do so some errands.'

'I hope you're not going to do anything crazy?'

'Before or after?'

'I'm serious.'

'I haven't spoken to Gail for two weeks. She'll be worried sick. I owe her a call just to let her know I'm still alive. She will also be able to make a few discreet enquiries about the whereabouts of Oleg Samsonov's London pied-à-terre. And I just remembered I have an acquaintance who drifts about in those circles.' He saw her confusion. 'Minor royalty, politicians on the make, football club owners and the like. The last time I saw her was at an exhibition Samsonov may even have attended. If nothing else, she'll know who his friends are. You've made me nervous about using the room phone. I'll wander around until I find a telephone box that works and call the office from there. Satisfied?'

'I'll let you know later.' She grinned and began un-buttoning her jeans.

An hour later, Jamie walked along the murky streets near the hotel lit by a warm internal glow and with a head that wasn't quite on this planet. The first telephone booth he found had the handset cord cut and the second wouldn't take his money. He cursed under his breath and carried on. Gradually, the glow faded. All around him people were going about their daily business oblivious of the enemy in their midst. Somewhere out there, a man was plotting murder. Probably more than one murder. Somewhere out there, a child might already be at the killer's mercy. He clutched his overcoat closer against the raw chill, but it wasn't only the cold that made him shiver. At times, he felt like a wraith, part-human, part-ghost, gliding through the midst of an unseeing crowd. He searched the faces and it seemed to him that he would know the murderer by his aura, and the murderer would know him in turn, because they had both been polluted by the taint of the Crown of Isis. The thought made him smile. This bloody thing is driving me off my rocker.

A figure appeared in front of him. 'Spare a fag, mate?'

Jamie tensed, his right fist curling into a ball with the third knuckle protruding, ready to make the straight-arm jab to the throat the instructors said would disable or kill with the single blow. Then he saw the flickering lids and dull eyes of the addict and the drooping, defeated shoulders of a man beyond help. Not even a man; the boy couldn't be more than seventeen. No threat here. He relaxed, shook his head – thought about handing over his spare change before remembering he needed it – and walked on towards the lights of Lancaster Gate.

The public telephone in the Tube station worked and he called Gail's home number first, waiting for a dozen rings before returning the receiver to its cradle. That probably meant she was working late. He called the office and this time it gave five rings before clicking to the answering machine. While he listened to his own voice telling him to leave a message after the tone, he made up his mind.

'Gail, Jamie here,' he said in that curiously stilted tone people use when they're talking to a machine. 'Sorry not to have been in touch, but as you can see . . . er, hear, I'm fine. Look, I need some info on a potential client. Rich Russian. Oleg Samsonov, O-Oscar,

L-Lima . . .' he spelled the name out phonetically,
'. . . address, telephone number, current whereabouts,
you know the form. Might be worth trying Charlie at
Bonhams, first, but be very discreet. It's important that
no one gets to know anything about this. Top secret,
okay? When you get it, e-mail the details to me. And
can you do me a favour and nip round to the flat
and see if there's anything that looks interesting in my
post. The spare key's in my desk drawer under the box
of business cards. Er, take care.' He hung up. What
would he do without that bloody woman? He was
walking back to the hotel when he remembered
something.

'Bugger.'

He reversed his direction. It wouldn't take long and
Danny would never know.

'. . . Er, take care.' In the darkened office overlooking
Old Bond Street, the impassive figure listened to the end
of the message before reaching with his gloved hand to
replay it. When he was certain he had every detail
memorized he stepped over the body crumpled into the
narrow space beside the desk and retrieved the key from
the drawer. He was barely conscious of the woman
on the floor as he made his way to the door. All she had
needed to do was answer his questions, but no, she
had to be a hero. She was an underling. A nobody.
Why had she felt the need to sacrifice herself for someone like Jamie Saintclair?

He closed the door behind him and looked down at the key in his hand. It had a brown label tied to it. '16C Kensington High Street.'

XLI

Paul Dornberger sat motionless in Jamie Saintclair's unlit flat absorbing the sights, scents and sounds around him. The instincts of the hunter and the ability to stay immobile were bred in him. He had spent countless hours in the freezing mud beside the pond on his father's estate waiting for the ducks to fly in. His father stayed in the hide, watching for any movement, and Paul knew that even the slightest twitch or attempt to ease his aching muscles would be punished. When he was older, they had travelled to the Highlands to shoot stags on the misty slopes of some Scottish mountain and he had squirmed through the gorse and the heather an inch at a time to get himself in place for the killing shot. The gillies had praised his marksmanship and his stamina, but he had seen the sidelong glances at his lack of emotion or feeling for the kill.

It took enormous effort and concentration to maintain this level of alertness and not allow the mind to be absorbed or tire or wander. A distant scratching noise caught his attention and his whole being focused on it like radar as his hand closed over the butt of the pistol that sat in his lap. His mind ran through the possible threats one after another, discarding each as they came. Not someone working on the lock, but a mouse or a vole nibbling at the skirting boards. The room's only illumination was provided by the orange glow from the street lights below. It meant he could make out the shapes of everything around him, but not the colours or textures that gave them their true identity. He knew there were paintings on the wall, but whether they were the work of Impressionists or Cubists was hidden in the gloom. Each piece of furniture was imprinted on the inside of his brain so that when the time came he would not trip or stumble, but could use them to his advantage. Likewise the layout of the apartment was as familiar to him as his own. The bedrooms to the rear beyond the kitchen – to the right – and the bathroom – left, one of them used as an office and equipped with a computer whose standby light produced a dull red line below the doorway. It was in the bathroom that he had placed everything he needed.

A siren sounded in the distance and drew closer; for a few seconds the room was bathed in a dozen shades of neon blue and then it was gone. He almost missed the sound of the lift opening, but the moment his ears caught the mechanical hiss he was on his feet and beside the door. A slight hesitation and then footsteps, wary and quiet. The sound of light breathing within two feet of his right ear. A liquid feeling in his brain as he felt the whisper of another mind seeking out his. He forced himself to relax. Tension slowed the reactions. Allow the mind to take control. Another pause before the muffled rattle of keys and the sound of one entering the lock. Counting down the seconds, he swapped the Glock from his right hand to his left, drew a spring-loaded leather cosh from his pocket. The door handle turned and the door opened inwards, the light from the hallway projecting a shadow across the floor of the lounge. He had removed the bulb from the light. By now a hand should be reaching for the switch. A voice screamed a warning inside his head. He raised the cosh as the shadow thickened and a figure appeared behind the painted wood. With astonishing power the heavy door swung into his face. But Dornberger was already moving backwards, allowing the threat to dissipate itself and rolling between a chair and a display case in a move that brought him to his feet ready to attack or defend as the situation required. There was no panic, only a constant revision of the circumstances. Saintclair had been quicker and more wary than he had believed possible, but that changed nothing. The art dealer was an amateur. Paul Dornberger had been trained from birth to deal death. He had lost the pistol and he could only pray his opponent didn't find it first. Attack. He weighed the cosh in his hand as the door closed and the shadow merged with the surrounding darkness. The soft sound of breathing merged with the shuffle of feet on carpet. He had a picture of the room in his mind and though he could see nothing he had a mental image of his opponent. He should be hesitant. Fearful. But what was this? A blur of speed moving towards him at hip height. He just had time to half turn and as the shoulder hit him a glancing blow the cosh was already descending. The shoulder was more solid than he had expected, but he heard a grunt of pain as the leather-wrapped steel struck. Even as the sound reached his ears he knew he'd missed his target, the kidney, and he was already moving away from danger as the other man swung a left hook towards his heart. The punch had all his weight behind it and threw him off balance, allowing Paul Dornberger to bring the cosh down on the point of Saintclair's shoulder. This time he felt the jar of a solid connection and he smiled inwardly because he knew his opponent wouldn't be able to use the arm for at least an hour. He was crippled and at his tormentor's mercy, as Dornberger had planned all along. What he hadn't planned was the skull that swung into his ribs with the power of a close-range cannonball. He heard the crack of breaking bone even as the pain speared through him like a red-hot bolt. His unconscious mind flared in wonder at the depths of unexpected endurance and violence his victim was capable of, but the conscious mind only had time to register his agony as the skull was followed by the rest of the body. Hard bone and solid muscle forced him backward and smashed him off the wall, creating a new ball of pain as the two men fell to the floor with a wooden chair splintering under their combined weight. This wasn't how it was supposed to be. He had had all the advantages against an opponent who should have been unprepared. Now he could smell the other man's breath as teeth snapped at his throat an inch from his jugular and the fingers of one functioning hand clawed for his eyes. But they had fallen with Dornberger on top and now he was able to get his right hand free. With a short professional swing he brought the cosh down on the forehead above the other man's eyes. Saintclair gave one convulsive shudder and was still.

Dornberger felt like collapsing on top of his victim, but the blow with the cosh had been little more than a tap and he knew he only had limited time. Still in darkness, he dragged the unconscious figure through into the hallway and turned left into the bathroom. The flat was part of an older building but the bathroom looked as if it had been recently modernized and contained a shower stall with a shower head fixed to the ceiling. He laid the unconscious body down on the tiled floor and pulled the cord that controlled the light switch. It took a few seconds for his eyes to adjust and when they did he felt the muscles bulge in his neck and an involuntary growl of suppressed rage escaped from his throat. Saintclair. It should have been Saintclair. Who was this man he had never set eyes on before, with the pale, almost albino looks, and cropped sandy hair? It took time to recover from the surprise, but he realized he had no choice but to go ahead with his original plan. There were things to be learned here, perhaps not what he had thought to learn, but they might be important. The intruder had Saintclair's key and he had fought with the speed and strength of a soldier or a martial arts specialist. The pain in Dornberger's ribs had subsided to a deep, throbbing assault and he knew what he was going to do next wouldn't help. He bent with a grunt and pulled the prone man's wrists together above his head and pinioned them with a cable tie. In the next movement, he heaved him to his feet and attached the tie to another that was already fixed to the shower head. The pain made him cry out, but he ignored it. He'd tested the head earlier and reckoned that it would take his victim's weight, unless he was able to exert pressure on it, which Dornberger didn't intend to allow him to do. When he was finished, the man who should have been Saintclair was suspended by the arms from the shower head with his head slumped to one side, snoring through his nose. Dornberger reached for the neck of the dangling man's shirt and ripped it apart, baring his hairless chest. He pinched the pale cheek hard, eliciting a small reaction. He pinched again.

Frederick opened his eyes to see a blurred figure looming in front of him. His aching head and the fire in his arms competed for his attention. After killing the woman he had come to the flat to wait for Saintclair. The attack as he'd entered had been a complete surprise, but he had known he could take the Englishman. What he hadn't expected was the strength and power he'd encountered, nor the cosh that had disabled him and eventually allowed his opponent to get the upper hand. Gradually, he became aware of his surroundings and he felt the first sharp thrill of fear. His initial reaction had been that, even though Saintclair had defeated him, he was in no real danger. The art dealer might rough him up a little – Saintclair might look like a typical English gentleman, but in the past he'd proved a tough, dangerous and intractable opponent – but then he would hand him over to the police. But as his vision cleared the man standing in front of him wasn't Saintclair, and the ice-chip eyes would have told him he was in trouble even if the short black plastic pole didn't.

'I see you recognize this. Good, I do not need to explain. First we set the ground rules.' The voice was businesslike and contained no hint of emotion. It reminded Frederick of his own. 'They are simple. I will ask you a question and you will answer. If you do not answer I will apply the prod. I will ask you again. If you do not answer, I will increase the power and apply the prod. If you continue to fail to answer I will apply the prod for as long as it takes, even if it burns a hole right through you. Nod if you understand.'

'*Verpiss dich.*'

'German, eh?' Dornberger nodded. 'That's a start. But no, I don't think I will fuck off.'

He peeled off a short strip from the roll of brown tape he always carried and slapped it without ceremony across Frederick's mouth.

'So, we begin.'

He placed the twin prongs against the German's flesh and pressed the power button.

Four hours later sweat poured off Paul Dornberger and his whole body ached. Frederick, as he knew him now, hung naked and the pale white skin was leopard-spotted with weals and burns, some of them still emitting wisps of smoke from the craters the cattle prod had created in the flesh. Christ, how could any man take what he had taken without speaking? Every name and every detail had had to be burned out of him. He now knew all about the neo-Nazi link and the vendetta against Saintclair that Frederick had come to complete. He knew about the woman Frederick had killed to get the key to the flat.

Frederick lived in a world of physical torment. He understood that there was little to be gained by holding out. He knew that whatever happened here he was dead. Still, everything he had ever been brought up to believe told him that he must never give in. By now he understood the only person he was protecting was Saintclair, a man he had vowed to kill. But that counted for nothing. Fight to the last man and the last bullet, that had been the watchword of the man he admired beyond any other. Only a weakling buckles. Still, the pain had been so terrible that his secrets had been torn from him one by one in throat-tearing shrieks of agony. He felt no shame, because his strategy from the beginning had been to create a series of defence lines, each of which could be given up so that the next could be defended for a little longer. He had been forced to choose one secret to protect above all others. There was no rational reason, apart from the importance Saintclair seemed to attach to it. He had come close, a gabbled reference to the telephone message, but if he went to his grave without divulging the name, he could hold his head high among the legions of Valhalla.

End it now, he prayed. *End it now*.

But Paul Dornberger had registered the lapse, cut off almost as soon as it began, as if the tortured man had only just realized its significance.

'The phone message. You said there was a name. What was it?' He removed the tape and there was an incomprehensible mumble from lips lacerated by Frederick's own teeth.

'I didn't hear it. Tell me again.'

This time the answer was clearer. '*Verpiss dich.*'

Dornberger shook his head wearily. '*Dummkoff.*' He gave Frederick's head a slap that was almost affectionate. He replaced the tape and swung the hanging body round so the back was to him. 'Tell me the name.' Frederick gave a shake of the head and Dornberger placed the prongs of the cattle prod carefully at the entrance of his anus and pushed hard. He felt Frederick shudder and when he pressed the button the tethered body bucked like a rodeo pony. When the tortured man had stopped shaking he peeled off the tape and held the prod in front of the tormented face.

'The name?'

Frederick uttered a single word. When he heard it, Paul Dornberger felt as if someone had applied the cattle prod directly to his brain.

XLII

Jamie came off the phone to Sir William Melrose. 'Junior Lieutenant Dmitri Samsonov won the title of Hero of the Soviet Union on the seventeenth of April nineteen forty-five, for what was described as suicidal courage in attacking an entrenched position on the Seelow Heights outside Berlin. He led his men across open ground to capture six machine guns and an anti-tank battery. He was the only survivor of the assault. Ten days later he won the Order of Lenin for doing something similar during the crossing of the Landwehr Canal.'

'Sounds like we've got our man. Oleg Samsonov has a son called Dmitri.' Danny's voice sounded oddly subdued. 'I guess this is where it gets complicated.'

'What do you mean?'

'The way I see it, we have two choices. Either we stake out his house and wait until our killer turns up looking for blood and the Eye of Isis—'

'Which could take forever and places an innocent family at risk.'

She nodded. 'Or we warn Oleg Samsonov that he's being stalked by a cold-blooded killer who will take any risk to get the diamond his father left him, and walk away and let the London cops take over.'

There followed a long silence while they considered the choice that was really no choice at all. Fisher leaned across the bed to kiss him on the lips.

'It was good while it lasted, Jamie Saintclair.'

He shook his head. 'It's not over yet. We still have a few days. I don't suppose we can just phone him and tell him?'

'Nope. Even if we got through to the man himself, which is doubtful, he'd think we were a couple of crazies. Somehow we have to convince him to meet us face to face.'

Jamie's friend Samantha had supplied them with the details of Samsonov's address. 'A great big Modernist cube of a house out by Regent's Park. Awful place, you can't miss it', adding that their chances of getting inside were 'slimmer than an After Eight mint, darling', which wasn't encouraging. They decided the quickest way to get there was by Tube to Baker Street, then take a taxi the rest of the way. Before they set off, they spent half an hour discussing how they might breach Oleg Samsonov's defences.

They walked towards Lancaster Gate and Jamie decided it was safe to switch on his mobile phone. A few seconds after he'd pressed the button it began to buzz like an angry hornet. He felt a terrible foreboding as missed call after missed call registered, all of them from the same number. Danny saw him go pale and stutter to a halt. 'What's up, Jamie?' He ignored her, fumbling for the buttons to access his voicemail. As he listened, he grew paler still.

'I have to get to the office.'

The forensic team had done their work and the body had been removed. Fine silver dust coated every surface, including the phones and the barren no man's land between Jamie's scattered dumping ground and Gail's perfectly aligned in-tray and computer. Without thinking, he moved the meetings diary so it was exactly parallel with the tray.

'Why? She never harmed anyone.'

The question was addressed to Danny, but it was the plain-clothes officer in charge of the murder investigation who answered.

'She was in the wrong place at the wrong time, sir. An accident of nature. Nothing in the world anyone could have done about it. You said she often worked late?' Jamie nodded without really thinking. He felt Danny's eyes on him. 'They would have watched her and seen that she was alone in the building. You're sure there's nothing else missing?'

'Just the petty cash. A few pounds. We don't keep any paintings or anything like that on the premises.'

The detective said something sympathetic, but Jamie's attention was caught by the sound of the answering machine. Another officer sat beside it listening to the message Jamie had sent. 'This is you, sir?' He took the silence that followed as confirmation and flicked the machine off. But Jamie could still hear the words ringing in his head. *Rich Russian. Oleg Samsonov, O-Oscar, L-Lima* . . . His eyes caught Danny's and he could see that she was thinking the same. They *knew*.

Paul Dornberger looked down at his father's body and listened to the tortured sound of his breathing. Like waves breaking across shingle, each intake seemed to take an age and each elastic pause between breaths threatened to be the last. For the past week it had been as if his whole system was fighting itself. Only the plastic tubes carrying liquid nutrition in and his body waste out kept him alive. The major organs fluttered in some limbo between life and extinction, uncertain whether they were required any longer. His was a world of pain, every nerve end exposed like a rotting tooth, and, despite the opiates the doctors prescribed to ease his way to the end, every moment was a torment that made him twist and turn and groan, sapping even further his fading reserve of energy.

'I can never forgive you for what you made me,' Paul said softly. 'But still you are my father. I will not fail you.'

He went to the floor safe and punched in the

numbers. The velvet sack was as he had left it and he picked it up and carried it to the bed. He retrieved the Crown from the depths of the thick cloth and held it for a moment, his chest thickening as he felt the suppressed power of it. Could an object feel? Could it demand? Of course not. Yet a voice inside his head harangued him to do what he must do, and it seemed to him that the voice and the Crown were one. *Soon*, he thought. *Soon you will be reunited with what is rightly yours.*

He took the Crown to the bed and placed his father's hands upon the metal. It had an instant effect. Immediately, the breathing eased and the groans melted away. He bent and kissed the clammy flesh of Max Dornberger's deeply furrowed brow before calling the front desk with the instructions.

Normally, he took a taxi to his work, but today he drove the car, a BMW X-5 with blacked-out rear windows, and parked it as close as he dared. He walked past the main entrance, a high wooden gate topped with spikes that provided vehicle access and was opened either automatically from inside by one of Oleg's fleet of limousines or by Gerard, who would be watching on the security camera that constantly scrutinized the area. Along the roadway beside the faceless security wall with its wired top, and round the corner to the staff entrance. Smile into the camera for Gerard. The slightly over-long pause that was meant to irritate him before the door clicked open to reveal Vince's mocking, disinterested eyes and the barrel of the MP-5 carelessly pointed in his general direction.

'Morning, Vince.'

'Somebody said you were sick.' The American made it sound like an accusation.

Dornberger shrugged. 'You know how it is. Miracle recovery. The boss wouldn't thank me for taking an unnecessary day off right now.'

'Sure.' Vince led the way to the security door at the bottom of the stairs.

Dornberger wore his normal business uniform of suit and dark cashmere overcoat and carried his briefcase in his left hand. As he entered the enclosed stairway, he used the briefcase to shield his right as he dipped into the custom-made inside pocket of the long coat. There was no rush. Just let it happen. His father had always planned for the possibility that Oleg Samsonov might need to be liquidated. He had played out this scene a thousand times in his mind. Practised it over and over again in the basement of the big, rambling house. The door at the top of the stairs clicked open. Kenny was in his usual position to the left of the entrance, with Gerard at the security screens just inside the door at the top of the stair. Gerard barely glanced up as Dornberger walked into the space between them. Kenny grinned and opened his mouth to say something. Dornberger calmly raised the silenced pistol from behind the brief-case and shot the Australian through the eye. In the same movement he turned as Gerard reacted to the sound and shot him in the head before his hand could get anywhere near the Glock on the desk. Blood, bone and brains spattered the wall and the former SAS man slumped over his keyboard. Kenny's body had fallen with an audible thump. Dornberger waited by the door-way connecting the security centre with the guards' living quarters, but there was no reaction. Satisfied, he opened the door and scanned the corridor. Empty. He walked swiftly across to the door of the living quarters, took a deep breath and walked through. Three of them, as normal. They were so used to him going back and forth to get his morning coffee that none showed any sign of suspicion. One on the bed and two at the card table. The two at the card table wore their pistols in shoulder holsters, while that of the man on the bed hung from a peg on the wall above him. Only the man on the bed glanced up. Dornberger walked towards the kitchen. He had planned for a dozen different scenarios, but they made it easy for him. When he was level with the back of the closest card player he lifted the pistol and shot his opponent between the eyes over his right shoulder, adjusting instantly to fire into the back of the nearer man's skull. He could hear the man on the bed scrabbling for his weapon as he turned, but by the time the guard's hand reached the pistol Dornberger had placed two slugs through his spine. As he fell back, Paul stepped forward and put a bullet in his brain. The temp-tation was to linger and admire his handiwork, but he forced himself to concentrate on his next move. Quickly. They're dead. Don't waste time checking. The timetable was set to allow minimal time for imponderables to intrude on the operational matrix. If he stuck to it, there was less chance of something going wrong. He walked out into the corridor, changing to a full magazine as he approached the offices. Mary, Samsonov's secretary, looked up as he entered, a frown on her face that would remain there forever as he brought the pistol up and shot her through the head at point-blank range.

Up the stairs, taking his time now. The only threat left was Vince at the gate, and he wouldn't leave his station without being relieved. Even if he tried to contact Gerard and received no reply, his first assumption would be that his comms were down. Irina appeared at the head of the stair. 'Paul.' Her face broke into a smile that turned into a frown as she remembered he shouldn't be in the house. He brought the pistol up and shot her in the left breast. The bullet threw her backwards and she fell, clawing at her chest. Without breaking stride he aimed the cylindrical barrel of the silencer between her eyes, but it seemed a sacrilege to mar that beautiful face and some impulse froze his finger on the trigger.

Oleg Samsonov must have heard something because he emerged from the gym area wearing a tracksuit and with a towel around his neck.

'Paul?'

Dornberger ignored him and allowed the pistol to slide towards the round-eyed presence that had appeared to his right. Dmitri.

'I'll give you one chance, Oleg. Get me the diamond

431

or I'll shoot him in the guts and we can listen to him scream.'

Samsonov's eyes flicked between the boy and the gun. Dornberger saw the questions going through his mind. Where were the guards? What had happened to Kenny and his men? The billionaire's screaming brain struggled to come to terms with what he was seeing. Outrage, fear and fury fought for supremacy, but it was fear for his son's safety that triumphed. The victor's instinct that made him the man he was told him to fight, but he knew he had no chance of reaching Dornberger before he shot Dmitri. The gunman's eyes told him everything he needed. They were the eyes of the hired killers who never left the Chechen Mafia bosses' side. He saw those eyes every day when Kenny gave his daily briefing. This was a different Paul Dornberger from the smiling aide who anticipated his every need. A moment of puzzlement intruded when he wondered how Dornberger had known about the diamond, but he thrust it aside. The only thing that mattered was Dimi and at the first sign of a threatening move Dmitri would die.

'Stay still, Dimi. Do not move.'

Dmitri didn't need to obey his father. He was frozen to the spot.

'The diamond, Oleg.' Dornberger moved so that he could cover father and son with the gun.

Samsonov edged his way towards the panic room. He formed half a plan to risk grabbing Dmitri and hauling him inside, but Dornberger preempted him by stepping forward to take Dimi by the arm. He reached the door and raised a shaking hand towards the keyboard.

'Careful.' Dornberger knew that if the wrong combination was entered an alarm would go off at the local police station. Oleg swallowed and carefully punched in the correct numbers.

'Good,' Dornberger said soothingly. 'Now the stone.'

The billionaire slid past the Van Gogh that had been his pride, but which now seemed to mock him. The painting half shielded him from Paul Dornberger's gun and he knew he could probably reach the door and take refuge either on the top floor or the floor below. Dornberger was unlikely to kill the boy while the father was free. But he couldn't take the chance. He would not leave his son alone with a psychopath.

He pressed a button on the wall that raised the safe to chest level and at the same time released a keypad on the side of the shining metal pillar. When he punched in the number the top of the pillar opened up in a series of smooth movements to reveal the prize within. The Eye of Isis.

For a moment he swayed in the glare of the Eye's brilliance. He remembered standing by his father's death bed as the old man had related the story in the same words the German prisoner had used. The Eye and the Crown. The passage to eternal life. His father, an old and hardened party man had laughed at the tale even as he coughed away his existence. It had never occurred to him to try to find the Crown, because to do so would have threatened the life he had created in Soviet Russia. But Oleg had been captivated by the possibility. Even then, he already had everything the world could offer. Yet he was a Russian, and as his own father's life slipped away he was presented with a vision of his own mortality. One day, he too would be lying on his death bed with his lungs filling up and his heart ready to explode. No amount of money would change that. Yet now he was presented with the possibility, however unlikely, that the moment could be delayed indefinitely. He had never told another living soul about the diamond, or the myth that made it so prized, but from that day on he had used his resources to try to reunite the Eye with the Crown. It occurred to him now, as he contemplated his own death and that of his son, that all the years of effort had been wasted. How could a man choose to live for ever when it meant he would watch the passing of his wife and children, and their children, for all eternity? It would take a harder and more flawed man than Oleg Samsonov to make that choice.

The diamond's seventy-five facets twinkled at him in the artificial light. It had a beauty and a depth that always moved him. Yet at this moment it was nothing more than a commodity. A commodity that he would use to buy his son's life. He picked up the egg-shaped stone in both hands and walked back out into the room.

'Now you must allow Dmitri to leave.'

Paul Dornberger laughed and shot him in the throat.

XLIII

By the time they reached the Samsonov house it was close to midday. Jamie paid the taxi driver and Danny scouted the front of the complex, taking in the wall and the gates.

'Maybe we should just knock,' she suggested as Jamie joined her.

He studied the wires on top of the wall and the security cameras covering every angle of the approach. 'The sign says vehicular access only,' he pointed out. 'It looks like they don't encourage visitors who don't have wheels. I have a feeling that if we walk up to that door on foot the only welcome we'll get will be from the Russian equivalent of a Claymore anti-personnel mine.'

'It would get their attention.'

'Mm, but only for as long as it took to sweep up what was left into a plastic bag.'

'Do you have a better idea?'

'Not at the moment.'

He took her hand and led her across the road to the gate. Normally, there would have been some kind of speaker system where the visitor could talk to whoever controlled the entry but it seemed Oleg Samsonov, or whoever was protecting him, was a man of few words. The only sign of life was a blinking red light beneath the security camera covering the entrance. Tentatively, Jamie approached the door and knocked. He repeated the action, harder this time, grinned at the camera and pointed at the door.

'Yeah, that should do it,' Fisher said, but he didn't think she meant it.

They stepped back and waited for a reaction, but the doors remained firmly closed.

'It looks as if they're not taking visitors today.'

'There has to be another entrance.'

They walked parallel to the walls on the other side of the road.

'Don't you think it's unusual that they haven't come out to shoo us away?'

'Maybe they get lots of visitors looking for a donation to the church Bring and Buy sale – like a yard sale,' he said before she could ask. 'Dear Mr Samsonov, the vicar and I wondered if you would like to contribute a couple of million to the spire restoration fund. Eventually they'd decide the best way is just not to answer the door at all. It works for me with Jehovah's Witnesses and Mormons.'

'If this is your way of putting me at ease, Saintclair, I think I prefer to be nervous.'

He took the hint and kept his mouth shut as they turned the corner and found another long stretch of wall that backed onto a road that ran along the outside of the park.

'Do you see what I see?'

'The camera?'

'There's one at this end and one at the other. The one in the middle can only be covering some kind of door.'

'You think we'll get a warmer welcome this time.'

'If we don't I may have to pole vault over that wall.'

'Sure.' She grinned, taking in the electrified razor wire along the top. 'I'd like to see that.'

They stayed on the far side of the road and it was Danny who noticed it first. The door, a sort of modern postern gate, was set flush with the wall but a narrow line of darkness showed at the far edge.

'Why would they leave it open?'

Jamie's stomach turned to ice. 'They wouldn't.' He glanced at the cameras at either end of the wall. 'Just keep walking.'

They carried on until they were almost parallel with the doorway.

'Maybe it's on some kind of chain.'

'Maybe.' He took a deep breath. 'There's only one way to find out.' He turned abruptly and walked straight towards the door. It was only open a few inches, so it was possible she was right, but he noticed something in the space at the bottom. At first he didn't recognize it, but gradually his mind turned the jumble of angles and shadows into the sole of a shoe. He looked from the shoe to the eye of the security camera. If someone was watching him now, there was nothing he could do about it. But if someone was watching, why hadn't they reacted to what was now becoming so obvious.

He felt Danny's breath on the back of his neck and the moment she froze as she saw the foot that was blocking the door.

'Stay here.'

'When hell freezes over, Saintclair.'

He pushed the door a few inches to reveal the slumped body of a man lying where he'd toppled after the bullet that had cratered his head threw him back against the wall. By his side, just out of reach, lay the kind of fancy modern machine gun favoured by armed cops and the Special Forces. Danny Fisher rummaged in her bag and he thought he must be dreaming when she came out with a silenced automatic. The gun stirred a vague memory.

'Where in the name of Christ did you get that?'

'From the guy who tried to kill you.' She shrugged. 'I figured it might come in handy. Looks like I figured right.'

There were several things he might have said to that, none of them complimentary, but this didn't seem the right time to mention them. Instead, he considered the door and what might be beyond it.

'What would a New York cop do in a situation like this?'

'She'd send in her partner to check out if the bad guy is still around?'

'And if he is?'

'Well, if things work out, I shoot him before he shoots you.'

Jamie took a deep breath. 'I hope you're a good shot?'

'The best.' She moved back, bringing the 9 mm up in a two-handed grip ready to cover him. 'Stay low, Sherlock, and be fast.' But he was already on the move, blasting through the door and throwing himself right in a shallow dive that took him across the body of the dead guard, picking up the sub-machine gun by its carrying sling as he went. A forward roll took him to the base of a cherry tree in the landscaped grounds and he brought the already cocked weapon to his shoulder ready to fire. The stubby barrel of the MP-5 quartered the surrounding area. Nothing. The ground floor of this side of the house was windowless, but the floors above seemed to be composed entirely of glass. A path led from the doorway he'd just come through to another in the wall of the building.

'Clear,' he called.

Danny moved cautiously through the door, pistol at the ready and her eyes alert for any movement. 'You all right, Sherlock?' she asked without looking at him.

'Now I know what it feels like to be a duck in a

fairground shooting gallery. What do you think?'

She thought about it for a moment, sniffing the air like an Indian tracker in a cowboy movie. 'I think this is all wrong. We should be surrounded by now. Where are the rest of the guards?' She moved back to the body and checked the throat for a pulse. When she was certain, she rummaged in the dead man's pockets and threw a second magazine to Jamie. 'We have a dead guy here who's been gone for at least fifteen minutes. Why didn't they react when he got hit? We have two gun-totin' nobodies running around playing soldiers among the flower beds of a Russian billionaire who likes his privacy. Why aren't we already dead or lying on the grass with the barrel of a Glock 17 in our ears?'

Their eyes turned simultaneously to the door at the end of the path. Fisher reached it first and studied the keypad set into the door jamb. 'We don't have the combination and this has got to be alarmed. Maybe we should try round the front?'

'Too late to worry about that,' Jamie said. 'Stand back.'

Puzzled, she did as she was told, jumping as the un-expected staccato rip of the MP-5 announced that Jamie had decided on a more direct approach. It was a heavy door, constructed of wood and metal, but not armoured. The gun had been chambered for .40 Smith & Wesson rounds and twenty heavy bullets chewed through the approximate area of the lock. Jamie took his finger from the trigger and in time-honoured fashion put his boot to the door.

Danny stepped past him with her pistol at the ready and pointed at the top of the enclosed stairway in front of them. 'Next time you try that, it would be nice to warn a girl, so she doesn't have to change her underwear.'

The first thing they noticed was music, so loud that it assaulted their ears. Some sort of brash classical symphony that Jamie vaguely recognized, but couldn't put a name to. They moved fast up the stairs to the second door. Jamie changed magazines and cocked the MP-5, but Danny Fisher pushed the door with the barrel of her pistol and it swung invitingly inwards. In front of them was a desk with a bank of monitors and an explosive pattern of blood on the wall beside it that told its own story. Jamie went first, taking in the body lying to his left in a pool of blood before Gerard came into view, his shattered head lying on the keyboard that controlled the monitors. It was obvious both men were dead.

'Don't touch anything,' Danny warned unnecessarily, forced to shout over the rising tempo and volume of the music.

'Tchaikovsky,' Jamie shouted back.

'What?'

'The music. It's Tchaikovsky's *1812 Overture*. The one with the cannons.'

Danny glanced at the spattered remnants of Gerard's brain on the wall. 'As if this wasn't already fucking insane enough.'

Beyond the second dead man a corridor led off towards the main part of the building. But there were more rooms that had to be checked before they could take it. When they reached the guards' living quarters Danny stared at the bodies.

'These guys are pros, but whoever did this took them out without blinking. The way I figure it is that the killer has got to be one of their own. It's the only thing that fits. The guys at the top of the stairs were hit before they could even twitch. Looks like these two,' she pointed at the men at the table, 'didn't even have time to go for their guns. The guy walks in. He smiles and heads for the kitchen. He reaches just about here.' She turned and brought the gun up. 'Pow, pow. By now the guard on the bed is reacting, but he's not quick enough, or maybe it's just that our guy is quicker.'

'What about the guard at the gate?'

She took her time to think about it and eventually came up with the answer. 'He didn't hit him on the way in. He hit him on the way out.'

'Then he already has what he came for.'

'We don't know that until we check, Jamie.'

But the certainty grew as they made their way through to the offices. The music had reached a quieter interlude and somehow their breathing and their steps slowed to match it, as if the reverence of the composer for his subject was reaching across the centuries. At first it appeared the offices were empty but the headshot that had taken out Samsonov's secretary had left its telltale pattern on the wall and they found her body lying beside her desk.

'Samsonov?'

'This must be where he works. The rooms where he lives will be up those stairs.'

Jamie went first up the broad wooden stairway, with Danny covering him from a few steps behind. With every step he took, the music gained volume as it lifted towards a new crescendo and with it rose the level of his foreboding. If the killer was still here, this was where he would hit them, when they were out in the open. And if he did, Jamie knew he was as good as dead. This man was a marksman with the reactions of a striking cobra. He would hit what he fired at. Maybe Danny would get him afterwards, but Jamie doubted that. For a fleeting moment he wished the bullet-proof vest that Shreeves had sent him wasn't sitting in a drawer in his flat. But he knew that he would have insisted Danny wear it even if he had brought it. As he reached the last few stairs the room opened up above him like a cathedral. It was vast. He crouched down, his eyes at floor level. A hundred hiding places in a space you could have played a football match in, and with room to spare. He reached forward with his left hand on the top step to steady himself and recoiled as his skin touched something cold and sticky. His fingers came away red. The view to his right had been obscured by the ornate carved banister and it was only now he registered the cube that dominated the centre of the floor and which corresponded with the one on the floor below. The only difference was that this one appeared to be open. Instinctively, he kept low and moved towards it.

The crash of a cannon made him flinch and he turned with his finger on the trigger of the MP-5 to find himself staring into Danny Fisher's wide eyes. The music was everywhere around them, coming from a dozen speakers, possibly more than twenty all over the house to which it must be being somehow streamed. The killer could step up behind them and shout 'boo' in their ears before he shot them and they'd never hear a thing.

He angled his approach so that he was shielded from the open door of the panic room. In front of it, a big man whom he recognized as Oleg Samsonov was lying on his back with his eyes open in a wide pool of darkening blood that had poured from the gaping hole in his throat. Beside him, with her head on his chest, lay the body of a woman who must be his wife. Jamie felt Danny Fisher's presence beside him, her body radiating the same conflicting emotions of rage and sorrow that racked him as he watched over a man and woman united forever in death. Belatedly he remembered that the couple had a young son, and he winced at what he might find in the safe room. He signalled Danny to stay back and stepped round the door with the MP-5 at the ready.

'Bloody hell!' His surprise was loud enough to compete with Tchaikovsky's artillery barrage.

'What is it?' Danny demanded.

But Jamie found he couldn't speak.

She joined him at the door. 'There are enough dead people here to start our own funeral parlour and you're excited about an old bunch of flowers?'

'Not any old bunch of flowers.' His voice was almost wistful, as if the golden glow of the Van Gogh had cast a spell on him. 'If you want to join the world of the filthy rich all we have to do is pick up that painting and walk out of here. I know a man who would pay half a billion dollars for it, no questions asked.'

'Snap out of it, Saintclair. If I wanted to be a crook I'd have done it years ago. The diamond's gone, huh?'

Jamie had noticed the distinctive metal compartment beyond the stand holding the sunflowers, but he found it difficult to take his eyes off the canvas. His mind was a whirl of conflicting emotions: despondency at their failure, anger at the pointless deaths of the billionaire and his guards, fighting with the art lover's joy of having a piece of pure genius more or less all to himself. *Snap out of it, Saintclair*. He shook his head to clear it.

'It looks that way. Why don't you see if you can put that racket off so we can hear ourselves think? I saw some sort of space-age sound system across in the corner that might be responsible.'

She opened her mouth to argue, but the look on his face changed her mind and she moved past him. He continued to stare at the painting and a few minutes later the music stopped abruptly.

'It's over then.' Her voice sounded sharp-edged

and loud in the silence. 'We can't just walk away.'

'No.' He was thinking that the boy was out there somewhere with the man responsible for all this. Responsible for how many deaths now? Why would he take the boy? Of course. The words came back to him. *You must spill the blood of a first born of good family beneath the first light of the sickle moon. Only then will the gateway to the next life open.*

He looked out of the window at the fading light. When was the new moon?

'Oh Christ.'

'What is it?'

'The boy, how—'

A long drawn-out groan emerged from the woman draped over Oleg Samsonov.

'She's alive.'

XLIV

They took Irina Samsonov between them and gently turned her over. One look was enough to tell them it was too late for the billionaire's wife. Blood oozed slowly from the wound in her left breast and the shadow across her pale features could only mean one thing. But somewhere deep inside Irina's indomitable Russian soul fought to keep her alive for another few moments. Her lips moved, but Jamie had to bend low over her to hear the words.

'My son,' she whispered. 'He has taken Dimi.'

'Who has taken him, Mrs Samsonov?'

'Paul . . . Paul Dornberger.' A tear rolled down her cheek. 'We trusted him. My husband paid his father's hospital bills.' With her last breath she whispered the name of the private hospital.

'How far?' Danny demanded.

'We don't know for certain he's gone there.'

'Paul Dornberger has the Eye, he has the Crown and

447

he has the boy, Jamie. It all adds up now. Where else is he going, unless it's to be with his father?'

Jamie fought to fit the name of the hospital to an area. When it materialized he realized there was still hope. He started for the stairs. 'Not far. It's on the other side of the park. Let's go.'

'We can't just call a cab.'

She followed him downstairs and along the corridor to the guards' living quarters where he remembered he'd seen a board with car keys on it. His hand hovered over a set with the prancing horse of the house of Ferrari on it, but eventually he picked one from a mass of Mercedes keys. When he'd made his choice he laid the MP-5 on the work surface and replaced it with the pistol from the nearest guard's shoulder holster, adding an extra magazine just in case. Common sense said the security men must have some sort of direct access to the garage area and they soon found the back stairs beyond another door from the kitchen. When they emerged into the underground garage they were faced with dozens of luxury cars all parked in rows and at least half of them were Mercs.

She glared at him. 'Which one is it, Sherlock?'

For answer he pressed a button on the main key and a black limousine in the front row beeped and flashed its indicators.

'That one, I'd say.'

When they were inside the car, he ran his hands over the controls. His knowledge of automatics was thin, but someone had told him they were easier than driving a manual. What could go wrong? He found out when he put the car into 'Drive' and his foot instinctively searched for the clutch, which turned out to be the brake. He heard Danny Fisher groan in frustration as they were hurled forward into their seat belts.

'Maybe I should drive?'

He bit back a comment about what had happened the last time she'd been at the controls of something and drove directly at the garage door.

'Er, shouldn't we open it first?'

'We're billionaires. We don't open things. They open for us.'

The door rose automatically and they drove out into the dull light of a November afternoon. The same happened at the main gates, which moved silently inwards as the big Mercedes S-Class approached. They drove onto Regent Park's outer ring road and Jamie hesitated.

'What's the problem now?'

'Right or left. Either way we're eventually going to hit heavy traffic at this time of day.'

'Go left. We'll worry about it when we hit it.'

He obeyed and gunned the big six-litre Maybach engine. As the car leapt forward he tried to explain. 'You don't understand. It could take us thirty or forty minutes and Dornberger has at least a thirty-minute lead on us. Whatever he's going to do he could have done it by the time we get there.'

'Well, get us close enough and we'll get out and run.'

'Too far,' he said. 'We need to find a shortcut.' They reached a junction where a paved walkway crossed the road and he put the big limousine into a screaming right turn.

'For Christ's sake, Jamie, you'll kill somebody,' Danny screamed as they roared into the wide open spaces of the park.

'In this weather it can't be too busy, and, with any luck, in this car they'll think it's Prince Andrew out for a drive.' He swerved to miss a shocked dogwalker and the driver's side wheels spun on the grass, but the Mercedes had some kind of stability control and they easily regained the tarmac. Belatedly, he switched on the hazard lights. 'Better safe than sorry.'

Off to their left was an odd-shaped flying saucer of a building on a low mound surrounded by cricket pitches. Jamie drove on, honking the horn at anyone who happened to be in the way while Danny waved apologetically at startled pedestrians oblivious of the fact that she was invisible behind the smoked-glass armoured windows. It was only a matter of time before some kind of park ranger spotted them, but soon they joined a wider walkway which led off to the right between an avenue of skeletal, leafless trees and within a few seconds Jamie swerved onto a roadway in a narrow gap between two cars.

'Not bad, Saintclair,' Danny said appreciatively. 'Where to now?'

'All I know is that the hospital is close to the Royal College of Surgeons, which can't be far from here. See if you can work the satnav.'

She fiddled with a screen on the dashboard. 'It says here the Royal College of Surgeons is miles away.'

'Not surgeons. Try physicians.'

'That's better. It's a little way to our right, on Albany Road.'

'All right, punch in the name of the hospital now. We'll park at the college and walk the rest of the way.'

The hospital was on a side street in a residential area not far from Munster Square. They passed a green-grocer's on the way and Jamie bought a basket of fruit tied up with a pink ribbon.

'What if it's not visiting time?'

'It's a private hospital,' he pointed out unnecessarily. 'Very civilized. It's always visiting time.'

They walked through the front door and up to reception with the bustling air of regular visitors.

'Max Dornberger's room, please.'

The nurse behind the counter smiled. 'If you could wait a second, please, we're just changing shifts.' A few seconds later she produced a chart and ran her finger down a list of names. 'Third floor, room eight. Who did you say you were?'

'We didn't. This is Mr Dornberger's niece from New York, I'm her partner.'

Before the nurse could say anything else, the lift door opened and they stepped briskly inside. Danny took the

451

pistol from her bag and pushed it in among the apples and bananas until only the grip was visible. She pressed the button for the third floor and took a deep breath.

'An apple a day keeps the doctor away, huh? Well, not for Paul Dornberger.'

Jamie cocked the pistol he had taken from the dead guard and folded his hands behind his back.

'We take no chances unless he threatens the boy.'

She stared at him. 'You know he's going to kill him anyway, don't you?'

'I won't be responsible for that child's death, Danny.'

The bell announced their arrival. 'Let's hope it doesn't come to that.'

They emerged into a corridor with the odd-numbered rooms on the left and the evens on the right. Room eight was the fourth door on the side overlooking the square. They stood side by side in front of the door. Danny's hand found the cool of the pistol grip and she held the basket in front of her like a shield. They could hear the soft murmur of voices inside.

Jamie reached for the door handle. 'There's no easy way to do this,' he whispered. 'If the boy is clear and Dornberger makes a move, shoot him.' Danny nodded. He noticed that she was holding her breath. 'Three, two, one . . .'

As they burst in the door side by side, Jamie began bringing the pistol round. Danny's finger tightened on her trigger. The occupants of the room were grouped by the bed and they whirled round at the unexpected intrusion, their expressions a mixture of surprise and shock. Danny's eyes vainly sought the child she knew should be here and she was a millimetre from firing when her brain screamed that the man by the bed was wearing a blue overall and the person lying on it was female.

'What the hell is going on?'

Jamie slipped his hand behind his back and hoped the male nurse hadn't seen the gun that had been about to blow his head off. 'Er . . .' His voice sounded as if it came from a long way off. 'We were looking for Mr Dornberger's room.'

The man frowned in annoyance. 'This room has been re-allocated to Mrs Gibson. Max Dornberger was checked out this morning by his son. You should have been informed at the front desk.'

'I'm sorry,' Danny apologized breathlessly. 'We wanted to surprise him.'

'Surprise? I don't know about Mrs Gibson, but I almost had a heart attack.'

They withdrew, still apologizing. The woman on the bed raised herself to one elbow. 'You could always leave the fruit, dear? I'm partial to a bit of pineapple.'

Danny produced a wan smile. 'I don't think you'd like this one. It's almost gone off.'

On the way out, Danny sweet-talked the receptionist into giving them the address where Dornberger's medicines were to be sent, so that she could visit her English 'uncle' at home.

The address she gave them was a small country estate out beyond the M11 in rural Essex. Danny punched the postcode into the car's satnav and a disjointed voice directed them north-east, through Holloway and Finsbury Park, up to Seven Sisters, where they turned due east.

'Can't you go any faster?'

'Certainly,' Jamie replied reasonably. 'I could stick the cruise control at thirty or forty miles an hour over the speed limit, but you can be the one to explain things when some traffic cop finds the guns we have no right to carry and the fact that this motor car is stolen from a Russian billionaire who just happens to have been slaughtered along with seven other people. That should go well.'

They were a few miles beyond Chigwell, crossing neat rolling countryside under a thunderous, threatening sky, when the voice ordered Jamie to turn right onto a country road, then onto a narrow lane. They drove for a further mile before it petered out into a mud track at a point where a surprisingly modern gate barred the way to a remote house. The estate was surrounded by a brick wall high enough to inform passers-by that they weren't welcome, but not to deter anyone determined to get across it. Jamie didn't see any high-tech security, but the apparent lapse was offset by the 'Beware of the Dogs' sign on the gate.

'You think it's real?'

'If this is the guy we think it is, I'm pretty sure you could bet on it.'

'In that case, you wouldn't happen to have any drugged meat on you?'

She gave him a thin smile and checked the magazine of the silenced pistol.

'We could call the police.' It was something they'd discussed earlier. Danny had called in the Samsonov killings, but she had been curiously reluctant to let them know about the location of the country house.

She shook her head. 'First, we don't know for certain he's in there.' She looked at the brooding clouds racing across the sky. 'Dark soon. If you're right about the significance of the new moon, I doubt we have time. We go in, get the boy and get out again.'

'It might not be as easy as that.'

She shrugged. 'You gotta start somewhere, Jamie. If we wait for your cops the chances are that Dmitri will be dead by the time they get here. I say we go, and we go now.'

There was no point arguing. By the time they were out of the car, the rain was slanting down and a distant flash of lightning lit the western skyline. Jamie pulled the thin jacket he was wearing closer around him, but Danny clicked the boot of the Mercedes and found a top-quality padded waterproof. Without a word, she threw it at him and he grinned acknowledgement.

'Okay, but I'll go in first. I've done this kind of stuff

before. OTC and the Brecons, and all that. We don't know what's on the other side of this wall, so when we go over, we stay together and we protect each other's backs. We follow the line of the drive towards the main house. Once we get there we'll have a better idea of where we go next. All right so far?'

For answer she cocked the pistol and jogged towards the wall. Thick foliage barred the way and by the time they reached it they were soaked. Jamie ran his hands along the top of the wall, checking for glass or razor wire, but there was none. He hauled himself up by the arms and straightened out, belly down along the top, keeping the lowest possible profile, before allowing himself to drop on the other side. Danny followed his example and they hunkered down in the shadow of the wall to get their bearings. The driveway to the house was off to their right, to their left was an open patch that seemed to be some kind of neglected garden. In front of them, covering the direct route to the house, was an orchard of ancient gnarled apple trees whose roots were hidden beneath the rough knee-high grass that carpeted the entire area.

Jamie led the way, leopard-crawling through the wet foliage. He'd felt a thrill of fear when he'd seen the warning sign. No one would willingly go up against the kind of dog Paul Dornberger was likely to keep about the premises. But now he was here it gave him a certain amount of reassurance. If Dornberger was relying on dogs it meant he wasn't relying on anything else, like the kind of motion-sensor equipment Bernie Hartmann had thought would protect him. It also made it unlikely that the long grass hid the kind of iron-jawed man trap that his imagination told him was sitting beneath every blade. He stopped and sniffed the air. Nothing; but that was what he would have expected. The weather was another bonus because not only would it hamper the dogs' sense of smell it would affect their hearing. With just a little luck they would make the house undetected. A peel of thunder was followed a few seconds later by a flash of lightning that turned the trees into an army of enormous, skeletal witches with twisted, grasping arms and long curling fingers, and he felt a shiver that was connected with some childhood memory. *Babes in the Wood? Fantasia?* He knew he would make quicker progress on his feet, with probably just as little, or as much, chance of being seen, but somewhere close by was Paul Dornberger and he was armed and dangerous and he could shoot the fleas off an itching hound. Why the hell did he think that? He tried to force the stupid thought back where it came from, but it was as if letting it loose had drawn them to him. Through the rain two enormous, hulking, four-legged figures padded into view a few yards ahead of him. He froze, but they lumbered to a stop and their red eyes fixed on him. It couldn't have been worse. Rottweilers. Devil dogs. Black-and-tan giants with broad shoulders and thick necks and jaws that were designed to crush a wolf's skull with a single bite. A low

growl confirmed that he'd been detected, but they must
have been trained not to bark because the following
rush was swift and silent. The first was almost on him
when something zipped past his ear like a turbo-charged
wasp and the lead attacker's head snapped back and it
somersaulted backwards as if it had run into a steel
wire. But there was no stopping the second and before
he could bring up his pistol its teeth clamped on his arm
and threatened to rip it from his shoulder, shaking its
head and using its powerful neck muscles. The only
thing that saved him was the padded jacket Danny had
given him; even then he felt the tips of those savage
fangs raking the flesh of his arm. It was like wrestling
with a crocodile and the way things were going there
would only be one winner. He smashed his free fist into
the beast's muzzle in a vain bid to force it off, but it
seemed to grow stronger. His vision was beginning to
blur when, in a moment of slow motion, he saw its eyes
widen and its skull expand until the back of its head
exploded in a spray of scarlet and white. With a convulsive shudder the Rottweiler went still, its enormous
weight pinning him to the ground. A dark figure
appeared from behind and heaved it clear.

'Can't lie about here all day, Jamie Saintclair, there's
work to be done.'

Jamie rose to his feet on shaking legs. He checked the
pistol to make sure the magazine hadn't been dislodged
and the familiar actions slowed his heart rate to a point
where the organ wasn't going to explode. It was almost

dark now and despite the storm to the east he could see a silver glow in the sky he knew was the first rays of the moon. Time was running out for Dmitri Samsonov.

Danny slipped easily through the trees and he ran to catch her up just as another flash of lightning illuminated the house properly for the first time. It was big, ugly and ramshackle, probably Victorian or earlier, with missing slates and peeling woodwork; neglected like the rest of the estate. The path through the trees brought them towards it at an angle, but half a dozen darkened windows covered their approach and any one of them could have Dornberger behind it watching their every move. Danny knelt at the base of the last crooked apple tree before the open ground of the driveway and Jamie crouched beside her. Together they studied the lower floor, looking for the best way to get inside.

Eventually, he put his mouth to Danny's ear. 'Stay here. I have an idea.' He slipped away into the darkness and reappeared after a minute or so with a rusting piece of metal. It was about two feet long, a narrow bar with hooks protruding at intervals; something that might have been made to string barbed wire, but had probably been used to support peas in the garden.

He led her to a small ground-floor window that looked as if it might provide light for a cloakroom. Fortunately, whoever owned the house had resisted the urge to improve its rustic charms by installing double glazing. The windows were old-fashioned sash and case affairs with cracked woodwork and layers of peeling paint. He put the end of the iron plate into the narrow space between the window and the sill. He had to use all his weight to prise the window upwards and it gave a crack like a small-calibre rifle as the thick seal of generations of paint surrendered to the assault.

Fisher winced at the sound, but she pushed him aside and silently squirmed through the gap he'd created. He followed her and for a few moments they stood in the pitch darkness listening to the sound of their own breathing until a flash illuminated their surroundings. It was fortunate they hadn't moved far from the window, because the small room was strewn with a domestic minefield of discarded household equipment. An old wooden ironing board blocked the way to the door, surrounded by boxes, a standard lamp and a collection of paint tins. Warily, they picked their way through the debris. Fisher groped for the door handle and eased it open. Beyond the door the house was in darkness, but in the gloom it was just possible to make out a wood-panelled hallway and stairs. They eased their way through into the hall, Fisher leading the way with her pistol held two-handed in front of her. Jamie gave an involuntary shiver. A permanent chill hung in the air as if the occupants preferred to live their lives without the benefit of warmth. Danny signalled that she was going to check a room off to her left and waved him on. He moved slowly, planting one foot at a time and feeling his way forward over the bare floorboards. The hall took a dogleg and as he turned the corner a giant figure loomed out of the darkness in front of him. The gun came up automatically and his finger tightened on the trigger. He was within a whisker of firing when the hooded attacker of his imagination transformed into an enormous stuffed bear with yellowing fangs and tiny obsidian eyes. Shaking, he lowered the pistol and stood for a moment, the surge of adrenalin draining away and leaving his body limp. All it needed was a few marching suits of fucking armour and they'd be starring in a nightmare version of *Bedknobs and Broomsticks*. Just for a second he felt the urge to scream out loud.

Someone else beat him to it.

He was moving before he even understood what he was hearing. At first he thought it must be Danny, caught in some awful demonic trap, but the scream was high-pitched and filled with visions of terror. A child's scream. *Dmitri*. A hand clamped on his shoulder and he turned to look into a pair of wild, staring eyes. Danny's face was twisted into a grimace of desperation.

'Stay still,' she hissed. 'We have to know where it came from!'

He shook his head, uncertain at first. Then some radar in his head clicked into operation and he knew. He pointed at the floor. The sound was from somewhere below. He signalled to her to check one side of the hall for the entrance to the basement, while he took the other. It didn't take long. One of the panels set into the side of the stair proved to be a door that led to a dank stairway. The stairs spiralled downwards and with Jamie in the lead they moved into the narrow passage.

At the bottom, they came to another door, identified by a thin frame of bright artificial light. Jamie's hand reached for the handle and Danny whispered in his ear: 'I'll be right behind you, Sherlock. Give 'em hell.'

He threw the door open and they froze. Was this some kind of hallucination?

In the cellar of his dilapidated English country house, Max Dornberger had created a replica of an Egyptian temple. Statues of jackal-headed Anubis and Horus, the hawk god, flanked the doorway. The floor was of paved sandstone and on the far side four steps led up to a carved throne set between two pillars. Each of the four walls was covered by marvellous multi-coloured friezes depicting more god-like figures conducting their hunts and holding court. The temple was empty.

In the silence, they could hear a muffled droning sound, as if someone was reciting a mantra.

'There must be another room.' Danny's urgent whisper brought Jamie out his reverie.

They searched the walls for a second door, but there was none.

'Look again. It has to be here,' he said. 'Dornberger is close.'

A tablet with two figures etched upon it caught his eye. The woman with the horned crown and the sun disc kneeling before a Pharaoh dressed all in white with green features.

'Isis and Osiris,' Danny whispered.

The woman's eye was the stylized symbol that had brought them here: a dark pupil on a white background, with the distinctive red tear in its corner. Without thinking, Jamie reached up and pushed the centre. Immediately the entire panel swung inwards.

XLV

Paul Dornberger watched in disbelief as the door to the killing chamber swung open. His mind rebelled at what he was seeing. No man could enter this room except himself or his father, or those who would soon be dead. The recitation that had been passed down the ages was almost complete, the Crown and the Eye had been reunited and through the opening in the ceiling, so cunningly concealed from outside, the thin sliver of a sickle moon was just coming into view. Only the final, irrevocable act was required to complete the ceremony.

Beside him, Max Dornberger lay on a rough trestle bed, clinging to life with every harsh breath. The doctors believed Paul had brought him here to die, but the opposite was the case. Tonight he would fulfil the quest of a lifetime. It did not matter how many had died to make it happen. All that mattered was that the Crown of Isis should live again through the one who had been chosen.

The Crown sat on the bed in front of his father. Dmitri Samsonov, his dark eyes wide with terror, was a tiny figure strapped into the chair that had shaped Paul Dornberger's life, his head forced back, the taut white flesh of his throat ready for the sacrificial knife.

In one swift movement, Dornberger picked up the pistol at his side, aimed and fired. The first person through the door gave a sharp cry and dropped to the tiled floor. The second shot missed its intended target, but by good fortune it smashed the gun from the man in the doorway's hand and with a cry of pain the figure stepped back out of the line of fire.

Dornberger recognized the woman writhing on the floor. He was tempted to finish her, but a glance at the opening above told him he had to hurry. Time was running out. He had minutes to complete the ceremony, no more. Keeping the gun on the doorway he resumed the litany of the ritual.

Jamie watched helplessly as Danny tried ineffectually to stem the bleeding from the gunshot wound high in her breast. His right hand vibrated like a tuning fork from the impact of the bullet that had knocked the pistol from his fingers. He had only got the briefest glimpse of what was happening inside the cellar, but it was enough. The chair with the boy held in its straps and tethers, sitting above the kind of enamel run-off you would see in an abattoir, told its own terrible story. His first instinct was to rush Dornberger, but he knew that was the tactic of despair. The man would shoot him down before he took three paces and afterwards he would kill Dmitri Samsonov and Danny Fisher. Time. He needed time to think.

'It's finished, Dornberger. Let the boy go. Whatever happens now your father is going to die. Nobody but you believes that mumbo-jumbo about the Crown, but even if it did work all it would mean is he'll spend whatever is left of his life in prison. Did you know that your father's name isn't even Dornberger, Paul? Did he ever tell you that he's actually a piece of Nazi scum called Bodo Ritter; a man who slaughtered more than twenty thousand innocent Jewish men, women and children? Bodo Ritter is something I'd wipe off my shoe, but there's hope for you, Paul,' he lied. 'Being brought up in this madhouse there must be a chance that you can plead insanity.'

The litany ended and Jamie heard a muffled cry. He risked a frantic glance round the door. Dornberger had laid the gun down, but now the knife was in his right hand, the razor edge against Dmitri Samsonov's cringing flesh. Jamie could see the veins pulsing in the exposed neck and he flinched at the thought of the slaughter that was about to occur unless he could find a way to stop it.

'The only thing that is finished is you, Saintclair,' Paul Dornberger's voice was eerily calm. 'What my father is or was means nothing. He created me in his own image to be capable of any act or make any sacrifice to restore the Crown and the Eye. Can you imagine how many have sat in this chair to make this day happen? How much pain this room has seen. Soon you will experience it, as I have done. Once the ceremony is complete, unless you surrender yourself I will shoot your mysterious companion to pieces. Naturally I will aim to cause her the maximum of suffering. Could you stand that Saintclair? Watching her squirm with a bullet in her guts. Hearing her scream for her life as the blood spurts from a severed artery. I do not think so. And when you are in the chair, we will discuss how you managed to discover the whereabouts of Berndt Hartmann and how you found your way here.'

'Keep him talking,' Danny hissed.

That was going to be easier said than done. Paul Dornberger kept glancing up at the opening in the roof. Jamie realized that the killer was operating to some timetable dictated by what he was seeing there and that might be measured in seconds. Even as he watched, Max Dornberger made a feeble movement towards the Crown, but the son nudged it away from his clutching fingers. Jamie closed his eyes. *Think*.

He stepped into the room. 'You don't have to do this, Paul. You have a mind of your own. I can imagine what happened to you here: what that man did to you and what he made you do. But it can stop, now. The Crown of Isis is stained in blood. But you have the power to make it clean again. End it here and you regain whatever honour your family ever had. End it here and you can be clean again.' Was there some kind of reaction? A hint of hesitation? 'We're all brothers under the skin, Paul. End it now and you can join the brotherhood of mankind again.' As pleas for mercy went, it was trite and hackneyed, but it was all he had. He gathered himself to commit suicide when it was rejected.

But trite or not, the words – a word – had triggered some kind of chain reaction in Paul Dornberger's brain. For a few precious seconds he forgot the sickle moon as the many deaths he had carried out here swam through his brain. The faces appeared one after the other, dozens of them, united in their terror and their hopelessness. But one face in particular, a face that had eluded him for a quarter of a century, suddenly created a freeze-frame image that caught and stayed. A boy's face, dull and trusting. An idiot, his father had said, as he handed Paul the knife, good for nothing but practice. His brother's face.

With a growl, he knocked the old man's hands away from the Crown and picked the golden treasure off the bed.

'It is not for you, old man. It was never for you.'

With his free hand he lifted the Crown of Isis towards his own head, the diamond glittering in the artificial light. Dmitri screamed again as he felt the increasing pressure of the knife at his throat. Jamie knew he had only one chance. Somehow Danny Fisher managed to push the pistol that had been trapped beneath her towards him and he made a dive for it. He had no time to aim. As his right hand closed over the weapon's butt he raised it and fired allowing instinct and experience to take over.

Dornberger had raised the Crown level with his face and there was a frozen millisecond before the bullet struck its target. The Eye of Isis shattered into a million pieces and the copper-jacketed slug continued on its course. The last thing Paul Dornberger saw was a blinding flash of light before the bullet took him directly between the eyes. Max Dornberger's eyelids snapped open and he lurched upright on the bed with the cry of a man being dragged down into the seventh pit of hell. The shadow was already upon him, and as Jamie watched it grew ever darker. In a matter of seconds, the man who had begun life as Bodo Ritter aged fifty years and with a final shriek he fell back dead.

Jamie lay exhausted for a few moments beside Danny Fisher's prone body before he remembered she might be bleeding to death. When he turned to help, her eyes were shining fever bright with agony and shock. A cursory examination showed she'd been hit in the fleshy part just below the angle of her right breast and shoulder. He realized with relief that it probably looked and felt worse than it was, not that she'd appreciate that for a while. He produced a handkerchief from his pocket and wadded it over the wound beneath her jacket.

A soft mewing wail reminded him that Danny wasn't the only one who needed his help. Dmitri Samsonov sat rigid with shock in the chair where he had been a millimetre from death, a thin red line showing just how close he had come. Jamie helped Danny to her feet and their shoes crunched on a billion-dollar carpet of splintered fragments as he supported her across to free Dmitri. The body of Paul Dornberger lay close by, the small hole in his forehead oozing blood and his face pierced with thousands of shards of carbon crystal.

They stood over him for a few moments, lost in their own thoughts. It seemed inappropriate that Dornberger's blood-flecked features should be relaxed and at peace; almost an insult to his victims. Jamie shuddered. Suddenly all he wanted to do was be out in the clean air. The very walls of the room oozed evil. How many people had died so this man and his father could pursue their demented fantasy? Danny sniffed and Jamie could tell that, despite her pain, she was equally moved.

She looked down at the glittering layer of shards beneath their feet and shook her head. 'Jesus, Saintclair,' she said wearily. 'Didn't anybody ever tell you diamonds are a girl's best friend?'

Epilogue

Jamie Saintclair was lying on a tropical beach with Danny Fisher's endlessly long, endlessly lithe body broiling to a perfect tan by his side when the buzz of his mobile phone roused him from the dream. He awoke in a cramped seat on the Paddington to Oxford train. Danny had recovered quickly from her wound and flown back to New York three weeks earlier and he was still surprised at how big a hole she had left in his life.

He checked the screen, hoping it might be a message from the New Yorker, but the caller ID said 'Det Shreeves', which took him a moment to turn into the Met officer who'd loaned him the protective vest that had saved his life. The message was equally cryptic: 'Daily Mail, page 17'.

The only newspapers available on the train were the brain-numbing free tabloids that littered the seats and luggage racks, so he had to wait until he reached the station before he could buy a *Mail* from the newsstand.

He flicked to page 17 and was wondering why Shreeves wanted him to read an article on Britain's Booze Culture when he noticed the headline at the bottom of the page:- ELECTRONICS TYCOON FOUND SHOT DEAD. The story said that the body of Howard Vanderbilt had been discovered in his tenth-floor apartment with a gun in his hand and a bullet wound in the head. It added that sources close to the investigation suggested that: '*prior to his death Mr Vanderbilt was being investigated over allegations of tax evasion and for suspected links to neo-Nazi groups and organized crime.*' Jamie had a momentary vision from what seemed another lifetime of a portly figure with a pony-tail and a 9 mm automatic pointed at his heart, but he wasn't quite sure how he should feel. He supposed it meant he could stop looking over his shoulder. No one was going to honour a contract put out by a dead man.

He threw the paper into the nearest bin and found his way to the taxi rank. Somewhere in there would be yet another story about the investigation at the Dornberger house, but he didn't need to read it to know the details. The discovery of the underground temple and the horrors that had taken place there had created a sensation. Every day brought a new revelation about the search for bodies in the grounds or the discovery of human tissue in the waste system. DNA tests had already brought the number of Paul and Max Dornberger's victims to at least twelve, although their identities remained a mystery. The boy intended to be their final victim was still in care. Overnight, Dmitri Samsonov had become the wealthiest child on the planet, and he was now the subject of a three-way tug of war between Irina's parents, a distant cousin of Samsonov, who also happened to be a prominent member of the Russian Mafia, and President Vladimir Putin, who had generously offered to adopt his old friend Oleg's son.

The taxi dropped him at the Ashmolean Museum. Inside, Athena was waiting exactly where she said she would be, among the artefacts in the Egyptian section. She smiled gravely when she saw him.

'Thank you for agreeing to come to Oxford to meet me, Mr Saintclair. I apologize, but it would have been inconvenient for me to travel to London.'

'I was a little surprised,' he admitted, 'until I remembered that Oxford has a long relationship with Isis.'

She laughed. 'You mean the rowing team, of course. Isis is the ancient name for the Thames, Mr Saintclair. I'm afraid Oxford has nothing to do with The Lady, no matter how much I should wish it. My association with this city is because I have been a visiting lecturer at the Faculty of Oriental Studies for many years, and the Ashmolean is a valuable research facility.'

To cover his embarrassment, Jamie unshouldered the rucksack he'd carried from London and removed the black velvet bag it contained. Athena drew a sharp breath as he placed the bag in her hands and she felt its weight.

'Is this . . . ?'

He nodded and her eyes glistened. She leaned forward with a sharp movement, like a bird pecking grain, and kissed him on the cheek. 'The Sisters of Isis will always be in your debt.'

'There is no need. I am just glad that it is back where it belongs . . . and sorry that I couldn't have done the same with the Eye.'

A sad smile touched her lips.

'I believe you and your friend were doing The Lady's work when you destroyed it, just as my daughter Klara was when she died trying to protect you. The Lady would not wish to be associated with something so defiled. There will be a new stone, clear and untarnished; untainted by the corruption of the old.'

Jamie covered his surprise with a smile of his own. The Eye of Isis had been beyond price. The cost of replacing it with a stone of similar quality was unthinkable, if such a thing ever came on the open market. 'I can put you in touch with a diamond merchant in Antwerp.'

The offer was made half in jest and drew a laugh from Athena. 'Oh, I doubt we will be buying it, Mr Saintclair. There are other ways of acquiring such things.'

He managed to suppress the image of another newspaper headline – one that said: MYSTERY RAID ON CROWN JEWELS – long enough to reach forward and shake her hand.

'Goodbye, and thank you again, Mr Saintclair. I must find a safe place for this. And if you ever need the assistance of the Sisters of Isis again . . .'

'I don't intend to be in a position where I'll need it,' Jamie assured her. His future plans included a long, stress-free rest, and a sun-kissed beach. Maybe somewhere like Florida where a certain New York detective might be persuaded to join him.

With a last glance at Athena as she walked through a door marked 'Private' he headed for the exit. It was only when he was outside that it struck him. The doorway had been flanked by two Egyptian steles carved from black granite, each inscribed with a familiar symbol.

The Eye of Isis.

Acknowledgements

As always, I have to thank my wife Alison and children, Kara, Nikki and Gregor for their unfailing support and encouragement. Special thanks go to our friends Shirley and Kenny Allan for yet again keeping me straight on my German. Finally to Simon my editor and his fantastic team at Transworld, and to Stan, my agent at Jenny Brown in Edinburgh.

James Douglas is the pseudonym of a writer of popular historical adventure novels. This is the second thriller to feature art recovery expert, Jamie Saintclair, the first, *The Doomsday Testament*, is also published by Corgi.

The first historical adventure featuring Jamie Saintclair . . .

The Doomsday Testament

James Douglas

1937, Hitler sent an expedition to Tibet in search of the lost land of Thule.

1941, Heinrich Himmler spent a huge fortune, and sacrificed the lives of hundreds of concentration camp prisoners, to turn Wewelsburg Castle in Germany into a shrine to the SS.

Art recovery expert Jamie Saintclair thought he knew his grandfather, but when he stumbles upon the old man's lost diary he's astonished to find that the gentle Anglican clergyman was a decorated hero who had served in the Special Air Service in World War Two. And his grandfather has one more surprise for him. Sewn in to the endpaper of the journal is a strange piece of Nazi symbolism.

This simple discovery will launch him on a breathless chase across Europe and deep into Germany's dark past. There are some who will kill to find that which is lost, and although he doesn't know it, Saintclair holds the key to its hiding place.